MEET THE FORTUNES!

Fortune of the Month: Toby Fortune Jones

Age: 28

Vital Statistics: Dazzling blue eyes, broad, strapping shoulders, strong arms that could hold a woman all night long…

Claim to Fame: Has a heart bigger than Texas.

Romantic Prospects: He's raising three foster kids *and* running a ranch. Are you kidding?

"I must be the king of bad timing. I finally meet a gal that's something special, and my nights are tied up with math homework and braiding pigtails. Angie is the first woman who seems to 'get' me. But let's be real. How many females are really in the market for a family of five? Forget about settling down—I haven't even been able to *kiss* her proper. How's a guy supposed to get to first base when there's always a first-grader underfoot?"

* * *

The Fortunes of Texas:
Welcome to Horseback Hollow!

D1396053

A HOUSE FULL
OF FORTUNES!

BY
JUDY DUARTE

Published in Great Britain 2014
by Mills & Boon, an imprint of Harlequin (UK) Limited,
Eton House, 18-24 Paradise Road, Richmond, Surrey, TW9 1SR

© 2014 Harlequin Books S.A.

Special thanks to Judy Duarte for her contribution to The Fortunes of Texas: Welcome to Horseback Hollow! continuity.

ISBN: 978 0 263 91274 6

23-0414

Harlequin (UK) Limited's policy is to use papers that are natural, renewable and recyclable products and made from wood grown in sustainable forests. The logging and manufacturing processes conform to the legal environmental regulations of the country of origin.

Printed and bound in Spain
by Blackprint CPI, Barcelona

Judy Duarte always knew there was a book inside her, but since English was her least favorite subject in school, she never considered herself a writer. An avid reader who enjoys a happy ending, Judy couldn't shake the dream of creating a book of her own.

Her dream became a reality in March 2002, when Mills & Boon® Cherish™ released her first book, *Cowboy Courage*. Since then she has published more than twenty novels. Her stories have touched the hearts of readers around the world. And in July 2005 Judy won a prestigious Readers' Choice Award for *The Rich Man's Son*.

Judy makes her home near the beach in Southern California. When she's not cooped up in her writing cave, she's spending time with her somewhat enormous but delightfully close family.

To my daughter, Christy Duarte,
who has been an awesome critique partner,
brainstorm wizard and editor. You are a creative
and talented author who will soon hold your first
of many of your published books in your hands.
I love you, T.

Chapter One

"Justin! Get down from there!"

At the sound of the baritone voice spiked with irritation, Angie Edwards looked up from the cash register, stopped totaling her mother's grocery purchases and looked across the Superette to see a little red-haired boy high atop the stock clerk's ladder.

She was just about to rush over to the child before he fell when she spotted Toby Fortune Jones standing near the bottom rung, waiting for the little imp to climb down.

Toby, who owned a small ranch just outside of town and volunteered his time as a coach at the YMCA in nearby Vicker's Corners, had become a foster parent to the three Hemings children last fall.

Who would have guessed that the hunky rancher had such a paternal side? Just seeing him with those kids each time they came into the Superette gave Angie pause. And it warmed her heart, too.

What didn't warm her heart, however, was her mother checking up on her. Again.

"Don't forget that you're always welcome to come stay at my house if you need to," Angie's mother said, drawing her back to the task and the conversation at hand.

Angie loved her mom—she truly did—but there was no way she'd ever consider living with the woman again. There were times she couldn't get her mom off the telephone or, in this case, through the Superette checkout line fast enough for comfort.

"That'll be fourteen dollars and seventeen cents," Angie said, after she'd finished totaling her mother's purchases.

Why would Doris Edwards, who now lived and worked in Lubbock as a real-estate agent, drive all the way into Horseback Hollow to buy fifteen dollars' worth of groceries?

To check up on Angie and give her another lecture, no doubt. Thank goodness no one had gotten into line behind her yet.

"You're twenty-four and you can't work at the Superette forever." Her mother reached into her purse for her wallet. "Not that you've worked anywhere longer than a few months, but how are you ever going to make ends meet if you're only putting in four hours a day? Your rent will be due soon. I hope you have enough money set aside to cover it."

She did, but just barely. However, she'd learned early in life that it was best not to share her worries or concerns with her mom. The woman stressed about things entirely too much as it was. And nothing Angie did would ever be good enough for a hardworking powerhouse like Doris Edwards.

"I'll be fine. Really." Angie glanced around the grocery store, hoping the owners—Julia Tierney or her parents, Mr. and Mrs. Tierney—weren't within earshot. When she saw that they weren't, she slowly released a sigh of relief. "I knew this was a part-time position when I accepted it."

"You put in your application at The Hollows Cantina like I told you to, right?" As Doris pulled out a twenty-dollar bill, Angie nodded her confirmation that she had reluctantly applied.

"Well, at least that's something promising. From what I've heard, it's going to be an upscale place to eat."

If truth be told, Angie really had no interest in waiting tables. She'd already done that gig and, as much as Angie liked to cook, the restaurant business wasn't for her. Unfortunately, working part-time at the Superette and filling in as a receptionist at the flight school and charter service barely enabled her to make ends meet. Thank goodness she'd moved recently and had worked out a deal with her new landlord.

"You realize," Doris added, "that with the Fortune name behind the cantina, and with Jeanne Marie Fortune Jones being related to royalty and all… Well, you know what that means. People with money will be eating there. So it'll be a good place for you to network and make some connections. Then again, if it's a husband you want, your prospects will be better there than here. After all, if you want to catch a big fish, you have to go where they're swimming."

Angie blew out a sigh. Her mother had been pushing her to get the college degree she'd never gotten for herself. And since Angie usually found jobs through friends or through a temp agency in Vicker's Corners, her mother had decided she lacked the ambition to succeed in life. So Doris had recently started pushing a white-lace and gold-band solution.

But Angie wasn't looking for love. Not until she had a good idea of who she really was and where she was going in life.

She just wished her mother's voice wasn't so loud, and that she wouldn't make those kinds of comments in public.

"Why don't you come over for supper tonight," her mother said, as she reached for her grocery bag. "If you do, I'll fix meat loaf."

Angie would rather have a root canal than spend the evening with her mom, especially if she was making meat loaf. The woman had never been known for her domestic skills. Or her parenting skills, for that matter. In fact, Angie had probably cooked more of the family meals growing up than she had.

But it wasn't the quality of the food that would keep her away. It was the heartburn and the headache she expected to get from the mealtime conversation. As usual, her mom was sure to point out that Angie's only hope—at least, as far as Doris could see—was for Angie to snag a gainfully employed husband. And there was no reason to believe tonight would be any different. They'd had this conversation at least twenty times in the past couple of months.

To be honest, Angie feared that at least some of what her mother believed might be true. Not that she needed a man to rescue her. That certainly wasn't the case. But for some reason, Angie just couldn't seem to get fired up about anything, which she found troubling. Because at twenty-four, you'd think she'd know what she wanted to do with her life.

Angie had never been good with decisions of any kind, as was evident by her résumé, which read like a copy of the Yellow Pages. But why pour herself into something when her heart wasn't in it? She always figured she'd know what she was meant to do with her life when she felt some sort of spark or passion. Until then, she'd just keep trying a little bit of everything and commit to nothing.

The sound of broken glass sounded from the first aisle, followed by a little girl's shriek.

"I'm sorry!" This came from a boy—maybe the one who'd been on the ladder. "But it wasn't my fault, Toby. Kylie pushed me into the stack of mayonnaise. I didn't mean to knock the jars over."

Angie reached for the small microphone to the right of her register. "Ralph? We'll need a cleanup at the front of aisle one."

Poor Toby. His foster kids were usually pretty well-mannered, but they were obviously having a bad day. At least, the middle boy was.

"Thank goodness you don't have *that* problem to worry about, Evangeline." Her mother shot a look of annoyance at the mayonnaise mess and then at the three children arguing over who was at fault. "Women like us were *not* meant to stay at home and raise a passel of rug rats. I can't imagine what Toby was thinking when he took in that brood."

The soft dark hairs on the back of Angie's neck bristled at her mother's familiar rant against children. *Just ignore it,* Angie thought. She knew better than to engage Doris in a conversation like that, especially in public.

"I'm sorry, Mom. I can't do dinner tonight. I already have plans." Angie just hoped her mother didn't ask what those plans might be because she'd probably spend the first half of her evening looking in her pantry trying to decide what to eat and the second half sitting in front of the television, wearing out the remote.

"Oh, really?" Doris perked up. "What are you doing tonight?"

So much for hoping her mother wouldn't ask.

As the next customer began to place his groceries on the conveyor belt, Angie tore her gaze from her mom and glanced at Toby, the man who'd gotten in line behind her. In spite of those gorgeous baby blues and the kind of face that made even strangers want to confide in him, Toby looked a bit frazzled today.

Funny. He usually looked so capable and put-together.

"I'll have to give you a call and we can talk more later," Angie told her mother. "We don't want to hold up the line."

"Sure, honey." Doris glanced over her shoulder. When she spotted Toby, she offered him a sympathetic smile. "You've certainly got your hands full."

"Just enough to keep life interesting—and fun."

Toby tossed Doris a boyish grin, then winked at Angie as if the two of them were in on a secret.

Being included, even in a make-believe secret, was enough to lift Angie's spirits and to trigger a smile of her own.

"We're going fishing," Brian, the older boy, said. "That is, if there're any fish left by the time we get to Cutter's Pond."

Toby placed a hand on the boy's shoulder. "Nonsense. Everyone knows the bigger fish are busy fattening themselves up and waiting for just the right person to come and catch them up." Toby winked at Angie again, and she realized he must have overheard her mother's comment about fishing for a suitable mate while working at The Hollows Cantina.

As her cheeks warmed, she looked at the small space under the cash register, wishing she could stuff her five-foot-seven-inch body into the square opening.

But why stress about it? It wasn't as though she'd set her sights on Toby as a viable romantic option. He was practically the guy next door.

She'd known the Jones family—make that the *Fortune* Jones family—forever. She'd gone to school with Toby's sister Stacey, although they'd never run in the same circles. She'd even double-dated with Toby's brother Jude a couple of times, but there'd never been any sparks, so nothing had ever come of it.

Toby was probably the only one of Stacey's hunky brothers Angie hadn't considered dating.

Not that he wasn't just as handsome as the others. Angie looked at his tall frame, lean and muscled from years of ranch work and extracurricular sports coaching. Yep, Toby Fortune Jones could definitely compete with his brothers in the looks department.

But Toby always seemed so confident and so sure of himself. And people who knew exactly what they wanted and went after it always intimidated her. Plus, the whole "Mother Teresa meets Dudley Do-Right" personality only made Toby seem all the more out of reach.

A guy like Toby would never be interested in someone like her. He'd want a woman who was down-to-earth, a woman who had her ducks in a row.

Someone who had dreams and plans to fulfill. Someone who wouldn't ever stress about what job she was going to try next.

Angie's mother reached for her grocery bag, causing Angie to break her bold perusal.

"Must be nice to have so much free time on your hands," Doris said to Toby. "Have fun."

Angie could see the disapproval evident on her mom's face. Doris Edwards didn't believe in burning daylight simply for fishing or spending time with one's family.

"We will," Toby told her. "You have a nice day, Mrs. Edwards."

As Doris headed to the parking lot, she turned back to look at what Angie was wearing behind the check stand. "And, honey," Doris said reproachingly, her voice quieter yet still loud enough for anyone within five feet of her to hear, "try to dress a bit more conservatively. Nobody is going to take you seriously with all those curves popping out everywhere. You look like you just got off a shift at a roadhouse honky-tonk."

Doris's smartphone rang, thankfully cutting off her insult to Angie's snug-but-comfortable jeans and her white T-shirt. "Gotta take this. You know, the client always comes first."

Angie started the conveyor belt as her mother breezed out the door in a conservative shoulder-padded power suit. She tried to smile through the mortification that warmed her cheeks and strained the muscles in her face. "Chips, soda, cookies… Looks like someone is planning a picnic."

Toby tossed her a playful grin. "Fishing on the lake is hungry business."

"It should be a nice day for it," Angie said, as she began to check out Toby—or rather, his groceries.

Not that there wasn't plenty to check out about the man himself—if she were looking.

Brown hair that was stylishly mussed, but not out of place. Dazzling blue eyes that were both playful and bright. Broad, strapping shoulders. Arms that looked as though they could pitch a mean curveball—or hold a woman tightly all night.

"I don't want to go to Cutter's Pond," Kylie complained, breaking Angie from her wayward thoughts. "You're just going to kill those poor fish. And I don't even like to eat them."

Brian rolled his eyes. "Don't be such a stinking crybaby, Kylie. We never get to do anything fun without you complaining."

Toby glanced at Angie and gave a little shrug. "Sometimes it's hard to find an activity or an outing they can all enjoy. It seems that someone always has an objection."

Angie smiled. "To be honest, I can't blame her a bit. I never did like putting a worm on a hook."

"You had to go fishing, too?" the little red-haired girl asked.

Angie offered her a sympathetic smile. "When my father was alive, he would take me to Cutter's Pond. And while I could usually count on getting sunburned and bit by a mosquito or two, there was always something special about spending time with my daddy."

"But I don't have a daddy," the girl said.

Angie's cheeks warmed. She'd only wanted to help, but had probably made things worse.

"You might not have a dad," Toby said, as he gave one of Kylie's lopsided auburn pigtails a gentle tug, "but you have *me*."

Toby's hands might be skilled at lassoing horses and throwing a football, but the poor man couldn't do a little girl's hair to save his life.

Still, these kids were lucky to have Toby. If he hadn't stepped up to the plate when their aunt had gone off the deep end and lost custody, they might have been separated and placed in different foster homes.

Justin, the boy who'd climbed the ladder, said, "Too bad we don't have a babysitter for Kylie. She's gonna wah-wah like a little crybaby and ruin our whole day." Justin made fake crying noises and rubbed his eyes to emphasize his overly dramatic point.

Maybe Angie could help out after all. "I only have to work for a half hour or so, and then my shift is over. If you don't mind leaving Kylie here with me, I'd be happy to hang out with her while you and the boys go fishing. We can do cool girls-only things that boys don't get to do."

"That's nice of you to offer," Toby said, "but you don't have to do that."

"Yes, she does!" Kylie gave a little jump and a clap.

Uh-oh. What had Angie done? Had she overstepped her boundaries—or bitten off more than she could chew?

"*Please,* Toby?" Kylie looked at her foster dad with puppy-dog eyes. "Can I stay here with Angie? Can I *please?*"

"If you're sure you don't mind." Toby's gaze zeroed in on Angie, and her heart spun in her chest.

What was that little zing all about?

Had that come from the way Toby was looking at her? Or from having second thoughts about what she'd just offered to do?

After all, she didn't know anything about kids. She'd been an only child and Doris definitely wasn't the maternal type. Plus, unlike some of the other girls she'd grown up with, she'd never even had a babysitting job.

But now that she'd made the offer, she couldn't very well backpedal.

"Of course I don't mind." Angie reached under the checkout stand for a stack of coloring pages and pulled out the top sheet. "The Superette is having a poster contest this month. All the kids have to do is color this picture and turn it back in for the judging. I have a few markers Kylie can use. Then, after I clock out, we'll be on our way for the best girls' day ever!"

Toby shot her an appreciative smile. "All right. We'll

probably only be a couple of hours. Where should I pick her up?"

Angie hadn't given much thought to what she'd do with Kylie, but since she didn't have any money to spend, they'd have to find something cheap to do at home. "I live in the small granny flat behind Elmer Murdock's place. Do you know where that is?"

"Sure do. Mr. Murdock owns the yellow, two-story house next to the post office. I didn't know anyone was living in that…unit in the back."

It wasn't common knowledge. In fact, she hadn't even mentioned the move to her mother yet.

Should she explain her living situation? Or better yet, make an excuse for it?

She decided to do neither.

After totaling Toby's purchases, Angie took his cash and gave him his change. Then she watched him leave the store with the boys, walking with that same swagger the other Fortune Jones boys possessed.

No, she'd never considered dating Toby in the past. And for the briefest of moments, she wondered why she hadn't.

After a fun but unproductive day at Cutter's Pond, Toby and the boys climbed into his truck. If they wanted fish for supper tonight, Toby would have to make another stop at the Superette and purchase a few fillets. As it was, he decided to make things easy on himself and to take the kids to The Horseback Hollow Grill for a couple of burgers. But first they'd have to pick up Kylie.

It had been nice of Angie to offer to babysit. The

afternoon had been a lot more pleasant with only the boys. Not that Kylie was a problem child. She was a sweetheart most of the time, but… Well, she had a tendency to get a little teary when things didn't go her way. But he supposed he couldn't really blame her. It had to be tough for a little girl growing up in a boys' world.

As he pulled his black four-wheel-drive Dodge Ram along the curb in front of the old Murdock place, he scanned the front yard, which looked a lot better than it had the last time he'd driven by. The once-overgrown lawn had been mowed recently and a sprinkler had brought the grass back to life.

The old house was still in need of repair—or at least, a fresh coat of paint and some new shutters. But that wasn't surprising. Elmer Murdock was well over eighty years old and living on his marine-corps retirement pay.

"Can we get out, too?" Justin asked.

"I don't see why not." While they'd all had a blast fishing, Toby knew the boys had been stewing over what kind of things might constitute a "girls-only" day. Apparently, the mystery of womanhood began early in a male's life.

He shut off the ignition, got out of the pickup and made his way to the path that led to the back of the house, where Mr. Murdock had built separate quarters for his widowed mother-in-law decades ago.

The "granny flat," as Angie had called it, was even more run-down than the main house. The small porch railing had come loose and was about to collapse, although the wood flooring had been swept recently.

A pot of red geraniums added a splash of color to the chipped and weathered white paint.

Brian and Justin lagged behind by several feet because they'd stopped to check out two different birdhouses in a maple tree. The birdhouse on the left was pretty basic, but the one on the right was three stories with a wraparound porch and looked like something straight out of his mother's *Southern Living* magazine.

Toby continued to the front door and knocked loud enough to be heard over the sound of Taylor Swift belting out her latest hit. He cringed, although he knew that, as a proud Texan, he should favor country music, even crossover pop artists like Taylor Swift. But his well-guarded secret was that he couldn't stand the stuff. He preferred his music with a lot more soul and a lot less twang.

When the front door swung open, Kylie, her face smeared with green goo, greeted Toby with a bright-eyed smile. "Guess what? Mr. Murdock and Angie had a nail-painting contest and I got to be the judge. And see, Mr. Murdock won because he painted the cutest little horse on my big toenail." She lifted her right leg high in the air in an effort to put her toe in front of his face.

"Yeah, well, Mr. Murdock cheated," came Angie's reply. "He took an hour to do it, using a magnifying glass and his model-airplane paint, which, by the way, isn't washable. That horse will never come off."

Toby couldn't actually see Angie, since she had her back to the door and was leaning over the arm of the sofa, a white container in one hand and a green sponge in the other.

Both amused and touched by the sight, Toby couldn't help but chuckle.

"Ooh, gross," Brian said, when he spotted his sister's face. "What happened to you?"

"I'm getting pretty—just like Angie."

Both boys began to hoot and howl.

Toby couldn't say that he blamed them. Kylie, who was a cutie-pie when she wasn't whining, looked like a pint-sized version of the creature from the black lagoon, walking around with a green face and her fingers and toes splayed out wide so the paint would dry.

The little red-haired girl stepped aside to allow them into the small house, just as Angie straightened. As Toby's eyes landed on Angie's face, it appeared as though she'd climbed from the same lagoon.

She smiled as if having green goop smeared all over wasn't the least bit unusual. "We didn't expect you back so soon."

"It certainly appears that way." Toby couldn't help but laugh.

"Just for the record, I did not cheat. You never established any ground rules." Elmer Murdock sprang up from the sofa Angie had been leaning over, the same green mud on his face. And Toby didn't know whether he should hoot with laughter or try his best to hold it back.

Was this the formidable retired marine who'd instilled fear in most of Horseback Hollow High School's youth with his loud shouting during football practices?

And for some reason, the old leatherneck didn't seem to be the least bit embarrassed at being caught having a facial.

Mr. Murdock slapped his hands on his hips and ze-roed in on Angie. "I didn't complain about *you* cheating when you used way more material on that Bird McMansion than I did during our birdhouse-building contest."

Toby quickly grabbed his ball cap from his head and pulled it lower over his face to cover his smirk. Was this the one-and-only Elmer Murdock?

His brothers would never believe this.

"You built that huge birdhouse outside?" Brian asked Angie. "I didn't know girls could build like that."

"Girls can do anything. Especially *this* girl." Angie pointed to her green-covered face. "I got an A in wood-shop when I was in high school. Give me a hammer, wood and nails, and I can build anything."

"Can you help me build my car for the soapbox derby?" Brian asked.

"Only if you want to win," Angie replied. Then she pointed to the sofa. "Have a seat, guys. Mr. Murdock has a few more minutes for his face to dry, but it's time for us ladies to wash off our masks. We'll be back in a Flash, Gordon."

"Hey," Brian said. "*Flash Gordon.* That's funny."

Toby crossed his arms and shifted his weight to one hip. Wow, Brian had been pretty quiet and distant ever since the state had stepped in and removed the kids from their aunt's custody. But he'd warmed up to Angie in about three minutes flat.

As Angie led Kylie across the small living area that served as both kitchen and sitting room, Toby couldn't help but watch the brunette who wore a pair of cutoff jeans that would have put Daisy Duke to shame pad across the floor. Her hips moved in a natural sway, her long, shapely legs damn near perfect. He remembered Doris Edwards's cutting potshot at the Superette and thought that from where he was standing, there was absolutely nothing wrong with Angie's curves.

He continued to watch her from behind until she and Kylie disappeared into the only other room in the house and shut the door.

Justin was sitting next to Mr. Murdock and reaching out his fingers to the wrinkled weather-beaten cheek. "Is that mud?" he asked the old man.

"Justin," Toby scolded, "keep your hands to yourself."

"Yeah, but this is sissy mud," Mr. Murdock answered casually. "It's supposed to clear your pores and detoxify your skin or some such bull. I'll tell you what, we never worried about our pores when we were covered in mud back in that wet foxhole in Korea. All we cared about was not getting our fool heads blown off."

"Wow, you got shot at in a war?" Brian asked as Justin started using the white container to apply stripes to his own eight-year-old face in a war-paint fashion that would make any Apache proud.

"Mr. Murdock," Angie yelled from the bathroom at the end of the small hall, "stop talking so much. You need to keep still and let the mask dry. Every time you talk, you crack it."

Mr. Murdock clamped his thin lips together in their perpetual grimace.

As Toby scanned Angie's small living area, he couldn't help but take note of the freshly painted blue walls that had been adorned with the oddest forms of artwork—

the label side of a wooden produce crate that advertised Parnell's Apple Farm, an old mirror framed with pieces of broken ceramic, a coatrack made out of doorknobs…

She'd placed a whitewashed bookshelf against one wall. Instead of books, it held various knickknacks. A bouquet of bluebonnets in a Mason jar sat on top. The furniture was old, and while the decor was kind of funky, the house had a cozy appeal.

"So you're running the old Double H Ranch?" Mr. Murdock asked Toby, lasting only a couple of minutes before he broke Angie's orders to stay quiet. It was hard to take the crotchety old man seriously with the green mud caked onto his face and his lips barely able to move.

"Sure am," Toby replied, warming up to his favorite subject—his ranch. "We have more than three hundred head of cattle now, and I've been doing some breeding."

"I used to do some roping back before I enlisted, you know. Could probably still out-rope most of you young upstarts. I should swing by your place and we could have a little contest."

What was it with this old man and contests? Apparently his competitiveness went well beyond the high-school football field.

Before Toby could politely decline the challenge, the door swung open and the girls came out.

Angie had apparently swapped the denim shorts for a yellow floral sundress, yet she was still barefoot, her toenails painted the same pink shade as Kylie's—minus the horse.

"We had a really good day," Angie said, her face clean, her eyes bright.

"We did, too," he said.

"Did you catch anything?"

"I'm afraid not."

"I used to catch all kinds of stuff out at Cutter's Pond," Mr. Murdock chimed in, while the boys continued to stare at the old swamp monster look-alike as if he were a real hero come to life. "Still hold the record for the biggest trout ever caught in Horseback Hollow. Nobody's beat me yet."

"Okay, Mr. Murdock, you should be dry." Angie patted her landlord on his shoulder. "You can probably go home and wash your face now."

"Roger that," the old coot replied as he shuffled toward the door and back to the main house. The former marine looked like a strong Texas wind would knock him over, and Toby doubted the man was in any shape to rope a tractor on his ranch, let alone a longhorn steer, although he'd never say so out loud.

Instead, he nodded at the interior of Angie's little house, at the freshly painted blue walls. "I like what you've done with this place. You certainly have a creative side."

"You think so? Thanks." She scanned the cramped quarters, too. "The house was empty for nearly twenty years, so it was pretty stuffy and drab when I moved in. I spent a couple of days cleaning and airing it out. I've also learned how to decorate on a shoestring budget, which has been fun."

"I can see that. You've done a great job. Where did you find this stuff?"

"Some of it was already here—like the furniture. I picked up the paint on sale when I was in Vicker's Corners the other day. Someone had ordered the wrong color, so it was practically free. I've also been picking up odds and ends at garage sales. Then I figured out a way to make them pretty—or at least, interesting."

"I'm impressed. You're quite the homemaker."

She brightened, and her wholesome beauty stunned him. Not that he hadn't noticed before, but he'd never seen her blue eyes light up when she smiled like that.

"To tell you the truth," he added, "I was surprised to hear that you'd moved in here. The windows had been boarded up for ages, and the weeds had grown up so high that most people forgot that there was a little house back here at all."

"Mr. Murdock and I were talking one day at the Superette, and he mentioned that he needed to hire someone to do some chores for him. I told him I had some free time. And when I spotted the little house, I asked if he'd be interested in renting it to me."

"I'd think you would have preferred to find a place that wouldn't have required as much work."

She shrugged. "Let's just say that, like Mr. Murdock, I love a challenge. Besides, his sons live out of state, so he's all alone. Plus, this way, I can look out for him and let him think he's looking out for me."

Toby had always thought Angie was a bit shallow, although he couldn't say why he'd come to that conclusion. Probably because he'd heard a few people say that she was flighty. But apparently, he'd been wrong. There was more to her than he'd given her credit for.

He also owed her for taking care of Kylie today, although something told him she wouldn't accept any money for doing it. So it seemed like the most natural thing in the world to say, "We're going to have burgers at The Grill. Would you like to join us?"

And it seemed even more natural for her to respond, "Sure. Why not?"

Chapter Two

The Horseback Hollow Grill, which was attached to the Two Moon Saloon, wasn't much to shout about when it came to eateries. But it was one of the only options in town. Fortunately, they served the juiciest burgers and dogs, fresh-cut fries and a mean grilled-cheese sandwich.

As Angie climbed from Toby's lifted truck, she couldn't help but smile. If her mom could see her now, the poor woman would be torn between deep anxiety and despair.

First of all, she'd be dancing on clouds to see Angie enter a restaurant with one of the Fortune Jones men, even if it was only The Grill. Doris assumed all the Fortunes were wealthy beyond their wildest dreams, although local rumor had it that the Horseback Hollow branch of the family hadn't struck any gold.

According to what Angie had heard, Jeanne Marie Fortune Jones had been adopted. And when her birth brother, James Marshall Fortune, had found her last year, he'd given her a portion of his stock in the family company. But when she found out those shares were supposed to go to his kids, she'd refused it.

Nevertheless, even with a boatload of cash, a man with three kids wasn't the catch Angie's mom had been hoping she'd snag.

Of course, this wasn't a date by any stretch of the word. Toby had only included her in the family plans because he was a nice guy. And Angie had accepted because she'd had nothing better to do and was on an especially tight budget these days.

As they entered the small-town restaurant, where artificial flowers in hammered coffeepots sat on old-style tables with rounded edges encased in silver metal, Angie realized they weren't the only ones in Horseback Hollow who'd decided to pick up a quick meal tonight. The place was certainly hopping.

Toby nodded toward an empty booth by the window, one of the few places to sit that weren't taken.

"Can we play in the game room for a while?" Justin asked.

Angie remembered the small arcade in back—if you could call it that—from her own school days. Back then, The Grill was *the* place to hang out if you were a teenager in Horseback Hollow. It probably still was, so she couldn't blame the kids for their eagerness to drop coins into the video-game machines.

"What do you guys want to eat?" he asked.

"I'd like grilled cheese," Kylie said, "but only if they have real bread and square cheese."

Angie cocked her head slightly. "What's she talking about?"

Toby chuckled. "We stopped at a place in Lubbock one day, and they brought out a sandwich that had been made with focaccia bread and several fancy kinds of cheese. It was the restaurant's claim to fame, and it cost a pretty penny, but Kylie didn't like it. By 'square' cheese, she means good ole American slices, individually wrapped."

"Aw." Angie smiled. "I'll have to remember that."

"I want a corn dog and fries," Justin said.

"Got it." Toby turned to Brian. "How about you?"

"I want a cheeseburger, but I don't want onions or lettuce or pickles. But ask if they'll give me extra tomatoes."

"Since we've got that out of the way, here you go." Toby reached into his pocket and pulled out a small handful of quarters. "Why don't you start with these? I'll get some change after the waitress takes our order."

While the kids dashed off, Toby waited for Angie to slide into the booth, then did the same.

As she settled into a middle spot, he removed his ball cap, as any proper Texan gentleman would do, leaving his brown hair disarrayed and close to his head. She was tempted to reach out and finger-comb it.

Or maybe she just wanted to touch it and see if it was as soft as it looked.

Odd, though. He didn't appear to be the least bit... mussed. He actually looked darn near perfect.

As if completely unaware of her perusal—and why

wouldn't he be?—he reached across the table for the menus and handed her one, ending her silly musing.

But as she opened it up and scanned the offerings— burgers, hot dogs and sandwiches—her options, while too few by some people's standards, still seemed too difficult to narrow down.

This was the part about eating out that she dreaded. She could never decide on what to order, especially when there were other people with her.

Since she didn't want Toby to think that she was indecisive, she did what she'd learned to do on her other dates. Not that this was a date.

Or was it? Did *Toby* think it was a date?

The waitress, a tall brunette in her early forties, approached. "What'll it be?"

Toby placed the kids' orders, then asked Angie, "What would you like?"

She gave her standard reply. "I'll have whatever you're having."

But when Toby ordered the double bacon cheeseburger, the large onion rings, fried pickles and jumbo peanut-butter milk shake, she realized she'd have to rethink her strategy if she ever went to another restaurant with him again.

Where was she going to put all that food?

"Maybe you'd better not bring me those pickles," she told the waitress.

The woman nodded, then made a note on her pad. After she left them alone, things got a little quiet. Actually, too quiet, since Angie tended to get bored easily.

So she said, "Looks like the kids will be busy for a while."

He smiled. "I remember when those games were brand-new. Fifteen years later, and they're still entertaining kids."

"You might not believe this," Angie said, "but I was a whiz at Ms. Pac-Man. There weren't too many people who could outscore me."

"Not even Mr. Murdock?"

At that, Angie laughed and shook her head. "Please don't tell him. I've never met a man more competitive than he is. If he finds out, I'll be forced to defend my title."

"Wow! A *titleholder?*" Toby tossed her a heart-strumming grin. "Who would have guessed that I'd be sharing a meal with a real live champion?"

"Yeah, well, it'd be nice to have a more worthwhile claim to fame than 'Top Scorer on Ms. Pac-Man.'" Angie settled back in the booth. Even the praise over what little she had achieved in life didn't do much in the way of soothing her embarrassment over her mother's public criticism.

"I'm sure you have plenty of things to be proud of," he said.

Their gazes met and held for a moment. Her smile faded, and she broke eye contact.

She was also a champ at changing subjects.

"The kids certainly seem to be settling in," she said.

"They seem to be. It was tough for a while, though. Justin was acting out and getting in trouble at school, but he's doing better now. And Kylie no longer has nightmares. Brian still holds back a bit, although I can understand that. It's hard for him to trust adults. Each one he's ever had to depend on has abandoned him—one way or another."

She'd heard a few scant rumors about the kids, but she didn't know what was true and what wasn't.

"What happened to their mother?" she asked.

"She was diagnosed with cancer right after Kylie was born and died just before her first birthday. Justin was only two at the time, so Brian's the only one who was old enough to remember her."

"What about their dad?"

Toby glanced toward the arcade, where the kids continued to play. Still, he kept his voice low. "From what I understand, he wasn't the kind of guy who could handle responsibility. When Ann, their mom, found out that she was pregnant with Kylie, he left her. And no one has heard from him since."

"That's so sad." Angie had always been close to her father, and when her parents had split up, it had crushed her. Losing her dad to cancer two years later had been even worse.

"After Ann died," Toby continued, "the kids went to live with her sister. But Barbara wasn't prepared for the challenge of raising two toddlers and a five-year-old. She drank as a way of escape. And the kids seemed to exacerbate her stress—and her need for the bottle."

"When did the state step in?" Angie asked.

"Last year, when Justin's behavioral problems in school escalated. The authorities were called in to investigate, and that's when they found out how bad things were at home. Shortly after that, Barbara was arrested. At that point, she was ordered to get in-patient treatment and the children were placed in separate foster homes. I hated the thought of them being split up. Family is important. And they'd lost so much already. So I volunteered to take them in."

"That was a big step for a bachelor."

He shrugged. "My mom was adopted. It just seemed like a natural way to pay it forward."

There it was again. Toby's altruistic personality. Everything about him was too perfect. Even his slightly mussed hair, which she was still tempted to reach out and touch.

It had a bit of a curl to it. Was it *really* as soft as it looked?

Oh, good grief. Get a grip, girl. She forced herself to stop gawking at him and to keep the conversation going. "So how long have you had them? About six months?"

"Yes, and I'll be the first to admit that it was a big adjustment. But it's getting easier. I actually like having them around. The ranch was too quiet before. You probably can imagine what it was like for me, growing up with all my brothers and sisters. I'm used to noise. Sometimes I feel as if I can't concentrate unless the decibel level is over ninety-five."

Actually, Angie couldn't imagine what any of that had been like. She didn't have any siblings. So her house had always been as quiet as a tomb, unless she had friends over.

"It was the talk of the town when you got custody of the kids," she said. "Most people didn't think it would last."

"My buddies certainly didn't think it would."

"How about you?" she asked. "How are you holding up?"

"I'm doing all right, but it's put a real cramp in my social life."

Angie smiled. "You mean with the guys—or romantically speaking?"

"Romance? What's that?" Toby laughed. "Actually, if I were even in a position to be looking for a relationship, I'd be in a real fix. Most women go running for the hills when they hear I have three children, even though the situation is supposed to be temporary. Other women look at me as if I'm some kind of hero. But even then, when they're faced with the reality of dating a man with the responsibility of three kids, they don't stick around long."

Point taken. Toby was making it clear that he wasn't looking for a relationship. Therefore, Angie now knew this clearly wasn't a date.

"Yet here you are," she said, "out with the kids having burgers, when you could be having a few beers at the Two Moon Saloon and dancing with Horseback Hollow's most eligible bachelorettes. From what I remember, you were always a pretty good dancer."

"I still am. Maybe I'll prove it to you sometime." Now, that was a challenge Angie looked forward to. And while the boyish grin on his face suggested that he was teasing, for a moment, for a heartbeat, she'd suspected that he'd been a wee bit serious.

And if they were ever to lay their secrets out on the table, she'd have to admit that she wouldn't mind dancing with him, holding him close, swaying to the slow beat of a country love song, her body pressed to his...

"Seriously, though," he said, drawing her back to reality, "if I wanted a beer, they'd serve me one in here. But I have enough on my plate without having to worry about dancing and courting the ladies, too."

"I hear you." And she did—loud and clear. He'd said it twice now, which was just as well. *Really,* it was. "I'm not looking for love, either—although my mother seems to think I should be."

"Doris is really hard on you. Why is that?"

"Because she's lost all hope of me making a financial success of my life. So if I can't be the money-making ballbuster she envisions, the least I can do is marry one."

"Well, then, Doris can rest assured that you'll be safe from me. I'm definitely not raking in the dough."

Safe from him? Toby couldn't be more obvious if he was wearing a blinking neon sign. She wanted to say, *Okay, I get it. You're not interested in me.*

But she supposed it wasn't necessary. Neither one of them was in any position to enter into a romantic relationship right now—with anyone.

"I wouldn't let your mother drag you down," Toby said. "You seem like a happy person. So whatever you're doing must be working for you."

Well, not exactly. While she wasn't miserable, she'd be a lot happier if she had a full-time job—or at least some direction.

"I'm doing just fine," she said.

Before Toby could respond, Kylie ran up to the table. "Brian won't let me have a turn driving the race car. He said it's 'cause I'm a girl. And 'cause my feet won't reach the pedals. But they will if he lets me sit on his lap."

"I have an idea," Angie said, as she slid out from behind the booth. "I'm going to show you how to play a better game. One that you can play all by yourself."

"You're coming in pretty handy," Toby said.

Angie laughed. "I'm just paying for my supper."

"At this rate, I'm going to owe you breakfast, too."

For a moment, just like the comment about dancing together had done, the overnight innuendo hung in the air. And while they both might have laughed it off, there'd been a brief moment when their gazes had met, a beat when she suspected that neither of them had taken the promise of an early-morning breakfast lightly.

Toby hoped the waitress brought their food soon. Not only was he hungry, but he was down to his last few quarters and wasn't about to ask for any more change than he had already. Since taking in the kids six months ago, his coin contributions alone could go a long way in refurbishing some of those old games and buying a new one.

He took a sip of his milk shake and watched the kids and Angie return to the table—out of quarters again, no doubt.

"You're pretty good at Ms. Pac-Man," Brian told Angie, as she slipped back into the booth.

"Thanks." She winked at Toby. "I used to be a lot better, but I'm getting rusty in my old age."

"You aren't that old," Justin said, taking her far more seriously than she'd intended. "Maybe if you came here to practice more often, you'd be supergood again."

Angie laughed. "I'm afraid my days of playing in the arcade are over."

"That's too bad," Justin said. "I'll bet you could hold the world record."

"I'll have to remind my mother that I actually have some talent the next time she worries about my future prospects."

"Here you go," Toby said, as he rationed out a few more of the coveted coins to the kids.

Then they dashed off, leaving him and Angie alone again. It was nice getting to know her, getting a chance to see a side to her he'd never realized was there. He didn't think he was the only one in town to have misconceptions about Angie Edwards. Heck, even her own mother didn't seem to appreciate her.

Toby hadn't liked the way her mom had talked to her today, especially in front of other people. But he supposed that wasn't any of his business. He'd always had a sympathetic nature. In fact, his brothers often ribbed him, saying he was a sucker for people who were down on their luck. Some of that might be true, although he didn't see Angie that way.

Sure, maybe she wasn't a superambitious go-getter. But she seemed to have a good head—and a pretty one at that—on her shoulders. And something told him that she'd find her groove in life soon.

"You know," he said, "it's not too late to go back to school."

"No, it isn't. But you're looking at a woman who'd joined the Toastmasters Club, the Teachers of Tomorrow, Health Careers and Future Farmers of America when I was in high school. I was even a member of the French Club one semester. I couldn't decide on a direction then, and I'm no closer to having one now. So I can't imagine spending the time and money to take classes without a goal in mind. So far, my motto in life has been 'just keep on keeping on.'"

"Well, if it makes you feel any better, I think that motto suits you pretty well. You're a lot of fun to be with. And you have a great ability to adapt. I'm sure you'll figure something out."

"Yes, but as each week passes, my mother gets more and more stressed about my future."

"How about you?" he asked. "Are you worried about it?"

She tossed him a pretty smile. "I'm doing just fine."

He didn't doubt that she was. "Then that ought to settle it."

She took her glass, wrapped her full lips around the straw and took a slow drag of her milk shake, making him think about somewhere else her mouth could be…

What in blazes was wrong with him? Angie Edwards wasn't the woman for him. He needed someone who was solid and stable, someone who was willing to take on three kids. And while Angie could probably handle anything life threw at her, she didn't seem like the type who would stick around for the long haul.

And even though everyone in town, including his family, thought that his taking on the Hemings kids was a temporary thing, Toby had gotten attached to them, and he wasn't planning to give them up unless their aunt insisted on taking them back. And even then, he wasn't sure if he'd step back without a fight. But from what he'd gathered from the social worker, their aunt Barbara wasn't the maternal type.

So if he had any chance of keeping them, he needed a partner who would be just as committed to the kids as he was.

Still, that didn't mean Angie wasn't an attractive woman. What she might lack in commitment, she more than made up for with sex appeal.

Yet the more time he spent with her, the more intriguing he found her.

Why hadn't he looked at her that way before? Well, of course he'd noticed her looks. He wasn't blind. But he'd never been the kind of guy to date someone just because of her physical appearance. He'd been interested in the woman on the inside.

Of course, after talking with her this evening, he had to admit that he was curious about what made her tick.

Even though they'd both grown up in Horseback Hollow, he really didn't know very much about her— except in the way that most folks in small towns knew stuff about each other.

Up until today, he and Angie had never said more than a few words to each other in passing.

Before he could ponder it any further, the waitress brought their food. While she was placing the plates on the table, Toby excused himself and went after the kids.

Moments later, they were all seated at the booth. The boys began to dig in, but Kylie merely looked at her plate and frowned.

"What's the matter?" Angie asked.

"It's too much. I don't want it."

"Oops," Toby said. "The boys are such good eaters that I sometimes forget about her. She isn't actually all that fussy, but I think she gets overwhelmed when her plate is too full."

"What if you share with me," Angie said. "Would that help?"

When Kylie nodded, Angie took a knife and, with a careful slice, cut the grilled cheese into quarters instead of halves. "I like smaller triangles. Don't you?"

The little girl smiled.

Angie reached for a section. "Can I have some of your fries, too?"

Again, Kylie nodded.

Toby would have to remember that trick.

Next, Angie took the knife, then sliced her double bacon burger in two. "When the waitress comes by I'm going to ask her for a to-go box."

"What are you going to do?" Toby asked. "Take that home for lunch tomorrow?"

"Actually, I thought I'd offer it to Mr. Murdock. He likes a late-night snack when he watches television. And I thought it would be a nice surprise."

So she was thoughtful, too—especially with kids and the elderly.

Toby took a bite of his burger, relishing the taste. No one made them better than The Grill.

"Can you hand me the mustard?" Angie asked.

Toby reached for the bottle that stood next to the menus on the table and handed it to her, thinking she was going to apply it to the portion of the burger she intended to eat. Instead, she poured a glob onto her plate, dipped one of the French fries into it and took a bite.

"Most people prefer catsup," he said. "Miss Edwards, you're proving to be quite a novelty."

She smiled. "'Always keep 'em guessing.' That's my motto."

Toby laughed. "You have a lot of mottos, I'm learning."

She tossed him a pretty smile.

"Can I try that?" Justin asked. "Pass me the mustard, too."

"I'm not going to be able to eat all these onion rings," Angie said. "Does anyone want to help me out?"

"I've never had them before," Brian said.

She passed her plate to him. "You should at least try one. You might be missing a real treat."

Ten minutes later, Kylie had eaten three-quarters of her sandwich. Justin had finished off his corn dog and decided that he preferred dipping his fries in mustard rather than catsup. And Brian had wolfed down most of Angie's onion rings.

Then the kids dashed back to the arcade with the last of the quarters, leaving the adults sitting amid the clutter of nearly empty plates, wadded napkins, dribbles of soda pop and a melting ice cube.

Toby studied Angie in the dim light of the least romantic restaurant in West Texas.

Why in the world hadn't he taken the time to get to know her sooner, when his life hadn't been complicated by three children?

He supposed one reason he'd steered clear of her

was because his brother Jude had once dated her. And for that reason, Toby had considered her off-limits.

Yet, when the kids returned to the table, high from their final top-ranking scores on Ms. Pac-Man, the sound of Angie's infectious laughter, as well as the way she pulled Kylie onto her lap and gave her a squeeze, made Toby think he'd better have a talk with his newly engaged brother.

There were a few questions he needed to ask Jude. Because maybe, just maybe, this funny and beautiful woman wasn't entirely off-limits after all.

Chapter Three

Ever since Angie had joined him and the kids for dinner on Saturday night, Toby hadn't been able to stop thinking about her. By Monday morning he was racking his brain, trying to come up with an excuse to see her—other than stopping by the Superette to pick up groceries, although he was tempted to do just that.

Then, while driving the kids to school, he had a lightbulb moment.

Brian, who was seated in front, was craning his neck and peering out the windshield at a plane flying overhead.

"Look at that one," he said, pointing it out to his younger brother, who sat in the back with Kylie. "Wouldn't it be cool to fly an airplane?"

And bingo! Toby had the perfect solution.

"How would you like to talk to a real pilot and see some planes up close?" he asked Brian.

The oldest boy had been unusually quiet and introspective since moving in with Toby, but when he glanced across the seat, his mouth dropped open and his eyes lit up in a way they'd never done before. "That would be awesome. Do you know one?"

"My cousin Sawyer and his wife, Laurel, own the new flight school and charter service. Laurel is actually the pilot. She was even in the air force."

"No kidding?" The boy's jaw dropped, and his eyes grew wide. "For *real?*"

Most people in town were more impressed with Toby's connection to the Fortune family, rather than the lovely woman one of his cousins had married. "Yes, for *real.* I'll give Sawyer a call this morning and ask for a tour."

"For all of us?" Justin asked.

"And for me, too?" Kylie chimed in. "If it's a girl pilot, I want to see her."

Toby laughed. "Yes, we'll all go. After I drop you guys off at school, I'll try to work out a good time for us to go. But no promises on when that might be."

And that was just what Toby did. Once the kids had gotten their backpacks, climbed out of the truck and headed for their respective classrooms, he called his cousin.

Sawyer's father, James Marshall Fortune, had been a triplet. His two sisters had been given up for adoption when they were very young. Josephine May was raised in England by the Chesterfields, a family that was both rich and royal. Jeanne Marie, Toby's mom, was raised in Horseback Hollow by loving parents who were common folk. But what they lacked in finances, they made up for in love.

Last year, Sawyer had met Laurel Redmond in Red Rock, where they fell in love. On New Year's Eve, they married in Horseback Hollow, where they now made their home. Sawyer and Laurel opened Redmond-Fortune Air, which served folks in this area. Laurel used to work with her brother, Tanner Redmond, who owned the Redmond Flight School and Charter Service back in Red Rock. They originally opened a branch of that company here, but with Tanner's blessing and Sawyer's capital, Laurel bought out her brother's stock and recently went out on her own.

When Sawyer answered the phone, Toby told him about Brian's interest in airplanes, then asked if he could bring the kids by the airfield sometime for a tour.

"Absolutely," Sawyer said. "Laurel flew a couple of businessmen from Vicker's Corners to Abilene this morning for a meeting, but she should be back before three."

"Is Angie Edwards working for you today?" Toby asked, as casually as he could.

"As a matter of fact, she comes in at one-thirty and will be here until four. Why?"

"No reason. I'd heard she was a part-time receptionist." Toby glanced at the clock on the dashboard, realizing he had a lot of chores to get done today. But no telling when Angie would be working at the flight school again.

"The kids get out of school at three," he told Sawyer. "So we'll head over to the airfield then."

And that was just what he did.

As had become his routine, Toby waited in front of the school when the bell rang. Only this time, he'd gone home so he could shower, shave and put on a new shirt and his favorite jeans.

"Did you talk to your cousin?" Brian asked, as he climbed into the truck.

"I sure did. And Sawyer said to come by today."

Whoops and cheers erupted from the backseat. Even the usually quiet Brian was beaming, confirming that Toby had just hit a home run.

So what if fulfilling a young boy's dreams to get to see the inside of a cockpit hadn't been his only motive? Besides, the kids had been talking about Angie nonstop—especially Kylie—and they were going to be just as excited to see her as he was. If he happened to talk to a beautiful woman and casually slip in a dinner invitation while they were at the airfield, then so be it.

"But let's set some ground rules," he told the kids. "You're going to have to mind your manners and not touch anything you're not supposed to. No running off—that means *you,* Justin. And the minute we get back to the ranch, you're going to have to sit down and do your homework. No complaints. Got it?"

A chorus of "got it"s and excited chatter filtered over the seat to him.

Fifteen minutes later, as the anticipation built in the cab of the truck, Toby turned down the county road that led to their destination.

Prior to the addition of Redmond-Fortune Air, the Horseback Hollow Airport hadn't amounted to much more than a small control tower, a couple of modular buildings, one of which housed Lone Star Avionics, several hangars and a relatively small airstrip.

But the brand-new building Sawyer and Laurel had built, with its gray block exterior, smoky glass windows and chrome trim, added some class to an otherwise small-town, nondescript airport that served both Horseback Hollow and nearby Vicker's Corners.

After parking next to Sawyer's new black Cadillac Escalade, Toby led the kids up the walkway and through the double glass doors into the reception area.

Angie, who was busy typing some letters at the reception desk, brightened when they came in. "Hey, look who's here!"

She greeted each child with a hug, but stopped short when she reached Toby. After all, what was required? Certainly not an embrace. And a handshake was much too formal.

They both settled for a smile, which worked out just fine.

"I heard you were coming." She turned to a guy in green coveralls who was seated near a potted ficus tree and reading a newspaper. "Pete, is Sawyer still out back?"

"Yep. He'll be in shortly." Pete lowered his newspaper and nodded at Toby. "How's it goin'?"

"Not bad."

Pete Nelson, a tall, lanky mechanic, worked for Lone Star Avionics and sometimes did side jobs for Sawyer and Laurel. Ever since Sawyer and Laurel opened up for business, the other employees at the airfield usually came over to use their break room, as well as the new fridge, microwave and coffeemaker.

"Taking a break?" Toby asked the thirtysomething air-force vet, trying to keep the hint of jealousy from his voice. After all, if he worked at the airfield, he'd be taking breaks in the office when Angie was here, too.

Hell, Toby didn't even work at the airfield, and he was looking for reasons to stop by the sexy brunette's places of employment.

"Just having a quick cup of coffee," Pete said. "Then it's back to the hangar."

"Hey, Justin," Brian said, as he wandered toward a table with a plastic-enclosed display of miniature-sized scale models of airplanes. "Look at this."

Kylie followed the boys, just as Sawyer entered the building.

"Hey, Toby." He extended his arm, and they shook hands. "Sorry I wasn't here when you arrived."

"No problem. We've been checking out the reception area." And the receptionist, who'd just bent over to reach into the lowest drawer of the filing cabinet.

Toby hadn't noticed before, but Angie was wearing a short black skirt. Well, it hadn't looked so short until she'd bent over and those long, tanned, shapely legs stretched out.

Wow.

Sawyer continued to talk, although Toby couldn't quite wrap his mind around what he was saying. Still, he nodded as if he'd heard every word.

When Kylie, who must have gotten bored looking at the miniature planes with her brothers, wandered over to Angie, Toby was about to call the little girl over to him and tell her that Angie was busy. But without missing a beat, Angie set her up at the desk with a stamp pad and paper, then went back to stooping and bending and flashing those long, shapely legs.

"Aw, so that's the way the wind is blowing," Sawyer said, calling Toby out.

"The *wind?*"

Sawyer lowered his voice to a whisper. "It's not the airplanes you're interested in. It's Little Miss Google. I'd wondered why you wanted to know if she was working today."

Toby tore his gaze from Angie, ran his fingers through his closely cropped hair and focused on Sawyer. "What are you talking about? Who's Little Miss Google?"

"Evangeline Edwards, our part-time receptionist and jack-of-all-trades."

Toby never had been good at lying, so he zeroed in on the subject he'd rather discuss. "Why do you call her Little Miss Google?"

"Because she's a walking version of the website. If you want any information about anything at all, there's a pretty good chance she knows it."

While Toby had never considered Angie to be dumb, she hadn't struck him as being exceptionally knowledgeable, either.

Had he missed something?

"You don't believe me? Watch this." Sawyer called across the open reception room. "Hey, Angie, Captain Schroder called a few minutes ago. Laurel wasn't around for me to ask, but he's flying his client's new Cessna Nav into Horseback Hollow. He wants to know how many feet per minute his descent should be."

Angie didn't look up from her work. "If his true airspeed is 75 knots, which is standard for most Cessna Navs on approach, our headwind component here is usually 15 knots. That would make his ground speed 60 knots, which you'd multiply by five for a rate of descent of 300 feet per minute."

"Thanks. I'll let him know." Sawyer gave Toby a little jab with his elbow, then tilted his head and lifted a single eyebrow as if to ask, *What'd I tell you?*

Toby had no way of knowing if what Angie had recited was true or not, but he figured it must be. Pete the mechanic hadn't argued the point. Of course, he still had his nose in the newspaper.

Moments later, Laurel Redmond Fortune came through the same back door Sawyer had entered. The lovely blonde greeted Toby with a hug, then gave her husband a kiss. "I'm going to grab a quick cup of coffee in the break room, then I'll give you guys that tour we promised."

"Take your time," Toby said.

As Laurel left the room, Pete lowered the newspaper he'd been reading. "Did you guys know that Herb Walker got busted for drunk-and-disorderly conduct last night outside the Two Moon Saloon?"

Sawyer gave Toby another little elbow jab, then said, "I wonder what kind of bail his wife will have to post for him."

"Normally, it would be twenty-five hundred dollars," Angie said, "but seeing how today is Monday and Judge Hanson doesn't approve of drinking on Sundays, drunk and disorderlies from the night before usually have to post four thousand."

Angie's position on her knees, as she placed the last

of the papers in the very back of the lowest drawer, gave Toby an excellent view of the rear end Doris Edwards had criticized days earlier. But Toby was so busy picking up his jaw off the floor that he was having trouble concentrating on those lovely curves.

How did she know those random facts?

When Sawyer and Pete started to laugh, Angie finally looked up and clued in to what was happening. "Were you guys doing that Google thing again?"

"What's a drunk and disorderly?" Kylie asked, reminding the adults that the kids were still hanging around.

"It's what Aunt Barbara got arrested for," Brian answered, displaying knowledge beyond his age.

The laughter suddenly ceased, and the adults sobered. Fortunately, Angie swooped in for the save. "Hey, Brian, Mr. Fortune said you could go sit in the cockpit of his brand-new Gulfstream. You can even touch every button and lever. And Mr. Nelson won't mind a bit putting them all back into place after you guys mess with them to your heart's content."

As a whoop went up from the kids, Angie cheekily smiled at her boss and the mechanic.

About that time, Laurel came out of the break room with her coffee. "Let's go, kids."

"I call first on talking on the headset to the people in the control tower," Justin said.

"I get to sit in the pilot's chair first," Brian countered, as he followed Laurel out the door.

"Wait for me," Kylie yelled as she tried to keep up with her brothers, who were already headed toward the hangar with Laurel.

The mechanic and Sawyer both gave Angie a look that promised they'd get even with her. But as far as Toby could see, they'd messed with Angie first.

It was nice to see that she gave back as good as she got.

"Laurel's going to need my help," Sawyer said.

"Mine, too." Pete set aside the newspaper, grabbed his disposable cup and followed Sawyer outside, leaving Toby and Angie alone.

Finally.

"How do you know so much?" he asked.

"I used to watch *Jeopardy!* a lot with my dad when he was sick, and trivial facts tend to stick in my brain. Plus, I did a lot of internet research when I was trying to decide upon a college major." She glanced at the clock on the wall, noting that it was four.

She straightened her desk, then shut down her computer. As she reached for her purse, she added, "Learning various oddball things is also a perk to changing jobs frequently. So I ended up knowing a little something about everything. Obviously, the flight stuff, I learned here."

As she pushed back her chair, he couldn't help noticing those long, tanned legs emerging from the skirt that no longer seemed too short.

"What about the drunk and disorderly?" he asked. "Is that from a job or from firsthand experience?" *Please don't let her be a party girl,* he found himself thinking.

"Do I look like the drunk-and-disorderly type?" She turned back to Toby. She must have noticed his gaze on her legs, because she crossed her arms and said, "Don't answer that."

"Sorry."

She didn't seem to be actually annoyed, though, because there was a spark of humor in her voice when she added, "Before that temp agency folded, they sent me to work at Señor Paco's Bail Bonds for a few weeks."

That was a relief. Not that he planned to actually date her.

Or did he?

"Aren't you going out with the kids to see the new plane?" she asked.

He'd much rather learn about Angie's control panel than some stupid airplane's, especially since it was four o'clock and she was leaving.

Who knew when he'd see her again, which brought out an unexpected sense of urgency, prompting him to blurt out, "Do you want to come over for dinner tonight?"

Dinner? At the Double H Ranch? With Toby and the kids?

The invitation had come out of the blue, and judging from the expression on Toby's face, Angie suspected that the question had surprised him as much as it had her.

"I'm not sure what we'll be having," he added. "I'll have to stop by the Superette and pick up something. But the kids need to eat tonight. And if you're not busy…"

"Actually, I have to stop by there to pick up my paycheck anyway. Do you want me to do the shopping for you?"

"That would be great." Toby reached into his back pocket, pulled out his wallet and peeled out a couple of bills. "Here's forty bucks. Pick up whatever you think the kids will like."

Great. The choice was hers, then?

Not only had she agreed to have dinner with him and the kids, she'd also agreed to plan the menu, which meant she'd be stuck trying to decide what to cook for a hungry man and three picky children.

What had she been thinking?

At least he'd given her the money to pay for the groceries. She wasn't sure how she would have been able to afford them if he hadn't.

"Do you know how to get to the ranch?" he asked.

She tossed him a smile. "I'm sure I can find my way there."

Ten minutes later, she was walking up and down the aisles of the Superette, grabbing packages and cans in record time.

Julia Tierney, who'd been working the check stand, laughed when Angie started laying items out on the conveyor belt.

"What's so funny?" Angie asked her friend and boss.

"Girl, I haven't seen you make such quick decisions on what to buy since that time you came running in here after that chili-pepper-eating contest with Mr. Murdock. You grabbed the first bottle of Mylanta you could find and drained it right in the middle of aisle three."

Sometimes, when Angie didn't have time to think about it, she could be rather decisive. And her tummy had been on fire that day.

She shook off Julia's teasing. "I'm picking up dinner for Toby and his kids this evening. And since I'm sure everyone's probably hungry, I don't have time to roam the aisles, stewing about what to cook."

Julia glanced at the items she rang up. "Pizza sauce, mozzarella cheese, pepperoni slices, mushrooms, ham, peppers, onions, ice cream, strawberries, instant bread mix. Looks like you'll be having homemade pizza."

"I figured it would be safe, especially if the kids can make their own."

"That's clever," Julia said. "I couldn't have come up with a better idea myself."

That was quite the compliment. Julia had always dreamed of going to culinary school or maybe getting a degree in restaurant management, but when her father suffered a heart attack, she'd decided to stick close to home and help out her parents with the store. So she'd given up her dream.

However, now that her father was better, it looked as though her dreams would finally come true. When Wendy and Marcos Mendoza finally opened up The Hollows Cantina in the next month or so, Julia was going to manage it.

"Yeah, well, I've learned that if you can't choose just one thing, it's best to have plenty of options available."

"Good idea," Julia said, as she totaled Angie's purchases.

"How are things going with the new restaurant?"

"Great. I love what Marcos and Wendy have envisioned, and it's really coming together. In fact, I was going over some of the job applications we've gotten and saw yours. We won't be scheduling interviews yet, but I wanted you to know that you're at the top of the pile."

"Thanks. That's nice to know." Angie helped Julia bag her purchases. "Who's going to take over for you here?"

"My mother's sister just retired from a cable-television company in Lubbock. So she's going to move in with my folks and help out for a while. I think it's all going to work out nicely."

"I'm glad to hear that."

"So tell me," Julia said. "This thing with Toby and the kids… That's a little intriguing."

Only because Julia was in love with Liam, Toby's brother. And she had stars in her eyes and thought everyone else should, too.

"We're just friends," Angie said.

Of course, she'd caught Toby staring at her legs a few times earlier today. And unlike a lot of other men she'd caught gawking like that, he'd seemed to be interested in more than just her appearance.

"Didn't I once hear you say that you never liked limiting your options?" Julia asked.

Yes, that was Angie. Her father had always told her that life wasn't an Etch A Sketch. That she ought to weigh each decision carefully, especially when it came to choosing a career—or a spouse.

Otherwise, she could find herself stuck in a really bad place.

She supposed that was why she'd never been able to settle on a college major or to find a job that inter-

ested her for very long—or a man worth making any
kind of commitment to.

Angie didn't respond to Julia's question. Instead,
she thanked Julia, took the two bags of groceries and
headed for her car.

No, Toby Fortune Jones wasn't in the running when
it came to considering romantic possibilities.

But if he wasn't an option, then what was he?

The answer came to her as she placed the pizza fixings
into her car and prepared to head for the Double H Ranch.

Toby Fortune was one fine cowboy who was far too
attractive for her own good.

Chapter Four

After Toby finished overseeing the homework hour, he told the kids they could watch television before dinner. Then he went into the kitchen to check the pantry. It wasn't as though his cupboards were bare. He could certainly rustle up something to add to whatever Angie planned to cook.

He'd no more than scanned the canned goods in the pantry when he heard a car pull up. Knowing it had to be her, he went outside to greet her.

As she climbed out of the driver's seat of a black Toyota Celica that had seen better years, let alone days, she reached into the back for the first of two eco-friendly bags. Her hair had been pulled back in a ponytail when she'd been at Redmond-Fortune Air, but it hung loose around her shoulders now—soft, glossy and teased by a light evening breeze.

She wasn't wearing anything different—just that black skirt and white blouse. Yet tonight, for some crazy reason, he found himself a wee bit... Hell, he didn't know what to call it—starstruck, stagestruck, dumbstruck...?

"Here. Let me help you with those." He reached for the bags, and she handed them over.

As they headed for the house, he said, "I'm sorry for not having stuff on hand to cook. When I lived by myself, I could go weeks without grocery shopping. But since the kids have been living here, it seems like I need to restock my fridge every other day."

She tossed him a carefree smile. "You should probably shop at one of those warehouse stores where you can buy in bulk and use a flatbed cart to haul your purchases to the checkout line."

"If I didn't have to drive clear to Lubbock to find one, I would. But then again, the kids wouldn't get to come into the Superette all the time and see you."

Toby chanced a glance at the woman walking next to him, wondering if she knew the kids weren't the only ones who'd miss seeing her.

"The kids are fun," she said. "I like it when they come in."

What if he didn't have children? Would she like it when he came in?

"Nice house," she said, as they entered the living room, which always managed to stay tidy because there wasn't a television set or a video game in sight. "I've always liked the ranch style."

Toby slowed his steps long enough to scan the white walls, the open-beamed ceilings, the distressed hardwood floors, the stone fireplace, as well as the leather furniture. "Thanks. I've been meaning to add a little color, maybe some Southwestern-style pictures on the wall, but I haven't gotten around to it yet."

"I'm sure the kids take up most of your free time."

"You got that right." He carried her purchases into the kitchen and placed the bags on the white tile countertop.

"What are we having?" he asked.

"Pizza. And just the way everyone likes it."

"Great idea. But I've never told you my pizza preference." There had to be some things even Ms. Google didn't know, unless she was psychic.

She tossed him a breezy smile. "I'll bet I even have your specific preference covered."

Something told him not to take her up on any wagers or else he'd end up in some wacky competition with her, just like Mr. Murdock.

But then again, Toby had always liked a good challenge. And Angie Edwards would prove to be one heck of one—if he were to pursue her.

"Hmm," she said, as she studied the directions on the box of instant bread-dough mix. "This might not be enough. Do you have any flour?"

"It's in the pantry. I'll get it. Is there anything else I can do to help?"

"You can wash the veggies, chop them up and put them in separate containers. Do you have a cutting board and knife?"

"Sure do."

While Toby got busy on his assignments, Angie began kneading the dough. Next they sliced the pepperoni and grated the cheese. Before long, they were moving around the kitchen seamlessly, almost as if they'd worked together a hundred times.

"So let me ask you something," Angie said.

Oh, no, here it comes, he thought. *She wants to know why I keep showing up at her workplaces and inviting her to hang out with me and the kids.*

"How do you do it?" she asked.

"Excuse me?"

"I couldn't help noticing your refrigerator door. It's plastered with papers—Kylie's artwork, Justin's B+ in spelling, the graph Brian created in math, not to mention that bulletin board with the YMCA flyers posted all over it. Then there's a list of dance classes and the schedule for swim lessons. I'm amazed that a single dad is so supportive of his kids. But what really blows me away is that LEGO-themed calendar you have on the wall."

"When I was a kid, our fridge was always covered in stuff like that. And my mom used to display all our awards and trophies throughout the house. She kept a bulletin board in the kitchen, too. Right next to the telephone. But why does the calendar surprise you?"

"Because almost every square this month is full. And just look at this list of YMCA classes. Nearly all of them are circled."

"You think that's too many?"

"Not for the kids. It's great for them. But the YMCA is in Vicker's Corners, which is a bit of a drive from the ranch. And I'm worried about you. I was an only child, with two parents. And it was all they could do to get me to school, the sitter and to any medical appointments."

"I have to admit, it's tough sometimes."

She crossed her arms, as if she was going to scold him, but she smiled and her eyes sparkled in mirth. "Toby, you're doing it to yourself. It's only April, and you have them in swim lessons? It's not even summer vacation yet."

"I know, but Justin can't swim. And he wants to go to camp in June. So I figured we'd better get started on those lessons so I won't have to worry about him." Toby shrugged and added, "Besides, I don't mind running them around. They've had it rough ever since their mom died. And they've missed out on a lot of things— like parents and a happy home. I just want them to see what it's like to have a normal family life."

"I think that's wonderful. So don't get me wrong. I'm happy for them. And I think it's awesome that you're providing them with so many opportunities, especially when you're the only one available to drive them back and forth. It's just that I know how much you must be sacrificing, and I'm not even talking about the cost of those activities."

Toby thought about the old beat-up car sitting in his driveway and the fixer-upper granny flat in which she lived. Apparently money was an issue for her.

He was pretty sure that Angie couldn't care less about his family's financial situation—or rather, the wealth most folks seemed to think they had by way of their rich relations. But he had reason to believe her mother didn't feel the same way.

So just in case he'd misread Angie, he figured it wouldn't hurt to let it be known that if a woman was looking for a wealthy "catch," she wouldn't find him living on the Double H Ranch.

"I want the kids to stay busy, even if that keeps me hopping. I hired a foreman early on to take on a lot of my work and responsibilities, which put another strain on the finances, especially since the Double H doesn't bring in that kind of money yet. So I've had to scrimp in other ways."

"Yes," she said. "I know."

He cocked his head slightly. So he'd been right? She was not only smart, but a psychic, too? No, that couldn't be right.

"What do you mean?" he asked.

She pointed to the bag of flour on the counter, which he'd picked up at the Superette because it was half the price of the name brand.

"Oh. You mean because I bargain-shop."

She laughed. "You didn't get a deal. That flour is too inferior for any proper baking, and it was aging on the shelf. So the price was discounted, but it still isn't selling—except to people who don't know anything about cooking."

"Oh, yeah? It seems to work well enough." Toby reached into the bag, grabbed a handful of flour and blew the mound directly into her pretty little upturned face. "See? It's light and airy."

"Oh, you…" Angie sputtered through the white dust covering her lower face, then quickly picked up a mushroom she'd been chopping and threw it directly between his eyes.

The vegetable struck him dead center. He laughed,

and she reached into the bag of flour—no doubt wanting to dust his face a ghostly white, just as hers was.

He grabbed her wrist to stop her, and she twisted, trying to pull free. Then, as their eyes met, she stopped. He stopped. For a moment, everything stopped—time, breathing, heartbeats....

No, not heartbeats. He could feel her pulse pounding in her wrist, under his fingertips.

Their gazes remained locked, and something passed between them. Before he could figure out just what the heck it was, Kylie ran into the kitchen, breaking the tension, as well as the silence.

When she spotted Angie, her eyes widened. "What happened to your face? It's a great big mess."

"I know." Angie laughed.

So did Toby. "She might be a champ at playing Ms. Pac-Man, but she's no match for Mr. Ranch-Man."

"Cute," Angie said. "Very cute."

He tossed her the dish towel closest to him. She caught it, then walked to the sink, dampened it and wiped off her face.

"Is dinner ready yet?" Kylie asked.

"Almost, honey." Angie grabbed a slice of Kylie's favorite American cheese. "Snack on this and I'll call you guys in just a couple of minutes."

"Okay." Kylie took the cheese, then dashed out of the kitchen and back to the family room.

Deciding to get their earlier conversation back on track, Toby said, "Actually, just to set the record straight, the Horseback Hollow Fortunes aren't rich like our cousins from Red Rock, Atlanta or the U.K. So taking on the kids did put me in a financial bind at first, but not for long. Someone apparently wanted to help out and donated money to cover those expenses and then some."

"That's amazing. What a generous gift."

"It certainly was. I wish I could thank them, but it was an anonymous donor."

"Could it have been their father or maybe one of their long-lost relatives?" she asked.

Toby snorted. "I doubt that. I'm more inclined to think that it was one of *my* long-lost family members."

"Who? Or would you rather not share that with me?"

"My best guess and number one suspect is James Marshall Fortune, Sawyer's father and my mother's brother. I think it was his way of indirectly giving my mom some of those shares of stock she returned to him last year. But I'm not going to push too hard to find out. If the donor wants to remain anonymous, then I'll respect that."

"Nevertheless, I still think it's wonderful that someone wanted to help the kids."

"That's how I see it, too. The money was actually given to me through an attorney in Lubbock, along with a note saying that it was to offset the costs I incurred by taking in the kids. But that I should spend it as I saw fit. That's what made me think the donor had to be my uncle." Toby raked his hand through his hair. "I wrestled with my pride for a while and was tempted to refuse it. But then I realized the kids really deserved it. And it would provide a better life for them. So I decided not to look a gift horse in the mouth."

"I assume it was a substantial amount."

"Enough to see them each through high school and

to pay for their college. So I put the money into a trust fund for them. It's invested and provides a monthly income that helps cover their expenses and pays for extra things like swim lessons and dance classes. Summer camp, too. Stuff like that."

"Wow. That's awesome." She tossed him a dazzling smile, then added, *"You're* awesome, Toby."

Angie gazed at him as if he'd just been awarded the Medal of Honor. And while he found her admiration touching, it also felt undeserved. So he lobbed a playful smile at her in return. "Yep. A horrible bargain shopper, but an awesome man."

Toby leaned toward the bag of cheap flour again and Angie threw up her arms in protection. "No, no, I give up. You are not only a good man, but a fine steward of your money. You make excellent shopping decisions. You should be on that coupon show on TV."

"Now I know you're full of it," Toby said, laughing along with her.

Teasing had been a way of life in the Fortune Jones household, and he liked that Angie was the kind of woman who found it so easy to banter.

"Okay," she said. "The ingredients are all set."

"Do you want me to call in the kids?"

"Go right ahead. I'll turn on the oven and get the drinks." Angie went to the refrigerator door, paused and stared at the most recent flyer. "Speaking of saving money, it looks like they're offering two free weeks of classes at the Y this month. Maybe I should check into that. I've always wanted to see what yoga is all about."

Toby didn't know if she was talking to him or to

herself, but apparently there was yet another interest she wanted to add to what had to be a lengthy list.

She tossed him a pretty smile. "Who knows? Maybe
I'll become a yoga instructor someday."

"Speaking of people who run around too much,"
he said, returning her smile with a teasing grin, "what
about you?"

"Me?" Angie tilted her head slightly and furrowed
her brow. "What about me?"

"You seem to change jobs a lot. Why not find a
good, full-time position and stick with it?"

"I will someday. But I want something that I can
feel passionate about. Maybe, if I keep trying different
things, I'll eventually find the career I'm best suited
for."

He hoped she came across it soon—for her sake.

And maybe for his. She really was easy to talk to,
and the kids adored her. If she were more settled, he'd
like to see where this relationship—if he could even
call it that—would go.

But he couldn't risk allowing himself or the kids
to get too close to someone who could be gone working on an oil rig or joining the military or going to
cosmetology school or wherever the wind took her
next month.

Unless, of course, Angie had already worked on an
oil rig and had crossed that off her to-do list.

If he didn't have the kids and didn't need her help,
he'd…

He'd what? Cut her loose?

That might be the wisest thing to do.

So why did he feel like reeling her in?

Because she was beautiful. And fun to be around. In fact, if he didn't have the kids to think about, good ole dependable Toby might even consider doing something wild and crazy—like having a one-night stand or a weekend fling with her.

Talk about something totally out of character for a guy like him.

But yeah, if he were footloose and fancy-free, that was exactly what he'd do.

As he took another glance at Angie, saw the glimmer in her eyes, caught a whiff of her citrusy scent…

Well, heck. If he had a babysitter willing to spend the weekend at the ranch with the kids, he just might consider taking Angie for a night or two on the town in Lubbock anyway.

The pizza-making station had been a smashing success. Altogether, they'd created three medium lopsided pizzas, one supersized with only meat, and one that was perfectly formed with every single topping.

Once the homemade creations came out of the oven, the kids could hardly wait for them to cool before they scarfed them down.

"Thanks for dinner," Toby said. "It was awesome."

"It sure was," Justin said. "I never made pizza before. It was fun."

"I'm glad you liked it." Angie turned to the boys. "Hey, guys. I don't suppose I could get you to do me a favor. After we get the kitchen cleaned up, I was hoping you'd teach me a few tricks on your PlayStation. I need a crash course."

"Sure!" Justin turned to his older brother, and the boys pumped their fists in the air.

"Seriously? You want a lesson from the kids?" Toby asked. "And why the big rush?"

"Mr. Murdock won his grandson's PlayStation from him in a poker game."

Toby lifted his eyebrow. "He gambled with a kid?"

"Long story. Anyway, he's been beating me left and right on Madden."

"Oh, great," Toby said, a spark of humor in his tone. "I thought I'd brought in adult reinforcement, but I've ended up with a fourth kid."

"Come on," Justin said. "Let's go, Angie."

"We have dishes to do first," she reminded him.

"No, you go ahead," Toby said. "I'll take care of the cleanup."

"Are you sure you don't mind?"

"After you pulled off such a successful dinner? Heck no. Besides, I'd hate to see Mr. Murdock get the best of you again."

She laughed, then took off with the boys.

Twenty minutes later, Toby reminded them that it was a school night.

"Aw, man," Justin said.

Angie wrapped her arms around his shoulders and gave him a squeeze. "You heard what Toby said. Maybe I'll come back another night, and we'll play again."

Toby let the kids stay up long enough to eat a bowl of ice cream topped with fresh strawberries for dessert. Then it was time for them to go to bed.

Overall, it was one of the best evenings Angie had ever had. At least since… Well, since she'd had dinner with Toby and the kids a couple of nights ago at The Grill.

Kylie approached the chair where Angie was sitting and placed a hand on her knee. "Will you read my Disney princess book to me before I go to bed?"

"I don't mind." Angie looked at Toby for the ultimate okay.

"It's all right with me. Each night at bedtime, I read a story to her. After that, I read a chapter out of *Treasure Island* with the boys. We're at a pretty exciting part, so it'll be nice to get back to where we left off."

What a nice family ritual. Angie was glad she'd been given a chance to take part in it.

By the time she'd read the princess story twice, gotten Kylie two glasses of water to drink and checked in the closet and under the bed for dragons three times, Kylie finally drifted off to sleep.

As Angie quietly sneaked out of the little girl's room, she wondered if she should wait for Toby, or just let herself out. Fortunately, she didn't have to make a decision.

Having finished his bedtime duties, Toby was already back in the living room, picking up ice-cream dishes and putting the sofa cushions and throw pillows back in place.

"Listen," he said, "I can't thank you enough for your help with the kids. When I do handle bedtime by myself, it takes another hour."

"The kids really are amazing." And Angie meant that from the bottom of her heart. She couldn't believe her mom had referred to those sweet, adorable children as "rug rats."

"Look at *you*," Toby said. "You're the one who's *amazing*. I can't believe how quickly the kids have taken to you. Brian even talked to you about the girls in his class, and Justin didn't try to sneak off to the barn once while you were here. And Kylie… Well, I can't even tell you how great it's been for her to be around a woman. My mom and my sisters help out whenever they can, but they've got such full schedules and lives."

Did he think Angie didn't have much of a life? Or was she reading too much into what he was saying?

"Anyway," he said, "you're great with kids. Are you planning to have some of your own someday?"

"I haven't really given it much thought." She'd never been around children all that much. And her mom hadn't made any big deal about motherhood— or parenthood, for that matter. So she'd never really considered it one way or the other.

She did have to admit, though, that being around Toby's kids had made her see motherhood in a brand-new light.

"I suppose I'd have to think about getting married first," she said. "And that's never been a priority."

Toby seemed to straighten at that. "You mean to tell me that you're twenty-four, incredibly beautiful, fun and smarter than an internet search engine, and there hasn't been a single guy who's come along and made you think about bridal showers and wedding cakes and the whole nine yards?"

Toby thought she was beautiful? And fun? And smart?

"I…uh…thought about it once, but it didn't work out." She hoped he wouldn't ask for details. She hated talking about it. And there'd been so many witnesses that inevitably the subject always seemed to crop up when she least wanted it to.

"What happened?" he asked.

So much for hoping.

"I dated this guy once. David. He wasn't especially handsome, but he was bright and had a great personality. I really liked him, so we dated a couple of months—which was longer than most of my relationships last. But one night, he ruined everything."

"What did he do?"

"He insisted upon taking me to the Two Moon Saloon, and when we arrived, a lot of my friends were there. Even my mom showed up, which should have been a major clue that something was off-kilter. But apparently, come to find out, my mother had been coaching him."

"Your mom *coached* him? What happened?"

"Apparently, with her help and encouragement, David planned this elaborate and romantic proposal in front of an audience. Everyone was expecting me to say yes. So I did. And then two days later, I gave him the ring back."

"Why didn't you want to marry him?"

"Everyone asked me that same question. The truth is, I didn't know. And I still don't. Heck, I can't even commit to a brand of shampoo long enough to take advantage of a two-for-one sale. How could I have made a lifelong commitment like that without feeling something?"

"You didn't feel anything for him? I thought you said he was a great guy."

"Yes, but I never had the zing. You know what I mean?"

"I'm not sure that I do."

"It's that heart-spinning, soul-stirring rush that you get when you know the other person is 'the one.'"

"I can't say that I've ever felt that way," he said.

"Yeah, well, I've never felt it, either. But I've read about it. And if I ever make that kind of forever-commitment to someone, I want to feel it. And I didn't have it with David."

"So you broke up with him."

"Um. Yeah. But I should have ended things way before I did." She blew out a sigh.

Toby didn't say anything. He just stared at her. But she knew what he must be thinking. It was the same thing everyone else always thought about her—that she was unreliable and scattered and wouldn't know a good decision if it fell from the top shelf of a Superette display case and landed straight on her head.

Suddenly embarrassed that she'd revealed so much, she realized she'd better regroup, which was her standard operating procedure when things got sticky or icky or whatever.

So she grabbed her purse and decided to bolt before she could change her mind, climb into Toby's lap and tell him that she was already feeling more for him than she'd ever felt for David.

And before he could respond by reiterating that he wasn't looking for a girlfriend or a potential mom for his foster kids.

"Anyway," she said, "I have to get home before it gets too late or I'll have Mr. Murdock out looking for me."

"Thanks again for dinner."

"You're more than welcome. I'll see you around town sometime."

She was just about to make her escape when he tossed her a smile that sent her heart spinning and set off a little...?

Oh, no. It couldn't be.

Surely, it wasn't.

But it certainly felt like a zing.

Chapter Five

Angie had been kicking herself the past two days for bolting from Toby's house the other night. He'd never even commented on her story about David, yet assuming he'd think the worst of her, she'd left before he could say anything.

Wasn't that typical? When the going got tough, Angie skedaddled.

But why had she been in such a hurry to escape? If he hadn't considered her to be flighty before, he probably did now.

She just hoped she hadn't ruined their friendship, because she really enjoyed her time spent with him and the kids. She was just about to close down the register and clock out when the subject of her thoughts for the past forty-eight hours approached with the kids in tow.

"We're getting ice cream," Kylie announced, as she placed a frozen chocolate bar on the conveyor belt.

"I thought an after-school treat was in order," Toby said.

If he'd wanted to avoid her, he could have stopped by The Grill for that ice cream. So obviously he hadn't thought that badly about her.

"What're you guys up to today?" she asked, as she rang up his purchase.

"I need to take Justin to the YMCA for his swim lesson," Toby said. "But Kylie's dance practice was moved up earlier in the day, which is a problem since I can't be in two places at once. And so, I wondered if there was any chance you'd be getting off soon."

"As a matter of fact, I am."

"I don't suppose you could do me a huge favor."

When he gazed at her with those big baby blues, she said, "Sure."

Anything, she thought.

"Can you either take Kylie to dance or Justin to the Y?" he asked.

"Actually, I'd planned to stop by the Y and check out that yoga class today. So I can take Justin with me, then bring him to the ranch when we're done."

"Great. That would sure help me out. And this time, I'll have dinner ready for you."

"Meals at the ranch could become habit-forming," she said.

"Maybe, but everything seems to go better when you're around." He flashed her a smile, and there it went.

An almost definite zing.

Twenty minutes later, Angie dropped Justin off with his swim instructor, a lanky teen who barely looked old enough to drive. She wondered if he was qualified to be giving lessons and certified in CPR, but she decided he must be or the Y wouldn't have hired him.

"I'm going to take my class now," she told Justin. "You'll probably get finished a few minutes before me, so change into your dry clothes, then meet me by the vending machines. I'll buy you a candy bar as soon as I get there."

"Cool."

She remembered Toby telling her that the eight-year-old wasn't a very strong swimmer, so she wanted to make sure that he didn't hang around the pool without supervision. He also had a habit of wandering, so she figured a bribe to stay at a designated location was a good idea.

Satisfied that Justin was in good hands—and that she'd thought of everything, Angie headed to the front desk to find out where the yoga class was being held.

A young woman, clearly the receptionist, pointed her down the hall.

Angie turned in that direction, her gaze scanning the entry of the building, just as Mr. Murdock pushed open the double doors and walked inside.

He was wearing a red T-shirt with Semper Fi printed in yellow letters in front. He also had on a pair of green-and-white Hawaiian-print swim trunks and blue flip-flops.

"Hey," she said. "What are you doing here, Mr. Murdock? Are you a member of the Y?"

"Just joined yesterday. My doctor says I gotta exercise. So I'm heading out to the aquatics area. Thought I'd swim a few laps. How about you?"

"I just dropped off Justin, Toby's boy, for his swim lesson. And while he's there, I'm going to take a yoga class. They're offering free classes this month."

"You and Toby are getting pretty tight," Mr. Murdock said, lifting a single gray brow in that paternal way of his.

"We're just friends. I've been helping out with the kids."

"Humph." Mr. Murdock folded his arms and rested them on his ample belly. "Is that what you call it?"

Okay, so she'd been questioning that herself, too. But she wasn't about to admit it—especially in public.

"No need for you to be jealous, Mr. Murdock." She gave the old man a wink. "My heart will always belong to you."

"Glad to hear that, Girly. I'm getting pretty used to having you around the house." Then he winked back at her and shuffled off toward the pool, leaving her to scope out that yoga class—which she'd better hurry to or she'd be late.

When the class was over and she'd released her last pose, Angie didn't stick around to talk to anyone. Instead she hurried to meet Justin and buy him that treat.

But when she reached the vending machines, he was nowhere in sight. Were there other places to get snacks in the building that she hadn't known about? Some that were outside?

Oh, no. Not by the pool. She'd tried to tempt him with a treat to keep him away from the water.

She quickly made her way out to the aquatics area,

which was directly behind the building. But after a quick scan, she still didn't see him.

Darn it. Where was he? She should have known better than to have taken that yoga class. She should have sat by the pool and watched his swim lesson instead.

Panic set in, raising her heart rate to the level of a full-scale cardio workout. She hurried into the building, but she didn't dare ask if anyone had seen him.

What if word got out that she'd lost him? Not only would that further perpetuate everyone's belief that she was unreliable, but social services might get wind of it. What if they investigated Toby and somehow found him lacking because he'd entrusted a child with a flaky, irresponsible friend?

Mere seconds later, both of those concerns paled when she still hadn't found Justin. Where could he be?

When she spotted the swim instructor coming out of the men's locker room, she nearly accosted him when she asked, "Have you seen Justin Hemings?"

"No, not since his lesson ended ten minutes ago."

Oh, God. He could have been kidnapped, whisked away from here by some predator. And all on her watch.

Angie rushed back to the aquatics area for one last look, the teenage instructor now fast on her heels.

The area had pretty much cleared, except for Mr. Murdock, who sat on the edge of the pool's shallow end, his feet dangling into the water, his face red, his breathing labored, his hand clutching his chest.

Oh, dear God. Poor Mr. Murdock was having a heart attack. What else could possibly go wrong?

"Call 911," she told the swim instructor. "That man needs an ambulance."

Then she ran to her friend to let him know that help was on the way. When she reached him, he pointed to the pool, where Justin's body lay at the bottom.

"No!" she screamed, as she leaped into the water, clothes and all. She grabbed the child, pulled him to the surface and dragged him to the steps. "I've got you, honey. I've got you."

Justin, whose eyes opened and grew wide, appeared dazed. Or was he confused? He looked at Mr. Murdock, gasped, then called out, "What was my time? Did I win?"

"Win?" Angie shrieked. "Win what?"

"Me and Mr. Murdock were having a contest to see who could hold their breath the longest."

In her panic to save the boy's life, Angie had nearly forgotten about Mr. Murdock. But several bystanders, as well as YMCA employees, had now gathered around the older man and were trying to help.

"Are you okay?" one woman who appeared to be in management asked the retired marine.

"The paramedics are on their way," the teenage swim instructor said.

"You won…that round," Mr. Murdock told Justin, his voice coming out in short little pants. "But give me…a second. We'll go…best two…out of three."

A *contest?* They'd been having a fool competition?

Angie, who'd always prided herself on being cool, calm and collected in a crisis, practically shouted, "*Nobody* is going back in that water. You two nearly scared the living daylights out of me. And the whole time you were only competing in a stupid challenge. I can't blame Justin for acting childish. But really, Mr. Murdock, you should know better."

Before the elderly man could respond or even catch his breath, the ambulance arrived, along with a hook-and-ladder truck. Two firemen brought a gurney to the pool, while a female paramedic carried her bag and placed it next to Mr. Murdock.

The tough old man waved her away, especially when she tried to attach an oxygen mask to his face.

Justin seemed none the worse for wear, thank goodness.

"Can I have a ride in the ambulance?" he asked one of the firemen.

"That depends," the fireman said, nodding toward Mr. Murdock. "Is this man your grandfather? And did you ride with him here today?"

"No, they're not related," Angie clarified. "And we're *not* riding in the ambulance. We need to go back to the ranch."

"Then can I see how you turn on the siren?" the boy asked.

"Maybe after we get this gentleman loaded up," the fireman said.

"Who, *me?*" Mr. Murdock asked, apparently realizing that the 911 call had been made for him. "I ain't going nowhere in no damn ambulance. And I don't need no siren. My ticker is just fine. I only got a little winded after a friendly competition with the boy."

"A competition?" the paramedic asked. "Maybe we should start at the beginning. What's going on here?"

Justin explained what had happened, going so far

as to tell them how Angie had tried to save his life, even though it didn't need saving.

"Mr. Murdock beat me the first round," Justin said, "but he taught me how to let the bubbles out my nose to keep the air in my lungs longer."

"Well, I don't think Mr. Murdock's lungs are doing so great right about now," Angie mumbled in frustration. Her worry now switched to the old man.

Mr. Murdock finally ripped the oxygen mask out of the female paramedic's well-intentioned hand and threw it about ten feet into the pool.

Then he pointed an arthritic finger at the poor woman only trying to do her job. "I *said* I don't need medical attention. What I need is a Scotch and a cigarette."

Angie wanted to tell the old man that she didn't think his lungs could take the extra stress of inhaling tobacco right this second. But before she could, he turned to her and said, "You done good, Girly. No one was drowning, but if the kid had been, your response time was the quickest I've ever seen."

A wet Mr. Murdock in a saggy bathing suit shuffled to his feet and dripped his way to the changing rooms with the paramedics still following him.

A 911 call was big news and everyone inside the YMCA had now gathered around the pool area to watch. There was no getting around it. She was going to be the talk of the town before nightfall.

Angie, her yoga outfit drenched in water and stuck tight to her skin, pulled Justin into her lap and held him close. Thank God everything had turned out okay.

Still, as she glanced at the oxygen mask floating to

the deep end of the pool, she sighed. What a day. She might have had the best of intentions, but she'd really screwed up.

How was she ever going to tell Toby that she'd nearly lost Justin—and that she just might be as flighty and irresponsible as everyone seemed to think that she was?

Toby had just pulled the chicken off his outdoor grill when the headlights of Angie's Toyota flashed, letting him know she was turning up the drive that led to his house.

He'd put Brian in charge of making the salad with the promise that if the kid could master assembling some easy dishes in the kitchen, Toby would teach him how to man the grill next time.

And it had worked like a charm.

When Angie and Justin climbed from the car, Toby called out, "You guys are just in time for dinner."

Neither of them spoke as they slowly made their way to the patio at the side of the house.

That seemed a bit odd.

Toby flashed Angie a smile, which she didn't return. And that was his second clue that something had gone wrong.

Why was her hair all wet and slicked back?

Uh-oh. Her clothes were wet, too.

Before he could ask, she said, "We had a bit of an incident at the pool."

"What happened?"

When she didn't give him a speedy reply, Justin answered. "Me and Mr. Murdock were having a breath-holding contest, and Angie thought I was drowning. So she jumped in the pool to save me."

Justin glanced at Angie, then at Toby, his eyes wary as though he was bracing himself for a scolding. But Toby was still waiting for Angie to say something.

Apparently, thinking he was off the hook, Justin brightened and really opened up. "It was pretty sweet, though. The firemen and paramedics came—with sirens and everything. But best of all, I beat Mr. Murdock at holding my breath. And then he cussed. And Angie yelled at both of us. And even though the fireman said I couldn't ride in the ambulance, but I could look inside, Angie wouldn't let me. But that's okay, because—"

Toby interrupted the boy's rambling dialogue and said, "Kiddo, why don't you go get some dry clothes on before dinner. I'll let Angie tell me the rest of the story."

There was no telling what all had transpired at the YMCA earlier, but knowing Justin's history of wandering off and Mr. Murdock's fierce competitive streak, Toby was able to piece a lot of it together.

After Justin ran inside, Toby turned his full attention to the soaking-wet woman. She'd better get out of her clothes, too.

Whoops. Now that was an intriguing thought. And an arousing one, seeing how the Lycra now covered her like a sexy layer of skin. But as tears filled her eyes, his thoughts cooled to sympathy.

Justin said she'd been angry earlier, but she appeared to be hurt now. Crushed, actually.

Uh-oh. This was bad.

What in blazes had happened?

"I'm *so* sorry," she said. "It's all my fault. I shouldn't have gone to that yoga class. I should've just stayed out by the pool with him. And then, when he wasn't where he was supposed to meet me, I thought of all the terrible things that could have happened to him, and I panicked. I guess you could say I had a meltdown, and everyone saw the whole thing."

"It couldn't have been that bad," he said.

"Oh, no? If I'd been on an E.R. reality show, the TV ratings would have shot through the roof. It was terrible, and I completely lost it."

She started rambling then, just as Justin had. And while her sweet face still looked confused in the aftermath of her unnecessary panic attack, the snug workout pants sent his testosterone soaring, and he nearly dropped the platter of grilled chicken he was holding.

Damn. If he didn't have his hands full, he'd pull her to him, wet Lycra and all, just to offer his comfort and whatever else he could.

"Salad's ready!" Brian yelled out the side door. "I'm starved. Can we start eating?"

"You go ahead and eat with the kids," Angie told him. "I'm not hungry. I need to go home and get out of these wet clothes. If you want to talk more about it, we can do that in the morning."

Then she turned toward her car.

"Wait!" Toby called to her back.

When she turned around, he said, "I'll give you some dry clothes and a glass of wine. You look like you could use both. And after dinner, you and I can sit down and enjoy some quiet time—adults only. Then you can tell me what happened. Or, if you'd rather, you can forget all about it."

Whatever would make her smile again.

That was, unless she wanted to get the hell away from him and the kids as fast as her toned legs would carry her.

And quite frankly, he wouldn't blame her if she did. After all, he'd known all along how it would end. And he'd implied as much to her a few days ago when they'd discussed his nonexistent love life.

Women saw him as some sort of Captain Rescue at first. And then they ran for the hills as soon as they came face-to-face with the reality of dealing with three kids, each of whom still had some issues after living in a dysfunctional household with their aunt Barbara. But they seemed to be getting through all that, especially since Angie had started coming around.

"You know," she said, "a glass of wine sounds great. Besides, if I go home now and run into Mr. Murdock, I just might ring his little ole leatherneck."

Toby laughed. At least her sense of humor was coming back.

He shifted the plate into his left hand, then slipped his arm around her shoulders. She leaned into him, and he gave her a gentle squeeze.

A guy could get used to comforting her, even when she was soaking wet. In fact, Toby might have just stood there, holding her all night, except he had children to feed.

"Come on," he said, as he led her to the kitchen, where the kids had gathered.

Once inside, he assigned them all chores so they

could eat sooner. "Check the rice steamer, Brian. Kylie, set a place for Angie. She's staying for dinner."

Kylie, who was down on her hands and knees, looked up from the floor, where she was picking up some dropped silverware. "I already set the table. Well, all but the forks and spoons."

Toby was about to warn her to get fresh utensils from the drawer, then he figured he may as well forget it since the housekeeper had been here today and had mopped the floor. So at least for tonight, the three-second rule for germ-free drops had become a three-minute rule, as far as he was concerned.

While the kids did as they'd been asked, Toby took Angie to his bedroom, where he began opening drawers, looking for something she could wear, something that might fit.

When he caught her looking at the king-sized bed in the center of the room, he wondered if she was thinking the same thing he was.

And just what *was* he thinking?

Right now, he didn't dare put it into words. Instead, he haphazardly handed her a worn-out Houston Texans T-shirt, along with a pair of his old cross-country shorts from Horseback Hollow High, which he figured would be too big.

If he had his way, he'd prefer to see her stay in those tight pants and sports tank. But they were wet. And even if they were dry, he had to find something else for her to wear—and quick.

It was killing him to see her looking so sexy and so vulnerable at the same time, especially since she was just an arm's distance and mere steps away from his bed.

"While you change," he said, "I'll get the wine."

Minutes later, everyone was sitting in their places when Angie came to the table. The kids must have picked up on her solemn mood, because they were so quiet you could hear a pin drop—or a man's heart beat, his blood race.

She'd rolled his shorts up at the waist to make them fit her. The shirt barely reached the hem of the shorts, making it look as though she wasn't wearing anything underneath.

Man, he needed to get a grip. There were kids present.

And thankfully, the kids soon began to chatter, because Angie remained quiet through dinner, sipping her wine and picking at her food.

When everyone else had eaten their fill, Toby said, "Okay, guys, no TV tonight. It's already time to pick up your rooms, take your baths and get ready for bed."

It really wasn't all that late, but Toby had waited long enough to get Angie alone.

With her being as pensive as she'd been at dinner, he hadn't expected her to help out with the evening routine the way she'd done the other night she'd been here. But she surprised him by stepping right up to the plate, which was nice. The kids liked having her around.

He did, too. But he'd have to be careful that nobody got too attached. Especially him.

When Toby finished reading the next chapter of *Treasure Island,* Angie was still with Kylie, so he went to the kitchen and started to clean up. He'd just loaded the dishwasher when she entered the room, her shoulders slumped.

"Come on," he said, wiping his hands on a dish towel. "The rest of this can wait until tomorrow."

After refilling her wineglass, he grabbed a cold beer out of the fridge for himself. Then they walked into the living room. The house was noticeably quieter with all the kids tucked in.

She took a sip of the chardonnay before practically collapsing on the sofa. He recognized the signs of an adrenaline dump. Or maybe she was just emotionally exhausted.

He sat next to her, and it seemed only natural to reach out, to touch her shoulder, to finger her hair. "Okay, tell me what's bothering you."

She let out a ragged sigh. "I feel as though I've let you down."

"Why would you think that? The way I see it, you took your responsibility seriously. I'm actually impressed."

"Thank you, but I never should have let him out of my sight in the first place." She closed her eyes.

"Don't blame yourself. The same thing happens to me at least four times a week. Justin is impulsive. He has a history of running off and doing his own thing, which led to some of the behavioral problems he was having at school. We've been working on correcting it, but he's eight. It happens. I should have better prepared you."

She shuddered, and he adjusted his body so he could pull her even closer. He reminded himself that she was upset and vulnerable now, but she felt so good in his arms. He stroked her back, his fingers unhampered by any bra straps. And with those long, tanned legs bare to her thighs, she was practically naked.

Aw, man. It would be so easy to take advantage of the situation. But should he?

Then what?

She had her head cradled against his shoulder, and he was tempted to kiss the top of her head—a gentle kiss meant to comfort. But something told him he wouldn't want to stop at gentle.

Or at the top of her head.

And kissing her would take their relationship to a level neither of them was ready for, not when three kids stood in the balance.

So he reined in his lust and didn't kiss her at all. But he probably should have taken the opportunity while he'd had the chance, because it seemed as though she was pulling away from him and getting to her feet before he knew it.

She was leaving? So soon?

"It's been a long day," she said. "I need to go."

He followed her to the door. He hated to see her go, but the fact that she was wearing his shirt and shorts gave him some comfort. If he wouldn't be sleeping with her, maybe his clothes would.

"Thanks for dinner and for understanding," she said, as she grabbed the oversized purse and the wet shoes she'd left just outside the front door.

When she straightened, their eyes met.

A good-night kiss crossed his mind, but he pondered the wisdom of doing so for a beat too long, because she said, "I'll talk to you later."

Then she headed for her car.

As he stood on the porch and watched her go, the sway of her hips and those long, shapely legs taunted him. He kicked himself for his lack of courage, his foresight and his strong sense of family values—or whatever the hell had convinced him to do the right thing and keep his lips and his hands to himself.

He'd had two opportunities to kiss Angie tonight, neither of which he'd taken. He tried to tell himself that he'd done the right thing, that he'd made the right call, but his libido wasn't buying it.

But wouldn't you know it? Once he'd lost his chance to kiss her, he wanted her all that much more.

Chapter Six

After Angie left, Toby went into the bathroom to take a shower and spotted her wet workout clothes hanging over his towel bar. He'd assumed she'd taken them with her, along with her purse and the wet shoes she'd left outside by the door, but apparently, she'd forgotten them after she'd changed.

He'd return them, of course, which would give him an opportunity to see her again soon.

That was a good thing, right?

Less than twenty minutes ago, he'd been tempted to kiss her. In fact, he'd been tempted to do more than that, right there on his living-room sofa—and despite having a house full of kids.

But that *wouldn't* have been good. He blew out a sigh.

As long as those three children were depending

upon him, he'd better not even think about having a woman spend the night. And since he hoped they'd be living with him until they each went off to college, he'd better get used to sleeping alone—unless he tied a cowbell around each of their necks.

The image of him doing that was actually kind of funny, and he might have even chuckled out loud if being twenty-six and facing the possibility of ten years of near celibacy wasn't downright unsettling—and unthinkable.

Surely it wouldn't come to that.

He ran his hand through his hair, then turned on the water in the shower, adjusting the temperature to warm—hoping cold sprays wouldn't be the only ones in his future.

Something told him this was going to be a long night, and that sleep would be a long time coming.

And he'd been right.

The next day, as soon as school let out, he surprised the kids by driving to the Superette and telling them they could each pick out a snack. As they unbuckled their seat belts, he reached for the plastic bag holding Angie's now-dry workout clothes.

Then he herded the happy kids into the mom-and-pop grocery store, riding pretty high in the saddle himself. No matter what he told himself, being with Angie always brightened his day.

Trouble was, once he got inside and the kids took off, he didn't see her at any of the checkout registers.

Where was she? He could've sworn that she worked at the market on Thursdays. But it was tough keeping up with her schedule. Had he been wrong? Was she working for Sawyer and Laurel today?

Dang. Was this what his life would be like if he were to actually date her? Would she always be working at some odd job, changing shifts frequently, possibly moving to another city?

She didn't have a history of stability, and no matter how many family conversations she livened up or how many heated looks passed between the two of them, nothing was going to change that fact.

Just when he began to realize he'd have to take the plastic bag back to his truck, Justin ran up and asked, "Can I have one of Angie's cupcakes? She put little race cars on top and everything."

"Slow down, Justin. What are you talking about?"

"I'll show you." The boy turned and dashed off toward the bakery section.

Toby followed him to the display case—and to Angie, who stood behind it, wearing a white apron tied around her slim waist.

"See?" Justin said, imploring Toby to tear his gaze from Angie and to look at the tray of cupcakes behind the glass enclosure, each one blue and topped with candy sprinkles and a tiny toy race car.

"You're a baker, too?" Toby asked her.

"It's a long story. The baker called in sick, so I stepped in. And when I spotted the toy cars stashed in one of the cupboards in back, I thought they might add a little more pizzazz. Apparently, the customers agreed because we sold the first batch already and the second is going fast."

"So can I have one for my treat?" Justin asked again.

"I want the one with the purple car," Kylie chimed in.

"All right," Toby said. "We'll take 'em."

"Do you want to eat them here?" Angie asked. "Or should I box them up for you?"

Justin, always one for instant gratification, said, "I want to eat mine right now."

Toby laughed. "I'll never hear the end of it if I make them wait."

Angie carried the cupcakes to one of the two small bistro-style tables, where the morning customers enjoyed their doughnuts and coffees. She set them before Justin and Kylie, then passed out a couple of napkins, just as Brian walked up with a highly caffeinated energy drink in his hand.

"I'm gonna just have this instead of a snack," Brian said, as he sat down at the table.

"Oh, no, you won't." Toby snatched the can out of the boy's hand. "Kids aren't supposed to drink this crap. It's not good for you."

"Mike Waddell drinks it all the time at school," Brian argued.

"Maybe so," Angie said, as she set a cupcake in front of the boy. "But Mike Waddell got detention last week for jumping out of his seat seven times during that movie in science class. He also had eight cavities at his last dentist appointment."

As the kids dug into their cupcakes, Toby followed Angie behind the bakery display case and lowered his voice. "How did you know that about Mike Waddell?"

"We live in a small town, Toby. People talk. Especially Brian's teacher, Mrs. Dawson, and Wendy Cummings, the dental hygienist." Angie glanced at the plastic bag he still held. "What's that?"

"The clothes you left in my bathroom." He handed them to her.

She flushed, then scanned the area as if they were making a drug deal and she didn't want to get caught. Then she stashed the bag in one of the drawers near the cash register.

Was she embarrassed? Whatever for? It wasn't as though she'd spent the night at the ranch and left her panties behind, although the thought of her doing that made him smile.

She lowered her voice. "And that's another thing people have been talking about and why I'm really back here in bakery and not out in front."

Because people thought she and Toby were...sleeping together?

"What are you talking about?" he asked.

"Several people who came through the checkout line asked me about the incident at the pool. They'd heard from a neighbor, who'd heard from a cousin, who... Well, you know how small towns are."

Yes, he did. And there wasn't much he could do to stop a rumor like that from getting out. But heck, if he was going to be the subject of gossip, it was too bad he couldn't have had a night to remember it by.

"Finally, around ten this morning, I asked Mrs. Tierney if she could man the cash register for a while," Angie said. "And so she let me work back here instead."

"All because of a little misunderstanding?" Toby shook his head. "That reminds me, though. How is Mr. Murdock?"

"He was here this morning, having coffee and holding court. He gave everyone a firsthand account of what happened. He…uh…also mentioned to Mrs. Rhodes, who was on her way to The Cuttery for her shampoo and set, that I've been helping you out a lot with the kids."

Should that be a secret? Toby wondered. Apparently Angie thought so because the pink flush on her cheeks deepened.

"Actually," he said, "you've been a godsend. And I really appreciate your help more than you can imagine."

"Even after yesterday?" she asked.

He laughed. "I told you before. I've had my share of bad days, too. It happens."

Angie glanced at the kids, who'd finished their cupcakes and were now racing their frosting-coated cars along the table, then looked at Toby and smiled. "To be honest, I've really enjoyed helping you, too. The kids are great, and I'm actually surprised at how much I like spending time with them."

What about their foster dad? Toby wanted to ask. *Do you enjoy spending time with him, too?*

But he knew better than to let things get personal, especially when he really did need another favor from her tomorrow. Besides, he'd picked up on what she'd left unsaid earlier.

If Mrs. Rhodes knew Angie was spending so much time with him and the kids, it wouldn't be long before all the other women getting their hair done at The Cuttery would start linking him and Angie romantically.

He really didn't mind what people said, but he didn't think Angie would like it, especially if her mom got wind of it. Doris Edwards had been pushing Angie to find a husband. And if the eligible men in town thought she was already taken, it might ruin her chance of going out with a guy who could offer her more than a cattle ranch and three foster kids.

Although the thought of her going out on a real date with someone else reared up inside of him, throwing him to the ground like an unexpected buck from a mild-mannered horse.

Maybe, in that case, he ought to keep her unavailable for a while—until he figured out where this thing was going. Or where he wanted it to go.

"I feel bad asking you this," he said, "but I'm in a bind. I'd ask Stacey, but she works and has her hands full with Piper."

"I'd be glad to help," Angie said. "What do you need me to do?"

"I have a meeting in Lubbock tomorrow afternoon, and I'm not sure when I'll get back. Is there any chance you could pick the kids up from school and take them home?"

"I have a few things to do, but it shouldn't be too hard to reschedule them. Let me work on that. In the meantime, don't worry about the kids. I'll pick them up from school. And I'll have dinner ready for you when you get home."

Well, what do you know?

He was back in the saddle again.

The meeting in Lubbock had gone later than Toby had expected, so he called Angie before he left town and told her to go ahead and feed the kids.

"Don't wait for me," he said.

"We're having spaghetti," she told him. "I'll keep a plate warm for you."

"Sounds good. Thanks."

"Did your meeting go well?" she asked.

"It sure did. I've been negotiating a deal on a piece of property that backs mine, and the man who owned it had refused to sell. But he passed away last spring, and his widow doesn't want to deal with it any longer. Her late husband thought it was a lot more valuable than it really is, so we had to agree upon a price."

"Great. We'll have to celebrate when you get home."

"Sounds good to me."

"Oh," she said. "I hope you don't mind, but I told the kids they could have a movie night after dinner."

"That's fine. I'll see you in a bit."

When the line disconnected, he turned on the radio, letting Gladys Knight fill the cab with her soulful voice as she sang about a midnight train to Georgia.

See, all you Texas country music fans. Willie Nelson isn't the only one who can sing about the Peach State.

The song had barely ended when his cell rang.

Toby glanced at the lit display, but didn't recognize the area code. Still, he turned down the volume on the radio, took the call and pushed the speakerphone button. "Hello?"

"It's Barbara Hemings, Toby."

The kids' aunt. He glanced in the rearview mirror, then pulled to the shoulder of the road and let the truck idle.

"Hi, Barbara." He wanted to ask her how rehab was going, but the woman sometimes became defensive, so he let it be. Besides, he had a feeling this wasn't going to be a social call, which was why he wanted to have his hands free in case he needed to make any notes about something she said.

"I heard about what happened at the pool the other day, so I put in a call to the case worker from child services. I'm waiting for her call back, but I thought you should know that just because I'm stuck in court-ordered treatment, I haven't stopped fighting for my kids."

They weren't *her* kids. And she'd had a lot of opportunities to fight for them, especially when she had custody, but she kept blowing it. However, arguing with her wasn't going to solve anything.

"I'm not sure where you're getting your information, Barbara, but that incident was blown all out of proportion. Justin was never in danger at the pool. The kids are all safe, and they're happy. And just so you know, I've already called Ms. Fisk and given her a heads-up about the situation. I'm sure she'll tell you the same thing when she calls you back."

"Toby, you're a young, single man with a tumbling-down ranch. And those kids can be a handful at times. There's no way you can handle them on your own."

Tumbling-down ranch? He'd turned the Double H around in the three years he'd owned it. And, thanks to the meeting he'd had thirty minutes ago, he'd be running more cattle next year, and that meant he'd be turning an even better profit—if things went according to plan.

"As I seem to remember," he reminded her, "you were single when you took the kids on, too. And my 'tumbling-down' ranch is a hell of a lot nicer than that cockroach-infested motel you had them living in when the state took them away from you."

"Yes, and that turned out badly. But I'm better now."

At least the woman was able to admit the obvious.

"Anyway," she added, "the kids need to be with family. And if they can't be with me for the next few months, then I want them with one of my relatives."

What family? If there were any Hemings relatives nearby, wouldn't they have stepped up by now?

"Do the kids even know these relatives?" Toby finally asked, his fingers gripping the steering wheel until his knuckles ached.

"No, but they're family, Toby. You of all people should understand about long-lost family."

She was talking about James Marshall Fortune coming to Horseback Hollow and finding his sister, Jeanne Marie, Toby's mom. Although, quite frankly, Toby was surprised that she even knew about that.

"I have a cousin in California," Barbara said. "I'm going to ask him to take the children until I get out of rehab."

Great. Another upheaval? And just who was her cousin?

"What's his name? What does he do?"

"His name is Rocky, and he's looking for work. His parole agent thinks he can find a job by the end of this month. His wife works at a hospital out there, but one of his conditions of parole is that he's not allowed to work at hospitals anymore, so that's out. But there are plenty of other places where he can get work."

His parole agent? He couldn't work in a hospital

anymore? If the cousin couldn't be trusted in a hospital then he sure as shooting couldn't be trusted with Brian, Justin and Kylie.

What made Barbara think that the children would be better off with some deadbeat cousin they didn't even know than they would be with Toby?

"I don't think that's in the children's best interest, Barbara."

"Honestly, Toby, it's not your decision. I thought you'd be a little more cooperative, but I guess the kids can't count on you for that."

The woman disconnected the call before Toby could throw the phone out his open window, which was what he'd wanted to do the moment he'd heard her voice.

He sucked the country air into his lungs and counted to ten, the way his pitching coach had taught him to do when he'd been on the mound.

Think. Whom did he call first? Ms. Fisk, the case worker? Or an attorney?

He glanced at the clock on the dashboard. Crap. It was too late to call anyone today. That would have to wait until tomorrow. He continued to sit in the idling truck for a while, his hands on the steering wheel, his thoughts on the troubling call.

Would the court decide that the kids were better off with a sketchy family member over a stable and caring guardian? It didn't seem feasible, but then again, anything was possible...

He did his best to shake off Barbara's threat, telling himself he didn't have time to worry about that blasted woman. He'd told Angie that he was going to be late, but he hadn't meant to completely abandon her with the kids.

After checking for traffic, Toby pulled back onto the road and accelerated.

At times like this it was nice to know he had someone to rely on, especially Angie.

People might think that she was flighty—and they might even be right. But either way, she was proving to be a real blessing.

A man could get used to going home to a woman like her.

Angie sure hoped Toby got home soon, because she was fading fast. She hadn't slept very well the past two nights, thanks in large part to the residual stress and worry from that 911 fiasco at the Y.

Even her mother had heard all about it and called, asking her what had happened. Sheesh. What a pain that conversation had been.

But at least Toby trusted her enough to ask her to help with the kids again.

It hadn't been easy to adjust her schedule to accommodate his, but she had. She'd worked a split shift at the Superette, going in early this morning. Then she'd left at ten o'clock to take Mr. Murdock to his doctor's appointment in Vicker's Corners. After that, she'd run over to Redmond-Fortune Air to type some letters for Sawyer. And it was back to the Superette for another two-hour shift, after which she purchased the ingredients she needed to make spaghetti for dinner.

She was nearly late picking the kids up from school, but she got there just in the nick of time. Then it was a quick stop at her house for the surprise she'd planned for the evening.

A couple of summers ago, she'd worked at an old movie theater outside of Lubbock. When the Red Raider Cinemas went out of business, the owner gave Angie a projector and several old movie reels. She'd always wanted to have an old-fashioned movie night under the stars, but she'd never gotten around to planning one. That was, until tonight.

Too bad she was about to nod off from exhaustion. She could really use one of those energy drinks Brian had wanted yesterday afternoon.

Hopefully, Toby would be home soon. He'd told her not to wait dinner for him, and they hadn't. At this rate, she was going to start the movie without him, too. Otherwise, she'd probably curl up on his sofa and nod off before he even got home.

She'd fixed him a plate and left it on the stove. Then she'd cleaned up the kitchen. She'd made popcorn, but had to make it the old-fashioned way, since Toby didn't have any kind of popper. She'd just salted a large bowl for them to share when Brian came in.

"We're all done," he said. "Me and Justin hung up the white sheet, just like you told us. And Kylie made beds for us on the lawn. You ought to see it."

Angie followed the boys out of the house, where they'd set up the makeshift outdoor movie theater. And, just as Brian had said, Kylie had, indeed, made them a giant bed—with every blanket, sheet and pillow she could possibly find.

"Did you leave any of the beds made up in the house?" Angie asked her.

"Nope," Kylie said. "Even Toby's blankets and pillows are out here."

That wasn't quite what Angie had in mind, which meant there was going to be a big mess to clean up afterward, when she doubted she'd have the energy to deal with it. But she wasn't about to scold the kids when the whole idea had been hers in the first place—and when they'd tried so hard to follow her instructions.

Besides, look how happy they were.

"Okay," she said. "Let's get this show on the road."

She'd just finished setting up the projector with the *Star Wars* film threaded in the proper slots, when Toby's Dodge rolled into the driveway.

"What's all this?" Toby asked, as he stepped out of his truck.

"Movie night!" Justin yelled, as he barged out of the back door in his pajamas and dived onto the bedding on the lawn, calling his spot.

Toby looked nearly as tired as Angie felt—probably realizing they'd have four beds to make up before anyone could go to sleep tonight.

Angie hoped she hadn't blown it by throwing the impromptu cinema party in his backyard.

Toby nodded to the old projector. "Where in the world did you get that thing? Wait, don't tell me. Does it have something to do with an old job?"

His grin and a glimmer in his eye teased her in a way that didn't make her feel quite so bad about her history of random employment. But she sidestepped his question and asked one of her own. "You look tired. Would you rather we do this another night?"

"And disappoint the kids?" Toby's grin blossomed into a smile, easing her mind. "No way. Let me get out of these clothes and put on something more comfortable."

Angie had been so busy reading into Toby's expression, which hadn't matched the upbeat tone of his voice when he'd called her earlier, that she'd failed to notice that he wasn't wearing his trademark jeans, T-shirt and cowboy boots.

He was dressed in black slacks, a button-down shirt and expensive dress boots. He looked sharp—and ready for a night on the town without the kids.

She wondered what it might be like to actually go out on a date with him—if they had a sitter.

That was, if he'd actually ask her to be his date.

As Toby headed into the house, Brian and Kylie followed Justin's lead, rushing outside in their pajamas and choosing their own spots to spread out on the blankets.

But Angie's thoughts were on Toby.

"I'll get the popcorn," she told the kids. "Showtime is in five minutes."

She made her way into the house slowly. She didn't want Toby to think that she was following him.

But what if he'd wanted her to?

Oh, get a grip. She was so sleep-deprived, she was becoming delusional.

She was about to carry the first load of refreshments outside when Toby stepped into the kitchen.

"Thanks," he said, his eyes contradicting the simplicity of his single word as they bored deeply into her own.

She tried to downplay the intensity in his gaze, as well as her efforts to provide a fun evening for the kids. "It was no big deal."

"Actually, it's a big deal to me. You have no idea how much I need this right now."

She thought Toby was going to pull her in for a hug, and she would have willingly gone—if he'd made the first move. But as her heartbeats pounded off the seconds and he didn't make the attempt, she realized it was probably more likely that one of the kids would come flying in the door to ask what was holding them up.

So she handed him the bowl of popcorn and grabbed the five ice-cream-filled mugs by their handles and led the way out the back door.

"So what are we watching?" Toby asked as he settled into the only spot the kids had left open, which happened to be right beside Angie.

"*Star Wars I*," Justin said.

"No, dude, this is *Star Wars IV*," Brian said snarkily, as if Justin was an idiot.

"How can it be number IV when this is the first *Star Wars* they ever made?" Justin challenged back.

Angie quickly explained the nuances of the *Star Wars* episodes before the boys came to blows across the blankets.

"So you're both right," she said.

The boys conceded, going back to their ice cream.

"Is that my bedsheet?" Toby asked as he studied the improvised movie screen nailed to the side of his barn.

"Well, the boys' sheets are dark blue, and Kylie's has a *My Little Pony* print," Angie defended.

"Why is there a big brown spot on it?" Toby asked, glossing over the fact that the boys had put nail holes into his sheet.

"Justin dropped his end in some manure while I was on the ladder trying to nail it in place," Brian explained.

"I'm sorry," Angie said. "I didn't know they were going to use real nails. And I didn't realize they'd dropped it in cow... Well, in...you know. I just thought you had stained sheets."

Toby looked at her as if she'd been the one to drop the manure outside the barn in the first place.

"Did you try the popcorn yet?" she asked, trying to get the conversation heading in a different direction. "I put extra butter on it for you."

Toby reached into the bowl. "That stain on the sheet makes it look like Luke Skywalker has melanoma on his face."

"What's 'melanoma'?" Brian asked.

"It's a kind of skin cancer," Angie answered.

The pillows looked so comfortable. Maybe she could just put her head down for a second and rest her eyes, maybe even doze off for a moment or two.

"My mommy died of cancer," Justin said.

"Is Luke Skywalker gonna die of cancer, too?" Kylie asked.

Oh, no. Angie hadn't meant to mention the C-word.

"Nobody is going to die tonight," Toby said, trying to save the day.

But that didn't make Angie feel much better. If her brain hadn't been so sleep-deprived, she might have thought before opening her mouth.

Here she was, trying to do something fun and nice for the family, but then she'd screwed everything up by reminding them of their dead mother.

No matter what she tried to do, it seemed that she only made things worse. Maybe Toby and the kids would be better if she ran for the hills and stayed out of their lives forever.

They'd be better off. But as she scanned the yard, taking in the sweet kids and the handsome cowboy who'd taken them in and given them a home, she wondered how she'd ever just walk away from them without looking back.

Or did she dare risk it all and stick around until she finally got things right?

Chapter Seven

The kids settled back on the blankets to watch the movie. Toby and Angie did, too, stretching out next to each other.

By the time Han Solo was telling Leia that he was in it for the money, Toby leaned over and whispered to Angie, "Is there any more popcorn?"

He hadn't eaten lunch, so he'd pretty much wolfed down the spaghetti Angie had set out for him, but it really hadn't quite filled him up.

"I'll run in and make some more," she said, getting to her feet.

He hadn't meant to put her to work. "You don't have to do that."

"Actually, I was about to fall asleep. It'll help me stay awake."

Toby followed her into the kitchen. She may not

need any help, but he saw an opportunity and decided to take it. With the kids so engrossed in the movie, he didn't know when they'd get another chance to be alone. And the longer he'd lain next to her, the more he'd craved some one-on-one adult time with her.

When she realized he'd followed her into the kitchen, she said, "I'm so sorry about bringing up the C-word earlier."

"Don't even give it another thought. Everyone slips up now and then. Besides, I was the one who brought up melanoma in the first place. And if it makes you feel better, the social worker told me that the kids need to talk about their mom. It's better for them to process her death in a normal, healthy way. When they lived with their aunt, they saw a bad example of hiding emotions behind the bottle."

Just thinking about Barbara reminded him of the unsettling conversation they'd had. He'd almost forgotten about it once he'd gotten home. Angie had a way of getting his mind off his trouble, which was one more thing he liked about her.

Should he tell her about the call?

He didn't consider the idea very long. He didn't want to dump any more on her than he had to, no matter how easy she was to talk to. She wasn't in this thing for the long haul anyway.

Besides, why did he want to think about Barbara when he had Angie in front of him now, standing at the stove, heating oil and popcorn kernels in a covered skillet?

When the corn began popping against the lid, she

moved the pan across the burner—back and forth, faster and faster—her breasts swaying with the motion.

Aw, man. If he didn't stop gaping at the mesmerizing sight, those kernels wouldn't be the only thing popping.

"Is the popcorn done yet?" Justin yelled from the open doorway.

If you were talking about being hot and bothered, Toby was certainly close to done.

"Just about," Angie called out to the boy. "I'll bring it out to you in just a minute."

Justin ran back to the movie, and Toby decided he'd better do the same before his thoughts got the better of him.

A few minutes later, Angie joined them in the yard, bringing the replenished bowl with her and settling back into her spot next to Toby. Even the action scenes, with swishing lightsabers, zooming X-wing fighters and intergalactic battles, didn't keep Toby from wanting to reach out and grab more than a handful of popcorn.

But he managed self-control.

By the time the credits started to roll, he looked over and saw that Kylie and Justin had fallen asleep.

"I guess we'll have to carry them in to bed," he whispered to Angie, who'd nuzzled into the pillow next to his.

But she didn't answer.

He leaned over and, while tempted to brush back the strands of hair that had fallen across her face and tell her the movie was over, he let her sleep.

Brian, thank goodness, picked up his blankets and

pillow and made his way into the house on his own. But Toby had to carry the smaller kids one at a time.

Thanks to Kylie's overzealous efforts to make them all cozy for the movie, the mattresses were completely bare. Remaking all the beds seemed like way too much work to do. So instead, he went back to the grass, retrieved a couple of blankets and put one over each of the sleeping children.

When he returned outside and saw Angie curled up under the stars, the corner of his comforter tucked under her chin, he stood there and watched her for a while.

Now what? Wake her up? Send her home?

Invite her inside?

He looked back at the house. Considering the bare mattress that awaited him inside, he figured, what the heck.

She looked so soft, so comfortable. Why not let her nap? He could certainly use a little snooze himself.

So he lay down next to her, just as they'd done when the movie had first begun. Then he pulled a blanket over the top of them. Surely one of them would wake up in an hour or so. At that time, they could each go their own way, she to her house and he to his own room.

And no one would be the wiser.

Toby might not be able to invite Angie to actually spend the night in his bed, but this seemed like the next best thing.

Angie wiggled backward, not quite ready to wake up from her dream.

When had her bed gotten so small and cramped?

Her back was pressed up against a warm wall, her bottom nestled against something hard.

Her waist was tethered down.

She didn't feel trapped or claustrophobic, though. Nor did she feel compelled to move away. Rather, she snuggled deeper into the cocoon of comfort.

Whatever had been clamped on her waist slowly traveled upward until it reached under her shirt and began to fondle her breast.

Ooh. Nice. She sighed and arched in contentment, her dream getting better by the minute.

A warm breeze whispered along her neck, as lips brushed against the sensitive skin below her ear.

She leaned her head back to provide more access to the mouth that was giving her such delicious pleasure.

Swish.

Swack.

Swish.

What was that flapping sound?

Angie didn't want to stir, didn't want to ever wake up, but the annoying sound wouldn't go away. She cracked her eyes open and saw something big and white floating up in the wind, then smacking down against the side of a huge, red barn.

A barn that looked a lot like Toby's.

Why was her bed in Toby's backyard?

Wait. Whose pink-pony-covered pillow was wrapped in her arms?

And whose hand held her left breast? Whose fingers had tightened over her taut nipple?

"You feel good," a sleep-graveled, baritone voice whispered against her ear.

Toby?

This wasn't a dream, was it?

Swish. Swish. Splat.

Were those water droplets that just sprinkled her face?

"What the—" Toby shot up, and his hand left her breast. "Oh, hell. The sprinkler."

Angie stared at Toby through wet lashes, fully awake now and trying to piece together why they'd been sleeping together outdoors, why he'd been holding her so intimately. But more water from a nearby sprinkler shot her in the face again, and Toby grabbed her arm, pulling her toward the house.

"We have to get this stuff inside. Everything's going to get soaked."

Angie, still dazed from her erotic sleep-induced bliss, didn't take the time to decide whether Toby had been fully awake or dreaming. Instead she snapped out of it long enough to run for the movie projector, pull the hefty old machine off the relocated patio table and lug it, extension cord and all, inside the kitchen, trying to dodge the shooting sprays of water as she went.

She set the reels on the table, just as Toby dropped the first load of wet blankets on the kitchen floor.

"Why are you guys all wet?" Kylie asked, walking into the kitchen before Angie could process what had happened outside on the lawn.

Angie waited for Toby to answer because she didn't think the words would form in her throat.

But a red flush on Toby's face as he reached down for one of the damp pillows and placed it in front of his waist suggested that her hormones hadn't been the only ones getting an early-morning workout.

She didn't know whether to laugh at his discomfort or run out of the room in embarrassment because, whatever had just happened—sleep-induced or fully conscious—their friendship had just taken a tremendous turn in an unexpected direction.

Maybe it was best if she got out of here.

She was usually good with smooth exit strategies, but she couldn't seem to get her brain to engage.

As much as she'd like to pretend this morning hadn't happened, she hated to leave Toby to face the music alone. And judging from the pink tint blossoming underneath his stubble-covered cheeks, he didn't quite know what to make of it, either.

"The sprinklers came on early this morning," Toby mumbled, not dropping the pillow. "So Angie and I were trying to get all this stuff inside."

"Why didn't you bring it in last night?" Justin asked, making his way into the crowded kitchen, oblivious to the strong but awkward sexual attraction swirling in the room like a Texas dust cloud.

"Sweet," Brian said, padding in to join them, his red hair sticking up on one side of his head. "You guys had a sleepover."

Oh, great. That wasn't going to look good in the social worker's report—if one of the kids happened to mention Toby having a woman spend the night while the kids were home.

Angie reached up to smooth her own sleep-tousled hair.

Maybe she should tell the kids she'd been out for a morning jog and had decided to stop in for breakfast.

She glanced down at her bare feet. No, they were

too smart to fall for that. She needed to nip this thing in the bud before everyone in town heard that she and Toby had slept together—which, technically, they had.

"It wasn't really a sleepover," she said. "I just dozed off while watching the movie."

"Then can Mike Waddell kinda fall asleep over here next Saturday after our baseball game?" Brian asked.

The energy-drink kid? Angie could only imagine the hyperactivity that would come along with that night. But at least the focus was now off her.

"We'll talk about it later," Toby said, finally releasing the pillow.

"If Brian gets a sleepover, then can I have a slumber party?" Kylie asked.

"How many girls do you want to come to your slumber party?" Angie asked.

"My teacher said that, if we have a party, we have to invite everyone from the class so we don't hurt anyone's feelings. And we have twenty-three kids in our class. But I don't want to invite Destiny Simmons because she told everyone my hair looks funny because I don't have a mommy to do it right."

That reminded Angie that Kylie needed a real mother figure, someone permanent. And not a fly-by-night female role model who'd nearly made love to a man outdoors in broad daylight, with three impressionable kids inside the house.

"Twenty-three kids?" Toby asked. "But that's counting the boys, too. You can't invite them to a girls' slumber party."

Kylie pointed at Angie. "But *you* had a *girl* over for a slumber party."

The tiny red-haired cherub in the princess pajamas had brought the conversation full circle without missing a beat.

And just as quickly, Toby opened the pantry door and changed the topic. "Hey, guys. We need to get our chores done early today. Why don't I make pancakes for breakfast? You can help me by setting the table and getting the juice out of the fridge."

Smart move. New focus.

While the children were distracted with setting the table and getting the orange juice out of the refrigerator, Angie decided it was the perfect time to sneak out of here.

She was such a coward. But she was doing what she did best—leaving before things got uncomfortable again.

So she slipped out the back, quietly shutting the door. When she walked by the kitchen window, Toby spotted her and lifted his eyebrows.

She gestured, then mouthed, "I have to go." It was a lame excuse, especially since she really had nowhere to go on a Saturday morning. But she couldn't very well stay here and play house with Toby and the kids.

He nodded as if he understood. Yet guilt, embarrassment, fear and other emotions she hadn't yet pegged all tumbled around in her throat, threatening to cut off her air supply.

She put her thumb to her ear and her pinkie to her lips, giving him the universal sign for telephone. Then she mouthed, "I'll call you."

Again, he nodded.

Then she climbed into her car before she could debate whether she really had any business calling Toby at all.

Ten minutes after Angie drove away, the cordless phone on the counter rang and Kylie answered it before Toby could make a grab for it. Was Angie calling him already? He could understand her wanting to get the heck out of Dodge this morning. He'd been tempted to jump in her car and go with her just to escape the curious eyes pelting him with unspoken questions.

What had he been thinking, spending the entire night with Angie like that? Better yet, what had he been thinking setting those damn sprinklers on a timer to go off at six in the morning? If they hadn't blasted them with water, Toby knew exactly what he would have done to Angie's sweet, warm and tempting body this morning. He wouldn't have stopped with a hand on her lush breast—that was for sure. Instead, they'd gotten sprayed with water like a couple of dogs someone had to turn the hose on to keep from going at it on the front lawn.

"Yeah, Aunt Stacey," Kylie said. "He's right here, fixing pancakes for us and Angie."

Obviously, Kylie still hadn't realized that Angie had left. Or that Toby was still staring out the kitchen window after her like a sad, abandoned puppy.

He tried to reach for the telephone before Kylie could tell his sister anything else, but his hands were full of slimy eggshells, which he'd have to rinse off first.

"Uh-huh," Kylie continued. "Angie and Toby had a

sleepover last night. And Toby got my pillow all wet, but that's okay because he said I get to invite my class over for a slumber party."

With his hands clean, but still wet, Toby took the phone from Kylie. "Hey, Stace. What's up?"

"Why did Kylie put *you* on the phone?" Stacey asked. "I wanted to talk to Angie."

"She's not here," Toby said, a bit more defensively than he'd intended.

"She left already?" Justin asked. "Aw, man. I wanted to ask her to help me build a spaceship out of LEGO."

"We'll see her later," Toby told the disappointed boy.

But the truth was, he didn't know when they'd see Angie again. Or if Angie would even want to see him after the way he'd been pawing at her this morning.

"Later, huh?" Stacey asked. "I heard the two of you have been spending a lot of time together lately, but I had no idea you guys were at the sleepover stage."

Toby covered the mouthpiece. "Brian, stir the pancake mix. I'm going to talk to my sister for a sec. But don't use the stove until I get back."

After giving all the kids an assignment, Toby walked into the living room so they wouldn't hear his line of defense.

Not that he'd done anything wrong. Had he? Maybe if he just explained what had happened…

Hey, wait. He didn't owe anyone an explanation.

When he reached the living room, he asked, "So how's Piper?"

Everyone knew Stacey adored her nine-month-old daughter, so he figured he'd change the subject to one of toothless grins and sleepless nights.

"She's fine," Stacey said. "Growing cuter and smarter every day."

"And how about Colton?" he asked, hoping he could get her talking about her new fiancé, one of the neighboring ranchers. "Have you guys set a date yet?"

"Colton is doing great, but don't try those distraction tactics on me. I'm one step ahead of you, big brother. You are *not* getting out of this one. What's going on with you and Angie Edwards?"

His sisters, Stacey and Delaney, were protective over all their brothers, but particularly Toby since his family always accused him of being a softy—and a sucker for a sob story. Not that Angie was a sob story.

"Nothing's going on," he said. "Angie's been helping me out with the kids. That's all."

"Are you paying her for babysitting services? Because I heard Angie's always looking for a new job. She never seems to stick with one very long."

"Not that it's any of your business, but no, I'm not paying her. She's doing it to be nice and because she likes the kids. And for your information, Angie is a very hard worker. Just because she hasn't found a career she likes doesn't mean she isn't a good person."

"I never said she wasn't, Toby. I was just telling you what I've been hearing around town. I went to high school with Angie, remember? She used to date a lot back then."

Toby felt a jostle of jealousy stir up again in his veins.

"What do you mean she used to date a lot? Like she was…" Toby didn't want to say anything that would be demeaning to Angie, but he didn't know how else to ask.

"Well, she didn't have a reputation for being fast or anything like that, but she was known as the Queen of the First Date."

"What does that mean?"

"It means she would go out with a guy if he asked her, but usually, they never made it to a second date. I don't know if it was fear of commitment or what, but she never went steady with anyone or took any of the guys seriously. She for sure never had sleepovers with anyone before. Or at least none that I heard about."

The envy died down a little bit inside him. At least he couldn't fault Angie for being choosy.

"Listen, last night wasn't a sleepover. It was just an accident. Nothing, uh, really happened."

He hoped his sister hadn't caught the hesitation in his voice.

"Aha!" she said. "Define 'nothing.' And 'really.'"

"I'm not defining anything." Toby looked back to the kitchen to make sure none of the little ears had made their way within hearing distance.

Stacey clicked her tongue. "You wouldn't be getting so defensive if your relationship was strictly platonic. So how far have you guys gone?"

Toby couldn't believe Stacey had just asked him that. "This isn't high school, Stace. We're not playing truth or dare. I'm not talking about my sex life with my little sister."

"So you're saying there *is* a sex life to talk about," she said, a spark of excitement lighting her voice as if she'd tricked a leprechaun into revealing the location of his pot of gold.

Embarrassment was an understatement. Toby remembered holding the wet pillow up to cover his arousal this morning when the kids came into the kitchen. He wished he had something to hide behind now.

He wasn't going to admit to anything. He'd said too much as it was and figured silence was his only option.

"So," Stacey said, apparently changing tactics, "the reason I called was to tell you that Mom and Dad are having a family dinner at their house tonight. And we'd like you to bring Angie."

"Why, so you guys can check her out and pump her for information? No way."

"Mom told me and Delaney you'd say that when we came up with the idea."

Great. His family was already plotting and scheming.

"That's why," Stacey continued, "Delaney is calling Angie right now and asking her to come over for dinner. Too bad she didn't pick up the phone a few minutes earlier. We could've killed two birds with one stone."

"I'm not coming to dinner tonight," Toby said. "And I'm not inviting Angie."

"Why not? If there's nothing going on between you two, then why try to keep her away from your family?"

Stacey had a point. Unfortunately, with the sparks that were jumping between him and Angie lately, he doubted a blind man would believe there wasn't anything going on between them.

And knowing his family the way he did, he was

sure they'd figure out something was up the second he, Angie and the kids walked in the door.

Hell.

"Okay," he finally conceded. "But let me invite her. And I'll only do it if you guys promise not to interrogate her."

"My, aren't you the protector. She's lucky to have you in her corner."

Toby didn't know about that.

"Oops," Stacey said, "Piper just smeared green beans all over herself. Gotta go."

Good, Toby thought. He was glad Stacey's baby had made a mess she'd have to clean up. That was what his sister got for butting into Toby's business.

He just hoped he didn't have an even bigger mess to deal with now.

Angie saw Toby's name displayed on her caller-ID screen. She'd been too chicken to call him after she said she would. What was the proper length of time one should wait to call the man they'd intimately nestled against all night long? Three days? Maybe there was an article in some women's magazine she could reference.

Ugh. She needed to get this over with. He was probably calling to tell her that they needed to see less of each other. That he wasn't looking for a relationship. He'd made that more than clear. The sooner she bit the bullet, the sooner she could get over him. Unfortunately, she didn't think she'd ever get over the feeling of his fingers stroking their way up her waist. Or his husky voice telling her how good she felt.

She tried to sound more upbeat than the groan stuck in her throat would allow when she said, "Hello?"

"Um, hey."

Couldn't he even manage a proper greeting? He must already be experiencing remorse at what they'd done and guilt over what he was about to tell her.

She should make it easy for him and call things off first, but she couldn't bring herself to say the words for him.

"Did my sister Delaney call you yet?" he finally got out.

"Not that I know of. But I haven't looked at my missed calls since I got out of the shower."

Why would Delaney be calling her? Had the rumors started already? Was Toby trying to do damage control? Maybe they needed to get their stories straight about her spending the night out at the Double H.

"Good. I wanted to talk to you before she did."

Uh-oh. This didn't bode well.

"It sounds like my family is doing a dinner thing tonight and they want me to bring you."

"Why would they want me there?" Unless they thought something was going on between her and Toby. Of course, she didn't know why his family would think that when she, herself, had no idea if there was anything going on between the two of them.

"They, uh, well, they're just curious about you since we've been spending, uh, so much time together and, you know…" Was Toby nervous? His voice tripped over the words like a shy schoolboy asking her out to prom. He was usually so confident. What had happened to all his swagger and self-assuredness?

"So they want to check me out?" She actually wanted to ask if they were trying to determine if she was good enough for their Fortune Jones standards. Angie had the feeling she wouldn't pass that test.

"It's really not a big deal. It's just a little family get-together. And I made Stacey promise that they wouldn't interrogate you or anything."

"Yeah, that's not exactly selling me on the idea, Toby." In fact, the implication that he probably had to wrestle the promise from his sister made it seem that much more likely that what his family had planned was a full-scale inquisition.

"Well, I figure we could either go to the dinner together and show a kind of united front, or we can sit back and wait for them to come into the Superette one by one and hound you for information."

That was a good point. She didn't relish being the subject of the Fortune Joneses' scrutiny, but she'd rather it be in the privacy of their family ranch than in public at her place of employment. She didn't mind working in the bakery on occasion, but she'd hate to have to hide back there for good.

"Plus," Toby continued, "the kids will be there and Stacey is bringing Piper. If we stick close to at least one of the children, we should be safe, right?"

Angie didn't know if he meant they'd be safe from the prying questions from his family or safe from their own raging hormones.

But she just wasn't sure she should go. She wanted to spend more time with him, but would this just make things more complicated? He sounded as if he was eager to have her there, which wasn't how a man would act if he was trying to break it off with a woman.

"Let me think about it," she finally said.

"Fair enough. I'll be at the baseball field most of the afternoon, so just give me a call on my cell when you decide."

She had no more than set her phone down on the counter when a preprogrammed ringtone sounded. The foreboding theme song from *Jaws* indicated it was her mother.

Doris had called her twice last night, and if Angie didn't talk to her mom now, the woman would think something was going on and make another surveillance trip into the Superette.

"Hi, Mom," Angie finally said, ending the crescendo of doom.

"Evangeline, I've been trying to get ahold of you since yesterday. Where have you been? On a date?"

Did her mom suspect?

Probably not. Doris didn't keep in touch with many people she'd known from when she'd lived in Horseback Hollow. They were too small-town for Doris's perceived cosmopolitan lifestyle. Not that Lubbock could be considered an epicenter of sophistication by most people's standards, but her mom liked to think she was a big deal now.

"I've just been really busy. Nothing new or exciting going on here."

"Good, because if you don't have plans tonight, there's a dinner dance at the country club here in Lubbock, and Margie Suttelheimer's grandson is going to be there. He's a corporate attorney, and his second di-

vorce was just finalized last month. Margie assured
me his prenup was ironclad. His ex barely got a dime,
so he's still worth millions."

Angie had never made a quicker decision.

"I'm sorry, Mom. I've already made plans for tonight."

She'd just have to tell Toby that dinner with the Fortune Jones clan was on.

At one minute after nine, Toby went out to the barn
for some privacy. Using his cell phone, he placed a call
to Ms. Fisk at child services, only to reach a record-
ing that said she was out of the office. So he left her a
voice-mail message.

Next he called the Lubbock attorney who'd first
contacted him about the money that the anonymous
donor had given him and he'd placed in trust for the
kids. Jake Gleason specialized in estate planning, so
if push came to shove, Toby would retain someone
else to handle the custody issue. But for right now, he
needed some professional assurance that Barbara had
only been blowing smoke.

Unfortunately, Jake hadn't been able to do much
to ease his worry. "It's hard to second-guess what the
court will decide in cases like yours. One judge may
consider stability a priority and look at how well the
kids are doing under your care and not want to move
them. But another might prefer to keep kids with their
family members."

Jake did, however, give Toby the names of a couple
of family-law attorneys.

As morning wore on, the only thing that had given

Toby a lift had been thoughts of Angie. Her bright-eyed smile and upbeat nature had a way of making him feel as though everything would work out fine—one way or another. So he hoped she still planned to join them at his parents' house.

By the time lunch was over and afternoon rolled around, he'd picked up the phone a couple of times to call her, just to make sure they were still on for dinner. After all, she'd been known to change her mind.

Finally, at three o'clock, he bit the bullet and called. When she answered, he asked, "Are we still on for that barbecue at my parents' house?"

"Sure. What time did you want to go?"

"I thought I'd pick you up around four."

"You shouldn't have to drive all the way into town to get me when your parents live closer to you. Why don't I drive to your place? Then I can fix Kylie's hair."

"That makes more sense. And Kylie would really appreciate a woman's hand with those pigtails. I can never seem to get them to hang evenly."

Angie laughed, and the lilt of her voice made him grip the phone tighter, as if he could draw her near and hold her close.

"While I was helping Mr. Murdock organize his closets, I found some ribbons in an old sewing basket. He said I could have them, so I'll bring them with me. I also baked brownies to take with us. I'm ready now, so I may as well head on over to your place."

"That sounds like a plan. I'll round up the troops, and we'll be ready when you get here."

"By the way," Angie said, "who's going to be at that family dinner?"

"My parents, of course. My sister Delaney and my

brother Galen. Stacey is the ringleader, so she and her fiancé, Colton Foster, will be there, along with her baby, Piper. I imagine my brother Jude and his fiancée, Gabriella Mendoza, will be coming. And of course Liam and Julia Tierney."

"It'll be fun to see Julia outside of the Superette," Angie said. "And it will be nice to see Stacey and Delaney again."

Toby hoped she still felt that way after his sisters began plying her with questions about their supposed relationship.

"It might be best not to mention my brother Chris," Toby said. "Unless someone else brings him up first."

"Why?"

He waited a beat, wondering why he felt inclined to even mention it.

"It's not as though there's a big family rift," he explained, trying to downplay things and to choose his words carefully. "It's just there were some hard feelings about him leaving Horseback Hollow and moving to Red Rock."

"That's really not a secret. There's been some talk around town. And Sawyer and Laurel made a comment about it at the flight school."

"What did they say?" Toby asked.

"Nothing really. They don't discuss things like that in front of their employees. But they said something in passing, and I connected a few dots. So I know that Chris is working for Sawyer's dad at the Fortune Foundation. But that's about it."

Toby didn't know much more than that, either, although he'd been tempted to go to Red Rock and talk to his brother face-to-face. But with him now having three kids, all of whom were in school and involved in outside activities, he wasn't free to make a trip like that without a lot of juggling and some careful orchestrating.

"I'm assuming that your parents aren't happy about his move," Angie said.

Toby didn't usually air family laundry in public, but he and Angie had become pretty close lately, so sharing his concerns came easily. "When my mom asked us to accept our roots by taking on the Fortune name, my dad was a good sport about it. But when Chris announced he was moving to Red Rock, my dad hit the roof. He felt as though my brother had completely jumped ship by leaving town and going to work for James Marshall Fortune. Things really hit the fan then."

There'd always been issues between Chris and their dad over the years, although Toby never had thought they were all that serious. But apparently, he'd been wrong.

"Don't worry about me saying anything at dinner tonight—or to anyone else," Angie said. "I may have my faults, but being a gossip isn't one of them."

"Thanks. I appreciate that."

Silence filled the line for a beat, then Angie said, "I'd better let you go. I'll see you in a little while."

As soon as they ended the call, Toby rounded up the kids and told them to wash up, change their clothes and get ready to go to Grandma and Grandpa's house.

They might not be related by blood, but his parents and siblings had accepted them into the Fortune Jones fold, just as though they were. And the kids, who'd been starved for love and affection, had been thrilled to have a family to call their own. So the last time they'd visited, his mom had suggested they not be so formal. "Why don't y'all call us Grandma Jeanne and Grandpa Deke?" she'd said.

The kids, who'd never really had parents, let alone grandparents, had jumped at the chance to become a part of Jeanne's brood. In fact, if you didn't know, you'd think there'd been a long line of redheads somewhere in the Fortune Jones family tree.

Toby did, however, realize that it could all come to an end one day if Barbara made good on her threat, and his gut twisted at the possibility. But he shook off the negative thoughts and tried to focus on the fact that the kids were thriving. And that their school would back that up if need be.

"Can I pack my backpack with things me and Piper can play with?" Kylie asked.

Toby smiled. Most little girls loved dolls, but having a real baby to play with? "Absolutely. Just let Aunt Stacey check out the toys first. You know how careful she is about the things Piper puts in her mouth."

"I will," Kylie said, as she dashed off to her room.

Toby glanced at the clock on the mantel. While the kids were getting ready, he'd take a shower. Angie would be here before he knew it.

Chapter Eight

Nearly an hour later, Angie arrived at the Double H wearing a white sundress that was wholesome, yet strappy and sexy at the same time—especially when paired with brown cowboy boots.

"Look what I have," she said, lifting a platter of gooey-looking brownies in one hand and a fistful of colorful hair ribbons in the other.

"Nice," Toby said, although he was far more focused on the sweet and lovely lady who stood in front of him, her blue eyes bright, her brown hair lying soft and glossy along her almost bare shoulders.

"Where's Kylie?" she asked.

"In her room. I'll call her." But before Toby could open his mouth, Kylie came dashing into the entry to greet Angie.

The two of them took off, and before long, Kylie

returned, wearing a pair of cowboy boots, just like Angie, her hair in princess-perfect pigtails.

"Let's go," he said.

It took only ten minutes on the county road to reach his parents' ranch. After driving through the white wooden gate, Toby followed the graveled road to the house and parked near the barn, next to the other cars and trucks.

"Looks like everyone beat us here," he said.

"Are we late?" Angie asked.

"Not really. But I have a feeling the women in my family were eager to be here when we arrived."

"Why?"

"Curiosity, I suppose." Toby shut off the ignition. "They know we've been seeing a lot of each other, and I'm afraid their imaginations are getting the best of them."

He could argue—and, in fact, he had argued—that he and Angie weren't dating, that she was merely helping him out with the kids. But sexual attraction and mutual interest were definitely flaring beneath the surface, and he wasn't so sure he'd be able to keep that a secret, especially here.

They all got out of the truck. As usual, the kids managed to pile out a lot faster than they ever climbed in.

"Don't forget to wipe your feet at the front door," Toby called out to them. "And don't barge in. Hang on until Angie and I get there."

"We won't," they called back in near unison.

Toby waited for Angie, as she reached into the cab and pulled out a denim jacket. Then she slipped into it, covering the white sundress that revealed a lovely set of tanned arms and shoulders. But as afternoon wore into evening, he knew there was a chance it could get chilly, so he couldn't blame her for being prepared.

Next he watched as she reached into the cab for the platter of brownies she'd brought.

"I'm sorry," she said, as she realized he was standing near the truck, waiting for her. "I didn't mean to be a slug."

"No problem." He actually liked watching her. But if he stared at her any longer, thinking about how much he wanted to pull her close, to kiss her before entering the house, it was going to take a whole lot more than an evening breeze to cool him off.

They walked together, meeting up with the kids at the front door, which was flanked by large pots of colorful flowers.

Out of habit, Toby took care to wipe his boots, just as he'd asked the children to do.

"My mom always made a big deal about us coming inside with muddy feet." He chuckled as he reached for the doorknob to let them all into the house. "I guess some habits are hard to break."

Toby's mom, with her silver hair pulled into a bun and dressed in her usual stretch-denim jeans and a pale blue sweatshirt, greeted them in the foyer. She gave Toby a warm embrace, then took the time to address each of the kids.

"Now, don't you look pretty, Kylie. Look at those yellow ribbons in your hair. And my goodness. What in the world have you stuffed in that backpack?"

"Toys to show baby Piper. Is she here?"

Jeanne Marie placed a hand on Kylie's head and smiled. "She certainly is. Aunt Stacey just gave her some bananas and peaches for a snack, which she's washing off her face and hands now. Why don't you go into the kitchen and see if she's ready to play."

"Oh, good," Kylie said, as she dashed off.

"And you boys are in for a big treat," Jeanne Marie told Brian and Justin. "Grandpa Deke fixed the rungs to the tree house and gave it a new coat of paint yesterday. And when Uncle Galen saw what he'd done, he attached a rope swing to one of those sturdy ole branches. You probably ought to go check it out."

"Cool," Brian said, as both boys hurried off.

Well done, Toby thought. His mother adored the kids, but it was plain to see that she had something up her sleeve. She'd sent them off happily so she could devote her full attention to Angie and to the interrogation process.

Now, with the children out of the way, she welcomed Angie with a warm shake of the hand. "I'm so glad you could join us. Toby tells me how helpful you've been to him this past week."

"It's been my pleasure. The kids are great. And in all honesty, Toby's so good with them, I'm not sure he even needs my help at all."

"Don't let her downplay her efforts," Toby said. "She's been awesome, whether it's playing beauty salon with Kylie or planning a make-it-yourself pizza night or watching a movie under the stars. And I would have really been up a creek yesterday without her."

"You don't say." His mom smiled, those blue eyes glimmering. "I'll tell you what, Toby. Why don't you check out that tree house and make sure Galen secured that swing right, while I take Angie into the kitchen. Since she's such a good helper, I'm going to rope her into helping the girls and I finish up with the burger fixings."

And just like a mama fox, Jeanne Marie had dispensed with Toby.

He could argue and insist that Angie stick close to his side, he supposed. But Angie was a big girl and had proved that she could hold her own. Besides, he wanted to check out that old fort he and his brothers used to play in. And on top of that, he trusted his mom and his sisters not to go overboard.

So he took his leave, walking out to the backyard, where his own interrogation undoubtedly awaited.

Angie followed Toby's mother out to the kitchen. She'd always liked the woman, but then, who in town didn't?

Jeanne Marie might come across as plain and simple, but there was more to her than met the eye. She had a quick wit, a gentle spirit and a kind heart. She also loved her husband and children dearly and was fiercely devoted to them.

Since working at the Superette, Angie had picked up on all of that. She'd even found herself a bit envious of the family's closeness. How could she not be?

She'd always wanted to be part of a big, happy family, but she'd been an only child. She and her daddy had been close, but he'd died five years ago.

Now that Angie was an adult, her mom sought the closeness they'd never quite had before. But Doris

Edwards was so determined to make Angie into the woman she wanted her to be that it was easier to avoid her, which was sad.

"I brought some brownies," Angie said, holding out the platter of chocolaty squares covered in caramel frosting and toffee pieces.

"You didn't need to do that," Jeanne Marie said, as she led Angie through the large-but-cozy living room. "But it was awfully nice of you. I try to have plenty for everyone to eat, but I have to admit, this family can really put away the desserts. So I doubt you'll have anything to take home except a few crumbs."

When they reached the kitchen, Angie saw Piper sitting in a walker on the floor with Kylie playing beside her. The little red-haired girl had made fast work of emptying out the entire contents of her backpack on the hardwood floor.

"You girls remember Angie," Jeanne Marie said to both Stacey and Delaney.

"Of course." Stacey, a bright-eyed blonde with a light spray of freckles on her nose, smiled. "We're so glad Toby finally brought you out to meet his crazy family."

Angie and Stacey had graduated from high school together, although they really hadn't run in the same circles. Stacey, who'd gone on to nursing school after graduation, had been more of an academic and tended to hang out with the smarter kids. And Angie had been all over the campus, hanging with the members of whichever social club she was trying out that semester.

"Thanks for including me." Angie placed the brownies on the sideboard, next to a Bundt cake in a covered dish and a plate of lemon bars. Toby's mom had been right. They were certainly dessert-friendly in this household. She hoped everyone was as sweet as the offerings on the countertop.

"Can I help you guys with anything?" Angie asked, noticing that Stacey was putting the finishing touches on a cheese-and-vegetable platter.

"Julia and Gabi are setting the tables outside," Delaney said, as she stirred something that appeared to be potato salad. "And we're almost done in here."

"Why don't you pull up a chair?" Stacey nodded to one of the empty barstools on the other side of the kitchen island. "Tell us what you've been doing with yourself since high school."

"Now hold off a moment," Jeanne Marie said. "It's only fair to offer Angie a glass of wine or some iced tea first. The least we can do is let our guest wet her whistle before you launch into a full-blown question-and-answer session."

When Jeanne winked at Angie, and her daughters laughed, easing the awkward tension, Angie couldn't help but join in the merriment. If Stacey and Delaney could make light of their overly curious natures, then so could she. Besides, she had nothing to hide.

Well, nothing except the fact that she had the hots for one of their brothers.

"I think I'll take an iced tea," Angie said, "but you guys keep doing what you're doing. I'll get it."

She'd no more than crossed the kitchen and was reaching for the pitcher when Justin rushed into the room, his eyes bright, his excitement impossible to ignore. "Angie, I was telling Uncle Galen about your candy brownies, and he wanted me to bring them out to the tree house so we can all try them."

If there was anyone who loved sweets more than the Fortune Jones family, it was Justin Hemings. And since he'd been eyeing those brownies and asking for a taste ever since she'd arrived at the Double H, Angie knew when he was still trying to finagle an early treat.

"You tell Uncle Galen that we have so many desserts to choose from that it's best if he waits until after dinner. That way, instead of having only one treat, he'll be able to try them all." Angie pointed to the counter holding the sweets.

Justin hurried over to look at his many options. His eyes darted from side to side, unable to settle on a favorite.

"Did you make all of these?" he asked Angie. Before she could answer, he looked at Jeanne Marie and continued. "Angie makes the *best* cupcakes with little race cars on the top. And she makes us pizza with our very own favorite toppings. And she puts extra butter on the popcorn because that's how Toby likes it best. She's the best cooker in the world. I'm going to tell Brian about the desserts. C'mon, Angie. You gotta come see the tree house."

And with that, Justin shot out the open sliding door, running as fast as he talked.

Angie looked at Toby's sisters, who both seemed eager to pounce on her with questions, but Jeanne Marie saved her by saying, "Let's go see the tree house. Then you can meet my husband. That will give my daughters plenty of time to strategize about what they want to ask you."

Grateful to have escaped what she was sure would have been a barrage of questions, Angie tossed them each a smile and went outside with Jeanne Marie to a built-in barbecue, where Deke was preparing to grill hamburger patties and hot dogs.

"Honey," Jeanne Marie said, "this is Angie Edwards, Toby's friend."

Deke, a tall, rugged man with a thatch of thick gray hair, turned to Angie and greeted her with a hint of a smile. "It's nice to meet you. We like it when the kids bring their friends home."

"I'm glad to be included," Angie said. "Where's that tree house I heard so much about?"

Deke pointed about fifty yards from the house to a huge tree where Toby stood with his brothers Jude, Liam and Galen. The men were watching Brian swing while laughing at something Liam said.

"The boys found that ole fort the first day Toby brought them to the ranch," Deke said. "But we hadn't realized how rotten some of that lumber had gotten until Justin fell and bumped his head a couple of weeks ago. So we wouldn't let them play on it until I could find the time to replace some of those old boards."

"Well, it looks as though they appreciate your time and effort," Angie said. "In fact, if I wasn't wearing a dress, I'd join them on that swing."

Jeanne Marie laughed. "And I might take a turn with you. When our sons were little, we used to have overnight campouts in that fort."

"You slept outside with them?" Angie couldn't imagine her mom doing something like that.

"I did until they stopped being afraid of the bogeyman. After that, whenever they had those campouts I stayed inside and enjoyed the peace and quiet with their daddy."

Deke grinned and gave Jeanne Marie a little pat.

It was heartwarming to see such a loving couple. She'd never seen her parents show each other any affection.

"Honey," Deke said to his wife, "can you please go in the house and get a clean platter for me to put the cooked meat on?"

"I'll get it," Angie offered. "Everyone else has a job to do. I better earn my dinner, too."

"Then you go on ahead," Jeanne Marie said with a laugh. "We wouldn't want you to feel excluded."

Angie started toward the house, just as Julia Tierney was coming outside with a pitcher of lemonade and a stack of red plastic cups.

"Hey," Julia said. "I heard you were coming. It's nice to see you outside of the Superette."

Angie smiled. "It's nice to be here. In fact, I've only been on the ranch a few minutes, but everyone has been so warm and welcoming. You're lucky to be a part of this."

Julia, who'd recently become engaged to Toby's brother Liam, had a glow about her these days. "I've really been blessed. I've fallen in love with the greatest guy in the world, and he has a wonderful family."

"You know," Angie said, as she stepped aside, "I'd better let you put that lemonade down before you drop it. Besides, I finally have a job to do and don't want Deke to think I'm lagging."

Julia smiled. "I'll talk to you later."

As Julia passed through the doorway and onto the patio, Gabriella Mendoza followed behind her, carrying a platter of lettuce leaves, tomato slices and other hamburger fixings.

Gabi was also sporting a diamond engagement ring these days, courtesy of Jude, another of Toby's brothers. The two had met after Gabi's father, Orlando Mendoza, had been seriously injured in a plane crash.

Orlando had been a pilot for the Redmond Flight School when the accident happened. And Gabi had flown out from Miami to be with him as soon as she'd gotten the news.

"Hi there," Gabi said. "It's good to see you again."

"Same here," Angie said. "How's your dad doing?"

"Much better. Thank you for asking."

"I'm so glad to hear that." Angie again stepped aside to let Gabi pass, then entered the kitchen, which was a bustle of activity as Stacey and Delaney laid out plates of appetizers to go outside.

"Your dad asked me to bring him a clean platter for the cooked meat," Angie said.

"I'll get that for you." Stacey went to a side cupboard and pulled out a large, ceramic platter. "But before you go, I do have a question for you."

Angie smiled. "Okay, shoot."

"In high school you were Queen of the First Date and president of just about every club they offered." Angie assumed Stacey was going to point out the obvious—that Angie couldn't commit to anything—until she added, "At times I was a bit envious."

No kidding? She hadn't meant to insult her? Stacey had actually admired her?

"I'm curious," Stacey said. "When you told Justin not to choose anything too soon, how did you come up with that strategy?"

It was a strategy, although no one had actually pegged it as such.

The other women in the kitchen—Julia and Gabi were now back—continued to move about, but their movements slowed and their side conversations stalled.

Angie had never tried to explain it to anyone before, but for some reason, she opted for candor now. "My dad used to tell me to be careful when making a choice, because once I made it, I couldn't change my mind. So I took that to heart. I try everything once, knowing that when I find something I'm passionate about, I'll stick to it."

Trouble was, she wasn't entirely convinced of that. If it turned out she was wrong, she could end up in some eternal revolving door of new beginnings and never find a happy ending.

"But you don't believe that, do you?" Delaney said. "I mean, everyone makes mistakes. It's not like you can't start over and have a second chance."

Angie had never talked about her childhood to anyone before, but being here with Toby's family had a way of making her lower her guard.

"Yes, I know that—intellectually. However, I grew up in a household with parents who remained in an unhappy marriage for my sake. And they drilled it into me that once a commitment was made, you had to stick to it."

"That's kind of sad," Delaney said.

"I know. My mom hated small-town life, so living

in Horseback Hollow nearly sucked the life out of her. And as a result, her unhappiness nearly sucked the life out of my dad."

"Is that why your mom eventually moved to Lubbock?" Delaney asked.

It was common knowledge that Doris acted as though she was better than everyone in town. And that she'd filed for a divorce and moved to Lubbock the day after Angie had graduated from high school.

Still, even when her mom had lived with them in Horseback Hollow, she'd commuted to work in Lubbock, which meant she was gone most of the time. And to be honest, she'd left Angie and her father emotionally even before that—or so it had seemed.

"My parents were mismatched from day one," Angie said. "And, if anything, it's made me not want to make any big decisions that I might regret for the rest of my life, especially when it came to a college degree or a lifelong profession."

"C'mon, Angie," Delaney said. "Don't you think you're taking your dad's advice to an extreme?"

"Maybe," Angie conceded. "But I've had a lot of cool jobs, tried a variety of things and learned a lot along the way. I can also handle just about anything thrown my way."

"I've heard about some of your job experience," Jeanne Marie said, as she entered the kitchen and breezed right into the conversation.

"What have you heard?" Angie asked.

"That you're more than qualified to do *my* job." Jeanne Marie laughed as she carried the big bowl of potato salad out the back door to the tables set up in the yard.

Angie looked at Toby's sisters and whispered, "What's your mom's job?"

The girls both laughed, and Angie began to wonder whether any of them would answer. Finally, Delaney said, "She was a professional stay-at-home mom."

Angie was at a loss. She could never be a stay-at-home mom. Not like Jeanne Marie.

When the girls finally got their giggles under control, Stacey asked, "Do you need any help deciding what to do with our brother?"

"No, not really. We never seem to have any time to talk about it. So I have no idea what he's even thinking."

Angie did, however, have a very memorable moment of waking in his arms—before the sprinklers ruined it all.

"You mean you've never had a proper date?" Stacey asked.

"I'm afraid not. The kids are always with us. And to tell you the truth, I don't know if Toby *wants* to date me."

"Oh, believe us," Stacey said, "he wants to."

Delaney beamed. "Just leave it to us. Stacey and I are just the ones who can make that happen."

A date? With Toby Fortune Jones?

Angie didn't know if she should run for the hills—or thank her lucky stars.

As the meat sizzled on the grill, setting off the aroma of barbecued burgers and hot dogs, Toby stood next to his father and Colton Foster, Stacey's fiancé.

Deke had roped his future son-in-law into helping

him man the grill, and the two ranchers had been discussing the rising cost of feed corn, as well as the new bull Deke intended to purchase.

But Toby couldn't seem to focus on the discussion at hand. Instead he kept thinking about the one going on in the kitchen, where the women had gathered with Angie.

"Excuse me," he said, as he stepped away from his dad and Colton.

The two men continued to talk while Toby strode across the patio to the insulated cooler that held a variety of drinks, including the ice-cold bottle of beer he snatched for himself.

So far, the family dinner at his parents' house seemed to be going well. The women had begun to carry out the food and place it on tables that had been set up on the lawn, which meant it would be time to eat soon.

Jude, Liam and Galen had gathered near the tree house, where they were probably still reminiscing about their childhood or predicting the likelihood of the Rangers making it to the World Series this year.

But Toby's mind was on the kids and the fear that he might lose them. He could honestly say that if Barbara were a loving and maternal woman who'd made a few mistakes and was trying hard to straighten her life out he wouldn't be so uneasy. After all, he probably valued family ties more than anyone. It was just that he'd never seen a maternal side to Barbara.

He thought about sharing his worries with his family, but he didn't want to talk about it in front of the kids. Maybe it was best to wait until after he'd talked to Ms. Fisk on Monday—assuming she'd return his call the day she returned to the office.

Either way, he couldn't very well stew about it all weekend. So he'd better shake it off for now and start mingling before people started asking him what was bothering him.

As he stood in the center of the yard, a beer in hand, debating which of the two male groups to join, a squeal of feminine laughter rang out from the kitchen.

What in the heck were the women talking about in there? He hoped the topic of conversation wasn't on him and Angie.

Should he check? Did Angie need him to bail her out?

No, they were all laughing, so it had to be something else. His presence would only remind them of the questioning they'd planned upon his and Angie's arrival. So it would be best—and safer—if he hung out with the men.

Opting for the rowdier group near the tree house, Toby returned to the cooler, reached in for a couple more Coronas and carried them out to his brothers.

Upon his approach, a big ole grin stole across Galen's face. "You're just the guy I wanted to talk to."

"What about?" Toby asked.

"About you and Angie. I hear things are heating up."

Toby wasn't sure where Galen had come up with that. He glanced at Jude and Liam, both of whom were smirking, and realized it was now his turn to get the third degree. But there wasn't much to tell—or much he was willing to talk about.

He offered up the extra two Coronas he held instead. "You guys want a beer?"

Liam and Jude both took one.

Galen crossed his arms, his grin bursting into a full-on smile. "Don't change the subject, little bro. We just want to know what's going on with you and Angie, especially since Justin told us you two had a sleepover last night."

Aw, hell. Toby had been afraid that was going to happen.

He blew out a sigh. "As nice as that might sound, I'm afraid Justin blew that all out of proportion. Angie stayed over, but it's not what you're thinking."

"Hmm." Liam crossed his arms. "So if it would have been nice, does that mean you're interested in her?"

So what if he was?

Still, Toby wasn't going to admit anything. If he did, he'd never hear the end of it. And besides, he and Angie hadn't even talked about whether they wanted their relationship or friendship or whatever the hell it was to progress to a level like that.

"You know what I think?" Toby said to Liam. "You guys have fallen in love, so you think everyone else ought to be feeling the same way."

"I'm still single and unattached," Galen said. "And I think there's definitely some big-time sparks going on between you and Angie."

"Okay," Toby said. "I'm attracted to her. She's fun to be with. But that's about all there is to it."

"Why aren't you pursuing anything more?" Galen asked.

All kinds of reasons. The kids, for one. Angie's inability to commit to anyone or anything, for another. But then again, that hadn't seemed to matter when they'd woken up in each other's arms this morning.

Of course, there was also the matter of Jude dating her in the past. And Toby didn't want to cross any weird fraternal boundaries or become romantically involved with a woman his brother had once been… intimate with.

Wouldn't that be one huge disappointment?

"Speaking of Angie," Toby said to Jude, "you dated her, didn't you?"

"I guess you could call it that. We only went out a couple of times. It ended pretty abruptly."

"What happened?" Toby asked.

"When Angie's mom saw her out with me one evening, she flipped out. Apparently, she thought Angie could do a whole lot better. Doris tried to lower her voice, but I overheard her refer to me as a 'Horseback Hollow Casanova' and ask if I'd gone through all the women in my own age bracket and had started on a new generation." Jude blew out a sigh. "Okay, granted, there was a six-year age difference, but come on. A whole generation?"

Knowing her mom, that didn't surprise Toby. So if he and Angie ever did start dating, he and Doris would have to set some definite boundaries.

"So it ended quickly," Toby said. "But how serious were you?"

"It never would have gotten off the ground. She was a little too indecisive for me." Jude laughed. "Don't get me wrong. She's a nice girl, and we had fun. But

I made the mistake of asking her which movie she wanted to see. If I hadn't picked one myself and taken her by the hand, we probably would have stood outside the theater all night."

Toby had never really seen that side of Angie. She always seemed to know just what she wanted when she was with him and the kids.

Feminine voices grew louder as the women gathered outside and his mother announced that it was time to eat.

"Brian and Justin," she called to the boys in the tree house, "go on in the house with Kylie and wash your hands."

As the boys hurried to do as they were told, Jude asked Toby, "Has Angie decided upon a career yet?"

"No, she hasn't."

"Don't let that stop you," Galen said. "Look at her. She's smoking hot."

His oldest brother certainly had that right. Toby studied the lovely brunette crossing the lawn in that white sundress. She had on the denim jacket now, as well as those cowboy boots. So she'd covered up her arms and shoulders. But she still looked good.

In fact, she looked amazing in whatever she wore—especially a wet yoga outfit.

"Let me know if you're not interested in her," Galen added. "If that's the case, I might ask her out myself."

Just the thought of Galen moving in on Angie sent Toby's senses reeling.

"All right, I'm interested," he admitted. "So back off."

Before his brothers could tease him further, he

headed for the tables and found seats for him, Angie and the kids.

As was typical of a Fortune Jones dinner, everyone ate their fill, including the variety of desserts. All the while, they told stories about growing up together, sometimes teasing, usually smiling or laughing.

When Toby could finally call it a day, he rounded up the kids and told them it was time to head home.

"Why don't you let Brian and Justin spend the night here," Galen said. "I think I'll camp out in that tree house for old times' sake. And it would be nice if the boys kept me company."

Before Toby could respond, Stacey chimed in. "And Piper would like to have her very first sleepover. Why don't you let Colton and me take Kylie home with us?"

"A sleepover?" Toby asked. "Piper is only nine months old."

Stacey smiled. "You're right. She doesn't stay up past seven. But then I'll get a chance to play with Kylie."

What was going on? Galen and Stacey were offering to keep the kids?

"I don't know about that," Toby said. "They don't have their pajamas or toothbrushes."

Galen elbowed him. "Come on, Toby. Real cowboys don't sleep in jammies. They sleep in their boots and clothes. What's the matter with you?"

Stacey edged forward. "Kylie can sleep in one of my old T-shirts. I also have a brand-new toothbrush she can use. What do you say?"

He didn't know what to say. The offer stole the words right out of him.

"Come on, Toby." His little sister gave him a wink. "You deserve a good night's sleep."

It took him a moment to realize what his crazy family was up to. And he didn't know if he should kill them or kiss them. But when he took a look at Angie, when he spotted the wide-eyed wonder, the look of surprise…

Well, it wasn't just the kids who were whooping it up and begging for the night to come.

Toby's hormones were right there with them.

Chapter Nine

As Toby's pickup headed down the county road that led to the Double H Ranch, Angie bit down on her bottom lip and stared out the windshield. It was the first time they'd actually been alone, and for some reason they both seemed to be at a loss for words.

Sure, they'd had a few stolen moments before, but this was different. There were no children to worry about walking in on them, no job to hustle out to, no errands to run.

It was just the two of them.

The silence in the cab was almost overwhelming, and if that weren't enough, Angie's heart was zipping through her chest, racing around as if it wanted to beat her and Toby back to his place.

But then what? Things were sure to be more awkward there.

Would he tell her good-night the minute they got out of the truck? Or would he invite her into the house?

He hadn't uttered a word since they'd left, so she had no idea what he was thinking. But whenever she stole a glance across the seat, the expression he wore suggested that he felt just as on edge and nervous as she did.

She'd like to put him—or rather both of them—at ease, but she was so far out of her element that she didn't know where to begin.

What she could really use was an icebreaker, but she couldn't seem to come up with anything clever to say or do. So she just sank into the leather passenger seat, trying to keep her eyes off the handsome rancher who'd been captivating her thoughts more and more each day.

When they finally turned down his drive and neared the ranch house, she spotted her car parked right where she'd left it. The old Toyota looked a little sad and lonely sitting there, and Angie was going to feel the same way if she drove off in it.

Think, girl. Say something.

"So," she finally said, the sound of her voice breaking into the silence. "What are you going to do with an evening all to yourself?"

At that, Toby turned, glanced across the seat at her and smiled. "It's been so long since I've had a night without the kids that I have no idea."

Angie tucked a strand of hair behind her ear and tossed him a carefree grin. "Then if I were you, I'd turn on the TV, choose a channel that doesn't play cartoons and eat ice cream straight from the container."

Toby shut off the ignition. In the dim light of the

cab, she caught a glimmer in his eyes and a flirtatious tilt in his smile.

Now there went a definite *zing*.

He stretched his arm across the seat, and his smile deepened. "If you were me, would you invite someone in to watch television and help you eat the rest of the chocolate ice cream?"

"Actually, that's exactly what I'd do. But instead of the ice cream, I'd offer her wine because she probably avoided anything alcoholic at the barbecue for fear she'd slip and say something that your sisters might misconstrue. But I'd also promise to let her control the remote."

Toby laughed. "The wine, I can do. But I'm pretty territorial about my remote."

Not bad for an icebreaker, huh?

Angie smiled, then reached for the door handle and let herself out of the truck. They walked together to the porch, and when Toby opened the front door for her and flipped on the light switch, she stepped inside.

The house was quieter than it had ever been, at least since she'd started coming to visit. Only now, the solitude made things awkward again. Without the kids around to act as buffers, she and Toby had to face each other and whatever they were feeling.

He led her to the kitchen, where he opened the fridge and pulled out the bottle of wine for her and a longneck beer for him.

"I had a lot of fun tonight," she said, as she removed a goblet from the cabinet. "Your family knows how to have a good time. And they're down-to-earth."

"If by 'down-to-earth,' you mean 'meddling,' then,

yes. They are." Toby filled her glass. After popping the top off his drink, he leaned against the counter in a sexy cowboy slant.

"They weren't meddling," Angie said. "They were a little curious, maybe. But friendly. And look at how helpful they were, offering to take the kids for the night so that you could have a break."

Toby chuckled, then lifted the Corona to his lips and took another swig.

Oh, sweet goodness. Those lips. Angie had never been so jealous of a drink container.

When he lowered the bottle, his gaze zeroed in on her. "You know why they offered to keep the kids, don't you?"

She hadn't wanted to speculate, but now that he'd brought it up, she supposed, deep down, that she'd known what they'd been up to. They'd wanted to give her and Toby some time alone.

Or rather, a *night* alone.

Gosh. It was sure getting warm in here. Had someone left the oven on while they'd been gone?

She slipped off her denim jacket and placed it on the back of one of the barstools. All the while, Toby continued to lean against the counter, watching her.

Why was he looking at her like that—as if there was a big ole elephant in the room and he was determined to circle around it and come right on over to her?

His gaze was only making her warmer, and if he didn't stop, she was going to melt into a puddle.

Hoping the wine would help her cool down, she took a gulp.

"Come on." Toby reached for her hand, his fingers

threading through hers and sending a flurry of little zings rushing all the way to her core. Then he led her to the living room.

Thank goodness they were walking. Her knees had turned to rubber, and she wasn't sure they'd hold her up much longer if she didn't shake them out and get the blood flowing again.

She could use some cool air, too.

When they reached the living room, he led her to the leather sectional, where she took a seat. Then he sat next to her, even though there'd been plenty of room to spread out.

That was a good sign, yes?

Or was it a bad one?

She wasn't quite sure. But either way, the heat from the kitchen had followed them into the living room, and she took another swallow of wine.

"My family was definitely meddling," he said. "They could have kept the kids last night—or the weekend before. But they wanted to spend some time with you first, to see us together, before they made the offer."

"So they were vetting me?" she asked.

"That's about the size of it."

"Hmm." Angie stared at her chardonnay as if it was the most fascinating wine she'd ever tasted. Then she took another sip. If she continued to drink at this rate, she'd finish what was left in the bottle—and be on the floor soon after that.

"I guess I should be flattered that they approve," she said.

He placed his arm along the backrest, close enough

for her to feel his body heat along her bare shoulders. "How could they not approve of you? You're bright, funny, sweet and genuine." He paused, then fingered a strand of her hair. "And you're so damn beautiful."

Zing! Zing! Zing!

Now her glass was empty. Where had all that cold wine gone?

"Aw, hell," he said. "I'd wanted to spend some time with you away from the kids. But now that I've finally got you alone..."

When he trailed off, she studied his averted gaze, his pained expression.

What had he been about to say?

That he wasn't interested in her? That she was nice as far as babysitters went, but there was no point in her being here if the kids weren't?

"But *now* what?" she prodded.

Whoa. Where had the double-shot of courage come from? Did she really want to hear what he'd been about to say?

Her heart went haywire while she awaited his answer.

Toby removed his hand from her hair, from the back of the sofa and leaned forward.

Uh-oh. Bad sign?

Then he raked his fingers through his own hair. "It's just that now it all feels forced. And expected. It's like every member of my family knows exactly what we're doing right this second."

Angie chuckled, the sound coming out in a nervous rush. "But we aren't doing *anything*. And even if we do decide to do something, whatever happens or doesn't happen is our secret. Nobody has to know."

Toby's brows furrowed, and a look of annoyance crossed his face. "Of course no one will know. Do I look like the type to kiss and tell?"

"Toby," Angie said, her tone the same one she used when one of the kids was out of line. "I'm not sure if you're the type to *kiss,* let alone talk about it."

Their eyes met for a moment, and then a slow grin spread across his face. "Oh, I'm the type, all right." Then he lowered his mouth to hers.

Angie turned into his embrace, eager to kiss him with the passion that had been building over the past week until it threatened to consume her now.

And she wasn't disappointed.

His lips were soft, yet demanding. And his taste, while cool and refreshing, was hot and arousing.

Breaths mingled, tongues mated and the kiss deepened, intensifying until they were making out on the sofa like a couple of teenagers who had the run of the house for the very first time.

As Toby tugged at the strap of her dress, slipping it off her shoulder, he stroked her skin, igniting a fire and an ache deep in her core. Her breath caught, and her zing meter burst, like a flash of sparklers on a Fourth of July night.

As she leaned back and sucked a gulp of air into her lungs, Toby trailed kisses down her neck, along her shoulder. The warmth of his breath, the skill of his lips, caused her back to arch. And she was…his.

Toby had wanted to get Angie into his arms ever since the day he'd seen her wearing those cutoff shorts and walking around with bare, freshly painted toes.

And judging from the wispy little pants and whimpers coming from her sweet lips, she'd been wanting him just as badly.

At least, she certainly wanted him now.

The ride home from his parents' house had just about done him in. He'd never been so tense in his life. Not just because the physical attraction between the two of them had built to astronomical proportions, but because they'd soon have a big decision to make.

If they took things to a physical level tonight, there'd be no going back. And he needed to know that they were both on the same page.

As much as it pained him, he pulled his mouth from hers and ended the kiss.

"I…uh…" He cleared his throat. "We…"

Hell, he didn't even know what to say. Seconds ago, when they'd been kissing, he'd been in complete control of his tongue. But now he could barely form a simple word.

Angie merely looked at him with passion-glazed eyes.

Finally he managed to spell it out. "If you think you might have second thoughts about where this is heading, now would be a good time to say it."

"If you're afraid I'll change my mind or have any regrets," she said, "don't be."

That was the answer he'd wanted to hear. So he captured her mouth in another heart-soaring, star-spinning kiss.

Somehow, without removing her lips from his, she managed to lift a knee, and in one swift movement, she straddled his lap and faced him.

As they continued to kiss, he ran his hands up and down the slope of her back, along her hips, caressing her curves, memorizing them.

The lovely sundress, once so damn sexy, was now in the way. Should he unzip it and do away with it?

As she began to rock back and forth, a movement that was sure to drive them both over the brink, he realized they could very easily make love right on the sofa if he didn't change tactics. So again he drew his lips from hers.

"Let's take this into the bedroom," he whispered. But instead of releasing her, he held her tighter, leaned forward and slowly got to his feet.

She wrapped her legs around his waist, holding on as he carried her to his room. He kissed her along the way, hoping not to step on any of the LEGO pieces or dolls that sometimes littered his hallway.

He meant to hold himself in check, but he couldn't seem to help himself from tumbling with her onto the bed.

As they stretched out, hands reaching, lips seeking, she sobered and pulled away. "Toby, wait."

Oh, no. She wasn't going to stop him now, was she? If so, this was one hell of a time for her to prove everyone right and change her mind.

"I'm not on the pill," she said. "And I don't have any…you know…protection with me. I wasn't really anticipating this."

Did she think *he* was?

He couldn't help but smile, as he rolled to the side, taking her with him. "I hope you don't think I was expecting this to happen, either, or that I planned to bring you back here and ravish you." He'd hoped to, yes. But he hadn't planned to. "I do happen to have some condoms, though."

She smiled. "So we have that hurdle covered."

"And just so you know, I've been weighing the pros and cons of where moving forward might take us."

"Maybe you're overthinking things," she said.

Had that come from the woman who seemed to overthink every little decision she'd ever had to make?

"It's really quite simple," she added. "Either you want me or you don't."

He ran a knuckle along her cheek. "That part *is* simple. I want you more than I've ever wanted another woman in my life."

Dang. Had he really admitted that to her? And was it actually true?

Yeah, he was afraid that it was.

"But then what?" he asked.

"If you're sure about what you want, then everything else will fall into place."

How could he argue with *that* logic?

Toby chuckled and slowly shook his head. Who would have guessed that Angie would be the one helping him make a decision?

But, in truth, he feared he'd decided he wanted her—and wanted this—long before now. And judging by the way she'd sat up, unzipped her dress and began to lift it over her head, so had she.

Toby reached into his nightstand drawer and pulled out the box of condoms he'd picked up at the pharmacy when he'd been in Lubbock yesterday.

Okay, so maybe he *had* done a *little* planning. And

after waking up with her on the lawn this morning in a state of arousal, he'd realized that purchase had been a good investment, since he'd thought—or rather, he'd hoped—an occasion like this might arise.

When Angie had completely undressed, she stretched out on the bed, her perfect breasts, her lush curves a tempting sight he'd never forget.

She was beautiful and sweet and, at least for this moment in time, completely his.

She reached for his belt buckle, letting him know that she was ready for him to join her, and he quickly removed his clothing, too.

"You're so beautiful, Toby. So perfect."

Him? She thought *he* was perfect? She was the beautiful one. The perfect one. And as he lay down beside her again, he used his mouth and his body to tell her just that.

When he entered her, making them one, she arched up to meet his thrusts. And as she peaked, as her nails dug into his shoulders, she called out his name, sending him over the edge of control.

They came together in one amazing kaleidoscope of color, then held on to each other, riding the ebb and flow of the wonder-filled moment to the very end.

Finally, as their breathing slowed to normal, Angie opened her eyes and smiled. "That was amazing."

"To say the least." Toby pressed a kiss on her forehead. "And I have to admit, it was probably one of the best decisions I've ever made."

"Sometimes," Angie said, as she ran a leg along his, "the right decision can't be made with a list and a spreadsheet. Sometimes you just have to follow your heart."

He'd followed his—right into Angie's arms. Trouble was, he feared she'd captured his heart and that he might never get it back, even if she decided she was no longer interested in what little he had to offer her.

After walking naked through the quiet house to the kitchen for the carton of ice cream to share in bed, they made love several times before finally falling to sleep in the wee hours of morning.

The next day, as sunlight peered through the open shutters of his bedroom window, Toby awoke with Angie in his arms, the tousled sheet doing very little to cover her naked body. There was no telling when they'd have the house to themselves again, so he decided to wake her with a kiss.

But before he could nuzzle her neck, the bedside telephone rang, dashing his romantic thoughts.

Angie shot up in bed, pulling the sheet with her, as if the ringing phone had not only awoken her but reminded her their night in paradise had ended.

Toby snatched the telephone receiver after the third ring. "Hello?"

"Hey," Justin said, his voice so loud Angie could undoubtedly hear. "What are you doing? Grandma made us wait until eight o'clock to call you, but we've been up since six."

Bless his mom for putting a time restriction on the morning wake-up call, but would waiting another thirty minutes have hurt?

Angie began to inch off the bed, a pink tint brightening her cheeks. She had a history of running off on him when they'd been caught in an intimate position, and Toby wasn't going to let her slip away from him this time. Not after last night. So he made a grab for the sheet she was tugging along with her, and she tumbled back to the mattress, practically landing on him.

A muffled "oomph" sounded from her lips, as he locked his arm around her and pulled her close.

"What was that noise?" Justin asked.

Before Toby could make up a reasonable explanation, Brian yelled, "Don't forget to tell Toby about the baseball game!"

"Oh, yeah," Justin said. "The reason I called was because Uncle Galen has tickets for the Lubbock Hubbers game today and said he would give them to us. So can we go? And can we invite Angie? Galen has five tickets, and the game starts at one. So can we? Please?"

Toby wondered how his brother had magically come up with exactly five tickets to a minor-league baseball game the morning after his sisters had concocted a plan to get him and Angie alone together for the night. Somehow, it didn't seem like a coincidence.

He put his hand over the mouthpiece and whispered, "You want to go with us to the ball game?"

Angie's second of hesitation was all he needed to make the decision for her. After all, she'd been the one to tell him to follow his heart. So now, in the aftermath of their incredible night together, he was going to keep following his. And he was going to encourage her to do the same.

"Okay, kiddo," he told Justin. "I'll call Angie at *her house* and ask her if she wants to go with us. Then I'll go by *her house* to get her before I swing by Grandma and Grandpa's house to pick up you guys."

He wondered if he'd gotten his point across that Angie wasn't with him.

But Justin didn't seem to care either way. All he said was "Don't forget to bring our gloves. I'm going to catch the first foul ball!"

"I won't forget."

When they'd said goodbye and the call ended, Toby went back to his very first catch of the day—a beautiful brunette he hoped wouldn't run off on him anytime soon.

Chapter Ten

Toby, Angie and the kids had a blast at the baseball game on Sunday, although Kylie, who'd eaten too much cotton candy, popcorn and too many mustard dogs, had thrown up in Toby's truck on the way home. But both Angie and Toby had gotten used to unpleasant surprises like that—and to rolling with the unexpected punches of life with children.

In fact, it seemed only natural for them to settle into a routine, with Angie spending more time at Toby's than at her own place.

However, Toby was expecting a visit from child services and thought it best to downplay their relationship. Angie, of course, agreed with him, especially since she wasn't sure how involved she wanted to be with him and the kids anyway. So she didn't spend the night with him again. But that didn't mean they weren't able to steal a kiss or enjoy a tender-but-secret embrace whenever they could.

For the next week, they tried to be discreet about the change in their relationship, but their happiness was hard to contain, and the secret began to leak out.

On the following Monday, while the kids were in school, Toby took lunch to her while she was working at Redmond-Fortune Air. She'd stayed so late at the ranch the night before, making out with him on the front porch after the kids went to sleep, that by the time she'd driven home, she'd barely gotten any sleep. And she'd hurried to work without having breakfast.

When Toby had called that morning and learned her alarm hadn't gone off, he'd known she'd be hungry. So he came sauntering in to the flight school carrying a take-out bag from The Grill.

Angie's heart melted at the sight of him, and her stomach growled at the aroma of pastrami and fries.

"What's in the bag?" Sawyer asked his cousin.

"I figured you weren't making enough money to feed your employees," Toby said. "So I brought Angie's lunch."

"Well, it's nice to see you've stopped using the kids as a pretense to schmooze with my most valuable employee."

"I brought one for you, too." Toby tossed one of the wrapped sandwiches to his cousin. "Maybe this will keep your mouth too busy to talk."

Sawyer laughed as he snatched the flying pastrami. "You're going to be buying a lot of extra lunches if you think you can keep the whole town from talking."

Sawyer had been right about that. Angie had heard

a few murmurs while she'd worked at the Superette the next day, although no one came right out and said anything directly to her.

Of course, Mr. Murdock did when she was getting ready to leave for work on Wednesday morning.

"Why don't you take my car," he said, pulling out his set of keys. "Leave yours here, and I'll change the oil for you. When I'm finished, I'll come down to the market and we'll trade."

"That's really sweet of you, Mr. Murdock. Thank you."

"I thought it'd be a shame if you had car trouble and got stranded on the road." He burst into a grin, then winked at her. "No telling how many miles you've logged on that car by driving out to that ranch at all hours of the day and night."

She could have downplayed the whole thing, but she realized people weren't dumb, especially the ones who knew her so well. The fact was, she was falling for Toby. And that was going to be tough to hide.

But would their happiness last? She hoped so, but she feared they were living in their own little bubble and that reality would eventually intrude.

She just hadn't realized it would happen so soon.

That very afternoon, following her yoga class and Justin's swim lesson—which, thankfully, went off without a hitch!—she entered Toby's kitchen to find him gazing out the window, his hands braced on either side of the sink.

The cordless phone sat on the counter beside the forgotten chicken-and-rice casserole she'd left for him to pop into the oven.

This wasn't good.

Angie told Justin to do his homework and to tell the other kids they'd be eating in thirty minutes. Then she placed the casserole in the preheated oven herself.

When Toby still hadn't moved or otherwise acknowledged her presence, she walked up behind him, slid her arms around his waist and pressed her face to his back. "I'm here if you want to talk about whatever's bothering you."

Toby turned and gathered her into his arms. "I know. And I love having you here. It's just that…" He blew out a sigh. "I got a call from child services. I need to talk to you about it, but not until after the kids go to bed."

The sound of a heated argument rising up in the family room about whose turn it was to use the computer forced Angie to lower her arms and ease out of their embrace.

"Do you want referee duty?" she asked. "Or would you prefer to make the salad?"

"I'd rather putter around in the kitchen alone until I can manage a happy face."

Uh-oh. That phone call hadn't been a good one.

She placed a hand on his cheek, felt the light bristle of his beard, then drew his lips to hers for a quick kiss. "I've got your back, Toby. Don't worry about the kids. I'll keep them busy until dinner is on the table."

Then she walked to the family room, where an old laptop had been set up for the kids to use for homework assignments.

I love having you here, he'd said.

Did that mean he loved *her?* Or that he just loved having her help?

They'd spent so much time together since they'd made love, which would lead Angie to believe that Toby definitely wanted to be with her. Yet, they hadn't had the opportunity for a repeat performance of that magical night, so she was feeling more insecure than she would've liked.

But within minutes of entering the family room, her insecurities disappeared. She was too busy setting time limits on the computer, helping Kylie with her word search and explaining the different biospheres to Brian. Then, of course, she had to explain to Justin that while she didn't mind inviting Mr. Murdock to dinner so he could share more war stories, tonight wasn't a good night for them to have company.

It was funny, though. When she was with Brian, Justin and Kylie, all of the other pressing details in life seemed so inconsequential. These sweet kids needed her and were way more important than her shift at the Superette or her mother's wish to see her married off.

As she herded the children and their freshly washed hands toward the kitchen table, she noticed that Toby had managed to slap on a smile of sorts.

However, he'd also added strawberries to the Caesar salad. Yuck. He knew better than that.

She suspected the telephone call with child services must have really knocked him off-balance because, despite his forced smile and attempts at conversation over dinner, he asked Brian several times what game they'd played during PE today. And then he promised Kylie that she could invite her three best friends to The Cuttery for a beauty makeover day tomorrow, just like Madison Rodriguez had done when it was her birthday.

How was he going to pull that off? Angie had already told him she was having brunch with her mom in Lubbock tomorrow, so she couldn't help him.

She supposed he'd have to ask Jeanne Marie, Deke or one of his sisters to help out, which made Angie feel a little insignificant. But she scolded herself for the crazy thought and shook it off.

What was the matter with her? She deserved a break, didn't she? And besides, shouldn't his mother or his sisters help him out once in a while?

As soon as dinner was over, she handled the bedtime duties alone, while Toby stayed in the kitchen to clean up.

When she finally returned, she stood in the doorway and watched him go through the motions, his mind still clearly on anything but what he was doing, as he wiped the casserole dish over and over again.

"I think that's as dry as it's going to get," she said. "Just leave everything and come with me."

When she reached out her hand to him, he laid the baking dish and towel on the counter. Then he let her lead him outside to the porch, where they took seats on the cushioned patio bench.

While she listened to the ranch sounds at night—cattle lowing, crickets chirping—she waited for him to share what had been weighing on his mind.

Finally, he said, "Ms. Fisk, the kids' case worker, called. Their aunt Barbara isn't ready to leave rehab, but she's been pushing hard to have the children shipped out of state to live with her cousin, a guy who's out on parole and who's never even met them."

The news slammed into Angie like a line drive to

the chest, and her stomach twisted. Toby stood to lose the kids? What would that do to them?

What would it do to *him?*

Oh, God. What would it do to her? She'd grown to love them, to care for them. To want the best for them....

"Did the case worker think that could happen?" she asked. "I mean, they're doing so well."

"She said it was unlikely, but that it could happen. I've read about cases that went badly. And bottom line? I'm just their foster dad. I'm not their blood kin, so I don't have much legal standing."

Angie took his hand in hers, letting him know that she was here for him, that she was worried and hurting, too.

"Did you tell the case worker your concerns?" she asked. "Did you mention how well they're doing, and that uprooting them wouldn't be good for them?"

"I laid out every argument I could think of. And she agreed with me, but her hands are somewhat tied. Apparently, that long-lost cousin in California wants to petition for adoption. And Ms. Fisk thinks the court would rather see the kids in a permanent home than in foster care."

Angie's stomach tossed and turned as she tried to make sense of it all.

"Why would a guy in California suddenly want to adopt three kids he's never even met?" she asked. "That seems like a mighty big step for someone to take."

"I agree. And I hope the judge will consider that question, too. That trust fund could very well be motivating both Barbara and her cousin to seek custody, especially since she knew about my mom's long-lost brother and her connection to the Fortunes. She'd also heard about the incident at the YMCA."

Angie stiffened, and her fingers, still held in the warmth of Toby's hands, grew cold. "You mean she heard about the day I flipped out and the paramedics were called?"

If she'd somehow caused a black mark upon Toby's case, she'd never forgive herself.

"I don't think the incident at the Y had anything to do with Barbara's call to child services and the petition for adoption. But someone in town has been feeding her rumors. And knowing her, the one rumor that she may have heard, the one that may have really caused a stir in her, was the one about the kids' trust fund."

"But you're the trustee. Don't you control the money?"

"That's the problem. I'm the trustee, but the kids' legal guardian is in charge of the monthly payments they receive—and they're substantial. Those classes and all the extras I've been providing them aren't free. Barbara may not know all of the details, but I'm certain she's after whatever money is available to her."

"That's too bad." Angie thought about how her own mother seemed more interested in earning a dollar than in being a stay-at-home mom.

"I'd never planned on using that money for myself," Toby said. "That's why I set it up for their guardian to have control of the monthly income. I didn't mind who had access to it, as long as they were looking out for the kids' best interests. But I hadn't realized Barbara's problems and issues went deeper than her alcohol dependency."

"And now there's her cousin to contend with," Angie added. "Who knows what kind of problems he has. Or what kind of parent or guardian he'd be."

"I've done some online research," Toby said. "And I can't believe any judge in their right mind would think that guy should have custody of them. The last thing they need right now is to move to a home with a man they don't know, a man who's on parole and can't even work at a hospital anymore because of whatever crime he was convicted of. And while I realize he may have paid his debt to society, those poor kids have had enough instability and unhappiness in their lives."

"So what are w...?" Angie cleared her throat, then coughed before she fully pronounced "we." The kids and Toby had become a big part of her life recently, but she wasn't entirely sure where she fit into their lives—at least, in the long run.

She cleared her throat again, then continued with the corrected version of her question. "So what do you plan to do?"

"If it comes to fighting for custody, Ms. Fisk thinks I can win, but she isn't sure. And a 'maybe' isn't good enough for me. It's not a risk I'm willing to take. So I'm giving the court another option. I'm going to talk to an attorney in Lubbock who specializes in family law. And then I'm going to petition for adoption myself. I'll show that I'm much better suited to raise those kids than some ex-con way out in California or a greedy aunt who can't seem to follow the rules in rehab."

While glad that Toby had a game plan and that he

felt more hopeful now than when she'd first arrived, Angie's shoulders slumped and she couldn't stanch the wave of disappointment that swept through her.

She might not have known where she fit into Toby's life, but apparently he did.

He'd just spelled out exactly what he planned to do, saying, "I."

And never once had he used the word *we*.

If there was one thing Angie hated, it was being late when meeting her mother. But she'd tossed and turned all night, thinking long and hard about Toby's dilemma, as well as her own. And she hadn't fallen asleep until almost dawn.

Needless to say, she'd overslept. So she quickly showered, dressed and pulled her hair into a ponytail. She figured she'd apply a quick coat of lipstick when she stopped at the first traffic light in Lubbock.

She'd no more than tossed her purse onto the passenger seat of her car when Mr. Murdock stepped out on his back porch, his cup of coffee steaming in his hands. He was wearing a bright yellow shirt that read Not As Mean, Not As Lean, But Still A Marine.

"Good morning, Mr. Murdock." She gave him a little wave as she slipped behind the wheel and strapped on her seat belt.

"Slow down, Girly." Mr. Murdock took his time as he lumbered down the steps, obviously intent on talking to her.

She'd told him yesterday that she was meeting her mom for brunch this morning. Didn't he realize that if she was even ten minutes late she was in for a lecture even the best mimosa couldn't dull?

When he finally made his way beside her idling car, he asked, "You tell your mama you're living here yet?"

"No, but I promise to do it today." And she would, even if it meant her mother would again offer to put a down payment on a condo in Lubbock for her.

Angie could hear it now. *There's no way I'll tolerate my only child living in some old-timer's run-down granny flat in Horseback Hollow.* In fact, her mom would be scrolling through the online MLS pages before the eggs Benedict arrived.

"Well, that's the thing, Girly. I don't see any need for you to mention that to old Doris."

Old Doris? Angie couldn't help but chuckle. If her mom could hear the eightysomething-year-old veteran refer to her as *old,* she'd be searching the internet for deals on Botox injections.

"Why the change of heart?" Angie asked her landlord. Just last month, Mr. Murdock had insisted that she stand up to her mother and become her own person.

Angie had tried to explain to the competitive man that she was passive-aggressive by nature. And that it was easier to nod her head and then do whatever she wanted to do anyway. So she was surprised that the old marine didn't want her to do battle at brunch today.

"Last night, while I was down at the VFW, Pete told me that the Jones boy was adopting those three kids."

"You shouldn't listen to gossip, Mr. Murdock. Especially from Pete. Wasn't he the one who told you that Ethel Gardiner was as bald as the cue balls in the Two Moon Saloon?"

"Yep. He did."

"And then you pulled on her hair, thinking it was a wig, and she smacked you silly."

"That slap won me five bucks." Mr. Murdock stood tall and puffed out his chest. "Her hair might have been dyed the shade of Pepto-Bismol, but I knew it wasn't no dang wig."

Angie wanted to laugh, but with her foot on the clutch, ready for her to slip the car into Reverse and back out, she was afraid a fit of giggles would cause her to stall the engine.

Besides, she didn't have time to waste getting off on tangents, so she steered the topic back to the original.

"What does Toby adopting those kids have to do with me telling my mother that I rent the granny flat from you?" she asked.

"Well, the way I figure it, since you spend about all your time at his ranch helping him with those young'uns, he'll convince you to move in with him before Old Doris ever finds out you ever lived here."

Thankfully, Mr. Murdock had the grace to turn and walk back to his house so Angie wasn't forced to come up with any sort of reply or denial. Instead, she backed out of the driveway and drove to Lubbock, hoping she didn't get a speeding ticket while she was at it.

As usual, Mr. Murdock had a funny take on things. But there was no way Toby would ask her to move in with him, especially now that he was seeking permanent custody of the kids. In fact, it looked as though their relationship—whatever there was of it—was going to have to take an even bigger backseat to the kids.

But she understood why. And she'd go with the flow. She'd have to deal with her disappointment later.

When she finally arrived at the quaint cottage-style bistro in Lubbock, Angie saw her mother's sedan parked in front. She found an empty space a few shops down the street, yet didn't immediately climb out of the car.

Dealing with Doris Edwards was nothing new. She'd been ignoring her instructions and advice for years. So why did she feel like backing out of the parking space and driving in the opposite direction—as far as she could from Lubbock *and* from Horseback Hollow?

The only thing stopping her from doing so now was a promise she'd made Toby. She'd told him she would pick up the children at the ball field and take them to dinner at The Grill so he could meet with some of his family this afternoon and talk about the adoption plans.

So she couldn't flake on him—or the kids, who would be looking forward to seeing her.

Steeling herself with a deep breath, Angie entered the restaurant and spotted her mom, joining her at a small table in back.

"You finally made it," Doris said. "I thought for sure that old wreck you drive around had broken down somewhere on the highway."

And there was the first insult of the day. But, hey, brunch wouldn't last more than an hour.

"I'm sorry I'm late," Angie said. "How are you, Mom?"

"I've never been better. And you'd know that if you came to see me more."

Insult number two.

"I wish I could come to town more often, but I've been busy lately."

"So I've heard. I talked to Ethel Gardiner on Monday. And she said that you've been spending a lot of time with Toby Fortune Jones and those kids he has running around his house."

Angie crossed her arms, suddenly not the least bit sorry about Mr. Murdock's bet with Pete. Ethel Gardiner deserved to have her pink locks tugged after spreading gossip.

"For the record," Angie said, "Toby's an amazing guy. Not many men would give up so much to take care of three children who weren't their own."

"That's just it," Doris argued. "Those kids *aren't* his own. It's unnatural. I mean, maybe if he used some of his family money and spent more time making something out of that ranch of his and less time playing daddy, he could be the right man for you."

Angie wanted to tell her mother that Toby didn't have any family money, but it really wasn't any of her business. So instead she signaled the waitress and ordered a much-needed cappuccino.

She normally would've spent twenty minutes reading every detailed item on the menu and trying to decide what to order. But since she wanted to get out of this restaurant as quickly as possible, she pointed to the frittata special—which was the first thing listed on the menu.

Her mother ordered plain yogurt, and Angie wondered why the woman would even bother coming out to eat if that was all she was going to have.

"You know," Angie said, "if you drove out to the

ranch and spent some time with Toby and the kids, you'd see things differently."

Had Angie actually suggested that? What would Toby say? He might claim to be easygoing, but having her mom around would probably be the kiss of death for their relationship—or whatever it was they had.

"Your defensive response is telling," Doris said.

"Telling?" How could it tell Doris anything when Angie didn't know what she was feeling herself?

"It sounds like you're trying to sell me on a ready-made family. You're not, are you? I mean, look at your history. You've avoided any kind of commitment in the past—and not just when it comes to relationships."

Angie couldn't argue with that.

"Besides," Doris said, "if you can't commit one hundred percent to those kids, then you shouldn't waste your time with their foster dad. It wouldn't be fair, especially if those children have lost as many people as everyone says they have."

Angie didn't normally see eye to eye with her mom, but those last words resonated loud and clear.

She didn't want to give anyone false hope, especially those kids.

"Plus, dear, you were meant to be so much more than just a mother."

Was she? She'd always thought that she was destined for more. After all, Doris had been telling her that for years. But she could still hear Jeanne Marie's words, still feel the way they'd warmed her heart.

...you're more than qualified to do my job.

Angie had been good at it, too. And she liked the kids. She'd even turned down some afternoon shifts at the Superette so that she could help Toby more with the carpooling.

But the Mama Angie gig had only been going on for a couple of weeks. Could she continue doing it for the next ten or fifteen years?

And did she even want to?

When the waitress brought their breakfast, Angie stared at the frittata placed in front of her. Why hadn't she ordered the stuffed French toast instead?

For some reason she found herself retreating back to her usual on-the-fence mode.

Was she up to the job of raising children?

Talk about long-term commitments.

What if the kids bonded with her, and then she skipped out on them?

Or maybe even worse, what if she stuck it out, like her mother had done when Angie had been growing up, and the decision to stay in an unhappy situation only made her life, as well as those of everyone around her, miserable?

No, in this case, her mother had called it right. Angie had never been able to commit to anything up until now. And those children needed stability in their lives more than anything.

Of course, Toby had never given her any reason to believe he envisioned her as a part of his long-term family plan. And the fact that he hadn't lanced something soft and fragile inside.

In what ways had Toby found her lacking?

Certainly not as a lover—or as a teammate, baby-sitter or friend.

But did he question her ability to make a lasting commitment to him and the kids? If so, she couldn't blame him for that. Because as much as she'd come to care for that precious little family, she had those same worries herself.

"I know you've never taken my advice in the past," Doris said. "And it's no secret that you pretend to listen— and that you think I'm pushy."

For some reason, Angie couldn't let that one go without commenting. "Listen, Mom. I love you. And I appreciate the fact that you believe you have my best interests at heart. But this is my life, not yours. You may have made some bad choices in the past, but they were yours to make—and yours to live with. Right or wrong, I intend to do the same thing. If you want to offer a bit of advice, that's fine. But then drop it. Please."

Doris sat there for a moment, then cleared her throat. "I'm sorry, Angie. Believe it or not, I really don't mean to interfere. I'll try to be more respectful of you in the future. And I'll be supportive of whatever you decide to do—even if it means going out to the ranch for a visit."

"Thank you. And for the record, I truly care for Toby and those kids. I actually love them. But deciding what to do about that isn't a simple decision for me to make. And no matter what I choose to do, I'll do it with my eyes and my heart wide open, knowing that if I make the wrong decision, if I end up hurt or disappointed in the long run, then so be it."

Doris placed her napkin in her lap, signaling it was time to eat and to put unpleasant matters behind them. "Since you understand the importance and are giving it a great deal of thought, I can respect that. So I'll drop the subject. I just hope that you will be able to make that decision quickly."

Her mother had never been more right.

Angie was facing the most critical decision she'd ever had to make—one that could prove to be life-changing and heartbreaking. And one she couldn't afford to stew about.

But instead of only having to consider the effects of her choice on her own life, her own heart, she had to consider what it would do to three children and to Toby, as well.

That being said, she really had to follow her heart, even if it was breaking. And that meant there was only one possible choice.

She had to step back and let them go.

And the sooner she told Toby the better.

Chapter Eleven

Toby's meeting with his family had gone even better than he'd hoped. When he'd laid out his dilemma and his plan, they'd all agreed to support him in a full-scale custody battle—if it should come to that—and in his attempt to adopt Brian, Justin and Kylie.

The only concern that had come up was the cost of legal fees, which could get expensive, but Toby had already talked at length to Jake Gleason, the attorney who'd drawn up the trust. So he was able to explain to his family that he, as the trustee, was allowed to tap into the principal at his discretion for any unexpected needs the kids might have. He'd also been able to assure them that securing a permanent home qualified as such a need.

So now Toby was on his way to The Grill. He intended to have a heart-to-heart talk with Angie while the kids played in the arcade. He wasn't looking forward to it, but he had to do it.

Over the past twenty-four hours, he'd been preoccupied with thoughts of the custody hearing and the adoption, but not so much that he hadn't sensed a very subtle difference in Angie. And he'd picked up on it again in the distant tone in her voice when they'd talked on the phone earlier.

He sensed that she was withdrawing from him, just as he'd suspected she would. And he really couldn't blame her. His life had taken a sudden and complicated turn, one their budding relationship wasn't prepared to handle.

Asking her to babysit or to fix Kylie's hair was one thing, but assuming that she'd want to take on even more responsibility or to actually become a permanent part of his and the children's lives was something completely different.

For one thing, she was still trying to find herself and her way in the world. How could he ask her to take on a burden she clearly wasn't ready for? Besides, she might want to have her own kids someday, and a large family was... Well, it was probably more than a woman who'd grown up as an only child would ever consider.

On top of that, they hadn't been dating very long.

Dating? He couldn't even call it that. One amazing night of lovemaking, no matter how amazing it might have been, wasn't the kind of romantic relationship Angie deserved. Not when the bulk of their time together was spent dealing with sick kids, spilled milk and squabbles over whose turn it was to use the laptop or the TV remote.

Heck, Toby had never even taken her out on a real

date, had never provided her with candlelight and roses. There'd been no nights on the town, no holding hands in the movie theater or dancing until dawn.

So allowing things to continue in the way they'd been going wasn't fair to her.

Knowing Angie, she was probably trying to figure out how to end things between them without hurting or disappointing the kids. So Toby would just have to make things easier on her. And, in the long run, he'd make things easier on all of them.

While the kids played in the arcade, oblivious to the custody battle that loomed, Toby would thank Angie for all she'd done for him. Then he'd let her off the hook, making the decision for her. If she wanted to stick around for dinner, they'd have one last meal together, then she'd go her way, and he and the kids would go theirs.

It sounded easy enough. He just hoped his voice didn't crack and reveal the ache in his heart that set in whenever he thought about her walking out of his life for good.

When Toby arrived at The Grill and spotted Angie's Toyota in the parking lot, his heart skipped a beat, and his breathing stalled. She'd probably been here awhile, since he was ten minutes later than he'd told her he'd be.

Yet he continued to sit in his truck, his hands on the steering wheel, wishing there was another way around what he had to do, but knowing there wasn't. Finally, he mustered his courage and opened the driver's door to let himself out. Then he headed for the front entrance.

When he stepped inside The Grill, he was met by Bonnie Sue Hillman, a petite blonde waitress.

"Angie is in the big booth in back," Bonnie Sue

said, "and the kids are in the arcade, going through quarters like crazy."

"Thanks. Have they ordered yet?"

Bonnie Sue laughed. "Angie's only been here for about fifteen minutes, and it takes her a lot longer than that just to study the menu."

As Toby made his way to the booth where Angie sat, another waitress stopped at her table. She said something to Angie and nodded. Then she whipped out her pad and pencil.

Toby approached, just as Angie said, "Brian will have the cheeseburger—well-done, no onions, lettuce or pickles. But he'd like extra tomatoes. And can you bring a side of mustard for his fries?"

As the waitress made note of it, Angie added, "Justin would like the corn dog, but instead of fries, he'll have onion rings with a side of ranch dressing. Kylie wants the grilled cheese with American—not cheddar. And can you please ask the cook to cut it into four triangles? If not, I can do that. She'd also like a bowl of strawberries—if you have them. When Toby gets here, he'll want the double bacon cheeseburger, fried pickles and a peanut-butter milk shake. He can share the onion rings with Justin. And I'll have the patty melt on rye and an iced tea with lemon."

Bonnie Sue, who'd followed Toby to the booth with a handful of menus, blew out a little whistle. "That's gotta be some kind of record. You'd think Angie's been ordering food for you guys for years."

It sure seemed that way. She'd picked up on a lot of their habits in a few short weeks. But then again, they didn't call her Little Miss Google for nothing.

Still, it tugged at his heart that the woman who'd

fallen into his life seemed to have somehow picked *him* up after that fall.

Angie looked up and spotted Toby. "Oh, you're here. I'm sorry. I probably shouldn't have ordered for you."

"No, that's fine. I'm glad you did." He slid into the booth and placed his hat on the seat beside him.

"How did it go?" she asked.

"Great. My family is behind me one hundred percent."

"I knew they would be."

Toby studied his hands, which rested on the table.

"Is something wrong?" she asked. "Do you want to talk about it before the kids come back?"

All right. This was the opening he needed. Now all he had to do was form the words.

He took a deep, fortifying breath. "Things will probably get pretty intense over the next few weeks and months."

"I know."

He paused a beat, then pressed on. "I realize you didn't sign on for all of this. And I want you to know that I understand. At this point, you can bow out gracefully before anyone gets hurt."

There. He'd said it.

Now all he had to do was wait and see what she would do with the ball he'd lobbed into her court.

Angie hadn't been sure how to tell Toby that she'd decided to back off, that she needed some space and time to herself. Then he'd broached the subject himself.

Not only that, he'd practically spelled it all out for

her, making it easy. But now that he'd given her a free pass…

Well…was taking a step back what she really wanted?

In truth, she hadn't been ready to walk away yet. But because she was afraid she'd change her mind down the road, which would devastate the kids, she'd thought it would be best to do it now.

And apparently, Toby felt the same way.

Yet now that he was cutting her loose, she felt an incredible sense of loss and fear that she stood to lose everything she'd ever wanted or needed if she didn't speak up…

Speak up and say what? That she didn't want to completely bow out?

That, in fact, she might not want to bow out at all?

"You're not saying anything," Toby said. "What are you thinking?"

"That I'd planned to take a step back and give you guys time to yourselves, but not because of the problems you're facing."

"Then why?"

"It's complicated."

Toby leaned forward. "I'm going to fight to keep Brian, Justin and Kylie. So things aren't temporary anymore. I'm making a commitment to them—one I hope the courts will make permanent. And as much as the kids—and I—would like you to be a part of that, I wouldn't even think of asking you to stick around for the long haul. It would be asking too much, and it wouldn't be fair."

Good. That was what she'd wanted to explain to him.

But the way he'd said it, the way he'd implied that it was just him and the kids from here on out—a family through thick and thin—made her feel as though she was the odd man out. And she wasn't so sure she wanted to be on the outside looking in.

She lifted her eyes, caught his gaze zeroing in on hers. Glossy. Intense.

His words told her he was letting her go and that he thought it was for the best.

Okay, she got that. But his pained expression said something entirely different to her heart.

Or did she just want to read something into all the emotions she saw brewing in his eyes?

"What's the matter?" he asked. "I thought you'd be relieved to have an opportunity to ease out of this relationship."

She should be. She'd come here intending to end things between them after dinner, then return to her own little corner of the world—the part-time job at the Superette, the twenty hours a week at Redmond-Fortune Air, the small little granny flat behind Mr. Murdock's house that she called home....

But was that cute little granny flat where she really called home?

Not when she woke up each morning in her own bed, thinking about Toby, seeing his face, hearing his voice. And whenever she thought about going home, it was always to the Double H, where Toby, the kids and one big mess or another always awaited her.

Come to think of it, no matter where she was— brunch with her mom, the Superette or at the airfield, her thoughts revolved around that precious, ragtag family. Even in her spare time, she planned meals she thought they'd like to eat and worked out better ways to balance their busy after-school schedules.

Just this morning, when she'd fixed her hair before her shift at the store, she'd wondered if Kylie was wearing the new headband Toby had bought her to use on days Angie wasn't there to braid her hair. She'd also wanted to tell Justin to practice his spelling words one more time and to remind Brian not to forget his backpack.

She'd gone so far as to pick up the phone to call Toby and offer her suggestions, but she'd been afraid that she was getting way too involved, especially if she was going to distance herself.

But as she looked at Toby now, as she saw his anguished expression, as she realized how difficult this was for him…

It was breaking his heart, and for that reason, it was breaking hers, too.

He was all on his own and facing a custody battle, one he might lose. But that wasn't the only thing hurting him.

Call it a zany sixth sense, but Angie could see it as plain as the summer sun at high noon. He was struggling with letting her go.

And she was struggling, too—right along with him.

All she wanted to do was to make his pain go away, to settle his fear, to strengthen his resolve.

And for some crazy reason, she didn't even question the fact that she might be wrong in her assumption about what he was feeling for her.

The solution to the problem, to *their* problem, had

never seemed so clear or so simple. All she had to do was to follow her heart.

Without a thought to the repercussions, the words rolled out of her mouth as loud and clear as the church bells on Sunday morning. "Toby, I think we should get married."

He blinked, and his lips parted. "What did you say?"

"Those kids need a loving, two-parent home. And you and I are the ones who can provide it for them. I want us to be a family. And if we go before the court together, I don't think the judge will turn us down."

"You mean you'd marry me because of the kids?"

Angie laughed. "I want to marry you because I love you. And because I love the kids, I want us to be a family."

Toby reached across the table and took her hand in his. "You love me?"

"Yes." How could she not? He was everything a woman could ever want in a man—loving, loyal, a family man... And he was the most handsome man in all of Texas—if not the whole world.

"Are you sure about that?" he asked. "You're not going to change your mind?"

"I've always known that when the perfect choice came along, I'd know it and that I'd jump on it. And that's what I'm doing. When I'm with you and the kids, I don't feel the least bit insecure or indecisive or flighty. I feel in control, at home, and..." She paused, realizing that was one word she needed to hear Toby say himself.

"And what?" Toby asked. "I hope you feel loved,

because I'm crazy about you." He slid around to her side of the booth and slipped his arm around her. "And I'm going to spend the rest of my life proving to you just how much."

Angie leaned into him. "I must admit, I felt loved and cherished on Saturday night."

He brushed a kiss on her cheek. "Honey, if we weren't out in public, I'd make you feel loved and cherished right now."

She laughed. "Something tells me our private times together, as nice as they'll be, aren't going to be easy to find. But I'll put some thought into it and figure out something."

"One thing I can do is to call Stacey and ask if she knows any reliable sitters we can hire on a regular basis. We're going to set aside one day a week as date night. I'd also like to plan some romantic weekend getaways."

Angie's heart swelled until she thought it might burst wide open. "I'm going to like being married to you, Toby."

"I'm glad, because the more I think about it, the more I like the idea of being married to you."

"It's too bad the junior college doesn't offer a crash course in motherhood," she said. "There's a lot I need to learn. Maybe I should ask your mom to tutor me."

"You're doing just fine. You've picked up plenty already."

"I'm not sure about that."

"Oh, no? You know which girls in Brian's class think he's cute and how many breaths Justin takes when he swims the length of the YMCA pool. It took you all

of fifteen seconds to figure out how to juggle the timing of Kylie's gymnastics lesson and still get the boys
to baseball practice on time. You're a natural—and a
fast learner. You've also come to know me pretty well."

She smiled and bumped his shoulder with hers. "Oh,
yeah?"

"You can read my mood like nobody's business.
You knew that I really wanted to beg you to stay with
me and the kids, even though I was trying to do the
gentlemanly thing and give you a way out. And, maybe
even more importantly, you know how to set my blood
on fire."

She leaned in and gave him a long, heated kiss that
could have set The Grill on fire if he hadn't drawn
back.

Toby ran his finger along her lips. "But you need
to know something. No matter what happens with the
kids, even if I lose them, I still want you for my wife."

"We won't lose them," Angie said. "I've set my
heart on it."

For the first time since Ms. Fisk had returned his
call and told him Barbara had moved forward with her
plan, Toby began to relax. With Angie in his corner,
how could he lose?

Before either of them could comment further, the
kids dashed back to the table announcing their high
scores and asking for more quarters.

"What do you think?" Angie asked Toby. "Should
we tell them?"

Justin pressed in front of his brother and sister. "Tell
us what?"

"Angie and I are getting married," Toby said.

"No kidding?" Brian asked. "Sweet."

"Woo-hoo!" Justin shouted, drawing the other diners' attention to their table.

Kylie clapped her hands and gave a little jump. "Can I be in the wedding?"

"Absolutely," Angie said. "You're all going to be in the wedding. We wouldn't have it any other way."

"So when is it?" Brian asked.

"We'll have to wait at least three days," Angie said. "That's Texas law."

Toby chuckled. "I suppose you picked that trivial piece of info up at one of your temp jobs?"

"As a matter of fact, I spent a few weeks working at a bridal shop in Vicker's Corners."

Miss Google strikes again.

"So how soon can I call you my wife?" Toby asked.

Angie tossed him a flirtatious grin. "How does next Saturday sound?"

"That long, huh?" He slipped his arm around her again and drew her close. "Saturday is fine with me. But don't you think you'll need more time to plan a wedding?"

"Yes, but I'd like to keep things simple. You may not believe this, but I can practically see it all unfolding in my mind."

"You're right. That *is* hard to believe, but I don't doubt it." He leaned over and kissed her again.

"Hey," Justin said. "Before you guys start smooching again, can you look and see if you have any more quarters?"

Toby laughed, then dug into his pocket and pulled out several. "Take these."

When the kids dashed off, Toby turned his attention back to Angie. "So you're not going to drag your feet and make me wait while you stew over bridal magazines and reception venues?"

"No, I won't have to. When I make up my mind, and my heart's in it, I don't drag my feet. I can tell you right now that I'd like to be married in your parents' backyard. And that I want Stacey and Delaney to be my bridesmaids. I've never had sisters, so I'm looking forward to having two right off the bat."

"I'm sure they'll be happy about that."

"Good. Then since we're both on the same page, I don't see a problem."

"Neither do I."

Well, other than having to wait until next Saturday to make love with her again. But he was going to work very hard at getting her alone before that.

"I don't suppose you've thought about a guest list," he said. "Saturday won't give us time to send out invitations."

"We'll keep it simple—mostly family, if that's okay. But with it being so soon, we'll have to call and invite people."

"I'd like my brother Chris to be there, but that's going to be tricky."

"Because of the hard feelings within the family?" she asked.

"Yes. Chris has always been both a black sheep and a lone wolf. I've understood that and known when to give him his space. After things blew sky-high, I knew he needed to do some airing out. So I gave him the time he needed, figuring that he'd contact me when he was ready to talk and move back into the fold."

"So will you call him?" Angie asked. "You could use the wedding as an excuse."

"It might be best to extend the invitation through Sawyer. That way I'm respecting his decision to distance himself from Horseback Hollow and from the rest of the family. Yet it's also a way to let him know that I still love him and want a relationship with him. I have a feeling he'll reach out to me at that point, even if he doesn't come."

"Do you think he'll stay away?"

"I hope not, but Chris has always had to do things his way. In the meantime, my dad will need to do some bending, too. So if I want to see any fences getting mended, I'd better start working on him."

"If anyone can talk some sense into your dad, I'll bet you can." Angie gave him a kiss. "Now let's get busy. I have a lot of work to do—and nine days doesn't give me much time."

She was right. But when it came to waiting for Angie to move into the ranch and become his wife in every sense of the word, nine days seemed way too long.

Toby had an appointment to meet with his new attorney in Lubbock on Monday at eleven o'clock. So while he was in the city, he decided to stop by the real-estate office where Doris Edwards worked.

Needless to say, she was surprised to see him.

"Do you have a couple of minutes?" he asked.

"Certainly." She led him down the hall to a small break room. "Would you like a cup of coffee?"

"No, thanks. I can't stay long, but I have a question for you."

"What's that?"

"I'd like to ask for Angie's hand in marriage."

Doris sat up a little straighter. "That's a bit of a surprise—and a little old-fashioned. What if I were to tell you no?"

"We'd get married anyway. I just thought I'd pay you the respect you deserve—and to ask that you do the same for us."

"I see." Doris sat back in her seat. "So have you proposed to Angie yet?"

"Actually, it was her idea. She's the one who first popped the question." A slow smile tugged at his lips. "She's going to call you when she gets off work today and talk to you about it."

"Have you set a date?"

"Saturday."

"So soon?" Doris stiffened. "Are you eloping?"

"We're going to get married at my parents' ranch. We're only inviting family and a few close friends, although I suspect it won't be as small as it sounds."

Doris perked up. "Will the Fortunes from Red Rock be attending?"

"They'll be invited, as well as those from Atlanta and the United Kingdom. But with it being such short notice, I'm not sure who'll be able to make it."

"In that case, don't you think it would be better to wait at least a month? That way, you'll have more time to plan a nicer event. I might even be able to get the *Lubbock Avalanche-Journal* to run a spread in the society pages."

"We don't want to wait."

"Oh, dear. She's not pregnant, is she?"

Toby groaned inwardly. Doris Edwards was certainly going to be a trial, but Angie was worth it.

"No, she's not pregnant. But don't worry—even though we only have a few days to plan, the wedding is going to be nice. My entire family is pitching in, and we'd like you to be as involved as you want to be."

"Of course I'd like to be included." Doris began to click her manicured nails on the table—plotting and planning, no doubt. "I'll also need to purchase a new dress to wear." She bit down on her bottom lip, then looked at him with hope-filled eyes. "Do you think your aunt Josephine May Fortune Chesterfield will come all the way from England? Goodness, I'll bet the cost of *that* flight will be incredibly expensive."

Toby reached out and placed his hand over his future mother-in-law's, stopping her from fidgeting. "Listen, Doris. There are a few things we need to get straight. I may be a Fortune by blood, and while my ranch is doing just fine and I'm financially stable, I'm not wealthy by any means. And I probably never will be. But I love your daughter with all my heart. We may never have the money that some of my family members have, but in everything that matters, Angie and I are rich beyond measure."

Doris smiled. "I understand. But you can't help me for being a little starstruck. I mean, the Chesterfields are almost royals in the U.K."

Toby didn't know about that, but at least Doris seemed to support his and Angie's union.

"Do you think it would be all right if I stopped by to see Jeanne Marie and Deke after I get off work today?" Doris asked. "I'd love to offer my services—and to do whatever I can to offset the cost of the wedding. I'm not rich, either, but I did set aside some cash for my baby girl's big day."

Toby didn't dare tell her that Sawyer had already offered to do the same thing. Or that Sawyer's dad, James Marshall Fortune, had agreed to pay for their honeymoon in San Antonio, the flight courtesy of Redmond-Fortune Air.

Doris might accept that Toby wasn't as rich as some of the other Fortunes, but she'd certainly place a boatload of value on his family connections.

"I'm sure my parents would be glad to have you stop by this evening," Toby said, as he stood, preparing to leave.

His talk with Doris had gone better than he'd hoped. She seemed to be looking forward to the wedding.

He just hoped she wouldn't place any unnecessary stress on Angie, especially on their special day.

Angie, Stacey and Delaney were going to shop for dresses in Vicker's Corners on Tuesday afternoon. Angie's mom, who'd been both supportive and excited about the upcoming ceremony, was coming along, too.

Who would have guessed that Doris would actually be looking forward to her role as mother of the bride?

Angie had a feeling her excitement might have something to do with knowing that there would be quite a few Fortunes present and that one of Toby's handsome brothers would be walking her down the aisle. But either way, it would make the day go by a whole lot smoother.

Her mom was also planning to purchase the bridal gown, which was nice. And as long as Stacey and Delaney were there to prevent her from going tulle-crazy, it should work out okay.

Before driving to the bridal shop to meet everyone, Angie stopped at Mr. Murdock's house to tell him about the upcoming wedding and to let him know that she'd be moving out in less than a week.

"So that Fortune Jones boy has finally talked some sense into you, did he?"

Angie smiled at the old man she'd grown so fond of in the past couple of months. "Yes, he certainly did."

Mr. Murdock turned and headed to the lamp table, where he kept his telephone.

"What are you doing?" she asked, a little disappointed that he'd walked off while she was still sharing the news of the biggest and best decision she'd ever made in her life.

"I need to call Pete," he said.

"Your VFW buddy? Why?"

"Because I told him you'd be tying the knot by the end of the month. But he thought those young'uns would scare you off. So now Pete owes me five bucks and two of his lucky bingo cards."

"Oh, no. Please tell me you didn't make a bet on my love life."

"Girly," Mr. Murdock said with a big ole grin, "I'd bet on you any day of the week."

Coming from him, that was a huge compliment.

He picked up a glass of amber-colored liquid from the table. "Can I get you some Scotch?"

"No, thanks. And you shouldn't be drinking it, either. You really need to cut back. Remember what your doctor said?"

He glanced at the glass, scrunched his face as though he was really giving it some thought, then returned the drink to the table.

She didn't think he'd go so far as to pour it out, though. She suspected that he was going to finish it as soon as she left.

"Listen," she said. "There's something else, Mr. Murdock. I'd like to ask you to be in our wedding."

"Huh?" He scrunched his craggy face, as if thinking it over, then pointed an arthritic finger at her. "I know you young kids today are all okay with this gender-role-reversal business, and I'll go ahead and be your brides-man or man of honor or whatever you equal-rights hippies are calling it nowadays. But I ain't wearing no pink tuxedo."

Angie suddenly wished she'd accepted the glass of Scotch so she could lift it to her face and camouflage her twitching lips. "I wasn't asking you to stand up with me in the bridal party, Mr. Murdock."

"No?"

"I want you to walk me down the aisle."

Chapter Twelve

Saturday finally dawned, bringing a cloudless sky, a lazy breeze and a buzz of excitement. It was a perfect day for a wedding.

As two o'clock approached, the guests began to arrive and mingle. Toby stood off to the side, taking it all in and feeling as though he'd been blessed beyond measure.

He surveyed the once-familiar yard, which had morphed into a festive, ranch-style setting for the outdoor ceremony, thanks to the rented lattice gazebo, the white chairs lined up on the freshly mowed lawn and the small stage where the DJ was setting up his equipment next to the portable dance floor.

Marcos and Wendy Mendoza, who planned to open The Hollows Cantina at the end of June, had volunteered to cater the event as a wedding gift. They'd flown in from Red Rock two days before and were already laying out their spread on the linen-draped tables that had been adorned with the bouquets of flowers Angie and his sisters had created yesterday.

Come to find out his new bride had once worked for a florist in Vicker's Corners. With all the random skills Angie had acquired at her temp jobs, she was proving to be surprisingly handy.

As Toby marveled at all the work everyone had done in order to get the family homestead ready and decorated for a wedding, he shook his head in amazement.

Last night, his parents had hosted a rehearsal dinner with many of the Fortunes in attendance. Not all of his newfound relatives had been able to drop everything and come to Horseback Hollow, but quite a few from Red Rock and Atlanta had actually made the trip. Even Amelia Fortune Chesterfield had flown in from England.

But there was one family member noticeably missing—his brother Chris.

Toby had planned to talk to Sawyer, but a few minutes ago, his cousin had stepped away from the crowd to take a phone call. When Toby saw that Sawyer had put away his cell, he crossed the yard and made his way toward the man whose charter service had been busy all week flying guests into town.

"You're just the guy I wanted to see," Sawyer said.

"Same here. Did you talk to my brother?"

Sawyer reached into his lapel and pulled out what appeared to be a greeting card. "He asked me to give you this before the wedding."

Toby studied the pale blue envelope, then slipped his finger under the flap and tore it open. After removing the card, he read the printed words that wished the bride and groom all the best as they started their lives together. It was signed: Love, Chris.

Sawyer again reached into his lapel. This time, he withdrew a white business envelope. "He also wanted me to give you this. Open it."

Toby did, finding ten crisp one-hundred dollar bills inside. The amount of the gift was staggering, and while he appreciated his brother's generosity, he actually would have preferred just the card and having Chris attend the wedding in person. But he wouldn't mention his disappointment to Sawyer.

Instead, he said, "Chris must be doing well in Red Rock."

"I think so. And he's sorry he couldn't be here, but he figured, under the circumstances, his presence would only put a damper on your special day. And that's not the kind of wedding memory he wanted you and Angie to have."

As much as Toby would like to argue, Chris had a point.

"He also said to tell you that, if you ever need anything, he's just a phone call away."

Toby nodded, knowing that his brother's heart was softening. And that it was in the right place. "Thanks for being the go-between, Sawyer. I really appreciate it."

"I just wish I could have done more to help smooth things over."

"He'll come around. Eventually." Toby folded the envelope in half and slid it into his own lapel pocket.

"Would you look at all of this?" Sawyer lifted his hand and gestured to the decorated ranch and to the happy people milling about. "Who would have guessed that you and Angie could have pulled off something like this so quickly?"

"She worked her tail off," Toby said. "We both did. But we had a lot of help. And we appreciate your contribution, too."

"Flying you to San Antonio for your honeymoon was the least Laurel and I could do. I just wish you and Angie were able to stay for more than a few days."

"Our attorney said we need to demonstrate that we're the best caretakers for the children, so we didn't want it to look like we were ditching them the first chance we got. Four days will be enough."

Plus, they would miss the kids while they were gone. Maybe, in late summer, the five of them could take a family honeymoon to Six Flags.

"When my dad offered to pay for your hotel room," Sawyer said, "he hoped you'd choose a more exotic locale for your honeymoon."

"San Antonio is a beautiful city. Besides, we won't have to leave the state. And if we need to, we can get home fairly quick."

"That makes sense."

"But speaking of San Antonio," Toby said, "it's only a short drive from there to Red Rock. I think Angie and I will rent a car and stop by the Fortune Foundation to see Chris while we're in the area. It's time I talked to him in person."

That family rift had gone on too long. And it was time to mend fences.

"Uh-oh," Sawyer said. "You're being paged."

Toby scanned the grounds and spotted Jude, who was motioning for him, indicating it was time to get this show on the road.

"I'll talk to you later," Toby said. "Thanks again for everything."

Sawyer placed a hand on Toby's shoulder and gave it an affectionate squeeze. "Congratulations, cousin. I hope you and Angie will be as happy as Laurel and I are."

"I'm sure we will be."

Toby crossed the yard, then took his place at the gazebo, near the minister. His brothers—minus Chris—and Brian followed behind him, lining up at his side.

Just as Angie had promised, the kids all played a special part in the ceremony. Brian took pride in his role as a junior groomsman, while Justin felt honored to be the ring bearer, especially since it had been explained that his was the most important job of all. And Kylie, of course, was delighted to be the flower girl.

Now all the hard work and last night's practice was coming into play.

As the music began, signaling the start of the processional, Justin started down the aisle, balancing the small white satin pillow that had been in the Jones family for generations in one hand and tugging Kylie's flower-bearing arm with the other.

The guests laughed at the struggling pair of red-heads who eventually took their positions in front of the minister.

"There's still flowers left in my basket," Kylie stage-whispered to Justin.

With that, her brother snatched the basket out of her grasp and emptied it, dumping rose petals all over Toby's black cowboy boots. Then he pointed to the pile and smiled. "Now when Angie walks down the aisle, she'll know where she's supposed to end up."

Several of the guests covered their mouths to hold back their giggles. But apparently Doris Edwards didn't find it funny, because she turned her "grand-dame of Lubbock" eyes on anyone who seemed to be laughing at her daughter's expense.

Doris hadn't made it out to the Double H for a visit yet, but she'd purchased Angie's wedding dress and had paid the extra fees for the rush alterations. So she was definitely coming around.

Of course, she'd been on her best behavior last night at the rehearsal dinner. She'd also just happened to bring along some colorful brochures of houses and various other properties she had listed for sale. Apparently Toby's soon-to-be mother-in-law was in her element socializing and networking with his Fortune family members.

Next in the procession came the bridesmaids—Julia Tierney, who was engaged to Liam, and Gabi Mendoza, Jude's fiancée, followed by Toby's sisters, Stacey and Delaney.

But all thoughts of in-laws and family members

dissipated in the light afternoon breeze when the first chords of the bridal march were played.

The moment Toby spotted his bride, his breath caught at the sight of her. She wore a strapless, form-fitting satin gown that hugged her womanly curves, and when she flashed him a dazzling smile his lungs filled with so much pride he could have floated to the moon and back.

As she began her walk down the aisle on Mr. Murdock's arm, he realized his life was about to change in the most amazing way ever. And he couldn't wait until they became one—from this day forward, now and forever...

When Angie reached the gazebo, Mr. Murdock, who wore his much-too-snug dress uniform, handed her off to Toby.

"Who gives this woman away?" the minister asked.

The retired marine, who'd stepped back to his place of honor in the front row, drew up to his full five feet four inches, placed his hand on Doris's shoulder and roared out in his best drill-instructor voice, "Her mother and I do."

Toby had to bite back a laugh when Angie's mom leaned away and looked at Amelia Fortune Chesterfield, who represented the British Fortunes, as if wanting to silently communicate that she wasn't even remotely related to the elderly man.

Yet when Angie slipped her hand in Toby's, when she gazed into his eyes, all thoughts of laughter ceased. He was about to marry the most beautiful, loving woman in the whole world. And when she smiled back at him, he didn't think he could say "I do" fast enough.

Angie had never been happier. And her confident smile lasted all through the minister's opening words and continued through their vows. She'd just married the most perfect man ever made, and she'd never been more certain of a decision in her life.

The moment they were finally pronounced man and wife and Toby kissed her, the Hemings kids, dressed in their bridal finery, let loose with whoops, hoots and whistles.

If anyone thought the outburst was out of place, it would be her mother. But when Toby's family joined in with cheers and applause of their own, Angie couldn't see how her mom could possibly complain.

As the happy guests finally quieted down, the minister said, "May I be the first to introduce you to Mr. and Mrs. Toby Fortune Jones."

Again, the applause and cheers rang out.

The music began, signaling it was time to proceed back down the aisle, and Angie blew a kiss to her mom.

As soon as she and Toby had cleared the last row of chairs, he asked, "Are you glad it's over?"

"The ceremony? Yes. But our lives are just beginning, and I've never been happier."

"Neither have I."

"For the record," she admitted, "I'm looking forward to saying goodbye to our guests and having you all to myself, though."

Toby stroked his fingers along the delicate satin

on her back. "That dress is beautiful, and it couldn't look better on any other bride. But I can't wait to get you out of it."

As he brushed a kiss on her lips, and the photographer snapped another picture, Angie wholeheartedly agreed. The wedding night couldn't come quickly enough.

While the photographer went to gather up all the family members for some formal shots, Toby pulled her behind an elm tree, not far from the tree fort.

"Listen, about our honeymoon," he started.

Oh, no. Would they have to cancel? Had something come up with the kids or the babysitting arrangement? Oh, well. They'd just have to make do. She refused to be disappointed on the happiest day of her life.

"Since we'll be so close to Red Rock," Toby said, "I thought we could take one afternoon to visit Chris."

"That's a great idea."

Toby told her about the card and the monetary gift. "I think it's time to find out how he's doing and how he's feeling about things. He isn't the black sheep some people see him as."

Angie glanced down at the platinum band sparkling on her finger. She was Toby's wife now—and as much a part of the Fortune clan as everyone else. So she was doubly invested in making sure all members were happy and getting along.

"Maybe Chris would just like to get to know his uncle better," she said.

"You might be right. But he's probably also attracted to a new and different lifestyle. He went to college, so he has ideas on new ways to do things. And my dad's an old-school sort. Chris doesn't think Dad respects him. And my dad thinks Chris has gotten too big for his britches. In reality, they're probably both right."

"Do you think you can help them make peace with each other?"

"I'm sure going to try."

A snapping twig sounded, and the photographer called out. "Here they are."

As the rest of the family followed behind, the photographer asked them to gather in the shade of the tree, but he continued to snap random shots at the crowd anyway.

"Is this everyone?" the photographer asked.

No, it wasn't everyone, but that was okay. With all the couples who'd been hooking up lately, there was bound to be another wedding and reception soon. And they could get a bigger group photo then.

Jeanne Marie moved in next to Toby and, between smiles for the camera, whispered, "I'm so sorry Chris isn't here. I feel as though a part of me is missing."

Angie's heart ached for her new mother-in-law. And while Brian, Justin and Kylie weren't technically her children, she could understand a mother's distress.

"Angie and I are going to stop and see Chris in Red Rock while we're gone," Toby told her. "I'll talk to him."

"Thank you, son." She leaned in and kissed Toby right as another flash went off. "While you do that, I'll start working on your dad. And when these wedding pictures come back, I'll make a photo album to send to Chris. Maybe it'll remind him how much his family loves and misses him."

"Good idea."

"Can I have your attention?" the photographer asked. "I'd like to get one shot of everyone together. Let's gather around this tree. It'll make a good backdrop."

"Hey!" Justin chimed in. "Let's take it by the tree house instead. That way, some of us can climb up there and look down on you guys."

The photographed ignored the child, but Angie didn't. "Before the day is over, Justin, I'll have him take a family shot of the five of us near the tree house."

"How come we can't all be up in it?" Justin asked.

Angie caressed the top of his head. "Because I don't think I'd be able to climb very well in this dress."

"Five bucks says you can." Mr. Murdock, who stood beside her, nudged her with his elbow. "And another five says that I'll beat your time getting up there."

Angie laughed. "I'm not taking that bet, Mr. Murdock. This is going to be a wager-free wedding."

Before long, the reception launched into a full-scale party, with the food and drinks flowing freely.

When the DJ called the bride and groom to the dance floor, he said, "Since they didn't have a song picked out, I'll play a country classic."

"Seriously?" Toby called out. "Don't you have anything by Aretha Franklin? I'd take her over Patsy Cline any day of the week."

The whole dance floor fell into a hush, and Angie shook her head, realizing her husband had just said the one thing bound to agitate Texans quicker than a piñata at a five-year-old's birthday party.

"I'll see what I can do," the DJ said.

Moments later, as the music started, Toby and Angie stepped out onto the dance floor. Before long, other couples joined them—Stacey and Colton, Jude and Gabi, Liam and Julia.

Even Toby's cousin Amelia Fortune Chesterfield had found a dance partner in Quinn Drummond, who owned a ranch neighboring Toby's.

Quinn held Amelia close as Etta James crooned out through the speakers. The unlikely pairing of the proper British noble with a Horseback Hollow cowboy brought another smile to Angie's lips.

She nodded slightly and whispered, "Apparently, there's something about a wedding that makes for the strangest dance partners."

Toby drew her close. "And some of the nicest."

"You've got that right, cowboy." Then Angie wrapped her arms around her husband's neck and kissed him with all the love in her heart.

Two days later, in the honeymoon suite at one of San Antonio's swankiest hotels, Toby woke up with his wife in his arms, her back to his chest, her bottom nestled in his lap. Just hours ago, they'd made love again.

It seemed as though they couldn't get enough of each other, and he had a feeling that was how it was always going to be.

Today they planned to drive out to Red Rock, although he wasn't in any big hurry to let go of his lovely, naked wife.

"Are you awake?" he whispered against her hair.

"Um-hum." She arched and stretched. "I was just thinking."

Toby pressed a kiss on her bare shoulder. "What about?"

"About you and me and all the kids."

"All?" He chuckled. "I guess three would seem like a lot to an only child."

"Actually, I was thinking about the younger ones— the babies we're going to have."

"Babies? How many do you plan on having?"

"Well, none by myself. I was hoping you'd be involved."

He laughed. "I'm in this thing all the way, honey. So we can have as many kids as you'd like."

"I was thinking that six would be a good number."

"Six total?" he asked. "Or six more?"

Angie turned to face him, her smile radiant. "I'd like as many kids as we're blessed with."

"So the woman who once feared commitment is now daydreaming about having babies?"

"Yes. Little cowboys who are just like you—strong and handsome, loving and wise. And little girls who, like your mom, know that real wealth lies in love and family."

"Okay, but we'll need to have at least one little girl like you. One who's as inventive and creative and loving as she is beautiful." Toby pressed a kiss on Angie's brow. "Have I told you how much I love you?"

"Seven times throughout the night, but I'll never get tired of hearing you say it."

"Oh, yeah? Then you're really going to like it when I show you just how much."

Then he took her in his arms and did just that.

Toby had no idea what the future would bring, but right now, he was going to cherish every moment of the present.

* * * * *

"Hi, honey, I'm home!"

Aiden heard her laugh and followed it to the nursery, where she stood on a ladder. "Be careful." He extended a hand to help her down. Good thing, because she faltered and fell into him. "See, this is why you need me," he said, catching her.

He pulled her closer and lowered his head toward her, hesitating, giving her a chance to object.

Their first kiss had been for the tabloid reporter. This kiss wasn't for show. This one had been a long time coming.

Need coursed through him, unlike any he'd ever felt. Never in his long history of women, each of whom was supposed to be the antidote for Bia. But there was no antidote.

There had always been obstacles between them—physical distance, engagements, his marriage and their jobs. Till now.

Enough was enough. This time he was claiming what was his.

* * *

Celebrations, Inc:
Let's get this party started!

CELEBRATION'S BABY

BY
NANCY ROBARDS THOMPSON

Published in Great Britain 2014
by Mills & Boon, an imprint of Harlequin (UK) Limited,
Eton House, 18-24 Paradise Road, Richmond, Surrey, TW9 1SR

© 2014 Nancy Robards Thompson

ISBN: 978 0 263 91274 6

23-0414

Harlequin (UK) Limited's policy is to use papers that are natural, renewable and recyclable products and made from wood grown in sustainable forests. The logging and manufacturing processes conform to the legal environmental regulations of the country of origin.

Printed and bound in Spain
by Blackprint CPI, Barcelona

Award-winning author **Nancy Robards Thompson** is a sister, wife and mother who has lived the majority of her life south of the Mason-Dixon line. As the oldest sibling, she reveled in her ability to make her brother laugh at inappropriate moments, and she soon learned she could get away with it by proclaiming, "What? I wasn't doing anything." It's no wonder that upon graduating from college with a degree in journalism, she discovered that reporting "just the facts" bored her silly. Since she hung up her press pass to write novels full-time, critics have deemed her books "funny, smart and observant." She loves chocolate, champagne, cats and art (though not necessarily in that order). When she's not writing, she enjoys spending time with her family, reading, hiking and doing yoga.

This book is dedicated with love to good friends
who are steadfast and true.

Chapter One

Being in charge had its perks. Today, Bia Anderson fully intended to cash in. After all, there was chocolate involved.

She lifted her chin a little higher as she walked up the petunia-lined path to the old bungalow located at the end of Main Street in downtown Celebration—the new home of Maya's Chocolates.

Nicole Harrison, a staff writer for the *Dallas Journal of Business and Development,* where Bia was the editor in chief, hadn't hidden her disappointment that morning. Bia had assigned her to the catch-a-greased-pig contest at the grand opening of the Piggly Wiggly over in Kenansville rather than the interview for the Maya's Chocolates business profile.

It wasn't the first time she and Nicole had butted

heads, and it probably wouldn't be the last. But that came with the territory. In the two months since Bia had taken the reins as editor of the paper, making tough calls that sometimes disappointed the staff hadn't gotten easier, but she just had to suck it up and do what she thought was best.

So what if they all thought she was hard as nails, lacking empathy and compassion?

What would they think when they found out she was going to be a mother? The wall immediately went up, and she told herself she didn't care what they'd say or do or how they'd smirk when they learned she was pregnant by *People*'s reigning "Sexiest Man Alive," Hugh Newman. The thought knocked the air out of her. And not in a good way; it was more like a sucker punch to the gut. Reflexively, her hand went to her belly.

She'd done the pregnancy test last night, finally pulling her head out of the sand after being two months late. She still hadn't quite wrapped her mind around the reality of it—although the unexpected pregnancy did explain why she'd been craving chocolate to the point of insanity.

At first, she'd blamed the cravings on the stress of the Hugh Newman debacle: a five-day lapse of judgment that had ended abruptly when the paparazzi started inquiring into the identity of the woman with the auburn hair in the blue sundress, with whom Newman had been seen *canoodling* in Celebration, Texas.

Canoodling? Did anyone even use that word anymore?

He'd been in town doing location research—

soaking up local color for his next movie. Also, he had accepted an invitation to emcee the annual Doctor's Charity Ball, which benefited the new pediatric surgical wing at Celebration Memorial Hospital. Bia had gotten an up-close-and-personal tutorial of why Hugh had been named Mr. Sexy when she'd had lunch with him to interview him for the paper (and you can bet Nicole Harrison hadn't been happy that Bia had claimed that assignment). Five minutes into the interview, Hugh Newman had charmed the pants off her. Okay, so maybe it had been more like an hour. God, she wasn't *that* easy.

Bia stepped onto the porch and tried the door. It was locked. So she knocked and waited for Maya to let her in.

Truth be told, Bia wasn't easy at all.

At twenty-eight years old, she'd only had two lovers. Her first had been Duane, as part of a six-year relationship that had ended in a broken engagement; the other was Hugh, an impetuous mistake she'd known wouldn't last. And, of course, it hadn't.

She just hadn't expected to walk away with such a personal memento of their time together.

Dammit, she'd simply wanted one taste of sexy. *One taste*—and she had been prepared to walk away. But one night became five and then the media had gotten wind of the affair and suddenly the entire world was dying to know the identity of the woman with the auburn hair in the blue sundress. Overnight, Bia had gone from relative obscurity to the top of *XYZ Celebrity News*'s most-stalked list.

She did a hasty scan of the area looking for skulk-

ing media-types. It was a beautiful day. Shoppers were
wandering in and out of places like On a Roll Bakery,
Three Sisters dress shop, Dolce Vita Gourmet Grocery and Barbara's Beauty Salon. But the area was
all clear of lurking *XYZ* minions. Oh, they were gone
now, thank God. The paparazzi had lost interest when
Hugh's camp had explained that the redhead in the
blue sundress was simply his tour guide.

Nothing to see here, folks. Just a tour guide.

Liar, liar, sexy pants on fire.

At least they hadn't called her an escort.

What had really burned was when Hugh's people
had offered to pay her to keep her mouth shut. She
didn't want his money. But she did want her privacy
back. That's the only reason she'd agreed to play along
with the tour guide charade. Still, she told them to pass
along the message that Hugh could keep his money
and the insult it implied.

Within hours of explaining Bia away, Hugh and his
longtime on-again, off-again starlet girlfriend, Kristin Capistrano, announced that they were, indeed, on
again. *How lovely for them.* Then the tabloids devel-
oped instant amnesia about the "tour guide" and were
all ablaze with the news that they had a "liftoff" and
that "Hugh-stin" certainly did not have a problem.
The pair proclaimed they were deeply in love and—
surprise surprise—that Kristin would be costarring
with Hugh in the movie that was filming in Celebration, Texas. The one for which he'd been soaking up
the local color when he'd met Bia.

Bia's mouth went dry as she thought of the scandal it would cause if anyone found out the sexiest man alive was her baby daddy.

She clenched her fists, digging her nails into her palms. As far as she was concerned, Hugh Newman was dead to her. But the blue line on the pregnancy test had resurrected him.

Now she wasn't sure what to do... Except that, ready or not, she was going to have a baby—and she was going to keep it.

There was no question about that. Bia was adopted, and she'd often wondered why her birth mother had chosen to give her up rather than trying to make it work. Her mother and father—the ones who had adopted her—had been good people. At least her father had been. She hadn't really known her adoptive mother. She'd passed away when Bia was five, leaving her adoptive father to raise her.

The strong, silent type, he'd never been much of a talker. He'd bristled the handful of times she'd asked about her birth mother. So she hadn't pressed it.

Her dad had passed away last year, and now more than ever she wished she knew more about her roots. Maybe it was time to start digging. She'd need to know...for her child's sake. Health history and all that.

Bia rapped on the door again, shifting her weight from one foot to another. Across the street, a friend of her father's called to her and waved. She waved back.

Thank God her father wasn't alive to see what a mess she'd made of things. She sighed.

It had just *happened*. When she'd sat down to interview Hugh, she'd been the picture of professionalism. At first she'd been immune to his notorious charms.

Then he'd started putting the moves on her. Heavy-duty flirting. With her.

Hugh Newman had been flirting with *her*.

That was all it had taken for her resolve to melt like pure cane sugar in hot-brewed tea.

They'd used protection. Every single time.

That's the part she couldn't quite comprehend. How this could have happened when she'd been so careful?

Thinking about it made her feel nauseated.

She gave herself a mental shake.

She'd made her choices. Now she'd have to live with the consequences. Still, if she could just have one do-over in life, she'd turn back the clock two months and stay the heck away from Mr. Sexy. She'd let Nicole be Hugh Newman's *tour guide*.

She knocked on the door yet again, this time a little harder. Where the heck was Maya?

Above Bia's head hung a weathered, hand-painted wooden sign that boasted, Maya's Chocolates— Happily Ever After Starts Here. It swayed and squeaked on the lazy breeze of the warm May afternoon. The words, written in gray-blue calligraphy on a whitewashed background, were underlined by a fancy, scrolling arrow that pointed toward the door.

Happily Ever After. Right here, huh?

Nice thought.

She tried the door again, this time giving it a firmer tug and then a push, but it was locked tight as a tick. She shaded her eyes and peered in the glass front door. No one was in the showroom. All the fixtures seemed to be in place, but they looked empty.

Hmm, that was curious.

The store's grand opening was scheduled for next week. Bia thought that a good bit of the merchandise would be in place by now.

Had Maya forgotten their appointment? If they didn't let her in to start the interview soon, Bia couldn't promise that anyone was going to have a happily ever after. Bia glanced at her cell phone to check the time. Okay, so she was a couple of minutes early, but it was warm outside. She was feeling a little dizzy and beads of perspiration were forming underneath her silk blouse and starting to run down the crevice of her back.

Certain foods and smells—like coffee and the noxious traffic fumes wafting up from Main Street—made her feel ill. That, along with the chocolate cravings and, of course, the missed periods, were what had finally sent her to Dallas to purchase the in-home test. She couldn't purchase it in the local drugstore. Word would get around faster than if it had been aired on *XYZ*.

She blinked away the thought and refocused on the mental list of interview questions she would ask Maya…if she ever answered the door.

Bia was just about to dial Maya's phone number when, through the panes of glass on the front door, she saw the woman hurrying toward her in a flurry of long red spiral curls and flouncing green scarf and skirt. She was wiping her hands on a dish towel, which she flung over her shoulder as she opened the door with a breathless greeting.

"*Bonjour!* You're here!" Maya's lyrical accented voice rang out and mingled with the sounds of chirping birds and traffic. "I hope you have not been waiting long. I was in the kitchen putting the finishing touches on a surprise just for you. Come in! Come in, *cher!* Please, come in."

A surprise? For me?

"I hope it's chocolate," Bia said.

"But of course it is." Maya smiled as she held open the door for Bia and motioned her inside. A cool gust of air that smelled like rich dark chocolate greeted her and took the edge off her queasiness. Bia breathed in deeply.

"Well, then, in that case, you're forgiven." Bia grinned. "I have been dreaming of your chocolate since the Doctor's Ball. It was the first time I'd tasted it. In fact, for the past several weeks, I've been craving chocolate like crazy, but the over-the-counter stuff just isn't doing it for me. I think you've spoiled me for all other sweets. I just learned that Baldoon's Pub offers your Irish cream truffles on their dessert menu."

"Indeed they do," Maya said over her shoulder as Bia followed her into the house. "I like to hear that I've spoiled you for other chocolate. You might say that's the theme of my business plan."

The front room was set up as a shop with a refrigerated glass case in the center of the space. Like the shelving fixtures, the case was empty, Bia noted with chagrin. But it was surrounded by lovely silver-veined marble counters that housed a cash register and supplies to wrap purchases. Even if there was a decided dearth of chocolate, the place looked fresh and clean and light with its white paint, whitewashed wooden floors and yards of silver tulle draped elegantly across the ceiling. The look created an ethereal cloudlike effect.

Again, Bia breathed in the delicious aroma of chocolate, and her stomach growled. Since the cases and shelves were empty, she had to wonder if she was imagining the scent. Or had Maya piped it in for effect?

"Where's the chocolate?" Bia finally asked. "Don't you make all your goods on the premises? If so, how are you going to fill the cases and shelves before the grand opening?"

Maya glanced around the room. "I suppose it does look rather empty in here, doesn't it?" She sighed and went behind the wrap stand. "Alas, the increased demand for chocolate has forced me to be less hands-on with the manufacturing process. I still make some special made-to-order candy—like this batch I made especially for you this morning."

She presented a three-tiered glass-and-silver dessert plate brimming with confections in various shapes and colors. Bia's mouth watered at the sight.

"I thought I smelled chocolate in the air. But then I worried that I'd simply imagined it."

Maya laughed. "It is a lovely fragrance, isn't it? Some say the mere smell of chocolate causes a woman's body to release hormones that simulate the feeling of falling in love."

"Ha! All of the feelings and none of the heartache," Bia said. "Sounds like the perfect relationship. I just wish chocolate didn't love me back so much. It tends to stay with me. You know, right here." She patted her left hip.

"I don't know what you're talking about, you are reed-thin. You have nothing to worry about."

"Gosh, makes chocolates, gives compliments…I think you and I could be good friends."

Maya's eyes shone. "I certainly hope so."

"You will have chocolate for the grand opening, won't you?" Bia asked.

Maya nodded. "Of course. I was fortunate enough to find a stateside manufacturer who was able to duplicate my family recipe in bulk, the one my grandmother used to start the business three generations ago. The candy for the shelves and case will be delivered the day before we open. That way it will be as fresh as can be. We'll have to work extra hard to get everything in place, but it will be worth it."

Maya gestured toward the plate. "But please, don't let me detain you. Help yourself."

Reverently, Bia approached the manna. She paused to give the illusion of self-control, so that it didn't look as if she was about to bury her face in all that deliciousness. But then she found herself genuinely appreciating the sheer artistry of Maya's offering.

Yes, this definitely could be the start of a beautiful friendship.

Maya placed a silver cocktail napkin on the counter next to Bia. She also produced a small crystal pitcher of water, a matching glass and a plate containing bread, crackers and apple slices.

"What is this?" Bia asked.

"These are the palate cleansers for the chocolate tasting," Maya said. "To fully discern the differences between the chocolates, you must cleanse your palate between each tasting."

Oh. Bia suddenly felt a little out of her element. "You treat chocolate like some people treat wine?"

"Pourquoi pas?" Maya asked.

"You're right. Why not?"

"May I recommend that you start with the chocolates on the first tier? It has a lower percentage of cocoa and a milder taste. The chocolate on the upper tier will overpower those on the bottom. I suggest you let the chocolate melt on your tongue rather than chewing it, and in between different bites, enjoy a bit of apple or bread washed down by the water. That way you will taste all the nuances of each piece."

Maya gestured to the plate and gave Bia a few more tips on how to proceed: to observe the chocolate, to smell it and to break it, feeling the way the pieces of solid chocolate snapped, before finally tasting it. Those were all indicators of good quality.

Finally, she said, "That is enough instruction. Please enjoy."

Bia started to choose a chocolate from the bottom, but she paused. "Will there be a quiz when I'm finished?"

Maya laughed her perfect, crystal laugh. Bia breathed in deeply, savoring the mélange of scents from the plate. For the first time in a long time, a sense of peace and well-being washed over her.

"Only questions about which are your favorites," Maya answered.

"It's all gorgeous. I'm sure they will all be delicious."

First, she selected what looked like a classic chocolate truffle dusted with cocoa powder. She bit into it, and flavor exploded on her tongue. She closed her eyes and had to make a conscious effort not to let a moan escape.

Oh, Maya was wrong. This chocolate didn't simulate love; it was better. Way better. Better than kissing. Better than sex.

Oh, my God, I'm in public and I'm making virtual love to a French truffle. And I don't care.

She opened her eyes, and her gaze automatically found the dessert plate. She was tempted to pluck up another piece—a handful—even before she had finished the first. Somehow she managed to restrain herself.

She popped the rest of the first truffle into her mouth. She had the same urge to moan over the chocolate. It was too good. So she quit fighting and gave in to the unadulterated pleasure.

Finally, after blissfully indulging in several pieces from each level, Bia forced herself to take a step back. She had to put some space between herself and her vice. If she didn't, she was going to eat too much. Although, with the lingering flavors of chocolate, orange, cinnamon and cloves teasing her taste buds, that seemed unlikely. With one last wistful glance at the candy, she said, "That was delicious, Maya. I wish I could say I'd eaten myself sick, but I think I may want more later."

"And you say that like it's a bad thing?"

The two laughed like old friends.

"Your decor looks exquisite. Who did your decorating?"

Maya beamed. "Thank you. I did it myself. I tried to give the front of the house a similar feel to my shop in St. Michel. Similar, but maybe a touch more modern. More American. I wanted it to feel like home, since I will be spending a great deal of time here."

"Let's see," Bia said, flipping through her reporter's notebook, searching for the brief bio she'd gathered on Maya. "You're from St. Michel in Europe. Are you moving to Celebration?"

Maya stopped, considering the question. "I will be here for the time being. Because my heart is telling me Celebration is where I belong right now, especially while I am getting the new location off the ground. I must make sure it does well."

Bia jotted down more notes and anecdotes for use in her story. "Who is looking after your St. Michel shop while you're away?"

"I have promoted my assistant, Grace, to the managerial position. If anyone knows the shop as well as I do, Grace does. I trust that the place is in good hands."

Maya paused again, as if weighing her words. "As you can imagine, the Celebration location will need much tender loving care while I get the business off the ground."

Bia nodded. "I'm curious, though. Why in the world did you choose Celebration, Texas, as the location of your first U.S. retail store? I mean, no offense to this town. It's a great place. It's my home. But of all the places in the world…why Celebration?"

Maya's eyes shone as she regarded Bia, and for

the first time Bia noticed that the older woman's eyes were a gorgeous shade of hazel infused with intriguing flecks of amber and green, accentuated by the color of her skirt. The same mossy color was also echoed in the silk scarf that she had artfully arranged around her neck. *Leave it to the French,* Bia mused. They could create something enchanted out of a yard of silk and a bolt of tulle.

Maya's hair was magical, too. Bia's hair, when left to its natural devices, was almost as curly as Maya's. But Bia straightened hers since it never wanted to do the same thing twice. A few months ago, she'd opted for a keratin treatment so she wouldn't have to fight with it during the humid days of summer. It was only May, but the oppressive damp-heat days were already bearing down on them, as if someone were misting the entire town with a gigantic vaporizer. At this rate, by the time August rolled around, humidity would hang in the air like a billowing stratus cloud. Thanks to the magic of keratin, at least Bia's hair was armed and ready to take on the summer…and the pregnancy.

Oh…the pregnancy.

She swallowed hard and blinked away the thought.

"Why Celebration?" Bia urged.

She looked up from her notepad and caught Maya staring at her with an odd expression. In an instant the look was gone, replaced by Maya's placid, Madonna-like smile.

"I have…friends here. Do you know Pepper Meriweather, A. J. Sherwood-Antonelli and Caroline Coopersmith?" Maya asked.

"I know Caroline. Her husband, Drew Montgomery, is my boss."

Maya gave a quick flick of her wrist. "Of course he is. Well, I met Caroline, A.J. and Pepper through a mutual friend who went to school with them. This was a few years ago, before any of them were married. They'd come to St. Michel to help another friend. Margeaux Broussard? Do you know her?"

Bia shook her head and continued to furiously scribble notes as Maya talked.

"Anyhow," Maya continued, "the girls had come to St. Michel with Margeaux to help her make amends with her father, from whom she'd been estranged for the better part of her life. Once they'd accomplished that mission, they returned to Celebration, luring my good friend Sydney James away from St. Michel with the promise of a job with Texas Star Energy right here in Celebration."

Bia raised her head and looked at Maya. She knew Sydney pretty well, since the woman had just married Miles Mercer. Miles was good friends with Bia's best friend, Aiden Woods. The four of them got together a lot. Bia would've called it double dating if she and Aiden had been a couple, but they weren't. She'd known him since kindergarten and cared too much about him to ruin their relationship by dating him.

"Texas Star Energy, huh?" Bia said.

Maya nodded and quirked a brow that seemed to indicate she knew all about the scandalous demise of the corrupt energy empire. Bia had been the reporter who had broken the story that had started the conglomerate's unraveling. In fact, her investigative reporting and subsequent awards had helped her clinch the editorship of the paper after Drew Montgomery had decided to give up editing to focus more on the publishing end of the paper. But Texas Star was in the past. It was a can of worms Bia didn't want to reopen.

"So, you followed your friends to Celebration?"

"Oh, *mais non*. It's a little more complicated." Maya pursed her lips. "At first, I visited them. I attended each of their weddings. In fact, some might say that I even had a hand in bringing each of them together with their soul mates."

"You introduced them?"

Maya gave a noncommittal one-shoulder shrug. How very French her gestures were. But wait…hadn't Drew met Caroline at a wedding…? Yes. It had been Caroline's sister's wedding. It had been right around the time that everything was coming to a head at Texas Star.

"Technically, *non*. I didn't physically introduce them. It's another complicated story, really."

"You're full of complicated stories, aren't you? If you'd care to expound, I'm here to listen…. That's what I do."

Maya studied her as if she was deciding whether she would take Bia up on the offer of a listening ear.

"Well, I do love to talk." Maya laughed, an infectious sound that made Bia smile.

"Over the years, the girls—Pepper, A.J. and Caroline—have become very dear to me. So, I've always looked out for them, and that's how I had a hand in bringing them together with their soul mates."

Again, Bia paused and looked up at the woman.

Soul mates. There was that word again. Bia filed soul mates in the same category as happily ever after. She wasn't sure she believed there was such a thing, especially after being left at the altar by the man who should've been her *soul mate* if there was such a thing. Nope, in her book, love was an urban legend. People talked about it. Some even claimed to have experienced it, but *real* love—the kind that grafted your soul to another person's for better or worse, the type that could withstand bleached-blonde strippers and the relentless paparazzi—had managed to elude Bia her entire life.

Actually, she'd read somewhere that soul mates weren't always lovers. Sometimes they were parent and child, sometimes best friends. If that were true, the closest thing to a soul mate she'd ever had was Aiden. Their relationship had survived some pretty treacherous hurdles. It had actually transcended sex. That's probably why it worked. They hadn't ruined things by getting physical.

God knew there had been plenty of times Bia had been tempted to give in to his charm. The guy was gorgeous—in a more rugged and down-to-earth way than Hugh's pretty-boy looks. Women found Aiden irresistible. Since college, he'd had a constant rotation of babes. None of them serious.

Then he'd gotten married. It had lasted two years before they'd called it quits and he'd reverted back to his freewheeling ways.

He wouldn't talk about what had happened. All he would say was that he hadn't cheated. "It just didn't work out."

His smorgasbord of women had been the main reason Bia had kept Aiden in the friend zone. Well, that and the fact that he'd thrown the bachelor party that ended with the stripper that had broken up her engagement.

Still, despite all Aiden's faults, Duane and Hugh were long gone, and Aiden was still there.

She put her hand on her stomach. And he would be the first person she told about the baby.

"…and I came to Celebration to see each one of them say I do," Maya continued. "Each time I visited, I was drawn to this town. As time went on and I visited more, I knew there was a reason I was supposed to be here."

For a moment, Maya looked wistful. Bia studied her, taking a mental snapshot and hoping she could somehow convey Maya's mood in the article.

"Would you care to elaborate?"

A warm smile reclaimed Maya's delicate features. "At home, in St. Michel, I'm known as *un marieur*."

"I beg your pardon," said Bia.

"A matchmaker. I am a third-generation chocolatier by trade, but matchmaking, you might say, is my passion. Some people believe my chocolate is magical."

Bia stopped writing and looked up. The cinnamon and clove from the last piece of chocolate still lingered on the back of her tongue.

"So, you're telling me your chocolate is enchanted? What? Do you sprinkle in love potions or something?"

"I would claim nothing of the sort. My chocolate is all natural. Everything is on the label, except for a few proprietary blends."

"The love potions?"

Maya raked her hands through her hair. "Oh, I should not have said that. Please don't print that in the profile."

"Why not? It will probably drive business through the roof. Everyone wants love."

Well, almost everyone.

As if confirming Bia's thoughts, Maya did her one-shoulder French shrug.

"What?" Bia asked. "You don't believe that?"

"I do believe there is someone for everyone. You, for instance. You've had your share of setbacks, but there's someone for you. In fact, you've already met him."

Whoa. Whoa. Whoa. If she was going to start asking about the Hugh Newman debacle, Bia would shut that down very quickly. Instead of waiting to get caught in the pickle, she turned the tables.

"Is there someone special in *your* life?"

Maya paused and drew in a slow, thoughtful breath.

Ha. It's not so comfortable to be on the receiving end of the dating game rapid-fire, is it?

"Alas, even though my intuition is generally good when it comes to pairing up others, it doesn't work so well for me personally."

"So, does this *intuitive gift* of yours carry over into other areas? Would you go as far as saying you have the gift of second sight?"

Maya laughed. "If I had the second sight, I would've already won the lottery. I wouldn't be agonizing over rollout budgets and marketing campaigns. But that's strictly off the record, *oui?*"

"Fair enough," said Bia. "Back to the business of chocolate. I understand this is the first of two new Maya's Chocolates that you're opening stateside. Where will the other location be?"

"I want to get the one here in Celebration off the ground, and then I'll look into opening another, possibly in New York. However, it's important that I ensure the fiscal health of the current locations. Especially the one in St. Michel. That's where my grandmother started the business. It has been a fixture in downtown St. Michel for three generations. All of the recipes have been passed down through the years from mother to daughter."

"And will you continue the tradition?"

Maya nodded.

"Do you have children?"

For a fraction of a second, Bia thought she saw a shade of sadness color Maya's eyes.

"Come with me," Maya said. "I want to show you something."

The woman led the way to the kitchen, which was hidden behind a double-layered curtain made of silver gossamer backed by heavy white satin. When Maya parted the drapes, allowing Bia her first glimpse behind the scenes, Bia half expected she would glimpse the great and powerful Oz or some other secret to which mere mortals weren't privy. If they were, wouldn't every chocoholic have her own in-home chocolatier?

But when Bia stepped over the threshold, she didn't see anything that looked extraordinary. In fact, the kitchen, with its sterile stainless-steel countertops and run-of-the-mill industrial sink, refrigerator and gas range, looked quite...ordinary. Well, with the exception of the gleaming copper pots hanging on a rack over the sink, and the adorable pink-and-black box that was festively tied with a ribbon and waiting on the counter. Bia eyed the package.

It looked like a box of Maya's famous chocolate.

For her to take home? She had to bite her tongue to keep from asking the question out loud.

As if Maya had read her mind, she picked up the package and handed it to Bia. "This is for you."

"Ah, thank you," Bia said.

She gestured around the kitchen with a motion of her hand. "So this is where the magic happens?"

Pride straightened Maya's already admirable posture. "*Oui.* My mother and grandmother passed on those copper pots over there. That's what I wanted to show you. The recipes are proprietary, guarded jealously and handed down through the generations with the copper pots and the family Bible, from mother to daughter to granddaughter."

She walked over and took down one of the three gleaming vessels, running the pads of her manicured fingers lovingly over its shiny surface. "My grandmother gave them to my mother, and, in turn, my mother gave them to me. Everything in this shop is brand-new, but I brought these with me as a symbol of the past, to remind me of the importance of family. I use them to make special smaller batches. Personal chocolates. Like those you sampled earlier and the box you will take home."

"Thank you," Bia said.

But the burning question, the one that Maya had quite deftly skirted, was the one about children. While Bia hated to assume, she couldn't bring herself to press Maya for an answer. Wasn't it obvious? If Maya had an heir, she would've said so. Judging by the look on her face when Bia had originally asked the question, she knew she'd struck a nerve. No, it was definitely better not to go there.

"Your grandmother founded the business? She named it Maya's Chocolates?"

"She did."

"So, you were named after the family business?"

"No, I was named after my grandmother. Her name was also Maya."

A bittersweet taste caught in the back of Bia's throat, replacing the cinnamon and cloves. How lucky Maya was to be so connected to her past. It was a luxury that might not be afforded to Bia, unless she chose to go out searching for the woman who'd given her up all those years ago. Would it really be worth it? Walking into someone's life, disrupting—or possibly upending—the world to which they'd become accustomed?

If an attempted reconnection ended in rejection, maybe it would be better to leave well enough alone. She'd had a happy childhood with a father who'd done his darnedest to give her the best life he was capable of giving. Maybe there was something wrong with wanting any more than that.

She put her hand on her stomach. If Bia could get blind health records from the adoption agency, maybe it would serve everyone best to look forward rather than backward.

"Do you have extended family who will carry on the Maya's Chocolates tradition in the future?"

"That remains to be seen."

There was that look again. Bia glimpsed it before Maya turned away to hang up the copper pot.

She was just about to ask Maya to clarify the *remains to be seen* comment, when a patch of cold sweat erupted on the back of Bia's neck. She tugged at the neckline of her dress. Good grief, it felt as if someone had turned up the heat in the kitchen at least twenty degrees. A dizzying wave of nausea passed over her, and she grabbed on to the edge of the counter to steady herself.

Maya reached out and touched Bia's arm. "Are you all right? Let me get you some water and a chair so you can sit down."

Maya pulled over a wrought-iron chair from a small glass-topped table for two that stood in the corner of the kitchen. Bia had been so busy ogling the box of chocolates she hadn't noticed the dining set until now. Shaking, she lowered herself onto the seat. What the heck was wrong with her? She'd heard of morning sickness, but it was midafternoon. This was ridiculous. She'd just have to power through. She had so much to do she didn't have time for the indulgence of a sick day. As she'd done since she'd first felt the symptoms, she made the choice to buck up and push through.

Mind over matter. She always managed to feel better when she decided not to think about how she felt, not to give in.

Maya returned with some ice water. Bia gratefully accepted it and took a sip. She pressed the cool glass to her forehead. It helped.

How embarrassing was this? She took a deep breath and reminded herself she just needed to tie up loose ends for the article and then she could leave. She might even work from home for the rest of the day as she wrote the story.

"Thank you, Maya. I'm sorry about the interruption. I'm just feeling a little light-headed."

Maya walked over and put a cool hand on Bia's cheek. The breach of personal space was a little startling, but at the same time, it was sort of touching.

"No fever," Maya said. "Here, give me your hand."

Bia hesitated for a moment, then complied. Maya held Bia's hand. If the hand on the cheek had been a little weird, this made Bia want to squirm. But the thought of moving caused a new wave of nausea to crest.

"Any chance you could be pregnant?" Maya asked with the same casual tone she might use if she were asking if Bia had ever tasted chocolate-dipped bacon.

Bia jerked her hand away from Maya's and tried to stand up, but the rush of blood to her head landed her right back on the chair—hard.

"That's a very personal question," Bia insisted as alarms sounded in her head: Maya and her intuition. But what audacity for the woman to even suggest something like that to someone she barely knew?

Bia stood, this time more carefully. "I need to go."

"I didn't mean to upset you," Maya said. "Please

know everything is going to be okay. You have to believe that—"

"I'm just under the weather," Bia said, a little too
irritably. "It's nothing to be alarmed about."

Bia turned to leave but dropped her notebook as she
tried to hitch her purse up on her shoulder.

Maya swooped down and retrieved the notebook
before Bia could reach it. "Bia, I'm sorry." Maya
handed it to her. Bia took it with a quick jerk of the
hand. "Really. I didn't mean to upset you."

"Don't worry about it. I'll have Nicole Harrison call
you if we need anything else for the article."

Maya nodded solemnly. "Please forgive me if I have
overstepped my bounds. But I have to say this. Please
know you and the baby are going to be okay. Hugh
Newman may be the father of your child, but there is
another man who will love you and your baby the way
you deserve to be loved. And that's not all."

"Oh, yes it is," Bia said, backing away.

"Your family cares about you deeply and will rally
around you during your pregnancy. You have absolutely nothing to fear."

*Okay, this is the last straw. Who does this woman
think she is bringing my family into this, as she spouts
her woo-woo nonsense pretending like she knows
what's going on? She obviously has no idea what she's
talking about.*

But if so, how did she know Bia was pregnant and
that Hugh was the father? Conjecture? A lucky guess?

"This is none of your business," Bia said. "I'd appreciate it if you'd stop with the advice."

Maya's face turned scarlet. As Bia passed through

the curtains into the front of the shop, Maya said, "Bia, I'm sorry. I would never say or do anything to hurt you. Not on purpose."

Bia stopped and whirled around, looking Maya in the eyes. "Hurt me? You don't even know me. So please stop talking like you do. Stay out of my business, okay? Stay out of mine, and I will certainly stay out of yours."

Chapter Two

"I'm pregnant, Aiden."

Aiden Woods sat at Bia's kitchen table across from her, weighing his words before he spoke. He was inclined to make a joke—something about not being ready to be a father or that pregnancy was impossible since they'd never had sex.

Ha-ha?

Nope. Not funny.

For once in his life the filter of good sense kicked in before he stuck his foot in his mouth. Besides, one look at Bia's ashen face told him she wasn't joking.

"B?"

She didn't sleep around. So he had a pretty good idea who the father was. *Hugh Newman, the bastard.*

He wouldn't wish the guy on anyone, much less some-one he cared about.

"Are you sure?" The question sounded absurd to his own ears. But what else was he supposed to say? *I'm sorry? Tough break? Princess, I tried to warn you that Hugh Newman was a horse's ass with a pretty face, but did you listen? No, you didn't.*

"Yes, I'm quite sure. Three pregnancy tests don't lie." Her eyes welled up with tears.

Damn. Not the tears. Aiden fumbled for a minute. Then he reached across the table and took her hand. As the waterworks began to roll, she held on like he was her life preserver.

"God, I am so stupid, Aiden. How could I have gotten myself into this mess? How could I have let this happen?"

"Hey, hey, it's going to be okay." He got up and went around to her side of the table and slid onto the built-in banquette, putting his arm around her. She cried on his shoulder for a solid five minutes.

When Bia had called him at nine-thirty that morn-ing asking if he was free, if he could get away because she needed to talk to him about something important, he'd left the taping of *Catering to Dallas,* the reality television show that he produced, in the capable hands of the show's director, Miles Mercer, and met Bia. No wonder she hadn't wanted to meet him for coffee at the diner as he'd initially suggested. She wasn't a drama queen, so when she'd asked—and Bia never asked, not something like this—he knew it was important, but he'd never imagined a bomb like this.

Damn.

"Does Hugh know?" he asked, handing her a paper napkin from the holder on the table.

Bia wiped her eyes.

"No. You're the only person I've told. Well, you know and Maya LeBlanc *guessed*."

"Who is Maya LeBlanc?"

"She owns the new chocolate shop that's opening downtown. When I interviewed her yesterday, she took one look at me and asked me if I was pregnant."

Aiden squinted at her. "How the hell did she guess something like that?"

"I wasn't feeling well. I had a sinking spell and almost passed out. She must've put two and two together. Really, it wasn't such a stretch. Kind of personal of her to ask, but she did. Of course, that was after we'd been talking about her being highly intuitive. Maybe she was trying to prove a point about her intuition. I don't know."

"Did she guess who the father is?"

Bia flinched. "Absolutely not." She wrung her hands. "Well, sort of. But I didn't confirm that she was right. Come to think of it, though, I didn't even confirm that I was pregnant."

"But she knew it was Hugh? What is this woman, psychic or something?"

Bia inclined her head to the side and pierced him with impatient eyes. "If you think about it, after all the press Hugh and I got, that isn't such a stretch."

"Is she the one who tipped off the press back in March?"

Bia blinked. "Maya? I can't imagine that she would

do something like that. I mean, what would she stand
to gain?"

Aiden shrugged. "*Someone* tipped them off. We
don't know who. It sure seems like she's fishing."

"Well, if the press finds out that I'm pregnant, we'll
know who told them."

Aiden nodded. "When are you going to tell Hugh?"

Bia took a deep breath, held it for a minute and then
let it out audibly. She propped her elbow on the table
and rested her forehead in her palms.

"You're going to tell him, aren't you?"

She didn't look up.

"Bia, you have to tell him."

"I don't *have* to do anything, Aiden. I can't even
think right now. My head feels like it is about to ex-
plode."

"I understand," Aiden said. "But he's the father. He
deserves to know."

She gave a little growl. "I didn't ask you to come
here to lecture me."

That was his cue to back off. A woman he'd gone
out with a couple of times had told him that sometimes
women didn't want men to solve their problems; they
just wanted them to listen. Seemed kind of ridiculous
when a perfectly good solution to the problem was
right there in front of them.

"I get that, but come on, B. If I got a woman pregnant, I'd want to know. It's as much his child as it is
yours."

She rolled her eyes, which looked emerald green
through the tears.

"You and Hugh Newman are two completely dif-

ferent animals, Aiden. I didn't tell you this, but—"
She grimaced and shook her head as if she could take
back the bait.

"You didn't tell me what?"

She grabbed another napkin and blew her nose.
"This is so embarrassing...." She closed her eyes for
a moment, as if gathering her courage. "In the midst
of the media frenzy, when the press was going crazy,
making me out to be some sort of mystery girlfriend,
Hugh's people offered to pay me to keep quiet."

Aiden shrugged. "That's not so out of character
for him."

"No, you don't get it. *He* didn't call me. He had his
people do it. Somehow, I don't think he will be very
happy to hear from me now."

Aiden balled his fists. He'd worked with the guy
years ago when he was in Hollywood. Aiden had been
a production assistant on one of his movies in the
early days. The guy was a jackass, out for no one but
himself.

"Well, if you call him and he ignores you, you've
done your duty. Once you let him know, it's off your
shoulders. But, B, if he wants to be part of the baby's
life, you have to let him. A kid can change a guy. Give
him a chance. If he wants nothing to do with the baby,
you're free to walk away."

He couldn't believe he was defending Hugh Newman.

"God, you're bossy," she said through a fresh
stream of tears.

"But you know I'm right."

She nodded. Then squeezed her eyes shut as she put her head on his shoulder and sobbed again.

"Hey, it's not that bad. I'm here for you. I know it's a shock, but you're strong. You can do this."

Once again, he slid his arm around her shoulder and she nestled into him as if she belonged there. His heart twisted, but he ignored it and lowered his head so that it rested on hers. Her hair smelled like coconut and something floral that made him breathe in a little deeper.

They stayed like that for a few minutes, until she pulled away. She reached for another napkin, wiped her eyes and blew her nose again. "You're right. I have to call him. The sooner I do it, the sooner it's over."

But she just sat there and didn't get up to get her phone.

"You have his number, right?"

She nodded. "Well, I have *a* number for him. I haven't talked to him in two months, since everything erupted. You know, it's funny, the other day I almost deleted his number, but I didn't."

"Why not? Were you harboring hopes of a second chance?"

She made a disgusted *tsking* sound and gave his arm a little shove. "Hardly. I didn't delete it because I got tied up with something else. I've been too busy at the paper since then to give him a second thought. I certainly haven't been pining over him, Aiden."

"Good to know," he said.

"Why is that good to know?"

"Because I don't want to see you get hurt again, B. I mean, you have to let him know about the child, but

I don't want you to harbor any expectations. I don't want you to get hurt."

"He *didn't* hurt me."

He studied her for a minute, doing his best to read her, but she'd put the wall up. She was good at that, shutting out people and situations so that they didn't get under her skin. This was only the second time he'd seen her cry. The other time was when she'd broken up with Duane. He would've held her then, too, but she'd blamed him for hiring the stripper that Duane had slept with two nights before their wedding. It took some time for their friendship to heal, but she'd finally acknowledged that if it hadn't happened then, it would've likely been someone else. Better to find out before the wedding than after they'd been married for a few years.

Aiden hated that he'd played a part in anything that had hurt Bia. But he knew Duane didn't love her the way she deserved to be loved. He had made his decision and he'd suffered the consequences.

"What do you think Hugh will say when I tell him?" she asked, her voice sounding unusually small.

That was a no-win question. The Hugh he knew was probably the last person who wanted a kid, especially with someone who couldn't advance his career. Bia was salt of the earth, the tenacious girl-next-door type. A woman any normal guy would fall over himself to be with. She was smart, funny and loyal to those she cared about. And he'd realized too late that he'd loved her all his life.

"I think what's more important is what you're going

to say. How you pose it to him sets the tone for his response."

She opened her mouth but closed it again, sitting back against the banquette and sighing. "I don't know what to say." She threw up her hands and let them fall into her lap.

"Tell him the truth. Cut-and-dry."

"Hi, Hugh. It's Bia Anderson. Remember me? No? Well, I was your Celebration, Texas, tour guide. Yeah, right, that one. The one your people offered to pay to be quiet. Funny thing, I'm pregnant. Yeah, that's right. You and I are going to be parents. Isn't that great news? I'm sure that's changed your mind about me—makes me so much more attractive, doesn't it?"

She rolled her eyes. "I've got nothing, Aiden."

He didn't know what to say. Usually, Bia had no problem saying what was on her mind. That's what made her a good reporter and had gotten her the top job at the paper. It was a rare circumstance that she was hesitant to make a call or speak her mind.

Of course Bia didn't know what to say. She didn't play contrived Hollywood games, which was one of the many things that Aiden loved about her. It was why this was so hard for her.

"Let's think about this," he said. "He'll probably be shocked. Be prepared for that. He might need some time to digest things before he's able to wrap his mind around it."

Bia chewed her thumbnail.

"And there's always Kristin. If he's really in love with her, this is going to make things pretty rocky for them. If he told her the tour guide story, she'll probably be pretty upset."

Bia snorted. "Heaven forbid we upset Kristin Capistrano."

Aiden held up his hands. "Hey, I'm just trying to help."

"I know you are. I'm sorry."

"There's always the possibility that they're not in love," he offered. "At least not with each other. They're filming a movie together in a few weeks. The relationship is good press. Just watch. But be prepared. He may want to keep things quiet about the baby until after the premiere. Don't be surprised."

Bia blanched. "That could be a year."

Aiden touched her arm. It was warm and soft. Her skin broke out into goose flesh on contact. He tried not to read anything into that. Instead, he reminded himself that she was pregnant. With another man's child. Somehow, that just made him feel more protective of her.

"But if he's any sort of human being, he will man-up in due time."

They sat quietly for a moment. The only sound in the kitchen was the hum of the refrigerator and the faint tick of the old-fashioned red enamel rooster clock that hung over the banquette.

"I know I've already told you this, but my dad did a great job raising me. Still, I always felt as if I were missing out because I didn't have *two* parents. A kid deserves *two* parents."

"You're preaching to the choir," Aiden said. "Your dad was more of a father to me than my own."

Aiden's dad had left the family when Aiden was nine years old. The age where every boy needs a father figure most. Aiden had spent more time at the Andersons' house hanging out with Bia's dad, Hank, than at his own. Hank had taught him how to throw a football, taken him fishing and taught him how to drive a car with a manual transmission.

"If Hugh wants to be part of the baby's life—or even better, if he wants to make a life with us—I'd be willing to consider it."

Aiden had to grit his teeth to keep from telling her not to count on it. Because Aiden knew if he said it, he'd be the bad guy. The jerk. No, he'd just keep quiet and let Hugh speak for himself. Maybe the guy would surprise everyone. Fat chance, but stranger things had happened.

"So, you'd be willing to make that sacrifice, huh? Living with the sexiest man alive? Wow, you're such a martyr, Princess. Such a martyr."

She rolled her eyes at him. Then she nestled into the crook between his arm and shoulder, that place where she fit so well.

"What's next, after you call Hugh?"

"I have a doctor's appointment Thursday."

"What time?"

"Why?"

"I'll go with you."

"You don't have to do that, Aiden."

"I know, but I want to. I'll be there for you, for moral support.

Cell phone in hand, Bia went into the bedroom and shut the door. Aiden was waiting in the kitchen. He'd said he understood that she needed to be alone when she made the call.

She wondered if he was standing guard, making sure she actually went through with it. She eyed the window, contemplating crawling out of it. But she knew that although she might be able to run away now, she'd never be able to escape the truth. She might as well make the call while Aiden was there. Besides, he would know if she chickened out. He had this uncanny way of reading her.

After what had happened with Maya yesterday, she wondered if she was too much of an open book or too transparent, but that had never been the case before. In fact, if anything, most people accused her of being too closed, too prickly. Maya's correct guess that Bia was pregnant had been a fluke. That's all there was to it. She would just need to make sure Maya didn't say anything to anyone else. She would go talk to her again later that week.

But right now, first things first. She needed to make the call.

Her hand was shaking as she picked up the phone and pulled up Hugh's number in her contacts. She wanted to laugh at the irony—how many women would pay to have Hugh Newman's private number, to hear his voice over the line? But this was a call that she dreaded more than any she'd ever placed.

She stared at her phone screen for a moment, at the ten-digit number and the small thumbnail photo of Hugh's face in the top left-hand corner of the page.

Her finger hovered over the call button, but she was paralyzed. She couldn't press it.

Maybe she should send him a certified letter?
Right.

That was the big chicken's way out. She didn't
know what address to send it to, and, even if she did,
she had no guarantee he would be the one to open
it—certified letter or not. The rules that applied to
the little people didn't always hold true for people like
Hugh and his set.

"Oh, for God's sake," she muttered under her
breath. "Just call and get it over with."

Her shaking finger came down hard on the call
button. She held the phone to her ear before she could
change her mind. For a few seconds, there was no
sound and she was just about ready to pull the phone
back and make sure she'd actually dialed the number. But before she could, she heard the ring, distant
and tinny.

Bia paced the length of the room as the phone
rang…four times before an automated attendant picked
up. A generic, robotic voice informed her, "The person at this number is not available. Please leave your
name and number after the tone."

Not even a promise that the person would call
back at his convenience. But the one thing that robo-
attendant did get right was that Hugh was not available—not physically or emotionally.

Bia hung up. No way was she going to leave such
a personal message on his voice mail. For that matter, she didn't even know if the number still belonged
to him.

She slumped down on the bed and stared at the
phone's flat black screen.

Now what?

She should've known that he wouldn't pick up. Why would he? It wasn't as if he'd been waiting for her to call. She half expected to get a call back from his assistant, the one who had offered to pay her off—

That gave her an idea.

She brought up her call log and scrolled through it. Sure enough, there was the assistant's California number. What if she called him and asked him to have Hugh call her back? That it was a matter of great importance... Yeah, but there was no way she would make it past the guard dog without revealing what the call was about.

Wait a minute.... She stood up. Recently the paper had run a story on a phone app that manufactured *disposable* cell phone numbers, but for the life of her she couldn't remember the name of the company. She hadn't written the story. She'd edited it and probably seventy-five other articles since then. Still, she knew how she could find it. She called up the phone's browser and typed "how to disguise your cell number." The first link at the top of the list was for the company the paper had profiled.

She downloaded the app, got a disposable number with a California area code and dialed Hugh again.

Miracle of miracles, he picked up on the second ring.

"Hugh Newman."

It was now or never.

"Hugh, this is Bia Anderson. From Celebration, Texas."

There was complete silence on the other end of the line.

"Please don't hang up. I don't want anything from you, but I do have to tell you that I'm pregnant and you're the father."

She heard him exhale. At least he was still there. He'd gotten the message.

"This is a bad time." His voice was heavy with annoyance. "I'll call you back."

Chapter Three

The message was waiting for Maya when she logged into the Facebook page she had set up for Maya's Chocolates.

Hello, Maya! I'm so happy to learn that you are opening a shop in the United States. I had the pleasure of tasting your chocolate almost thirty years ago when I was in St. Michel. And sure if it hasn't been haunting me ever since. I will be in the Dallas area next week and I will stop in and say hello. Charles Jordan

While she wasn't inundated with fan mail, she did get a piece now and again. There was nothing out of the ordinary about the message. Except for the line, *And sure if it hasn't been haunting me ever since.*

Something about the turn of those words had been haunting *her*.

They called to mind a man she had known long ago. Actually, it was about twenty-nine or thirty years ago that Ian had been in her life. *Huh.* Another coincidence. But he'd disappeared just as fast as he'd appeared and swept her off her feet.

The memory weighed heavily on her heart.

Maya clicked on Charles Jordan's name, eager to see if she could find any more information on his profile page. But he didn't have a photo of himself for his profile picture. Instead, he had a generic picture of a snowcapped mountain range.

The page had been created a couple of years ago, but there hadn't been much activity. There were no other pictures and his list of friends was not open for the public to view.

Maya grappled with an uneasy feeling. Mr. Jordan's words, *And sure if it hasn't been haunting me ever since,* rang in her mind. In her head, she'd heard them in Ian's voice. They were as clear as if he'd spoken them an hour ago.

Ian Brannigan. Her Irishman. Her love.

He'd simply left one day, never called and never come back. For a long time, she had been so numb she could barely function. Then she had gotten angry. That's when she'd called his family in Dublin for contact information. Even though several years had passed by that point, Maya had been ready for an explanation. That's when the real heartbreak started. His mother had delivered the sad news that Ian was dead. He'd died in an accident on his way home from France.

That's why he'd never called. That's why the future she'd hoped they would have together never happened. That's why she'd never been able to fall in love with anyone else.

Ian had taken the largest part of her heart with him on that cold October day. And the rest of it had died nine months later when the nurse took their baby girl from her arms and whisked her away.

She was barely eighteen years old. She wasn't married, and the baby's father had obviously abandoned them. Or at least that's what everyone had thought then. But he hadn't abandoned them. It was both crushing and vindicating to learn that Ian hadn't abandoned them. He hadn't even known that she was carrying his child when he'd kissed her goodbye that last time.

However, that didn't change the fact that Maya was an unwed teenage mother, a disgrace to her family.

Her mother and grandmother made arrangements for her to go away for a while. She was allowed to come back after the baby was born. That way no one would ever be the wiser, the family name would be saved and they could hold their heads up high.

Maya knew that she could hope all she wanted to, but this Charles Jordan, no matter the imagined similarities, was not her Ian Brannigan.

Once again, Maya clicked on the message balloon icon and reread Charles Jordan's message. She was just about to type a quick reply when she heard a knock at the front door.

She wasn't expecting anyone, but she made her way

from the kitchen to the front of the store to see who was calling. To her surprise, it was Bia.

Things had ended on such a horrific note the other day that Maya quite honestly thought it would be a very long time before she heard from Bia again.

She gave a friendly wave to test the waters. To her relief, Bia waved back, even if she wasn't smiling. The wave had to be a good sign. At least she hoped it was. She would find out soon enough, she thought, as she opened the door and greeted Bia with the warmest American greeting she could muster. She didn't give her the customary French greeting, a kiss on each cheek. She had a feeling she needed to tread lightly.

"Hello!" Maya said. "I am so happy to see you. I wasn't expecting you after what happened yesterday. I'm so sorry, Bia. But I'm so glad you've come back."

Interesting, Maya pondered. *First, I'm thinking of Ian, and now Bia shows up. Perhaps the universe is trying to tell me something.*

But given this second chance and how easily Bia was frightened off yesterday, Maya was determined to take things slowly. She would build the relationship before she broke the news.

"I'm sorry I overreacted yesterday," Bia said. "But I have to ask—and I need an honest answer—how did you know I'm pregnant?"

Maya shrugged. "Intuition, I suppose."

"So, it was a lucky guess," Bia replied.

"If that's what you would prefer to call it. Shall we go into the kitchen where we can sit down and talk?

I'll make you a cup of hot chocolate. You need your calcium."

Bia held her ground. "First, I need your word that you will not tell a soul about this. If you think the media went crazy when they thought Hugh and I were seeing each other, this will blow up in both of our faces. Especially after he lied about the nature of our... *acquaintance.*"

Maya's brow creased in a look of what seemed to be genuine concern. "Of course you have my word. This is a very private matter. I want you to know that I am here for you. I promise I will not do anything to put you or your baby in emotional jeopardy."

"I need to ask you something, and, again, you must give me an honest answer."

Maya nodded. "Please. Anything."

"Have you ever said anything to the press about my previous relationship with Hugh Newman?"

Maya recoiled and looked genuinely shocked by the question. A good sign, as far as Bia was concerned. Still, she had to look Maya in the eyes as she asked. Just as Maya had a sixth sense about people, Bia could intuit when people were lying. Bia's gut was telling her that Maya was telling the truth.

Maya put her right hand over her heart. "I swear to you. I have not said one word. I did see the two of you together at the Doctor's Ball, but I would never gossip about you. I would swear this on my mother's and grandmother's graves."

"Thank you, Maya. I believe you. And I believe that you will keep your word about not talking to a soul other than me about my current situation."

Maya held up her right hand. "I solemnly swear. Now, let's have some hot chocolate. Yes?"

Maya's version of hot chocolate was like nothing Bia had ever tasted before. It was nearly as thick as melted chocolate and tasted so good it curled Bia's toes.

Le chocolat chaud, Maya called it.

Bia called it divine. She had to pace herself to keep from gulping it. To that end, she tried to employ some of the tasting principles that Maya had taught her yesterday. She sipped the drink and let the warm liquid flow over her tongue.

"Umm, is that cinnamon I taste?"

Maya nodded.

"There's something else I can't quite identify...." Bia closed her eyes and rolled the liquid around on her palate.

"I added a tiny dash of cayenne and a few flecks of *fleur de sel.*"

"Salt and pepper," Bia noted wryly.

Maya laughed her laugh that seemed to set Bia at ease, and the world seemed a little brighter. Bia didn't have many close girlfriends. She'd always related better to guys. She simply didn't enjoy the drama that always seemed to go hand in hand with women. On occasion, Bia had been accused of being too direct— one of the qualities that made her a good reporter, of course. But Maya hadn't been offended by Bia's head-on approach. Come to think of it, Maya had been pretty direct herself yesterday.

At least they understood each other.

"Have you had a chance to think about what you're going to do?" Maya asked.

"About?"

"The baby, of course."

"I'm having this baby. I'm twenty-eight years old. I can handle it. I was adopted. Actually, I just found out a few months ago, just before my adoptive father passed away. I had a good childhood despite my adoptive mother dying when I was five. Her husband—my father—never remarried. So, essentially, I grew up without a mother. My father was very good to me, but I can't help but wonder lately why my birth mother didn't want me. I have no information about her. I'm not sure whether I should go digging or not."

"I'm sure she would be thrilled to connect with you," Maya said. "At least you'll never know until you try."

"What? Is that your intuition speaking? I can't be *sure* that she would be thrilled. I mean, she gave me up. For all I know, she might have a family of her own. They might not know about me. I might be that unwelcome surprise from her past popping up at the most inopportune time."

"But you can't be certain of that, either. For all you know, you could be missing out on a second chance at family."

Bia shrugged. "But there's no way to know that for certain."

"There's no way to know that you won't walk out of here and get hit by a car, but the likelihood of disaster is slim. What I'm saying is, if you are open to having your birth mother in your life— Are you?"

Bia nodded.

"Good, then keep an open mind. I think it would be especially important to meet her now that you have a little one on the way. For that matter, have you talked to the father?"

Bia grimaced. "I spoke to Hugh briefly. Told him the situation. He told me it wasn't a good time to talk and that he would call me back. But he hasn't. I don't really expect him to."

Thoughtfully, Maya ran her finger around the rim of her demitasse cup. "At the risk of—how do you say it—sticking my nose in where it doesn't belong? Hugh Newman may be the father of your child, but he is not the right man for you."

"Story of my life," Bia murmured.

"Make no mistake, there is someone out there for you. He is already in your life. You simply must learn to see what is right in front of you."

Thursday afternoon, Aiden was leaning against his car, which was parked in the lot of Bia's doctor, waiting for her to arrive.

When she finally did, she got out of her car and said, "Aiden, you're here? I told you not to come."

Her words said one thing, but the way she said them confirmed that he'd been right to not let her face her first doctor's appointment alone.

"I thought you might want some moral support."

She smiled. "I'm a big girl, Aiden. I can handle this." Then she hugged him and whispered, "Thanks for being here. I don't know what I'd do without you."

He put his arm around her as they walked from the

parking lot into the lobby. To the untrained eye, they probably looked like a happy couple eager to get the lowdown on their first child. He could play that role, especially if Hugh wasn't going to.

"Have you heard from Hugh?"

She stiffened, pulled away ever so slightly. "No. But he knows. And he knows how to reach me and where to find me."

"Ball's in his court, then," Aiden said as he opened the office door and stood back so Bia could enter.

Two other women, both obviously further along in their pregnancies than Bia, waited. Both had men with them, and Aiden was instantly reassured that he'd made the right decision to come along. No doubt Bia would've soldiered through on her own, but she shouldn't have to face this alone.

"I'm going to go sign in," she said. "Go ahead and sit down and I'll be right back...with mountains of paperwork, no doubt."

He sat down in a chair across from one of the couples. The woman looked as if she were smuggling a basketball under her dress. Aiden looked away, trying to imagine what Bia would look like that far along. She'd be gorgeous.

"Is this your first child?" the woman asked.

"Uhh..." Obviously, she'd caught him staring. But she didn't seem annoyed or put off. Her husband was reading the newspaper and didn't seem to notice that Aiden had been scoping out his wife's belly. Good thing.

Rather than dive headlong into an explanation, he simply said, "Yes. It is." After all, he hadn't been party to another pregnancy before. She hadn't asked him if he was the father.

"Congratulations to you and your wife." She beamed at him and clasped her hands over her belly. "You have some exciting months ahead of you. Years actually. Kids will change your life."

Yep. So I've heard.

He nodded. Pondering the thought of Bia as his wife as she walked toward him, clipboard in hand. She stirred in him a feeling that was equal parts primal lust and Cro-Magnon protective. He'd always been attracted to her. Hell, if he were honest with himself, he'd admit that he'd always been in love with Bia Anderson.

He just hadn't been able to admit it to himself until his roommate Duane had taken an interest in her at that party their freshman year of college. He couldn't remember who threw the party or what the occasion was, but he would never forget what she looked like standing there kissing Duane. At that moment, something inside him shifted and snapped into place. By the time he finally woke up and realized what had been under his nose all his life, she was off-limits. So, Aiden had settled for a friendship because it was better to have her in his life under restricted terms than not at all.

Duane never had treated her right. He used to think Aiden was joking when he said things like, "Too bad you saw her first, man," and "If you don't treat her right, I'm going to take her away from you." They would all laugh and then Aiden would try to get interested in some other girl. Inevitably, those relationships never worked out. Bia thought he was the world's biggest player. And he would laugh it off and say, "None of them compare to you."

And she thought he was joking.

He'd come here, taken the *Catering to Dallas* gig, to be near her. Things had been going well between them. The best way to describe them was platonic with chemistry. They were solid, and he wanted to take things slowly, let the relationship develop naturally. And then Hugh Newman came to town, proving it had been a dumb idea to take things slowly. It had been a grave miscalculation to not move at the speed of Hugh.

As Bia sat down in the chair next to him, the nurse called back the woman who had been talking to him—Sandra something...he hadn't caught her last name.

"Good luck, you two," she said as she and her husband walked toward the waiting nurse. "This truly is the beginning of the happiest time of your lives."

"Thanks," he said. "Nice talking to you."

"Making friends, already?" Bia murmured. "You are such a flirt."

"I wasn't flirting," he said. "I was just being cordial. They think we're married."

Bia rolled her eyes at him. "Obviously they don't know who they're dealing with. You, with your commitment allergy. I'm surprised that you didn't run screaming for the door after she said that."

"That hurts, B. Like a stab right through the heart. You know I'm committed to you. You're the only woman in the world for me."

She made a *tsking* sound and gave his arm a little shove and muttered, "Spare me." Then she refocused on her paperwork, but she was smiling as she wrote. He noticed that she had left the spot on the form that asked for the name of the child's father blank. He thought about asking her what, if anything, she was going to tell the doctor, but he decided to wait until after the appointment.

"Obviously, we make a good couple," he said. "We fooled them."

"Yeah, well, welcome to the grand illusion. When a man and a woman come to an OB-GYN office together, they're usually involved. We just happen to be part of the slim minority who aren't."

"We should stop pretending and get married, Bia."

She didn't look up from her paperwork, but she laughed. "Says he who is allergic to monogamy. Don't joke about marriage, Aiden. Some things are sacred."

"Who says I'm joking?"

This time she pierced him with an exasperated look. "Settle down and quit distracting me. I have to finish filling out this paperwork before they call me back." She started writing again. "Besides, you don't have a ring. You can't propose to a woman without a ring."

He pretended to pat down his pockets, looking for a ring. "Touché. You got me there."

She did have him. Heart and soul. He'd never realized just how deep his feelings for her ran until recently. If only he could tell her without the comedy routine. Easier said than done.

A few minutes later, the nurse called Bia back.

Aiden followed her to the door. "I haven't finished my paperwork," she said.

"That's not a problem," the nurse said. "Maybe your husband could finish filling it out for you while we're getting you ready to see the doctor?"

"He's not my husband," Bia said.

The nurse smiled, and she looked from Bia to Aiden. "Well, okay. Do you want him to come back with you?"

She asked the question as if he would be entering a restricted-access area.

"Oh…" Bia glanced at Aiden and then back to the nurse. "I guess he can wait out here. Would you mind, Aiden?"

"Probably a good idea." The nurse smiled at him and took a step closer. "The first visit is always the longest. The doctor will want to go over the genetic history of your family and that of the baby's father. It will take a while, but if you'd like to wait, let's get you something to drink—would you like coffee? A soda?"

He felt Bia pull away from him emotionally. She had a strange look on her face, and he wasn't sure why. Probably just nerves. This was suddenly becoming very real, and she wanted to go back there alone.

"Aiden, I'm fine. Why don't you go back to work? There's no sense in you waiting."

"I don't mind. You might need me."

She softened, but the wall was still in place. That same wall that kept him a safe, platonic distance away. "It was so sweet of you to come. But really, I'm fine. Please go."

* * *

The nurse left Bia standing there while she fetched coffee for Aiden.

How utterly unprofessional. If the woman hadn't been wielding needles—once she'd made sure Aiden was comfortable—Bia might have schooled her on the meaning of a proper time and a place for everything. When a woman was walking through the door for her first obstetric appointment, it definitely *wasn't* the time or the place for the nurse to flirt with the man who had accompanied the pregnant woman. Just because he wasn't her husband didn't mean he was fair game.

Aiden seemed absolutely clueless to the effect he had on women. Sometimes she wondered if that cluelessness was more a case of playing dumb like a fox. *I'll be so disarmingly charming and oblivious to how gorgeous I am and see how many women I can lure in.*

He did it all the time, whether he was cognizant of it or not, and it made Bia crazy. He dated women long enough for them to fall for him and then he got the heck out of Dodge.

Since college, Bia had witnessed the never-ending parade of bimbos who were crazy for him. In fact, Bia was willing to wager that Aiden could give Hugh a run for the number of women he was stringing along.

The nurse, for example. The pregnant woman in the lobby… Well, that probably wasn't the same thing. She looked like she was about to pop and her husband was sitting right there. Still, the pregnant one could be filed in a subcategory of looking but not touching, which was fine.... Actually, it all was fine. She had no claim on him.

Since Aiden had moved to Celebration to work on *Catering to Dallas,* there hadn't been as many women. But he hadn't been there that long, and work kept him pretty busy. What little free time he had, he tended to spend with Bia. She'd come to think of herself as his safe haven.

They'd been friends for so long that she prided herself on being the person with whom he could hang out without fear of her getting the wrong idea or coming back with expectations.

That's not to say that Bia didn't find him attractive. For God's sake, he was probably *the* sexiest man she'd ever met. Sexier than Hugh Newman, hands-down sexier than Duane. A big part of what made him sexy to her was that she knew all the facets of Aiden. She'd seen the soul behind the one-hundred-watt smile and the smoldering I-want-you-now glances.

If there wasn't so much history between them, so much water under the bridge, he probably would've had her flat on her back a long time ago—and much faster than Hugh Newman. The difference was Hugh hadn't mattered.

A piece of her soul would die if she lost Aiden.

They hadn't gotten to this point overnight. The wine of their friendship had been maturing for years. And it had withstood nearly insurmountable mishaps.

When she'd found out Duane had slept with the stripper that Aiden had hired, she'd blamed Aiden. She had called off the wedding and sent Duane packing, but she blamed Aiden for enabling his friend. *Two nights before the wedding. Two nights.*

She'd had to cancel everything: the church, the caterer, the guests, the wedding hall. Her father had lost a good fifteen grand thanks to one night of someone else's utter stupidity.

The only reason she and Aiden were still talking today—and were as close as they'd become—was because Aiden had proven that Duane's actions had hurt him almost as much as they'd hurt Bia. Aiden had cut ties with Duane, but he hadn't left Bia alone until she'd accepted his apology. Once they'd cleared that hurdle, Aiden had never left. But they'd also agreed to never talk about the Duane–stripper fiasco again.

There had been a couple of times when Bia had been tempted to test the bounds of their friendship…to quench her curiosity about how his lips would taste… or how his hands would feel on her body…how he would feel inside her body.

She shivered at the thought and pulled the paper gown closed at her neck. But he was her friend. She shouldn't even go there mentally. Especially when she was sitting in a doctor's office pregnant with another man's child.

She took a deep breath and exhaled away the inappropriate thoughts about her friend. Her *friend.*

Even if she wouldn't allow herself to cross the line with Aiden, she was allowed to resent Nurse Flirty for so brazenly flirting with him. *Yeah, honey, you may pack a scary syringe, but if you want to get to him, you've gotta go through me.*

Finally, the doctor knocked on the door. He entered

the room, accompanied by—*oh, joy*—Nurse Flirty, who immediately turned her back on Bia and busied herself at the counter on the far wall.

"Hello, Ms. Anderson," said Dr. Porter. "It's nice to meet you."

He washed his hands and then shook Bia's hand before picking up her file.

"This is your first pregnancy?" he asked.

"It is," she said.

"I notice you left the space on the form for the father's name blank. Would you mind telling me why?"

Well, yes, she minded. She really didn't want to talk about him.

"He may or may not want to be a part of the child's life," Bia said. "That remains to be seen. So, until I know, I would prefer to leave him out of it."

The doctor rubbed his chin. "Regardless of whether or not he is part of the child's life, the baby will have his genes. It's important that we know as much about him as possible for your child's health. I'd prefer for his name to be part of the records."

A slow burn started in the pit of Bia's stomach. Maybe it was hormones; maybe it was this particular doctor's office. She'd chosen it because it was close rather than trekking all the way to Dallas for her checkups, which, according to everything she'd read, would be much more frequent than her annual checkup. She might need to rethink this decision since she wasn't feeling very comfortable.

"Dr. Porter, the baby's father is prominent, a celebrity who isn't local, and all communication thus far indicates that he doesn't want to be part of the child's life. I will do my due diligence and gather his medical history, but I'd like to keep his name out of the official records."

Bia noticed that the nurse was now facing her, unapologetically taking in every word of their conversation. Bia frowned at her, and she turned back around.

"Well…it's not optimal," Dr. Porter said. "But as you wish."

There was a knock at the door and another nurse stuck her head in. "Excuse me, Dr. Porter. May I see you for a moment? I'm sorry to interrupt, but there's an important matter."

"Certainly." He looked irritated, but he said, "Excuse me, Ms. Anderson. I'll be right back."

When the door had closed, the nurse turned back around to Bia. "I'm sorry—I just have to ask. Is Hugh Newman the father?"

"I beg your pardon?" Bia said.

"Is Hugh Newman the father of your baby?"

"You've got to be kidding me." Bia said.

"It's just that I knew you looked familiar and when you said the baby's father was a celebrity, I remembered seeing you on *XYZ* with Hugh. He is such a hottie. I'm such a fan. Don't worry—I won't tell anyone. You know, with HIPAA laws and all, I could get into big trouble if I told anyone."

Was this some sort of joke? Was she being *punked* for one of those reality television shows? Because this was the most surreal doctor visit she'd ever experienced in her life.

First, Nurse Flirty all but gave her number to Aiden

and now she was prying into a subject that Bia had clearly stated was a closed subject.

"It is him, isn't it?" the nurse said.

"Umm…I have to go," Bia said, getting to her feet.

"Dr. Porter isn't finished with your appointment yet. He'll be right back."

"That's okay. I'll make other arrangements. I need to go back to work. Would you please step outside so I can get dressed?"

"I'll go find Dr. Porter for you. It will only take a moment. Please don't go anywhere."

However, in less than a minute, Bia was dressed and in the lobby, where Aiden was still sipping the cup of coffee Nurse Flirty had fetched him.

"That didn't take long," he said. "What's wrong?"

"I'm leaving," Bia said and quietly let herself out the front door before the reception staff realized what was happening. She would call later, but now she needed to get out of there and rethink her plan. She'd call her doctor in Dallas and make the trip if that's what it took to maintain her privacy. Actually, she wondered, was privacy a thing of the past post-Hugh?

"What is going on?" Aiden repeated once they were in the parking lot.

"This is obviously not the right doctor for me," she said. "I didn't want to name the baby's father and they took issue with it."

"I noticed you left it blank," Aiden said. "But shouldn't that be your call?"

"You'd think. Actually, the doctor accepted it. I made the mistake of saying that the father was a celebrity who didn't want to be involved, and after Dr. Porter left the room for a moment, your girlfriend asked me point-blank if the father was Hugh. And she kept pressing it. So, I walked out."

"My girlfriend?"

"The nurse who got you all tucked in with juice and cookies while I was waiting."

"She's not even my type."

"She's female. I thought that was your type."

"Are you jealous?"

Maybe a little. Bia looked away. "No. I'm irritated."

"I don't blame you." He reached out and touched her chin with his finger, gently turning her head so that she was looking at him. "I'd be mad, too. That was pretty audacious of her."

Bia glanced up at him. The way he was standing so close to her, with one hip braced against the car, touching her and gazing at her so intently, she actually thought for a delusional moment that he might lean in and kiss her.

Her gaze fell to his lips, and she was suddenly a little too warm. Given the way everything had been imploding around her, she knew better than to go… there. As tempting as it might have been. She obviously wasn't herself. She took a step back.

"I'll say. I'll call my doctor in Dallas tomorrow—"

Her phone rang.

Bia sighed as she fished it out of her purse, fully expecting the display to show Dr. Porter's number. She had no intention of answering, but when she pulled out her phone to silence it, a number with a California area code lit up the screen.

Chapter Four

Bia let the call go to voice mail and waited until she got home to pick up the message. She wasn't about to have this conversation with Hugh in a doctor's parking lot. Plus, there was a very good chance that Hugh hadn't placed the call himself because it wasn't his number. Or at least not the number where Bia had reached him.

She was right. The person who had left the message was a guy named Steve Luciano, Hugh's attorney. It stung down to the quick that Hugh couldn't even be bothered to call her back himself.

The slippery jerk. How could she have been such a poor judge of character to let herself get blinded by a handsome face and lines he'd probably used on dozens of women to get exactly what he wanted?

The first thing she did after she picked up Luciano's message was call the office and tell them that she was going to be back later than she'd expected.

Then she went into the kitchen and made herself a cup of tea. She had to get her head together. Obviously she wasn't thinking clearly. She'd blown up at Maya in the middle of their interview the other day. Today she'd walked out of a doctor's appointment. Normally, she was stronger than that. Strong enough to resist the need to put someone like Nurse Flirty in her place.

She didn't know whether to blame it on the hormones or if the unexpected pregnancy had completely knocked her for a loop. Either way, she had to get a grip on this situation. Ignoring it wasn't going to change it.

For Bia, a cup of tea was a soothing ritual. Boiling the water, measuring out the tea leaves, letting the brew steep—all the steps forced her to slow down and take a breath. She set out the bone china cup that had belonged to her grandmother, probably the one person other than Aiden who had understood her best. After her mother had died, Bia used to spend summers with her Grandma Dee. It was always a magical time. They would read books together and have tea parties.

Grandma Dee was the one who had taught her how to brew tea and how emotionally healing it could be. When she drank from her grandmother's teacup, it was almost as if she were having tea with her even though she'd been gone more than eight years now.

Once the tea was ready, Bia took her cup, a piece of the chocolate from the box that Maya had given her the other day and her phone out to the table on the redbrick patio area in the backyard. When she was settled, she debated whether or not she would even return Steve Luciano's call.

It didn't take a genius to figure out that Luciano had called to set the tone—to intimidate. Maybe even to scare her off so that the situation might magically disappear in a *poof* of second thoughts since the lawyer was involved.

Well, she didn't like this any more than Hugh did, but it wasn't going to go away. They had to deal with it. As Bia took a bite of chocolate—this piece tasted like it was infused with lavender—she let it melt on her tongue and then took a small sip of her Earl Grey and let the flavors mingle. By the time she'd finished the piece of chocolate, she felt a little more like herself.

It made her regret how she'd blown up at Maya the other day. Especially thinking about how Maya couldn't have been nicer when Bia had gone in the next day to talk to her. In the same spirit that she hadn't run away from that unpleasant situation, she needed to handle Hugh the right way, too. To do this right, she needed to start by calling back Mr. Steve Luciano.

She played his message. His voice had a no-nonsense tone with just a hint of intimidation. The message was pretty straightforward: "Hello, Ms. Anderson, this is Steve Luciano, legal representative for Mr. Newman. Would you please call me back at your earliest convenience?"

At my earliest convenience? How genteel.

She fortified herself with the last sip of tea, took a deep breath and hit Redial. When a receptionist picked up, it suddenly hit her that she might not be able to get him right on the line.

"Yes, hello, this is Bia Anderson returning Steve Luciano's call."

She hoped that they wouldn't have to play several rounds of telephone tag before they finally connected. Lord knew this wasn't a call Bia wanted to take at the office, but she certainly couldn't wait around the house for him to call her back. If he wasn't available, she'd tell him he had to call her back after seven o'clock.

"Yes, Ms. Anderson, Mr. Luciano is expecting your call. Please hold and I will put you right through."

Oh. Well...okay.

"Thank you," Bia said in her steadiest voice.

Luciano was on the line in less than thirty seconds. Bia imagined that might be a record.

"Hello, Ms. Anderson. Steve Luciano here. Thank you for calling me back."

Did I have a choice? "You're welcome."

"Let me start by saying that Mr. Newman is deeply concerned about this situation and he appreciates your discretion, that you kept this quiet. However, I must admit that I'm surprised you contacted Mr. Newman again since you refused our generous offer a couple of months ago. When I offered to pay you for your... tour guide services. Have you reconsidered my initial offer?"

Bia was a bit taken aback. "I haven't reconsidered anything, Mr. Luciano. I don't want his money. I'm pregnant. It was simply a courtesy call to Hugh to advise him of the situation. And it appears that he's handed me off to you."

"I see. As I said, please know that Mr. Newman appreciates your discretion in this matter. He asked me to convey that he wants nothing but the best for you and your child—"

"His child," Bia corrected.

"Of course, you must understand that we have no proof that he is, in fact, the father. Not that I'm doubting you, of course."

"Of course. I suppose you'll just have to take my word on it."

"I see. Mr. Newman is very busy right now—"

"As am I," Bia said. "So why don't we cut to the chase?"

"Of course."

Of course. I see. I see. Of course. It was all a bit grating.

"I suppose that would be where you come in," said Luciano. "Exactly how much do you need to make this problem disappear?"

Bia stood and began pacing. "Excuse me? What exactly are you suggesting?"

"I'm not suggesting anything."

"Listen, Mr. Luciano. The only reason I called was to do the decent thing and let Hugh know that he is going to be a father. I'm going to have this child. Surely you weren't suggesting otherwise."

"Of course not. But I am strongly advising that you think twice before you try to extort money out of Mr. Newman."

She stopped. "Wait just a minute. You were the one who asked me how much I needed to make this go away."

"Yes, Ms. Anderson. If you must know, you are not unique in your claim. Last year alone three women claimed they were carrying babies fathered by Mr. Newman."

The bastard. Is he out there scattering his seed across the land?

"I'm sorry to hear that. Whether he's the father or not, there are innocent children involved. Children who deserve parents who love them and did not choose to be in the middle of a battle."

Luciano was silent on the other end of the line. He was probably employing the "he who speaks first loses" tactic.

"Let me make this easy for you and Mr. Newman. All I want to know is whether he wants to be a part of this child's life or not."

"Ms. Anderson, as I said before, I can't answer that question until we have DNA proof that the child is in fact his."

"Then I'll take that as a *no*. Tell Mr. Newman he has nothing to worry about. I've done my duty with this phone call. As far as I'm concerned, he is waiving any and all parental rights. Tell him the baby and I will be perfectly fine without him."

When she hung up, a huge sob escaped her throat. Only then did she realize that tears were streaming down her cheeks. She sat at the patio table and put her head in her hands and sobbed. The tears weren't for herself, but for this child, who had not been conceived in love and had been rejected even before he or she had come into the world.

"That's not a very good start to life, little one," she whispered.

She sat up and wrapped her arms around her middle, protectively hugging her unborn child. She stayed like that until she'd shed the last tear.

Then it was almost as if a switch had flipped inside her. They would be fine. She and her baby would be perfectly fine on their own. This child may not have been conceived in love, but she would love the child enough for two parents. Sure, if she'd had the choice she would've brought a child into the world under different circumstances, but this was the hand they'd been dealt.

She would make darn sure that she made the most of it. As she sat there, looking at the trees and flowers in the yard, landscaping that her father had done—her father, a man who was no blood relation to her, a man who had raised her on his own in the name of all that was decent and kind and right. She suddenly realized that she was probably better off having been raised by someone who wanted her rather than resented by someone whose DNA she shared.

No doubt, it would be a challenge being a single parent, but she would pay forward what her father had done for her.

She was going to be a mother.

"I'm having a baby." She said the words aloud, letting the true meaning sink in and flow through her.

This baby would be loved and wanted and cherished.

Bia went into the office on Saturday to catch up. She didn't mind being there alone. In fact, she liked the peace and quiet. She could leave her door open and lose herself in her work—something she hadn't been able to do in ages.

After pouring herself a cup of coffee and turning on the television in her office to an all-news channel, she settled at her desk and turned down the volume on the TV with the remote so that she could barely hear it.

It was the best kind of company for a day like this—quiet when she needed to concentrate, yet she could look up and glimpse what was going on in the world when she wanted a quick break. Even though she loved to be in the thick of the newsroom hubbub, she loved the occasional day of solitude. Right now, with all that had been going on, it was especially good to have time to breathe, time to regroup and center herself.

She took out her notes for the business profile on Maya's Chocolates. She needed to write that story first and get it ready to go for the next edition. Amid all the craziness, she hadn't sent a photographer over to get a picture of Maya.

Good grief. She had to get her act together. Since she was going to be a mother, it wasn't going to get any easier than it was right now. The carefree days of thinking only of herself and her schedule were numbered. That was okay. It was part of this next chapter of her life. Her hand found her still-flat belly and rested there. She'd make it work.

She opened a fresh document on her computer and poised her fingers on the keyboard. Usually by now she would have composed the story lede; she would've written it in her head so that it flowed onto the page when she was ready to begin the article. But since interviewing Maya, she hadn't had a sane moment to rub two thoughts together, much less compose the first paragraph of a news story.

The history of the business was what immediately leaped out at Bia. The beauty of how it had been handed down through the generations—from mother to daughter to granddaughter seemed like a great way to start...maybe working in the imagery of the copper pots....

Bia's gaze focused on the TV as she moved words around in her head. There was so much happening on the screen. The ticker of news snippets below the anchor, the collection of small boxes highlighting the other stories—it all amounted to the visual equivalent of white noise: such an overload of info that none of it registered...until the ticker at the bottom changed to a breaking news alert that nearly made her heart stop. *Actor Hugh Newman dead at age thirty-five.*

Bia blinked at the screen, unsure if she'd read it right. She grabbed the remote and, with shaking hands, used the DVR control to pause the news program. She stood up at her desk so she could see the television better and rewound the show to the place where the breaking news alert had begun.

She pushed Play. Her vision became white and fuzzy around the edges as her fear was confirmed. Hugh was dead...car accident in the Hollywood Hills...alone in the car. No further details available at the moment....

* * *

Aiden's condo was less than a quarter mile from the paper's office.

"Are you home?" she asked.

Thank goodness he was.

In a fog, she grabbed her purse and keys, locked the office and set out on foot to go to the only person she could talk to about this.

Hugh wasn't exactly her favorite person these days, but she would've never wished something as tragic as this to happen to him. He was only thirty-five years old. He couldn't be dead. He should've had more than half his life ahead of him.

It was surreal. And cruel. Before she walked out of the building that housed the office, she stood with her arms crossed, digging her fingernails into the flesh of her arms, hoping to wake herself up. Desperately hoping and praying that this was all a bad dream and she would wake up and realize everything was fine.

She cut across the parking lot behind the office building. She noticed that the hose that had always seemed out of place in an office parking lot had unraveled and was leaking again. She'd have to tell her boss, Drew. He rarely came into the office during the week anymore, but sometimes he washed his car in the parking lot on weekends—despite how he could afford to take it to a professional to get it cleaned and detailed. He was that kind of hands-on guy, she thought as she walked through the grass that separated the lot from the sidewalk. She was doing her best to keep her mind on anything but the bombshell she'd just heard.

Hugh is dead.

Dead.

She felt as if she sort of floated along the path. She couldn't cry. She couldn't feel her legs, either. She reached up and swiped at her face to make sure the numbness that had overridden the rest of her body hadn't caused her to not feel the tears. But her face was dry.

She was on autopilot, driven by a force that she couldn't control. But she must not have been completely out of her mind, because about three quarters of the way to Aiden's place, she became cognizant of a car driving very slowly behind her. She glanced back at the nondescript white sedan. She didn't recognize it, and the way the sunlight was reflecting off the windshield, she couldn't make out the driver's features.

Celebration, Texas, was probably one of the safest places in the Southwest. She'd never been hesitant to get out and walk, and, in fact, if she had the choice to walk rather than drive, she walked. It really was her preferred mode of transportation. Still, it unnerved her to have this car poking along behind her.

The street leading to Aiden's house was two blocks off Main Street and mostly residential. There were people outside mowing lawns and washing cars; kids were playing ball in one of the yards across the street. If the person following her was up to no good, there would be plenty of witnesses and people to come to her aid.

Even so, when she got to the next driveway, she walked a few steps up the driveway toward the house and stopped, fishing her cell phone out of her purse. If the person was following her, he or she would ei-

ther stop, too—but she would be at a safe distance—
or would drive on by.

The car slowed to a stop at the foot of the driveway.
Bia quickly dialed Aiden's number. Maybe the person
was lost. Maybe he just needed directions.

The person sat in the idling car. A red pickup truck
pulled up behind the white car, honked and finally
zoomed around it.

"Hello?" Aiden's voice sounded on the other end
of the line. Still, the car sat there.

"Hey, it's me," Bia said. "Strange thing. A car's
been following me. I'm only about two houses away
from you. Would you mind coming outside just in case
I need some help?"

"Do you want to stay on the line with me or hang
up and call nine-one-one?"

Someone opened the passenger side of the white
car.

So, there was more than one person. Her heart thudded. So much for the earlier numbness. Her mind flit-
ted to Hugh and the tragedy, and she couldn't help
wonder if somehow this had something to do with
him. But what?

The person who got out of the passenger side of
the car was a small man who looked vaguely familiar.
The minute he said, "Bia Anderson"—it was more of
a statement than a question—she knew exactly who
had been tailing her.

It was the same scumbag who had hounded her
when the "woman in the blue sundress" scandal
started when Hugh had been in Celebration two
months earlier.

Oh, boy. As the guy aimed a small video camera at her, Bia knew what was coming next and she looked for an escape route.

"Hello, Bia. Joey Camps from *XYZ Celebrity News.* How ya doin' today?"

As Joey walked toward her with the camera, Bia glanced around. The only escape route was around the hedge and across the lawn. She turned her back and made her way to the opening in the shrubbery. She heard Joey's footsteps behind her.

"Oh, come on. Don't be that way. I just wanted to ask you to say a few words about Hugh Newman. Tragic loss, isn't it?"

Did the guy have no decency?

Bia knew she was being filmed, but she kept her head down and her sights set on making her way across the lawn to the opening in the hedge that would let her out onto the sidewalk.

"Nothing to say about your good friend? We're trying to put together a memorial segment for the show."

Bia knew that was a lie. They would probably use the uncut footage or maybe pair it with a clip of Kristin mourning Hugh's loss. Her heart ached for Kristin. She didn't want her to be left brokenhearted. Despite everything that had transpired, she hoped that Hugh had known true love with someone.

"Come on, Bia," Joey pressed. "Just give us one statement about Hugh Newman and we'll leave you alone."

"I barely knew Hugh. He was only in Celebration for five days. Still, I'm deeply saddened to learn of his accident. It's a tragic loss."

"But, yeah, weren't you like his girlfriend when he was here?"

"No. I was his...*tour guide*." She lifted her chin defiantly.

Joey snorted. "I'd like to know what kind of tours you're offering because my sources tell me you're pregnant."

The previous numbness overtook Bia again. As she skirted the hedge, looking back at Joey in horror, she almost ran headlong into Aiden.

"Are you pregnant with Hugh Newman's baby?" Joey asked.

The world slowed down into a hazy sort of slow motion as Bia watched Aiden put his hand up and block the creep's camera shot. He put his other arm around Bia to shield her.

"Get that camera out of her face. Let's set the record straight once and for all. There was never anything serious between Bia and Hugh Newman because she's engaged to me."

"Engaged? To you? Since when?"

As Aiden walked Bia back to his place, he put his hand out to block the camera again.

"It's none of your business. Get out of here. Leave us alone."

"Where's the ring?" the guy persisted

"Get out of here." Aiden's voice had an edge.

"Well, at least tell us your name." Obviously, the guy was a veteran at obtaining the news at all costs. Predators like him gave the media a bad name.

"At least kiss your fiancée for us. If you do that, we'll leave you alone."

Aiden stopped and turned to the guy. "Then you'll get that camera out of our faces?"

"Deal," said Joey.

Before she could protest, those lips that she'd contemplated the other day closed over hers. At first, his kiss was surprisingly gentle. He was so tender, tasting like a hint of coffee and something else, something uniquely Aiden. Reflexively, her lips opened under his. As passion overtook her, the gentle kiss morphed into a hard, punishing hunger that consumed her. She wanted the kiss to last forever. She reveled in it, letting it block out all the ugliness of the day. In that moment she wanted this little white lie that Aiden had just told to be true. Right here, right now, she wanted to be Aiden's fiancée. Because Aiden Woods was nothing like Hugh Newman. He was kind and protective and one heck of a good kisser....

Then the kiss ended. Breathlessly, Bia pulled away. The spell was broken. She stood for a moment, her vision slightly blurry, her heart racing, her equilibrium thoroughly thrown. She looked at Aiden, then at Joey, who had finally put down the camera. Then back at Aiden, still feeling the weight of his mouth on hers. All she could do was turn and make a beeline for the sanctuary of Aiden's condo.

Chapter Five

"What the heck did you just do, Aiden?"

When Aiden had first stepped between Bia and the jerk who had been bothering her, her face had been as pale as death. Now, as she collapsed onto the sofa in Aiden's living room, patches of pink stained her cheeks.

As she pressed her fingertips to her mouth, Aiden memorized how her lips had felt, the taste of her, the way she'd kissed him back.

"I got the guy to leave you alone. He stopped asking about Hugh, didn't he?"

"Right, but you also just kissed me in front of the whole world. And you went on record saying we're engaged. What are we supposed to do now? Do we say 'just kidding'!"

She *had* kissed him back, but he knew better than to point that out right now.

"And how did he know that I'm pregnant?" Bia scooted up to the edge of the chair. "Only two people know. You and Maya."

"I sure as hell didn't say anything to anyone. Really, Bia? Do you think I would betray you? What would I stand to gain besides buying myself a whole lot of grief?"

Hell. As soon as the words were out of his mouth, he wished he could take them back. Despite the fact that it was true.

He could tell what she was thinking by the way her eyes flashed: the bachelor party. The night that Duane had been unfaithful. The night that she thought Aiden had led her fiancé astray. It had been a test, and Duane had failed. He didn't deserve a woman like Bia.

She stiffened, sat up straight. "You kind of have a history of that, don't you?"

"Once. You're still blaming me for something that happened once. And, by the way, did I ever mention that I wasn't the one in charge of Duane's actions that night? I thought we agreed to not talk about this again. What I inferred from that agreement was that you accepted that Duane had a will of his own and you had acquitted me. You can't randomly pull this out and use it when you want to skewer me."

She closed her eyes and held up a hand, waving off his words.

A moment later she said, "It's the same guy that was harassing me two months ago, when Hugh was here the first time. Obviously, he has a source who feeds him information."

"So, did this scumbag fly in from L.A.—or wherever the *XYZ* offices are—just to get this film clip?"

"I don't think so. Sometimes the media contracts stringers. They're freelancers who work on an as-needed basis. I'll bet the guy is local. Someone tipped him off the first time Hugh was here a couple months ago, and now he's back at it because of Hugh's accident."

Bia squeezed her eyes shut, the pain evident on her pretty face. It was too bad that this had happened to Hugh. He wasn't exactly an honorable guy, but this... No, not this. Aiden stood and went into the kitchen. He poured two glasses of ice water and brought them back into the living room. He handed one to Bia.

"Thanks," she said. "Putting everything into perspective, I think the news of our *engagement* is going to get lost among the hysteria over Hugh's death. So, I guess it's not the world I'm worried about as much as I'm worried about how we're going to explain this to your mom and our friends and coworkers."

They both sat in silence for a moment.

"I mean, what? Will we *break up* and be one of those couples who remain good friends?"

"Why does everyone's opinion matter, Bia?"

She raked her hands through her hair and continued as if she hadn't heard him. "Just when I think things can't get worse, they do."

"Was kissing me that bad?"

She wouldn't look at him. For a fraction of a second he thought about telling her how he'd wanted to do that a long time ago. How he *should've* done it. Maybe then the situation would be different.

"Why are you doing this, Aiden?" Bia asked.

"I guess I was channeling my inner Prince Valiant," he said, trying to keep the sarcasm out of his voice. She'd kissed him back. He'd felt it as sure as he could feel his heartbeat speed up thinking about the way she'd felt in his arms. The way her lips tasted. "I did it to save you. You're welcome, Princess. Let's just ride this out until the media move on. Okay? There could be worse things."

"Aiden, I don't need to be saved."

"Then why did you call me?"

She was staring at her hands resting in her lap and she gave a quick, one-shoulder shrug.

"I can't have a fake engagement," she said.

"Then I guess we can simply tell everyone the truth, that I did it to save you from the paparazzi."

She rolled her eyes at him. He gritted his teeth and looked away, waiting for his mounting irritation to dissipate. When he looked back, she was staring at him with the most heartrending tenderness he'd ever seen. But it only lasted a moment.

"Do you really think you can fix the engagement you broke up with a fake one?"

"That *I* broke? That's a low blow, B. Do you really want to go there again? I didn't force Duane to cheat on you. If he was any kind of man, he wouldn't have done what he did."

And if he was going to cheat, it would've happened with or without the bachelor party. He didn't say it, but it was hanging in the air, as palpable as if he'd written the words in black marker on the living room wall.

He softened his tone. "Bia, I'm really not a bad guy."

Bia stared out the window a few moments longer before she looked at him. "I know you're not, and I know I have to stop bringing that up. I'm sorry. I appreciate what you did for me out there."

He nodded, feeling as if they'd just made some kind of breakthrough but trying to keep his face neutral. She'd never admitted that before now. It felt like a small victory.

"It's just that…what are we supposed to tell everyone? Your mom, for example? How are we supposed to explain it when we don't get married?"

"Don't worry about that now."

"Of course I'm going to worry about it. Are we going to tell your mom that you're the father of my baby? The one the *XYZ* scumbag asked me about on film? Because if we—or *I*—deny the pregnancy, she and everyone else are going to find out I was lying sooner or later."

She fisted her hands and dug the heels of her palms into her eyes.

"Aiden, this is so messed up. I'm not ready for everyone to know I'm pregnant. I haven't even come to terms with it myself."

"They were going to find out sooner or later," Aiden said.

"Yes, but before this, I was able to deal with it on my terms. Now, it's ready or not."

Aiden moved from the chair to the couch. He took

her hand, and she let him. "We'll figure something out, but for now, don't you think it's better to have someone to lean on through this? At least until the pressure is off?"

She didn't say anything, just looked at him.

"Bia, let me be that person."

Again, she didn't say anything, just stared at him for a long intense moment. Finally, she fell back against the couch and the right corner of her mouth quirked up. "You should know me well enough to know I'd never get engaged without a ring."

"I can take care of that. What kind of a man doesn't give his fiancée a ring?"

He fell back next to her and nudged her with his elbow, a playful gesture to make her smile. She did, even if it was just a half smile, a Mona Lisa smile. He was suddenly aware that their faces were so close that if they each just leaned a little bit he could kiss her again. But she'd have to meet him halfway. He wasn't going to do this by himself.

Right now, it felt as if she wasn't budging. She wasn't even moving her gaze from his. His fingers flexed with the need to reach out and touch her, to trace the line of her jaw from her chin to back to where the bone disappeared behind her ear. He wanted to kiss her there and see if she'd budge then…budge right into his bed.

But, instead, he asked, "Hypothetically, if you were getting engaged, what kind of ring would you want?"

"Hypothetically?"

He nodded.

"I'll show you. Hold on a sec." She pulled her

smartphone out of her pocket and pulled up something on the internet.

"Hypothetically, if I were to get engaged, I'd like this one." She handed him the phone, and he saw a picture of a ring with a deep-set round diamond surrounded by smaller stones. He noticed that there were also thumbnail shots of wedding dresses, flowers, wedding decorations, what looked like ceremony venues.

"What is all this?" he asked. "Is this the wedding you planned with Duane?"

"Absolutely not. It's completely different."

At the risk of rehashing the past, he asked, "So, what happened in the past didn't poison you against marriage?"

"No, if it didn't poison me against *you,* why should it poison me against marriage? I mean, it certainly made me not want to marry Duane, but I'd love to get married someday. I want a family—and I'm obviously getting that sooner than I thought."

The faraway look in her eyes changed to one of sorrow. She clasped her hands over her stomach. "But I guess this might be a game changer."

"Not with the right guy." He continued scrolling through her wedding photo gallery. "So, women do this in their spare time? They plan weddings?"

"For the record, a girl can dream."

"For the record, I get that. I guess. The princess is a hopeless romantic. I've never seen this side of you before."

Their gazes locked again, and the way she was looking at him almost made him want to bridge the distance—cover the ground for both of them—and kiss her again. If she hadn't looked away, he would've done it.

But the sea change reminded him that being fast and reckless with Bia wasn't the way to go. The chemistry was there. It always had been, but now it was starting to age into something viable.

Patience, Grasshopper. Patience.

"I think I have a pretty good idea who is leaking this personal information to the paparazzi," she said. "I'm going to find out today."

Later that afternoon, Bia pulled into the Maya's Chocolates parking lot. She hadn't even called ahead to say she was coming because she wanted to look Maya in the eyes when she asked her the question. If Aiden wasn't the one who had leaked the news about the pregnancy, it had to be Maya or Nurse Flirty. Somehow her gut was telling her that despite Flirty's wandering eye, she didn't seem the type who would break laws and betray a patient's confidentiality.

But God, who could you trust these days? Someone had alerted the media. Bia would be able to tell by Maya's reaction if she was the guilty one.

Bia was relieved that Maya's car, a bright yellow Volkswagen Beetle, was in the lot. She steered her navy blue Volvo into the parking space next to Maya's car. The parking lot ran alongside the bungalow. It probably used to be a side yard years ago, when the place was a single-family home. A couple of men were working at the far end of the small parking lot. It looked as if they were doing some carpentry work. Probably something last-minute for the grand opening.

Bia sat in her car for a moment, replaying in her head the last conversation she'd had with Maya, trying to remember if she'd said anything that should've been a tip-off that she was going to talk to the media. Bia couldn't recall anything. In fact, Maya had been warm and sympathetic. She'd been a friend. It was strange this so-called friendship she'd formed with this woman who'd seemingly come out of nowhere to open a business in the middle of nowhere. What was even more peculiar was that each time Bia had doubted Maya, something had reeled her back in. Which was why she was there right now. Rather than just writing her off and avoiding her.

No, she had to see Maya's eyes when she asked her the question.

Maya was all smiles when she answered the door and let Bia in.

"*Bonjour!* What a wonderful surprise." Maya leaned in and planted a kiss on Bia's cheek. "And your timing is perfect. I just got back from lunch and running some errands. Come in. Have you had your calcium today? Shall I make us some drinking chocolate?"

Oh. At first glance things seemed to be okay. Normal. Maybe she was good at bluffing? If she was, then it meant things like right and wrong didn't matter to her. But it wasn't fair to judge Maya guilty until she asked her straight-out.

Maya was already walking ahead of Bia, gesturing her to follow her to the kitchen. Bia did.

Right away, Maya busied herself gathering the items for the hot chocolate. "Did you need some more information for the article?"

"No, actually, I came to ask you a personal question."

Maya stopped pouring milk into the copper pot, set down the milk carton and turned her full attention to Bia.

"Sure," she said, her eyes sparkling, actually looking a little hopeful. "Ask me anything."

Rarely at a loss for words, Bia was unsure how to start. So she decided to begin gently, from the beginning.

"Did you hear the news about Hugh?"

The smile faded from Maya's face. "I'm sorry to say I did. It's such a tragedy. I didn't want to say anything in case you didn't know."

"Yes, it is a tragedy," Bia said, keeping her gaze trained on Maya's face. "I was at work when I heard the news. I was pretty shocked."

"I can imagine. Did you ever get a chance to talk to him?"

"No, I didn't get to talk to him personally. But when I heard, I decided to walk over to a friend's place that is only a couple of blocks away from my office. On the way, the same guy who accosted me the last time Hugh was in town was waiting for me outside. He and his driver followed me to my friend Aiden's."

"Oh, I'm so sorry," Maya said. "The last thing you needed at a time like that was someone—how do you say it?—barging in on you in your time of sorrow." Her face bore the look of genuine sadness. Not the oops-I-did-a-bad-thing kind of sadness, but more of a genuine, from the heart, sorry-for-a-friend's-troubles expression.

"I know. It was pretty awful. He was pointing a camcorder at me while he was quizzing me about how I felt after learning about Hugh's accident."

"For shame." Maya sounded truly incensed.

"That's not the worst part." Bia paused to see if she could pick up on any perceptible change in Maya's demeanor. But the woman held steady.

"What?" she asked. "What happened?"

"Somehow the guy knew I was pregnant."

Maya gasped. "How? How did he know?"

"I...don't know. The only two people I told were you and Aiden. I know Aiden didn't tip him off. In fact, he almost punched the guy when he wouldn't leave me alone. It will probably be on the next episode of *XYZ*."

"What is this *XYZ* that you speak of?"

"It's a tabloid television show. You've never heard of it?"

"No, I haven't. It is not my kind of television program, you see."

Again, Bia watched Maya closely. She simply frowned and resumed making the hot chocolate, but she didn't act nervous or defensive.

"So, you didn't see the show the first time the guy was harassing me? Back when Hugh was in town for the Doctor's Ball?"

Maya shook her head and stirred, holding the copper pot by its handle. "I read about the accounts of you and the actor, but I didn't see it on television."

"Well, you didn't miss anything important. The footage they shot today will probably air tomorrow night. I'm DVRing it because I don't know if I can bring myself to watch. But what I want to talk to you about is who could've tipped off this guy? How did he know I'm pregnant?"

Maya frowned and tilted her head to one side, as if she was thinking, genuinely trying to solve the puzzle. "This Aiden you speak of, you are one hundred percent sure he is trustworthy?"

"I would trust him with my life." Bia couldn't blunt the edge in her tone.

Maya's face softened. "You would? He is that good to you?"

Bia nodded.

"I would like to meet this Aiden who means so much to you."

"Why?" Startled by this suggestion, Bia mentally backpedaled a little bit. Was this Maya's way to distract her, to throw her off course? A sleight of hand to get her talking about Aiden or anything else to divert her attention?

"Why? I am just interested in this man who has captured your heart."

"What? Wait. No! You have this all wrong. The relationship I have with Aiden isn't like that, and that's not what I came here to talk to you about. Maya, if you and Aiden are the only two who know about my pregnancy, and I know for a fact that Aiden didn't tell anyone... Well, you do the math."

Maya regarded Bia for a moment. Her expression was inscrutable. Then she turned and took two demitasse cups down from a cupboard and poured the chocolate.

"I can see how this might look to you, but I can assure you that I am not the one who alerted the press."

"If not you, then who? I mean, how can I believe you didn't?"

Maya carried the two cups on saucers and set them on the table. "Please have a seat, Bia. There is something I must tell you. I didn't want it to come out like this, but, given the circumstances, you must know now."

What? Was Maya going to confess?

Had she needed the money to finance her new location—not that two stories about an actor's affair with an ordinary no-name would bring in the big bucks.

Bia remained standing. "Look, we don't have to drag this out. If you tipped him off, just tell me. Fast and simple. I need to know."

"Sit down, Bia." Maya's voice was calm. "This is not about the tabloid reporter. This is an entirely different matter."

Something in Maya's voice had Bia lowering herself onto the chair. If it wasn't about *XYZ*…she was almost afraid to know.

"About a year and a half ago, your father contacted me."

Bia did a double take. "My *father?* How did you and my father know each other?"

Maya looked away as she picked up her chocolate and sipped it. "Actually, we never met. Not in person. But when he was diagnosed with cancer, he contacted me to tell me. You see, he knew he was terminal and it was very important to your father that you not be alone in the world after he passed on."

Suddenly, Bia felt as if she'd slipped and had fallen down a rabbit hole. She could see where this story might be headed, but she couldn't let herself land there until Maya said the words.

"So…my dying father contacted you, this person he'd never met, and asked you to look out for my well-being? I'm a grown woman. I've been living on my own for years. Why would he do that?"

"Because, Bia, I am your birth mother."

Now Bia was free-falling down the rabbit hole. She had never felt so out of control of her life. And it just kept getting worse. When was it going to stop? When was life going to quit punching her in the stomach long enough so that she could catch her breath and grasp all the changes that were happening? It was as if the universe had taken her life, turned it upside down and was continuing to shake her until everything that had ever made sense fell away from her world.

"I know this is a shock, but please say something," Maya said.

What? What am I supposed to say? Why did you give me up? Why are you back now? Are we supposed to pick up and act as if we've always had a relationship?

"My father contacted you?"

"Yes. He told me of his condition but asked me not to contact you until after he was gone."

"If he wanted…this—" Bia gestured back and forth between them "—why wouldn't he introduce us? Why wouldn't he have been part of our reunion? I don't understand."

Maya's expression was as gentle as a Madonna's. "Probably for the same reason he couldn't tell you himself that you were adopted. He told me about the letter he was leaving for you for after he'd passed. He'd arranged for his attorney to notify me once he'd passed on. I didn't want to tell you this way, Bia. I wanted you to get to know me better before I told you. Especially given your pregnancy and Hugh's death. It's a lot to digest."

"I just don't understand why he had to do it that way," Bia said. "Finding out that I'm adopted didn't change the way I feel for him, but I was disappointed that he couldn't tell me himself."

"I wish I had the answers for you, but I hope this helps you believe that I would never betray your confidence. Especially not to the media."

Bia had so many questions. Why did Maya give her up in the first place? What was she expecting now? But another more pressing question remained. "Then who did?"

"Perhaps I can help you get to the bottom of it?"

"How would you do that?"

"I don't know, but I can think about it. I want to be a part of your life, Bia. I want to catch up on all I missed out on with you and to know my grandchild. Will you let me?"

It was too much, too fast, too soon.

"I need time to think, time to process everything." Bia stood. "Please excuse me. I need to go now."

Chapter Six

"How is it that you always seem to know when I need you?" Bia asked.

Aiden stood in the threshold of Bia's house. She looked sexy in those jeans that hugged her in all the right places. He had an almost uncontrollable urge to lean in, draw those curves against him and kiss her. He reminded himself that even though he had made up his mind that she would be his, she wasn't quite ready yet. If he rushed things, he might blow it. It was best to take things slowly.

That's why he'd hesitated today when he'd found himself at the jewelry store looking at diamond rings. He'd walked away and come back three different times before he'd convinced himself that buying a ring was the right thing to do.

If he was going to make this happen, he needed to do it right. So he'd purchased the ring.

"Guess I'm just talented that way. So, you need me, huh? Was the jackass back?"

Bia shook her head. "Something different. Just when I think that all the crazy things in the world that can happen have laid themselves at my feet, *bam!*" She clapped her hands together. "Something else jumps out at me—like a scary clown in a jack-in-the-box."

She stepped aside and motioned for him to come in.

"I met my birth mother."

Aiden stopped and turned around. "What?"

"Yes. Well, actually, I've known her for a couple of months now. Only I had no idea until today. She wanted to wait until—" Bia made air quotes with her fingers "—*the right time* to tell me."

"And she decided now is the right time?"

Bia nodded.

"Who is she?"

Bia closed her eyes and took a long, slow deep breath. The tension was evident on her face. Aiden wanted to pull her into his arms and assure her that everything would be okay. He'd make sure of it. Come hell or high water.

"It's Maya." Bia's usually strong, confident voice was a whisper.

"Chocolate-maker Maya?"

Bia nodded, looking so fragile, as if she might break at any moment.

"You saw her today, and she thought now was the *right time?*"

Bia told Aiden about what had transpired with

Maya after she'd left him. "She hadn't planned on telling me today. But I went to see her and asked her if she was the press informant. That's when she told me. She promised she would never betray me. Now that I've had a little bit of time to step back and think about it, I get it. Sort of. But I told her I need some time to process everything. In the meantime, that brings up an entirely new conundrum. If neither you nor she told the *XYZ* guy, who did? The only other people who know are Dr. Porter and your nurse girlfriend and the others in the office—they could've been talking among themselves."

Aiden grimaced. "She's not my girlfriend. Especially not if she spills secrets like that. You know, it's against the law to leak medical information."

"I know." Bia smirked. "At first, I couldn't put it together. It didn't make sense. I'd never met anyone in Dr. Porter's office. I figured it had to be the same person who tipped off the tabloid a couple of months ago. So, the likelihood of someone in that office being the *XYZ* connection seemed like a stretch." She held up her index finger. "But then, I went to the *XYZ* website and found out there is a 'hot tip' number. They offer a reward for stories that end up on the air. Anyone can call in the scoop. So, the person who tipped them off about my doctor's appointment didn't necessarily have to be the original informant. Really, once a story like that is out, people are looking for the least little anything to call in a tip. Especially if there's a chance of a financial reward."

"If you really believe you can trust Maya, it almost

has to be someone in Porter's office. Seems like they're the only suspects, doesn't it? How do we prove it?"

"I have no idea. I thought about calling Dr. Porter and telling him what's happened, suggesting that he have a talk with his staff, just in case, but then I thought better of it. I decided I don't want to go there. It's too big of an accusation without proof positive. Plus, it would only draw more attention to the situation. I'm just going to leave it alone, switch doctors and keep my head down."

They looked at each other for a silent moment.

"Have you thought about what we are going to say when people ask when we're getting married?" Aiden asked. "We should probably talk about this so we have our stories straight."

"All we have to tell them is we haven't set a date yet."

"So, you're saying you want to move forward with Plan Engagement?" Aiden asked.

Bia's throat worked, and then she raised her chin and gave a single resolute nod. "I think so. I mean, I don't see any other way around it. Since it's likely that the reporter is still on high alert."

"Then I need to ask a favor," Aiden said.

"Sure," Bia said. "Anything. God knows you're making a huge sacrifice for me by going through with this charade. I can't imagine what this is going to do to your love life."

His gaze fell to her lips and then found her eyes again. *You have no idea. Not yet, anyway.*

"Before the show airs tonight," Aiden said. "I want to tell my mother. I don't want her to hear it on television. And what about Maya? Did you say anything to her?"

Bia shook her head.

"You don't want to tell her before she hears about it through the mass media?"

"Aiden, I don't know what I want to do about her yet. I need time to think. I mean, you haven't even met her yet. She knows about you, but—"

"You told her about me?"

"I told her you were my best friend."

There was something in her expression, something in her eyes, that made him believe *best friend* was a good thing. It wasn't *friend zone* best friend. It was best friend with a whole lot more potential.

"You do need to tell your mom." Bia sighed audibly. "I just can't quite make peace with telling her we're engaged when we really aren't. I know I said I wanted to go through with it, but I've met your mother. I just have a bad feeling that she's going to see right through this scheme. I wish there was some way around that."

"That really bothers you, doesn't it?"

"Well, yes. It should bother you, too. Unless you make a habit of lying to your mother?"

"That's a low blow," he said. "You know I don't."

"I know," she said. "I'm sorry. It's just…one more thing that feels as if it's spinning out of control."

"Okay. I know how to fix this," he said.

"Do tell."

He walked across the room and pulled Bia to her feet.

"What are you doing?" she protested.

He dropped down on one knee and took her hands in his. "Bia Anderson, will you marry me?"

"Aiden, stop it."

He knew her so well that he'd anticipated that she would balk at the suggestion…at first. "Bia, I am proposing to you. If you don't want to lie to my mother, I would suggest that you accept my proposal. It's as simple as that. Say, 'Yes, Aiden, I'll marry you,' and then we will be engaged. There you go. No lying to anyone."

"But we're lying to ourselves."

"Only if you believe that's what we're doing."

"What? Are you saying this is real?"

He didn't answer her.

"What about the tiny little detail of the wedding that will never happen?" she asked.

"We will just have to cross that bridge when we come to it. Come on, B. Live for the moment."

She frowned. "I know that's your philosophy, Aiden, but I have to start thinking about the future."

"The immediate future is that reporter who is still lurking out there. Do you want to deal with him? Do you want me to explain to him that I was just protecting you when I said we were engaged? Because he's not going to go away unless he thinks he doesn't have a story. If word gets around that we told him we're engaged and we're not, then he's going to be on you like white on rice, until he proves that his initial hunch was right. So, I'll ask you one more time. Bia, will you marry me?"

She opened her mouth to say something, but no

sound came out. She clamped her lips shut, a perplexed look on her face.

"It's a simple yes or no question, Princess," Aiden said. His knee was starting to ache, the remnants of an old college football injury. "This offer is only on the table as long as my knee can stand this cruel and unusual punishment. So what's it going to be, yes or no?"

She blinked at him, looking a little stunned.

"Aiden, if we do this, we have to do it right."

"Isn't that what we're doing?"

"Well, yes. Sort of. But what I mean is if we do this…this…" She gestured between them with her hand. "You have to play the part."

"Right. And that means?"

"I mean, you can't be engaged to me and be seen around town with a bunch of different women. Even if this isn't *real,* I don't want a replay of what happened with Duane. Everybody was talking about it, and I looked like a fool. I don't want to go through that again."

"I understand. I promise you're the only woman I will be seen with, Bia. Now, for the sake of my knee, can we please get on with this?"

She nodded. "But wait. We need a ring."

"If we had a ring, would you say yes?" he asked.

"I don't want you to go out and buy one. Wait, hold on a second. I have an idea." She left the room and returned a moment later with a small white box.

"This is a birthstone ring that my mother—er…my adopted mother wore." Bia opened the box and showed Aiden the thin gold band with a small purple stone.

"My father gave it to me a long time ago, but it's a

little bit too big. I never wore it because I was afraid it would slip off my finger. I didn't want to lose it."

Bia gazed at the ring. "After she died, there wasn't another woman in the world for my father. That's why he never remarried."

Aiden knew the feeling. There was only one woman in the world for him. No matter how he'd tried to get over her, his heart had always belonged to Bia. Always had, always would.

"It's not a diamond engagement ring," he said.

"That's okay."

She could be so stubborn sometimes. He was surprised that she wasn't holding out for exactly what she wanted. It took a little fun out of his plan. He took the ring box from her, took it out of the box and studied it.

"This is nice," he said. "It has a lot of sentimental value. But the way I see it, there's two problems. First one is it doesn't fit you. It might slip off your finger. It would be a real shame for you to lose it since it means so much to you. The second problem is that it's not an engagement ring. Any fiancée of mine would wear a diamond ring."

He pulled the small black box out of his jacket pocket and opened it. "I was thinking something like this might be more appropriate."

Bia gaped at him with large green eyes. "Aiden, what did you do?"

"It looks pretty good, doesn't it?" he asked.

"Please tell me this isn't a real diamond. Because I know you wouldn't go out and buy a diamond ring for this."

"I would if I had extra cash lying around begging

to be spent," he said. "It's as real as we want it to be. Like I said, my fiancée will wear a ring we can both be proud of."

"You would really do this for me?" she asked. "Swear off other women for a while and pretend to be engaged to me?"

He smiled. "Apparently so."

Bia was finally silent, fresh out of conditions, even if she did look a little overwhelmed. Aiden got back down on one knee and took her hand in his.

"Bia Anderson, will you do me the honor of being my wife?"

She stared at him for a moment. A vague light seemed to pass between them, and then the air in the room shifted.

"Yes, Aiden, I will."

As he slid the ring on her finger, he silently vowed to hold her to that promise.

Sunday evening, Bia sat in her living room alone with a cup of herbal tea, prepared to watch the fateful edition of *XYZ Celebrity News.*

Aiden had wanted to come over and watch it with her, but Bia had told him she had to do this alone. With all the other hoopla surrounding the *XYZ* reporter ambush, Aiden's fake but all-too-real-feeling proposal and the discovery that Maya was her birth mother, she hadn't even had time to properly mourn Hugh.

It was the strangest feeling. She wasn't in love with Hugh. In fact, she really hadn't even liked the guy during his last few days on earth, after he'd shirked his responsibilities to her and the baby. But the facts remained that he was the father of her child and he was much too young to die. It felt odd—sad and odd—to contemplate that he was no longer in this world.

As she lifted her cup to her lips, the light caught the diamond on her finger, making it wink and glint. After she took a sip, she returned the cup to its saucer and held up her hand.

It hadn't escaped her that just before Aiden had slipped the ring on her finger, he had changed the wording of his proposal and asked her to be his wife.

It had felt real. The earnest look on his face and the intense way he'd looked her in the eyes had caused her breath to hitch and made her stomach do an odd somersault. If she didn't watch it, she could let herself get caught up in the fantasy. Not only was Aiden a devastatingly handsome guy; he made her feel safe and cared for…and the side of her that had let its guard down had felt electric as he'd slipped the ring on her finger. She reminded herself that she had to make sure she kept both feet firmly planted in reality. She couldn't forget herself.

While Aiden was a great friend, falling for someone like him was a recipe for heartache. God knew—between Duane and Hugh—she'd had enough of that for a lifetime.

She put her hand on her stomach. She was going to be a mother. That was a total game changer. Now she no longer had the luxury of taking stupid chances. Now every decision she made had to have her child at its heart. Since the mishap with Duane's bachelor party, Aiden had taken great pains to prove himself a top-notch friend. No matter how handsome, sexy and downright tempting she found him, she couldn't afford to take a chance that risky. Because there were fewer things riskier than trying to get Aiden to commit to a long-term relationship.

The red and black of the *XYZ Celebrity News* logo caught her attention as it flashed across the screen. The show was starting. Her stomach knotted as she picked up the remote and unmuted the TV.

Here we go.

Hugh's accident was the lead story. The verbal subheadline: "Was Hugh Newman out *celebrating* the news that he was going to be a father before his fatal crash?"

Seeing his photo emblazoned with his birthdate and death date made it real. Her eyes filled with tears. As crazy as it sounded, somewhere deep in Bia's subconscious she'd hoped that this would somehow turn out to be an urban legend that had gotten out of control. One huge publicity stunt. She had no idea why seeing it on this skanky tabloid show made it feel official to her and real—other than the fact that these skeevy reporters were the ones who had drilled to the heart of what was real when they'd reported her affair with Hugh the first time. Sure, they were easily diverted by Hugh's camp and a total curtailing of contact between the two of them, but they'd gotten it right.

The camera captured the grim-faced *XYZ* ringleader as he sat leaning back in his chair, with his legs propped up on his desk, managing to restrain himself from cracking jokes as he and his minions dished about the few details they'd managed to uncover about Hugh's accident.

Blahblahblahblah car crash. *Blahblahblahblah* returning from party. *Blahblahblahblah* waiting for toxicology reports. *Blahblahblahblah* alone in the car.

Next, they broke to a shot of Kristin Capistrano sobbing hysterically. Bia's heart went out to the woman. If love could be weighed in tears, Kristin had been in deep.

Then, there it was—the somewhat blurry photo that had made the rounds two months before: Bia in that blue sundress. She made a mental note to donate it. If it wasn't such a nice dress, she'd burn it. She and Hugh were sitting at a patio table at Bistro Saint-Germain in downtown Celebration. They did look rather cozy the way they were leaning into one another. Bia was smiling, and Hugh looked as if he was playing with a wisp of her hair. As an *XYZ* minion rehashed the history of Bia and Hugh, his fellow minions made snide comments about the nature of the *tours* she allegedly gave. Of course, they couldn't remain somber and dignified for long. Someone had to go there, had to say it, "Well, at least we know she's not an *escort* in the old-fashioned sense of the word. We've learned that Hugh Newman's—" he cleared his throat "—*tour guide* is actually a pretty smart cookie. She is the editor of Celebration's local newspaper. I don't know when she finds time to offer private tours."

Yuck. Yuck. Yuck. Did they have no respect? No dignity?

And then the coup de grâce: Bia flinched as her own image appeared on the screen. She felt sick as she relived the way the *XYZ* minion harassed her, dogging her every move. And then there was Aiden. He swooped in, put one arm around her and stretched out the other, momentarily blocking the camera's view with the palm of his. Then he stepped back and claimed she was his fiancée.

Her stomach gave an unexpected little flutter at Aiden's protectiveness.

"Get that camera out of her face. Let's set the record straight once and for all. There was never anything serious between Bia and Hugh Newman because she's engaged to me."

"Engaged? To you? Since when?"

The flutter intensified as she watched the kiss they'd shared replay in living color on the television set. She could feel the weight of his lips on hers—just a little chapped and extremely skilled...what with all the practice he'd had.

It was like an out-of-body experience watching herself kissing this man who had become her best friend. A friend with whom she'd struggled through a love-hate relationship to get to the point where they were now.

Why is it feeling an awful lot like love now?

She shook away the preposterous thought.

This was *Aiden.* He certainly had never been Prince Charming. Prince Charming probably wasn't such a darn good kisser.

In the background now, they were saying something about how Hugh and Kristin had been scheduled to film a movie in Celebration, "a quaint, picturesque town that harkens back to simpler days."

Ahh, simpler days. The days before she'd met Hugh

and started having inappropriate thoughts about her best friend.

"However, with the recent turn of events, the future of the film is uncertain. For now, inside sources say the film is shelved. At least until they can figure out who will take over the role that Newman had been cast to play."

So many things were uncertain.

Life itself was fragile and tentative. You could spend your whole life protecting your heart so that it never got trampled on again, so that someone like Duane or Hugh didn't misuse it or hurt you. You could spend your entire life being careful and then die alone unbroken and unfulfilled.

She glanced down at her left hand. The diamond winked at her. Maybe it was time to explore the possibilities and live a little.

Chapter Seven

"Congratulations, Bia," said Nicole. "I can't believe you didn't tell us you were engaged. We had to find out on national television? You're so unromantic."

Nicole smiled, but underneath those perfect white teeth Bia was sure there were fangs ready to come out and bite her.

"You know me," Bia said as she made herself a cup of decaffeinated tea in the newspaper office's break room. "I'm generally a private person. If it makes you feel any better, Aiden and I hadn't really planned on announcing our engagement on national television. It was just one of those things."

"But are you...?" Nicole patted her belly.

"Am I what?"

Thank you, XYZ. The questions of the day had

been about the engagement and the pregnancy. The ultra-brazen had even gone as far as to ask who the father was—Hugh or Aiden.

Bia had leveled the ones who had had the audacity to ask with a stare that had made them wish they'd kept their mouths shut.

"I mean, there's private and then there's *private,*" Nicole said. "No one even knew you and Aiden were dating. Or that you were—"

Bia pierced her with a look that stopped her mid-sentence. Then she took a quart of half-and-half out of the refrigerator and stirred some into her tea. "As I said, Nicole, I'm a very private person. I don't like to discuss my personal life at work. And speaking of. Both of us need to get back to it."

She turned and walked to her desk. All the while, she could feel Nicole's gaze burning holes into her back. Bia had to admit, the woman's tenacity was one of the things that made her a good reporter. She seemed to have a sharp bull detector and she wouldn't let an issue drop when she had a hunch she was right. Ha. Maybe Nicole should get a job with *XYZ*.

As Bia sat down at her desk, she felt bad for thinking that about her employee. When the scrutiny wasn't turned on her, Bia admired Nicole's tenacity. But when she wouldn't take no for an answer (which was usually when she didn't get what she wanted) or the tables were turned, Bia wanted to ship the woman off to parts unknown.

Well, Nicole could ask all the questions she wanted. Bia wasn't required to answer.

She clicked on the email icon on her computer and

checked the damage that had accrued in the time that it took her to get her tea.

Twenty-six new emails. Before she even opened them, she could tell that five of them were from other news outlets requesting interviews.

Thanks to *XYZ* announcing to the world where she worked, she'd been inundated by the curious and the newshounds alike.

For heaven's sake. What part of engaged to another man did they not understand? She highlighted each of the emails and clicked the spam button. "There. That's better."

She was screening all her calls today, as well. She'd set the phone to automatically and silently deposit all calls into her voice mailbox. Otherwise, how was she supposed to get any work done? That's why the sound of her desk phone ringing startled her out of her concentration.

It was Candice, the receptionist. "Hi, Bia, I just wanted to let you know that Mr. Montgomery just arrived and he is on his way back to see you."

Drew Montgomery. Her boss. *Wonderful*...though she should have seen a visit from him coming from a mile away. Strange that he hadn't tried to call her first.

"Thank you, Candice."

Bia stood and met Drew at her office door.

"Hi, Drew, good to see you. Come in, please." She put on her most professional smile, determined to prove that nothing had changed in the newsroom. Despite how she had found herself in the news lately, everything was under control at the *Dallas Journal of Business and Development*.

Drew stepped into her office and took a seat in one of the chairs across from her desk. She shut the door. Once she'd reclaimed her seat, Drew said, "So, I understand congratulations are in order."

Reflexively, Bia's thumb went to the back of her engagement ring. She glanced down at the diamond. It was still a bit startling every time she saw it on her finger.

"Thank you," she said, deciding to let Drew take the lead in the conversation.

"I see your *XYZ* buddy was back," he said. "Do you need any help with that?"

Bia squinted at him, unsure what he meant. "I'm pretty confident the most recent ambush was the last, given the sad turn of events with Hugh Newman."

"Yeah, that was pretty shocking," Drew said. "And sad."

Bia nodded.

"I don't foresee any reasons for *XYZ* to need to interview me in the future. Now that Aiden and I are engaged, I'm no longer newsworthy."

"Yeah, about that," said Drew. "I've known for a long time that the guy is crazy about you, but I had no idea the two of you were serious."

His comment made Bia's heart race, and then she wanted to squirm. It wasn't like that between her and Aiden. That's why their relationship worked. That's why they were so good together. That's why they were such good—

She couldn't bring herself to say the word *friends* anymore, and that just about gave her a panic attack.

Now that her dad was gone, Aiden was all that she

had. If she lost him because of this… Behind the desk her hand found her belly, and she thought of Maya.

Actually, she wasn't alone anymore. At least she didn't have to be.

A baby and her own birth mother, who seemed to be on such an even keel, so patient and kind. Even if she had been a surprise in Bia's life, Maya had the personal endorsement of her boss's wife. And Caroline's friends.

So much had changed, and it seemed as if more changes were happening on a daily basis. Maybe she needed to take a step back and give Maya a chance.

"Anything else you'd like to share?" Drew asked.

Bia knew that he was hinting about the pregnancy. He was a decent guy and wouldn't come right out and ask until she was ready to bring it up.

She glanced out the window that overlooked the newsroom. Everyone seemed to be busy—on the phone or pounding away at their computers. She might as well confide in Drew. He'd know about the baby sooner or later.

"Well, actually, yes, there is. I'm going to have a baby in about seven months."

"Congratulations to you and Aiden," he said.

She didn't correct him. She glanced at the ring that Aiden had put on her finger. Aiden was the one who had the most to lose—taking himself off the dating market, pretending to be the father of another man's child and being willing to make everyone think that he wanted to marry her. She needed to be grateful enough to graciously accept this ultimate gift of friendship he was offering her.

"Thank you, Drew. I promise nothing will change here. I plan to work up to my due date and then take minimal time off. So, I can assure you there's nothing to worry about."

Drew nodded. "I was never worried. I can step in and help pick up the slack while you're out, and I know Nicole is eager to prove herself around here."

I'm sure she is. "She's a real go-getter, isn't she? But we have a long time between now and my due date. So let's not worry about that now."

"The real reason I'm here is because Caroline wanted me to invite Aiden and you to dinner next week. Are you free?"

"Thank you. I'm sure we can make time. Let me talk to Aiden. I'll let you know."

Bia felt the weight of somebody's gaze on her. She glanced out the window into the newsroom, and saw Nicole, unsmiling and watching Drew and her. Bia held Nicole's gaze until the woman looked away.

Yeah, she's a real go-getter. For some reason, Bia didn't trust her. Usually, she admired ambitious women. However, Nicole elevated ambition to aggressive. It was a shame she had to be that way. Bia knew she needed to honor her gut feeling and watch her back.

Chapter Eight

Today was the day. Opening day for Maya's Chocolates.

Maya's stomach was all aflutter. She'd put a lot of time, effort and money into this venture. She hoped today would go smoothly.

Aw, who was she kidding? She didn't simply want it to go smoothly; she wanted it to be a smashing success. She had hired three full-time sales clerks. She'd spent the past two days training them and felt good about the team she'd created.

She glanced around the shop. Everything was in place. The chocolate had been delivered yesterday, and she had spent the entire day up to her elbows in cocoa making several batches of handmade confections for the special day. Being in the kitchen was also good therapy to keep her mind off the fact that she hadn't heard from Bia since she'd broken the news that she was her birth mother. Maya was determined to give Bia her space until she had the opportunity to come to terms with the news. She knew it was a lot to handle on top of everything else she had gone through recently. Maya simply wished that Bia could see that now of all times it would be good to have a family member—a mother—to help her through.

So Maya had decided to give her time to think about it, or she'd wait at least until after the shop's grand opening. If she hadn't heard from her by then, she might start thinking of another approach. She couldn't allow herself to think that Bia might completely shun her. Of course, it was a possibility, but she just wasn't going to go there.

Especially not today.

Maya glanced at her watch. It had belonged to her grandmother. So it seemed particularly appropriate to wear it today. It was as if her grandmother and her mother were there with her. The only person missing was Bia, but Maya had seen the article that had appeared in the *Dallas Journal of Business and Development* just as Bia had promised.

Maya told herself that was second best to Bia being there in person.

It was nine-thirty. The shop would open in half an hour. Maya straightened her scarf, fluffed her hair and said a silent prayer for a great first day.

She walked from the kitchen onto the shop floor. Her three sales clerks, Susan, Paulina and Meg, were chatting away excitedly. They immediately quieted and jumped to attention when Maya walked into the room. They were dressed all in black as Maya had instructed them. Paulina had a feather duster in her hand and was swishing and swiping it over the fixtures. Maya hoped the girl would be as conscientious after the newness had worn off the adventure and the dust had had a chance to settle.

"Good morning, my chickens," Maya said. "You three look lovely. Thank you for dressing appropriately and for being here on time. This is the beginning of a wonderful adventure for all of us, and I'm glad you are here with me. We will open our doors at precisely ten o'clock. I hope we will have so much business that it will prove impossible for us to take a break. However, I will make sure that you get some time to refresh. I have posted the schedule in the kitchen on the bulletin board above the table."

Maya was just getting ready to go over the procedure for utilizing the cash drawer when a knock sounded at the door. She turned around to see Bia standing there with an armful of flowers. Her heart nearly leaped out of her chest.

"Please excuse me," Maya said. "We have a very special visitor."

Maya worried the hem of her scarf as she made her way to the door to let Bia in.

She had come.

Bia was her *first-footer*. It had to be a fabulous sign. While the Scottish tradition of first-footing said that the first person to cross a home's threshold after midnight on New Year's Eve would determine the family's luck for the year, Maya thought it auspicious that Bia was the first person to cross her threshold on the first day of her new business. The employees had used the employee entrance in the back.

Maya opened the door and greeted Bia enthusiastically.

"I am so happy to see you," she said. "I can't even begin to tell you."

"These are for you," said Bia. She handed Maya the flowers.

"Thank you so very much," Maya said, bringing the mix of white flowers to her nose. The flowers, which were in a tall glass vase, contained freesia, carnations and lilies that were tied with a silver ribbon. "These will look lovely on the wrap stand. I can't believe I neglected to get fresh flowers."

"Do you see these?" Bia asked. She indicated green stalklike limbs sticking out in the middle of the flowers. Maya had thought it was greenery.

"It's lucky bamboo," said Bia. "There are nine stalks and they represent good fortune. Even after the flowers fade, the bamboo will thrive. It lasts for years. If not forever."

Maya was so touched that tears came to her eyes. She smiled at Bia. "Thank you so much for this." Her words caught in her throat, and she took a moment to gather her composure. "It means so much that you're here this morning."

"I couldn't let you open without sending good wishes and good fortune," Bia said as Maya set the vase of flowers next to the register. "Did you see the article in today's paper?"

"I did. It was wonderful. Thank you so very much. For that and for being here now."

"Drew tells me you're invited to the dinner party they're throwing. Are you going?"

"I wouldn't miss it."

"I'm glad," said Bia. "It will be good to spend some time with you. But you must be swamped getting ready to open the doors. Look, people are lining up already. I won't keep you."

Bia gestured toward the door, where a small crowd had gathered.

"You see—you're already bringing me good luck," Maya said. "Before you arrived, nobody was out there. Now look at them."

Bia hitched her purse up onto her shoulder. "Maybe once you get the business up and running, we can meet for lunch or coffee or something?"

Maya put a hand on Bia's arm. "I would love that. And, of course, there's always dinner next week."

Within an hour of the shop being open, the store was overrun with people. Maya and the staff had to keep going into the storeroom off the kitchen to bring out more chocolate to restock the shelves. It looked as if that lucky bamboo was working, after all. Or maybe it was the good fortune of her first-footer. More likely it was the attention that Bia had garnered through the article that had run that morning. Either way, Maya was grateful for the blessing of her daughter.

She rang up a box of truffles, a candy gift basket and a collection of chocolate bars for a woman who said she was buying the candy for her grandchildren. "That will be $106.42, please." As the woman fished in her wallet for two pennies, Maya thought she saw someone familiar out of the corner of her eye. A man. It was his posture. The sight nearly made her heart stop.

Ian?

It couldn't be. Maya knew that, although her heart didn't seem to understand. A knot of people blocked her view and she craned her neck to see around them. No luck, though.

Her heart sank.

How many times had she thought she'd seen Ian's face in the crowd before? Too many times to count. Ian was dead. He wasn't coming back. She knew that. It was probably just her imagination conjuring up his image on this special day.

If wishes were chocolate…

Hmm…

She'd have to remember that, maybe use it in an advertisement.

She forced her cheeriest smile as she thanked the woman for her purchase.

"How often will you have handmade chocolate?" the woman asked.

"Of course, it will depend on the demand, but I think I will try to make fresh batches twice a week." Maya gestured toward a silver guest book. "Would you care to sign up for our mailing list? That way I can let you know when the fresh batches of chocolate are available. I'll also be able to tell you about specials and events that we're having."

Maya thought about getting a neon sign to put in the window. One she could light up when the handmade chocolate was available. She filed that idea away with the ad idea.

"Absolutely," the woman said. Her Texas drawl made Maya smile.

As the woman was adding her name and email address to the guest book, Maya caught sight of the back of the man's head again.

"I hope you can read my terrible handwriting," the woman said. "That's an *o* right there, not an *a*. Can you read that?"

Maya glanced down and read the woman's name. "I can read it just fine. Thank you so much for coming in today, Mrs. Rogers. Please come back soon."

When Mrs. Rogers walked away and the next person stepped up to be helped, Maya asked Meg to take over at the register. Maya made her way through the cluster of people gathered around the shelf with the boxed chocolates. To her surprise, the man was still there. Her heart thudded as she approached him.

"May I help you with something?" She held her breath until he looked up and smiled.

Her heart sank. Of course it was not Ian. She had been crazy to let herself get carried away.

"Hello, Maya," said the man. His familiar greeting startled her. Especially because his words were laced with the hint of an Irish accent. She knew she was imagining things, because his voice sounded like Ian's. So much so that it made goose flesh stand up on her arms. She crossed her arms in front of her and ran her hands over her skin.

"Hello," she said, mustering as enthusiastic a greeting as she could. He was a customer. It wasn't his fault he wasn't the person she had been hoping to see.

The stranger held out his right hand for Maya to shake. "I'm Charles Jordan," he said. "I'm the one who sent you the Facebook message. We communicated back and forth a bit. Oh, or maybe someone else handles the social media for you?"

Maya extended her hand and shook his. "Oh, Mr. Jordan. How lovely to meet you. I am the one who answered your nice note. You said you would be in Texas. I'm so glad that it coincided with the opening of the store. Were you looking for anything in particular?"

He hesitated a moment. Their gazes locked. And there was something in his blue eyes that set loose the butterflies in her stomach.

His voice.

His eyes.

His posture.

It was all uncanny. He reminded her so much of Ian. And it wasn't just because she was wishing that he were there today. For goodness' sake, it had been nearly thirty years since she'd lost him.

Of course, not a day went by that she didn't think of Ian, but it was the rare occasion that she met a man who seemed to be his walking ghost. And even that wasn't right, because other than the eyes, the voice and the way he carried himself, he looked nothing like Ian. Not even Ian aged thirty years.

This man, this Charles Jordan, had a different nose, a different jawline, different cheekbones.

Her gaze fell to the open collar of his blue dress

shirt, where she glimpsed the wide, raised pinkish-white edges of a scar shooting diagonally toward his Adam's apple.

She glanced up. That's when she realized that he was staring at her, too, seeming just as mesmerized. She tore her gaze away, looking toward the shelves.

"We have some lovely gift baskets over here," she said. "And there's still some handmade chocolate left. Not much. I'm pleased to report that it seems to be flying off the shelves."

He was probably just a good soul. The world was full of them, if a person cared enough to look beneath the surface…past the scars. At least that was Maya's philosophy.

"Do you have any Borgia truffles?" he asked. "That's what I had the first time I visited your shop."

Maya's breath caught. *Borgia truffles?*

Borgia truffles had been one of Ian's favorites. The memory made her heart ache.

"No, I'm so sorry. I haven't made those in years. Goodness, probably close to twenty-five years." She'd run into a problem getting the blood-orange extract she used for them. It was only manufactured by one company, and they went out of business. After trying to no avail to find a suitable substitute, she'd finally shelved the recipe.

"I'm so disappointed," he said.

"So it has been a while since you were in the St. Michel shop?" she asked.

"Sadly, it has been much too long. You know how life tends to get in the way. Time goes so fast. Then all of a sudden you realize what's important."

What a strange thing to say.

In an effort to keep things light, Maya replied, "I must say it's quite exciting to say that one of my first customers in my new shop was a return customer from the shop in St. Michel. How about some chocolate-covered salted caramel?"

"That sounds divine," he said.

There it was again. That vague turn of cadence that sounded a bit Irish. But overall he had a decidedly American accent. She motioned for him to follow her to the center of the store so that she could wrap up his caramels.

"Where are you from?"

"All over the place," he answered. "Right now, Orlando, Florida."

"Didn't you say in your message that you are here on business?"

"That I did."

"How long are you in town?"

"Who knows?" He smiled. "Until my business is finished."

Maya knew she shouldn't pry, but she couldn't help herself.

"I must ask, I can't help but think I hear a slight bit of an Irish brogue when you speak. Are you from Ireland, or am I imagining it?"

He gave her a look that seemed to say touché. "That I am. Although I haven't been back in ages. I suppose you can take the boy out of Ireland, but you can't take Ireland out of the boy."

Maya began the process of placing chocolates in a

small box. "How many would you like? A half-dozen? A dozen? That's what I have left."

"I'll take them all."

"Are you enjoying yourself while you're here?"

"I am. I found a great Irish pub downtown. Baldoon's Pub. It feels like home. They even serve your Irish cream chocolate, you know?"

"I do know. It was an arrangement I was excited to make. I'd like to think that it gave the residents of Celebration a preview of what was to come when I opened the shop."

"Well, it seems to have worked."

She felt Charles's gaze on her as she wrapped up his purchase. It made her both excited and a little nervous.

Finally, when she'd finished, she said, "Anything else?"

Charles hesitated a moment. "Would you care to join me for a bite to eat sometime at Baldoon's?"

Maya's immediate reaction was a resounding yes, but caution kicked in before she could get carried away. She didn't know this man who seemed to appear from out of nowhere claiming to have been in her shop twenty-nine years ago.

Even though he reminded her so much of Ian, she had to be careful.

"Oh, goodness, that sounds lovely. However, I don't know when I will have a moment of free time right now. The shop is so new. It requires my constant attention."

Charles Jordan nodded solemnly. "A woman has to eat."

Maya was relieved when Paulina interrupted with a question.

"Excuse me, Maya. I have a customer who has a question that I can't answer. Would you mind helping her? She's in a hurry. She's in here on her lunch hour."

"You'll have to excuse me, please," Maya said to Charles. "Paulina, would you please ring up Mr. Jordan's purchase and have him sign the guest book?"

When she returned about five minutes later, Charles Jordan was gone. He had not signed the guestbook.

Aiden never imagined that a simple shopping trip for something like baby furniture could do so much for a relationship. For that matter, he never thought he'd find himself enjoying shopping so much. Funny how Bia had that effect on him.

The evening he and Bia had spent in Dallas earlier that week, shopping for baby items as if they were a couple, had brought them even closer in a million subtle ways. They were already close, but suddenly there was a new air between the two of them, new life in their relationship. They called each other several times during the day and spent evenings together.

In the past, they may have had dinner together once or twice during the week, and maybe they'd spent a weekend night together if something special was going on. But, of course, both of them had erratic work schedules. Lots of times when he was free, she was working, and vice versa. But when there was a work function, they always seemed to rely on each other as dates. Maybe it was because there had never been any pressure. Maybe it was because they had always enjoyed each other's company.

Now that they were engaged—or *fake engaged,* as Bia kept calling it—spending time together seemed to happen spontaneously, naturally. Spending time with her felt like going home. There was nothing forced or awkward about it. In fact, he'd never enjoyed a woman's company quite so much.

Now they ate dinner together every night. They went for evening walks, after which they would come home and watch movies together sitting side by side on the couch—no more him sitting in the chair and her lounging alone on the couch. Things between the two of them were relaxed and companionable—a phenomenon he had never experienced with anyone else. In the past, he'd always known when he'd spent *too much* time with a woman. He would be bucking for some alone time or time with the guys.

Now things were different.

He didn't know what it all meant, only that it felt good. It felt *right.*

After the *XYZ* spot aired, he didn't feel the need to explain away the engagement to his buddies. Sure, they'd asked, but he hadn't really given them an explanation. Nobody asked about the baby. Funny thing was, they didn't seem to think it was so strange that, all of a sudden, he was engaged to Bia. In fact, his buddy Miles Mercer had said, "It's about damn time you settled down. You two make a great couple."

Of course, Miles was happily married to Sydney James. So his perspective might have been a little bit colored. But he was also a good example of how good being with the right woman could be.

He knew they'd reached a different place in their relationship. They didn't really feel platonic, but it was different than it used to be. He couldn't get a read. He didn't know exactly where they stood or how this would all go down in the end, but that was okay. For now, he was content to let things ride.

There'd been no physical intimacy. Not even another kiss since the one they'd shared in front of the *XYZ* reporter. He had relived that kiss every day, but he wasn't going to risk blowing everything out of the water by trying it again. Still, despite the lack of a physical relationship, he felt closer to her than ever. Of course, she seemed to have her fair share of hormones, or at least that's what she chalked her occasional moodiness up to. But he had decided it would be a challenge to change her mood when she had her moments, and usually he was successful. The place where he really felt he was making the most progress was that she hadn't brought up the trust issues since he'd put the ring on her finger.

All these changes between them had added up to a trial run of what they would be like as a couple, and he hadn't felt the urge to pull away.

For him, that was huge.

Bia had always had a special place in his heart, but now she had taken up residency there. That was the reason he didn't mind spending a Saturday evening putting up shelves in the spare bedroom that would be the baby's room.

She had already started buying things and wanted

to get organized as soon as possible. Even though she wasn't due for another six and a half months, her job demanded a lot of her—a lot of overtime and sometimes unpredictable hours, depending on what she needed to cover for the newspaper.

When she had asked him to put up the shelves tonight, he hadn't hesitated. Toolbox in hand, he walked up the porch steps and let himself inside her house.

"Hi, honey, I'm home!" The one thing in their relationship that remained the same was that they could joke with each other.

"I'm in the baby's room," she called.

He followed her voice down the hall to the first door on the left, where he saw her standing on a stepladder getting something out of the closet.

"Be careful," he said. "Do you want me to do that for you?"

"I'm fine," she said. "But here—could you take this?"

She turned and handed him a medium-size cardboard box she had gotten off the top shelf of the closet. He took it from her, set it on the dresser and extended a hand to help her down from the ladder.

It was a good thing he had because she faltered on the last step and fell into him. He caught her, holding her in his arms.

She didn't say a word and gazed up at him, looking shocked.

"See, this is why you need me," he murmured.

He closed the circle of his arms around her and pulled her closer. He lowered his head toward her, hesitating a moment, giving her a chance to object.

Their first kiss had been for the benefit of the tabloid reporter. Whether they wanted to acknowledge it or not, that kiss had been fueled by temptation and attraction that had been building for years.

It had been a subconscious test. A justified pushing of the envelope to see if their relationship could go there. They had crossed the bridge. And not only had they survived; they seemed to be thriving.

His mouth fused to hers.

This kiss wasn't for show. This one had been a long time coming. Silently she confirmed that, kissing him back, allowing him to take the kiss deeper. She moved against him, sliding her hands up his arms, over his shoulders until her fingers laced around the nape of his neck, holding him.

A hot rush of need coursed through his veins, a need the likes of which he'd never felt before. How was it that each new step they took overwhelmed his senses even more, bringing on new feelings and desires—fiery, fierce and undeniable. Feelings he had never experienced in his long history of women. Because each woman he'd pursued was supposed to be the antidote to his feelings for Bia. Little did he know there was no antidote. There was no way out or around. Only through her could he be happy.

His hands slid down the length of her curves until he cupped her bottom and pulled her closer, reveling in how perfect her body fit against his. She moaned into their kiss.

Keeping one hand in place, the fingertips of the other found the waistband of her shorts and dipped beneath the cloth barrier that stood between them.

Obstacles.

There had always been obstacles between them—Duane or Hugh or Tracey or some woman he couldn't feel anything for except a cordial kindness, which always meant cutting her loose before the friendship outgrew the bounds of amity. Physical distance, engagements, his marriage and jobs had separated them, too. Until finally the job in Celebration had presented itself. He had been patient, not wanting to move too fast when he'd first arrived, because things seemed to be going well between them. And then there was Hugh.

Enough was enough.

He was claiming what was his.

Chapter Nine

When she closed the doors to the chocolate shop the end of the first week that it had been open for business, Maya was both exhilarated and exhausted.

Business had been steady the entire week. She was working hard to keep up with the demand—especially for her handmade chocolates. Bia had been in to see her a couple of times. During the last visit, she'd asked if Maya would like to meet Aiden.

Of course she would. Maya had noticed the engagement ring on Bia's hand, but she hadn't asked too many questions other than having Bia confirm that she was, indeed, engaged to be married. There would be plenty of time for details, but right now Maya didn't want to scare her off with too many questions. Even if she was dying to know every last detail of her daughter's life—past, present and future.

It was such a treat to look up from the wrap stand or from a shelf that she had been dusting to see Bia's smiling face. It meant that she was ready for a relationship. Maya could feel it in her bones.

The one person who hadn't returned was Charles Jordan. Perhaps his business in Celebration was finished and he had returned to Orlando before he could say goodbye. Or maybe she had hurt his feelings when she had declined his offer for dinner at the pub.

Whatever the reason for his absence, he had provided an interesting daydream: that somehow Ian was still alive. She needed to stop torturing herself with what could never be and focus on everything that was good in her life.

Even so, on her walk home, she found herself taking a detour. She ended up walking by Baldoon's Pub. While she was down here, she wondered, what could it hurt to pop into the place and check it out? She might even order a shepherd's pie to take home for her dinner.

The place smelled of fried food and beer. It was crowded, but then again it was Saturday night. It was nice to see other downtown businesses thriving.

Maya looked around. She didn't want to sit at the bar. Not alone. But she didn't want to take up a table, either. She was just about to ask the bartender for a menu when a familiar voice behind her said, "Those were the best salted caramels I've ever had in my life." Maya turned around to see Charles Jordan standing there. A strange excitement she hadn't felt in ages blossomed in her stomach. It was a dangerous feeling. She knew she needed to be careful. It wasn't so much that she was in physical danger as it was that her heart might be in jeopardy. She took a long hard look at the tall man clad in khaki pants and a white button-down shirt, his sleeves unbuttoned and pushed up his forearms, his blue eyes and dark hair that was graying at the temples. She saw his broad shoulders, so much like Ian's that it made her want to weep. She found herself a little tongue-tied as heat began to creep up her neck.

"Hello," she said, finally finding her voice. "I thought perhaps you had already returned to Orlando."

"No, I'm still here," he said. "I've been wanting to stop in to see you. However, I thought I'd best pace myself." He patted his middle, but his eyes hinted that he might not be talking about the candy.

"If you call ahead, I will make a fresh batch for you."

Charles nodded. "I'll be sure and do that. In the meantime, would you care to join me for a bite to eat? Seeing that you're already here and all."

He smiled at her, and there was a look in his eyes that pulled her right in.

"That would be lovely," she said and followed him to a table in the middle of the pub.

It had been ages since she had been on a— Would she even call it that? It wasn't a date. She was too traditional to consider this chance meeting a date. She had come here of her own free will to pick up her dinner. She just happened to run into…a friend. Dinner with a friend. That's all this was.

Charles ordered Maya the same ale that he was enjoying.

"How has business been this week?" he asked.

That was a good neutral topic, Maya thought.

"It's been fabulous," she said. "Exhausting, actually. I may have to hire more help if business keeps up at the pace that it was this week. Then again, I suspect some of the customers may have just been curious. I hope they will return. I suppose I'll just have to wait and see."

Charles had propped his elbow on the table and was leaning on his fist, gazing at Maya. His stare made her uncomfortable. It made her want to fill the silence with words. And she usually didn't ramble.

Despite the awkward silence, she forced herself to be quiet.

The server returned with her beer, tried to flirt a little with Charles and then left them alone to look at the menus.

"Do you believe in fate, Maya?" he asked.

What kind of question was that? She'd never really thought about it, although to some extent her life did seem a bit preordained. The chocolate shop had been passed down from one generation to the other. Her stomach fluttered as she thought, for the very first time, that she might now have an heir to continue the legacy. Then again, Bia had her own career. Her daughter had freedom of choice. Fate was not pushing her; it wasn't driving the train.

"That's an interesting question, Mr. Jordan."

"Are you always so formal?"

Maya shrugged. "Charles. Is that better?"

"Much."

"You remind me of someone," she said. "I keep trying to decide if it's because I remember you from your visit to the St. Michel shop. But that was so long ago. I've had many customers since then."

"Who do I remind you of?"

"Somebody from a long time ago."

"Did you care for this person?"

"A great deal." She suddenly caught herself, not sure she wanted to continue where this conversation was headed. "I must say, Charles, you're awfully forward to be asking such personal questions. Questions about fate. Questions about my past. What about your past? Do you believe in fate?"

"I believe that sometimes life puts us in a position where we don't have the luxury of choosing the path that we want to take."

"I'm not exactly sure what you mean by that."

"There's not an easy explanation."

He was looking at her so intensely that for a moment Maya couldn't breathe. Those eyes. Those blue, blue eyes. She'd only seen eyes that color—with flecks of silver and gold radiating from the iris—one other time. If she looked only at his eyes, she felt in her soul that this man was Ian. But that was impossible. She knew it was, and all the hurt that she had managed to shove away over the years sprang free from its trap, lodging in her heart and in the very blood that coursed through her veins.

She couldn't do this to herself. So much was going right in her life right now—the reunion with Bia, the new shop. Why was she going to torture herself with what she couldn't have when things were going so well?

Common sense said that she found Charles Jordan attractive. Why not try to start anew?

Why not? For the same reason she had never been able to love anyone else since the day that she found out Ian was dead. Charles Jordan reminded her of everything that she had loved and lost and would never have again.

It wasn't fair to him.

But what was she supposed to say? *I can't do this because you speak in riddles and remind me of my dead soul mate? Is that all I'm responding to? That you look like somebody who loved me and left me and took my heart with him?*

But you're a stranger who appeared out of nowhere. This just won't work.

"If you'll excuse me for just a moment, I need to—"

She stood up from the table and walked quickly toward the front door.

Bia's life felt fuller with Aiden in it. There was no doubt about that. Or about how these newfound feelings scared her more than just a little bit. All these years, she'd thought she had him figured out, but every day she was learning so many new things.

Every time they were together, she found out something new about him. Small things, such as how he liked pickles but did not like them on his sandwiches. He wanted them on the side. She'd never noticed that before. And that while he liked to tell her about his day, he needed a few minutes after work to unwind and change gears. In the past, they hadn't been around each other in these off hours, and she'd never realized just how much they could reveal about a person. One of the best things she'd recently learned about *bad boy* Aiden Woods was that he called his mother, who now lived in North Carolina, faithfully every Sunday afternoon. He had a deep connection with his family. When he talked about his mother, his sister and her family—they lived in the same small town as his mother—he exhibited a warmth and vulnerability that she never knew he possessed. These were just a few of the things she was beginning to discover and appreciate about him. And the more she learned, the more vulnerable she felt.

They were so natural together, and it didn't feel weird.

And that, in itself, was weird.

Her equilibrium was off, and she couldn't keep blaming it on the pregnancy hormones. She feared she was beginning to buy into the PR that she and Aiden were selling to everyone else, and she wondered if she should start thinking about an escape plan.

Just as Cinderella's ball had ended at midnight, she was beginning to realize that their own bewitching hour would come. How was this fairy tale that they'd spun supposed to end? Because good things always ended. And she needed to start thinking of a plausible way out before her heart got in any deeper.

Everyone knew them as a couple now. However, Aiden's friends and coworkers had mostly stayed out of their business except to offer congratulations. She appreciated the space.

However, tonight was the dinner party at Drew and Caroline's house. Miles and Sydney would be there, along with Pepper and Rob, and another couple—A.J. and her husband, Shane.

Venturing outside the intimate bubble world that she and Aiden had created, she feared that things were about to get really real. As she began to get ready for the party, she wished that she would have declined the invitation.

Nerves flew around her stomach like a swarm of dragonflies. It was the first time she and Aiden would be out as a couple with a group. Now that they were together, they would be invited to gatherings like this dinner party—things that couples did together. In the past, they'd never been included.

It was as if now that they were a couple they were somehow validated. That bothered her a little bit. She had been an interesting person before she had merged with Aiden. And the joke was on the others, since they weren't really a couple at all.

Tonight, they would be thrown together with actual couples, and she hoped it wasn't a recipe for disaster.

Her hair was done. She'd taken extra time with her makeup, and she'd chosen a green sundress paired with strappy sandals bejeweled with rhinestones. The dress, with its V neckline and full skirt, had always made her feel pretty. Now it accentuated the new fullness of her breasts. She paused a moment to appreciate her still slim waistline. All too soon it would be a thing of the past. At least until after she had the baby and could get back into shape.

She had to admit that despite her earlier trepidations, she felt sort of sexy getting all dressed up to go out. If she was completely honest with herself, she would admit that she was eager to see Aiden's reaction when he saw her.

It had been a long time since she'd felt sexy. And, it seemed, even longer since she'd been out on a date. If this even qualified as a date. Despite the rational side of her brain telling her not to make more of this than she should, it felt like a date.

She was at her jewelry box, selecting a simple pair of hoop earrings, when she heard the sound of the front door opening as Aiden let himself in.

"Hello!" he called.

Her heart pounded.

"I'm in the bedroom," she called. "I'll be right out."

She put in her earrings, then gave herself one last once-over in the full-length mirror.

"I have a bottle of merlot to bring with us tonight," Aiden called from the living room. "And a bottle of club soda for you."

He'd remembered the club soda.

Oh, it really did feel like a date.

Insecurity hit her like a tidal wave and threatened to knock her flat. Was the dress too much? Too low-cut?

She tugged at the V-neck.

People were used to seeing her in business attire or simple blue jeans and a button-down. Oh, well, this would be a definite change. She straightened her shoulders and lifted her chin, trying to remember how good she had felt just moments ago.

Ah, well, this would have to do.

Come on, you can do this.

She wanted to do this.

And what about the exit strategy that had sounded like such a good idea before Aiden had arrived with the club soda?

The club soda was for tonight. The exit strategy would have to wait for another day.

She walked out into the living room, her heels click-clacking on the wood floor in a way that made her want to shift her weight to her toes. But she didn't, for fear that she might lose her balance. She'd purchased the sandals on a whim when Hugh had been in town. She'd only worn them once—the night of the Doctor's Ball.

When she'd purchased them, she had been determined to change up her image. It had been a delusional moment, and look where it had landed her.

But the minute Aiden glanced up and saw her, the look on his face made her heart say, *Hugh who?*

His right brow shot up.

Bia's heart pounded, equal parts excitement and nerves.

"Hey, you," he murmured. He stood up, like the Southern gentleman she'd never known he was—yet another new revelation—taking in her appearance with an appreciative glint in his eyes.

She couldn't help but smile. "Hey, yourself," she said, suddenly feeling more like herself again.

It was amazing how he affected her that way. He made her feel appreciated, as if there were no other place in the world he wanted to be and no other person he would rather be with.

But she was no fool; she wouldn't delude herself into believing that he could be exclusively hers forever. Not Aiden. He was already doing so much for her—it wasn't fair to expect that of him.

Of course, when things were going so well the beast of doubt always had to rampage through.

She didn't want to ruin the night. She could confidently say that while she had herself together when it came to business, her love life was another matter altogether. She had a history of making bad choices: trusting Duane, sleeping with Hugh and getting pregnant. She didn't want Aiden to become a casualty of this charade.

As she stood there watching him watching her, she realized that she had been blaming him for the breakup with Duane because it provided a convenient barrier to keep her heart safe. She had made Aiden out to be the bad guy, making herself believe that his was the face of a player, that he was the guy who couldn't stand to see another couple happy—especially after he and Tracey divorced. It was easier to ignore her own feelings for him when she was holding him responsible for her breakup. But after spending so much time with him, after allowing him to kiss her senseless, all the reasons *why not* had fallen away. Her heart was naked and vulnerable with the reality that she had it bad for Aiden Woods.

She who was no prize—pregnant with someone else's child—had lost her heart to a man who could have anyone. And she couldn't afford to keep making bad choices about love because now it wasn't just herself that she had to consider.

She had to think about the baby.

Chapter Ten

The party at Drew and Caroline's house was a co-congratulations affair: congratulations to Bia and Aiden on their engagement and three cheers for a successful grand opening for the new location of Maya's Chocolates.

Maya sat back and watched and listened as her friends talked and laughed around the dinner table, leisurely sipping their wine, Bia sipping her club soda. They were in no hurry to get up. Even though she was the only one without a date, she loved being included, soaking up the positive vibe.

The shop wasn't open on Sundays. So she hadn't seen or talked to Charles Jordan since last night. She felt silly for having bolted on him, but Maya always trusted her intuition and it had been propelling her to leave.

Today, as she thought about it, she realized she hadn't felt in physical danger when she was with him—every nerve in her body was telling her that Charles Jordan was not a dangerous man, or at least not someone who wanted to cause her physical harm.

Heartache, however? That's what scared her.

And it's why she'd run.

She was too busy with the new shop, and the last thing she needed was someone who dredged up heartache to derail her focus.

And she certainly didn't want to think about it tonight.

She shoved Charles Jordan into the recesses of her mind, where he seemed to have taken up permanent residence, and shut the door on him.

The smell of homemade lasagna and garlic bread hung in the air. Even though Maya was stuffed, she savored the aroma. The pasta dish, made entirely from scratch, was a specialty of Celebrations, Inc., Catering, the company owned by Pepper, A.J., Caroline and Sydney.

No wonder their business was so good clients were booking four months in advance.

It warmed her heart to look around the table through the candlelight and see everyone so happy. Successful in business, happy in love. And to think that she'd had a hand in bringing together just about every couple at the table.

Pepper and Rob.

A.J. and Shane.

Caroline and Drew.

Sydney and Miles.

Rob's sister Kate and her new husband were also there. While she hadn't foretold that marriage—not in the same way she had with the other four couples—she'd had the pleasure of serving as the emcee for the bachelor auction where Kate had placed the winning bid for the date with Liam, who was now her husband.

Her gaze drifted to Bia and Aiden.

She'd just met Aiden tonight. He was handsome. A great guy, loving and attentive to Bia. Maya was so pleased when she'd learned that he had proposed to her daughter.

However, something was off.

She couldn't quite put her finger on it, but something between the two of them was different. At least it was different than the vibes between the other couples.

Maybe it was because Bia was her daughter and their relationship was so new? That might skew things.

Tiger Mother syndrome?

No, actually, that wasn't it. She liked Aiden well enough and from what she could discern, he was absolutely smitten with Bia. The downturn was more from Bia.

Hmmm...

Maya hoped that there would be many more opportunities for her and her daughter to spend time together so that they could talk and Maya could try and figure out exactly what was amiss.

The young woman was guarded. While the other girls had popped the corks on bottles of champagne and had fussed over Bia's engagement ring when she and Aiden had first arrived, Bia seemed to hold back emotionally.

Maybe she was simply reserved, the cautious type who didn't wear her heart on her sleeve for everyone to see.... Perhaps. But it felt like there was more to it than that.

Maya could feel it in her bones.

Of course, there was the matter of the baby's paternity, but Aiden knew about that, even if the others didn't. He was marrying her with full disclosure.

Thank goodness everyone at the party had the good grace not to mention the horrid tabloid show and the reporter who was still speculating and lurking around town.

Maya had never seen *XYZ Celebrity News* until Bia had told her about the ambush. Thank goodness she'd watched it, because the guy had shown up in her shop one day asking her employees questions—not about Bia specifically, but he was fishing for information about Hugh Newman—looking for information about the time he had spent in Celebration previously. He had asked if the girls had seen Hugh around and more specifically if they had seen him around town with any women.

Maya had shown the guy the door, threatening to call the police if he didn't leave.

"Who wants dessert?" Caroline asked. "I have red velvet cake and coffee in the kitchen."

Bia stood. "Caroline, let me get dessert. You've worked so hard today having us over. Please relax."

"Yes, Caroline, please do. I am happy to help Bia clear the table and get the dessert."

In a matter of moments, Bia and Maya were in the kitchen slicing the tall red velvet cake that Caroline had made and left on a plate on the island in the center of her kitchen. Maya was doing the cutting and Bia was using a spatula to transfer the delicious-looking cake to dessert plates.

"Aiden is nice," Maya said. "He seems to care for you very much."

Maya glanced up just in time to see a certain look in Bia's eyes that confirmed her earlier suspicion. But as quickly as the emotion flashed, Bia's wall went up and a placid smile masked whatever it was that had initially troubled her.

As soon as Bia had delivered the last piece of cake to the dessert plate, Maya took her daughter's left hand and looked at the ring.

"That's a gorgeous ring," she said. "How did he propose?"

Bia cleared her throat. "He did it the old-fashioned way. He got down on one knee and asked me to be his wife."

"Were you surprised?"

The placid smile transformed into a wry grin. "I can assure you, I have never been more surprised in my entire life."

"But he hadn't given you the ring when the reporter showed up that day harassing you?"

Bia's brow furrowed, and her gaze flicked to the door between the kitchen and the dining room just as a bubble of laughter erupted from the gang.

They were engrossed in another matter and couldn't hear what they were talking about in the kitchen. Bia visibly relaxed.

"No, the day the reporter ambushed me was the first time I heard Aiden refer to me as his fiancée. The ring came later. So, technically, maybe I was a little more surprised that time than when he gave me the ring."

Maya nodded. "I just want to be sure that you're happy."

"I'll be happy when the *XYZ* reporter is gone for good." She lowered her voice to a whisper. "I still haven't found out who tipped him off those two times that he came after me. Has he been back to the shop at all?"

Maya shook her head. "No, I think he knows better than to darken the door of my shop. There's nothing like the protection of a mother who senses her daughter is in danger."

The words hung in the air between them. Bia's expression was unreadable for a moment.

Finally she said, "I appreciate you looking out for me."

Bia set the sugar bowl and cream pitcher on a tray that Caroline had left on another counter. She gestured toward the dining room with her head. "They don't know the other bit of recent happy news, do they? That you're my birth mother. I mean, Aiden knows, of course. But nobody else. Do they?"

"No, they don't."

She stopped what she was doing and turned full attention on Maya. "All that time you were here in Celebration after my father passed away, you didn't tell them that was part of the reason that you were here?"

She'd never really told Bia that's what had initially drawn her here. However, it didn't really take a genius to put two and two together. "No, I didn't want you to hear the news from anyone but me. And I didn't want to tell anyone until I knew you were ready to talk about it."

"I think I'm ready now. Shall we tell them?"

Everyone at the dinner party had seemed even more surprised to learn that Maya was Bia's birth mother than by the news that Bia and Aiden were getting married—scratch that—that they were *engaged*. Of course they'd all had a chance to digest the engagement before the dinner party on Sunday night. So, if they'd been at all shocked by it, they'd managed to mind their manners when they were all together.

The evening had been a nice celebration.

It had happened after Maya and Bia had distributed the cake and coffee. Maya had simply said, "As if we don't have enough to celebrate, there's more good news."

Everyone had quieted down and turned their attention to Maya. "Not many people know this about me, but when I was eighteen years old I met a man who was the love of my life. We had a few happy months together. Then, sadly, he died in a tragic automobile accident. I was pregnant with his child."

Every gaze in the room was riveted to Maya.

"It was a different day and age back then, and since I was from a small provincial town, my mother and grandmother, who both had extremely traditional values, were horrified by my pregnancy out of wedlock. They sent me away to have the baby and arranged for the child—a baby girl—to be adopted by a couple who could not have a child of their own. I grieved the loss of my baby, just as much as I grieved the loss of my soul mate. And even though I knew there was never a chance that I would see my love again, deep in my heart I held out hope that I would be reunited with my child.

"Of course, it was a closed adoption. The adoptive parents were adamant about that. They didn't want to take the chance of me changing my mind. However, my mother had the foresight to ask the agency to give the adoptive parents my information just in case. Whatever she figured might constitute 'just in case,' I will never know. I didn't know then that the parents knew how to find me, only that they had taken my baby girl from me. I thought I would never see her again.

"Then about eighteen months ago, I received a letter from a man informing me that he was the husband of the couple who had adopted my daughter. His wife had passed away years ago. Now he was dying, and he didn't have long to live. He told me that it was his dying wish that his daughter—my daughter—should not be left alone after he died.

"If I had any desire whatsoever to know my daughter, he asked that I wait until after he was gone. But then he would be happy for me to be a part of Bia's life."

Everyone in the room had gasped at the revelation. But they were happy that they could be among the first to share the wonderful news. It was just sinking in that Maya was family. She was Bia's *mother*. It was comforting to know that Maya had not given her up voluntarily. She really hadn't had any choice.

Actually, if you wanted to look for the silver lining, Maya had chosen to give Bia a better life by giving her up to loving parents who desperately wanted a child.

Later that week, Bia pondered the thought as she pulled into a parking place at the grocery store. As she put the car in Park and reached over to turn off the ignition, she glanced down at the dashboard. A yellow warning light that she'd never seen before was illuminated. She took the car owner's manual out of the glove box and looked up the problem.

It turned out to be a bulb failure warning sensor, which meant that somewhere on the vehicle a bulb had blown or was about to.

Thank goodness it didn't seem to be anything serious. Aiden was working late and Maya was coming over for dinner tonight. Bia would ask him about it tomorrow. If it was something simple, she'd see if he could show her how to change it. If not, she could take it to the dealership.

She fished her shopping list out of her purse, got out of the car and locked it before walking into the store.

At the party, A.J. had given her a couple of recipes that sounded delicious: soy ginger–glazed salmon and Asian coleslaw. She was making them for dinner tonight. She was trying to be so careful about eating healthy for the baby. She figured salmon was a good choice. Plus, it would be quick and easy to put on the table.

Since it was something not in her usual recipe repertoire, she didn't have many of the ingredients on hand. It was okay; she was learning it was a good thing to try new things every once in a while. Her mind drifted to Aiden. This phase in their relationship was definitely something new. It felt as if she was walking out on a glass bridge. Her senses kept preparing her for a crash landing. Yet she was fine—something sturdy and unseen was holding her up. If she didn't look down, she just might be all right.

She needed to keep reminding herself of that. Or maybe she should just quit thinking about it altogether. Quit overthinking and live.

She was in the aisle with the cooking oils, searching for sesame oil, when she heard a voice behind her.

"Well, if it isn't Bia Anderson," the woman said.

Bia flinched inwardly before she turned around and saw a woman that Aiden had dated on and off for a couple of months. She had only met the woman one time, and she didn't remember her name. It was something like Judy…or Julie…or Juliet?

"Hello," Bia said vaguely, still racking her brain for the woman's name. There had been so many women, it was hard to keep track. Actually, she hadn't catalogued them, but this one was so pretty she stood out from the bunch. Tall, blonde and model-thin. Bia swallowed a pang of…what? Jealousy? Inadequacy?

"I'm Joanna," she said. "You probably don't re-member me. But I'm Aiden's old...um...Aiden and I used to...um..."

"I do remember you, Joanna. Yes, you and Aiden used to date. It's nice of you to say hello."

The woman with her Heidi Klum looks was perfect. If Aiden didn't want her, Bia didn't understand what he was looking for. If she wasn't good enough... Well.

"I understand congratulations are in order. I wanted to get a good look at the woman who finally snagged Aiden Woods's heart. May I see the ring?"

These words coming from tall, beautiful Joanna took Bia aback. Bia held up her hand, and, as the woman studied it, Bia had a chance to study her per-fect complexion, her wide-set blue eyes and other clas-sic features.

Good God, Aiden. If this woman isn't good enough for you, what in the world do you want?

Then Bia recognized the feeling she was fighting. It was regret. She certainly couldn't compete with Joanna. The escape plan that she'd been thinking so much about...she needed to get to work on that.

"It really is gorgeous," Joanna said wistfully. "It's just the kind of ring I knew Aiden would pick out."

Bia's expression must have betrayed her.

"Oh, honey, you don't have to worry about me. I tossed in the Aiden towel months ago. But I have to warn you, Lisa English is devastated. You might want to watch your back there. She's not going away with-out a fight."

Watch my back?

Was she kidding?

Joanna gave Bia a once-over that ended with a patronizing smile. It could have been described as pity.

"Good luck, Bia." The words *you're going to need it* went unsaid, but they hung in the air, as heavily as Joanna's perfume, after she turned and click-clacked her way down the aisle.

Chapter Eleven

An hour later, standing in her kitchen, Bia took out her angst on the green, red and napa cabbage, shredding it for the coleslaw and trying not to get sucked into a black hole of doubt.

The grocery store rendezvous with Joanna had been a huge reality check for Bia. The problem with being a realist was that she refused to delude herself. She and Joanna were two completely different breeds of women. And if Aiden didn't want Joanna…

Bia blinked away the nagging thought and reread the recipe, which called for slicing carrots into ultra-thin matchsticks. She focused on making each cut as precise and uniform as she could.

She was good at things like this—checking newspaper stories for grammar and fact. Following recipes and slicing vegetables into precise matchstick pieces. Logical things. Things that took precision and concentration. These were the things she had control over. This was her comfort zone, and that's where she was confident. But she had no more desire to put herself out there on the dating scene, head-to-head with women like Joanna and this Lisa English—whoever she was—than she wanted to get up onstage and try to outsing Christina Aguilera.

Joanna and Lisa were the type of women Aiden was attracted to. Beautiful, fashionable, trophy girlfriend material. That's exactly what they were. What the heck was wrong with Aiden?

Bia stopped cutting, realization creeping over her.

Aiden dated these women until they fell for him. Was he only into the thrill of the chase? He pursued women until they wanted him and then he got the heck out of Dodge…as fast as he could. It had even happened with Tracey after they'd gotten married.

Huh.

The symptoms sure did seem to fit the disease.

Maybe the chance meeting with Joanna was a good reminder that Bia needed to not get carried away. Even though kissing Aiden felt pretty darn right, she needed to take off the *lurve* goggles and see the situation for what it really was.

But for some reason, that didn't sit right with her, either.

Bia had just put the salmon in the oven when Maya arrived. She remembered what Maya had said that first day she had come to interview her: that Bia had already met the love of her life. That he was in her life, and all she needed to do was appreciate what was right in front of her.

Against Bia's better judgment, the completely senseless heart of her that she never allowed to have a voice was speaking up loud and clear: somehow, some way she wished that person could be Aiden.

Who else could it be?

And here she was talking to herself as if she believed in Maya's *woo-woo* proclamations.

All she had to lose was her heart. But before she could do that, she needed to know that she and the baby were safe. That she wasn't making another colossal mistake.

Maya greeted Bia with a big warm hug and what looked like a box of chocolates.

"Come in!" said Bia.

"I can't even begin to tell you how much I've been looking forward to this evening," Maya said. "These are for you."

Bia gratefully accepted the chocolates. "These will make a fabulous dessert. Thank you."

"I hope I'm not late," Maya said. "I came straight from work. But it took longer than I thought it would to close up shop for the day. I suppose I could have let the staff do it, but we're still getting used to each other."

"I'm sure that will happen in no time," Bia said. "But you're not late. I just put the salmon in the oven. Would you mind coming into the kitchen? I'm still working on another dish for dinner."

Bia noticed the way that Maya glanced around as she walked toward the kitchen. She seemed to be taking in all the details of her house. It was the first time Maya had ever been there. She tried to see the place through Maya's eyes: the living room with the big, overstuffed red sofa; the rustic plank wood coffee table with several magazines fanned out, a grouping of candles and a silk orchid plant that looked real; an entertainment center with a flat-screen TV. It was all her own furniture that she'd moved in from her apartment after her father had passed away. The only thing of his that remained was his old recliner, which was in dire need of reupholstering, and some of the paintings and family photos that still hung on the wall. While she'd done her best to make the house that she'd grown up in her own, she couldn't bring herself to part with those remnants of the past.

"You have such a nice home," Maya said.

"Thank you. I grew up in this house. Lived here all my life except for the years I was away at college and in my apartment when I came back to take the reporting job at the paper."

Maya walked over to the fireplace and picked up a frame that contained one of the few family portraits they'd had taken before Brenda, Bia's adoptive mom, had died.

"How old were you here?" Maya asked.

"I was three."

"Look at you with your red curls. You're such a beautiful child. You still are."

Bia smiled her thanks at the motherly comment.

She paused in the doorway, watching Maya set down the picture and glance around again, seemingly taking everything in.

"I'm just trying to imagine you as a three-year-old running around this house."

"Do you have any regrets?" Bia asked. "I mean, I know you were in no position to care for a child, especially since your family wasn't very supportive of your situation, but…"

As the words left her mouth, it struck Bia as odd that a family that had prided itself on passing a business down from one generation to another would be so willing to give up one of their own. Maybe they thought Maya would have other children.

Oh, well.

That was a long time ago, and Bia could read the sorrow in Maya's eyes.

"If I could do it over again, I would do it differently," she said. "But I'm a firm believer in not staining the present with regrets over the past." She took a deep breath, exhaled and smiled. "I always knew that I would see you again. I always clung to that belief. Now look at us. Here we are."

"Yes. Here we are."

This was her mother.

Her *mother*. Even though it had taken a while to wrap her mind around the fact that her father had kept the truth about her birth from her for all those years, he had been instrumental in bringing the two of them together.

As they made their way into the kitchen, Bia thought about how sometimes you had to look past the first impression to realize the beauty in something that at first glance might seem devastating.

"I just realized I've never asked you where you

live," Bia said as she busied herself measuring out ingredients for the coleslaw dressing.

"I have a small studio on the second floor of the shop."

Bia glanced up from her recipe. "I didn't even realize that the shop had a second story."

"It's more of a renovated attic space. But I have a nice full bathroom and a place to sleep. Actually, it's quite cozy. The best part is, I can't beat the commute."

The two of them laughed at Maya's joke, then exchanged stories and snippets of information, bringing each other up-to-date with their lives with broad brushstrokes covering the missing years. She really was happy to have this time with Maya…her mother.

The reality of it made her catch her breath each time she thought about Maya being her mother. At least, for the most part, it kept her mind off the Joanna incident. Occasionally, her mind would drift back to their conversation in the grocery store, but Bia would force herself to think about something else. She thought she was doing a pretty good job keeping a sunny disposition.

Still, somehow Maya seemed to see through the facade. "Is everything all right?"

Bia tossed the cabbage in the dressing. "Of course. Why do you ask?"

"You just don't seem like yourself tonight. Are you feeling all right?"

Bia nodded. "I guess I'm just a little bit tired. We just put this week's edition of the paper to bed last night. It always takes a lot out of me to get that done."

"Please let me help you with the rest of dinner," said Maya.

"It's a very simple meal," Bia said. "It's almost done. So, just have a seat and relax. You must be tired, too, after being on your feet all day."

"Well, if you won't let me help you with the cooking, while you do that, I'll set the table for you."

"That would be fabulous. And would you please put on the kettle for some herbal tea? I'd love some with dinner, but would you like a glass of wine?"

"Tea sounds perfect."

Bia showed Maya the drawer with the silverware and pointed out a basket of cloth napkins.

"Is Aiden joining us tonight?"

Bia inhaled sharply. The mention of his name had caused her stomach to do a little somersault. Oh, that wasn't good. She needed to stop doing things like that. She needed to stop remembering the feel of his lips on hers and the way his hands had taken possession of her body.

"No, he's working tonight. It's just you and me."

"Are you missing him?" Maya asked. "Is that why you seem a little blue?"

Bia threw a quick glance over her shoulder at Maya, who was fishing the silverware out of the drawer.

"Well, no. I wouldn't say that exactly."

Maya walked up and placed a hand on Bia's shoulder and gave a little squeeze.

Bia made a conscious effort to relax. "I think my hormones are knocking me for a loop. I don't know what's wrong with me."

"What do you mean?"

"I was at the grocery store after I got off work, and I ran into an old girlfriend of Aiden's."

Maya looked at her quizzically. "Did she upset you?"

"Yes, but it's not her fault."

"What did she do?"

Nothing. She didn't do anything. How did she tell Maya that the only thing the woman was guilty of was being gorgeous and dating Aiden?

Bia knew she was being ridiculous without even saying the words. It was the hormones. Was it the hormones that were bothering her? Or was it the fact that she wasn't telling the truth? Right now she wanted nothing more than to talk to Maya.

"May I confide in you?" Bia asked.

"This engagement isn't real. Aiden has agreed to do this to help me out."

Bia explained everything to Maya—how Aiden had spontaneously jumped to her rescue, and, while it was a quick fix for the moment, it had left them in a precarious position. It left Bia vulnerable to the media discovering that she was carrying Hugh's baby.

"We just need to give it some time. Until I'm sure that the tabloid reporters have gone away and aren't planning any more sneak attacks. We've talked about keeping this up until they decide what to do about the movie that Hugh was supposed to be in. Whether they will still shoot in Celebration or if they put the project on hold. Until then it seems pretty certain that the *XYZ* correspondents will be lurking."

Maya didn't look as surprised as Bia thought she

might upon hearing the news. She simply nodded and drew some water for the kettle, ignited the burner on the gas range and set the water to boil.

Bia took down her grandmother's china teapot and two cups and set them on a tray. She put four teaspoons of loose tea leaves into the pot.

"The two of you have been putting on a convincing show," Maya said as she set the table. "From the ring all the way down to the way he looks at you. The energy is right between the two of you. Whether you realize it or not, there is something special here. He's in love with you. Everyone can see it's so. Why are you making this so difficult?"

Bia flinched at the unexpected question.

"What makes you so sure that this energy, as you put it, is right? And what makes you think I am the one who is making this difficult?"

"Because I sense that you are the one who is holding back. How can you expect things to work out if you won't allow him to love you?"

"It's not that easy. I wish it were."

"Falling in love can be the easiest or the most difficult thing in the world. It all depends on what you make of it."

The teakettle whistled, and Maya got up to pour the boiling water into the teapot. As she stood over the steeping pot, she said, "You don't like to be out of control, do you?"

"Does anyone?" asked Bia. "I'm sure if a person could choose to be in control of her life and feelings or not, she would choose to be. Right?"

Maya brought the tray over to the table.

"Anytime a person falls in love, she feels vulnerable and out of control. It's much easier if you just go with it. Don't fight it."

Maya sat down across the table from Bia and poured tea into each of the cups.

"I wish it were that easy," Bia said.

"It's only as hard as you make it," said Maya. "You have to trust Aiden. You have to trust yourself."

"I guess that's the problem. Trust and I...we have a rather complicated relationship."

"Has he given you any reason not to trust him?" Maya asked.

Bia thought back to that night so long ago—the night of the bachelor party—and all the times in between that they'd talked about it. All the years she'd so desperately wanted to pin the blame on someone other than Duane. If she could, then maybe that meant that she hadn't been the one who'd made the mistake. But Aiden was right. The only one to blame was Duane.

"I used to think so," Bia said. "But no. Aiden has been nothing but wonderful to me. He's the one who came up with this plan to protect me. My problem is, I don't want it to ruin our friendship."

Maya sipped her tea thoughtfully. "Why would it?"

Bia told her about her newfound theory. That Aiden was only intrigued by the thrill of the chase.

"And you say this because he has dated a lot of women?"

Bia nodded. "A lot of beautiful women."

"You do realize that he ended things with each of them because they weren't the right women for him?

Otherwise he would be married and we wouldn't be having this conversation."

"Well, he was married once," Bia said.

Maya's brows shot up. "What happened?"

"I don't know. They got a divorce. He won't talk about it. They were married for a couple of years after college, when Aiden was living in Los Angeles."

"He will tell you in good time. Especially after the two of you are married."

"I don't think this will end in marriage," Bia said. "He made an impulsive action. I appreciate it, but I won't hold him to it."

Maya gave her a look like she wasn't convinced.

"You need to talk to him about it," Maya said. "Just be open about how you feel."

How could she be honest with him when she wasn't sure she could even be honest with herself about how she felt?

Thank goodness the stove's timer dinged, indicating that the salmon was finished and that line of the conversation was over. Bia got up to take the fish out of the oven.

While Bia was plating the meal, Maya didn't push the issue any further. That was a good thing, because Bia didn't want to talk about it anymore.

Still, she thought, as she retrieved the slaw from the refrigerator, it was nice to have Maya in her life. Someone to talk to. Despite all the years they'd been apart and the short time that they'd known each other, she felt incredibly connected to Maya. For that, Bia was grateful.

As Bia set a plate in front of Maya, her mother

smiled up at her. A feeling of gratitude washed over Bia in an unexpected wave.

"We've been talking about me all night," Bia said as she took her seat across the table from Maya. "It's your turn."

Maya gave a reticent one-shoulder shrug, dipping her head at Bia's suggestion. "There's not much else to say. I've told you most everything."

Maya took a bite of salmon and chewed it.

"You told me everything?"

Maya swallowed her bite and looked at Bia as if she was contemplating something. "This is delicious, by the way."

"Thank you, but don't change the subject," Bia said. "We're talking about you."

"There might be one thing that I haven't told you. A turn of events that has happened just since I've been in Celebration."

Bia leaned forward. "Is this about a man?"

Maya's left eyebrow arched and a sly smile spread across her face. "Maybe."

"There's no maybe about it," Bia said. "Either there's a man or there's not. Which is it?"

"Okay, so it's about a man. I'm just not sure how he figures. He scares me a little."

Bia's eyes widened. "As in fearing for your safety or he makes you feel vulnerable?"

"I don't know. Okay, I guess he doesn't make me fear for my safety, but I don't know him. He knows me, though. He sent me a message before the store opened saying he'd been to the shop in St. Michel. He's in town on business and…"

Bia propped her elbow on the table and rested her chin on her palm. "And?"

Maya answered her with another shrug.

"All right, Ms. You-Have-to-Be-Willing-to-Be-Vulnerable, I believe it's time you practice what you preach."

Maya laughed. "It's so much easier to give advice than it is to practice it."

Bia looked up at the ceiling. "Finally, my mother understands me."

They both laughed, and Maya told Bia about Charles, about how he had stopped by the shop on opening day and about how she had run out on him at the pub.

"Why does he make you so nervous?"

Suddenly Maya's face turned very solemn. "Because he reminds me of your father. Ian Brannigan was the only man I've ever loved. I haven't been able to feel anything for a man since I lost him."

"Until now?"

"I don't know. I don't know what I feel."

"I hear you. This vulnerability business isn't all it's cracked up to be, is it?"

"Not when you're the one sitting in the seat of vulnerability."

"Will you tell me about my father?" Bia asked. "I would love to know about him."

Maya's trademark placid smile returned to her face. A light the likes of which Bia had never seen on her mother's face ignited as she began to tell the story of how she fell in love with Ian. It dimmed as she recounted how he left one day and never came back, leaving her pregnant with his child, how she eventually learned of his accident.

"He never knew about you. I couldn't imagine him just running off without a goodbye. But when he didn't come back, I thought the worst. I was so mad at him for a long time, for breaking all his promises. He told me he would love me forever and then he just disappeared. The more I thought about it, the more it didn't make sense. It didn't seem like him. But then my mother sent me away and you were born. After I got home I got this crazy idea that I was going to find him. That once he knew about you, he would come back and we would be a family.

"So I called his family, and that's when I learned of the tragic news. It was like losing him all over again, only far worse and much more painful than I could ever imagine. It took me years to be able to smile again—and even then I might've just been going through the motions. I was dead on the inside until I got the letter from your adoptive father and there was the possibility of reuniting with you. My daughter."

Maya reached across the table and took Bia's hand in hers. "For the first time in decades, I am happy, truly happy. So I don't know if these feelings for Charles are an offshoot from the joy I am feeling from our reunion. These similarities that I see in him, the mannerisms, the turns of speech that remind me of your father might just be transference—my wanting to imagine your father here. That's why I need to be careful."

"From what you said, though, Charles sounds like a nice guy. Why not give him a chance?"

Maya pursed her lips and her left brow shot up. Bia was beginning to notice that as one of Maya's trademark expressions.

"I'll make a deal with you," Maya said. "If you give Aiden a chance, I'll consider doing the same with Charles Jordan. Do we have a deal?"

Chapter Twelve

The *Catering to Dallas* shoot wrapped at about nine-thirty, and Aiden was at Bia's house by ten-fifteen. He was surprised to see the yellow Volkswagen convertible in her driveway, but then he remembered that Maya was coming over to have dinner with Bia tonight.

The two women were standing in the foyer when Aiden walked in. They stopped in the middle of what they were saying, looking a little startled to see him.

"Hello," he said. He kissed Bia on the cheek and felt her tense and pull away from him ever so slightly. He took a step back, giving her a quizzical look. "I hope I'm not interrupting."

Maybe he should've knocked, but he and Bia had an open-door policy. Neither of them ever knocked when they entered the other's place. Especially not lately.

"No, you're not interrupting," said Bia. "I'm glad to see you."

Her words said welcome, but her actions were cool and distant.

"Maya and I were just talking about the chocolate business. She is going to show me how to make chocolate. Doesn't that sound like fun?"

"Yes, I am," Maya said a little too brightly.

That may have been the plan, but Aiden got the feeling that's not what they had been talking about when he had walked in. That was fine; they had a lot to catch up on considering all the years they'd been apart. Aiden was glad that Bia had Maya to lean on during the pregnancy. Every woman deserved to have her mother there when she went through life's rites of passage.

"I made salmon for dinner," Bia said. "It's in the oven. I kept it warm for you. Unless you're absolutely starving, I'll fix you a plate after I say goodbye to Maya. If you are starving, go ahead and help yourself."

"Thank you," he said. "You take your time. I can fix my plate. It was good to see you, Maya. Hope to see you again soon."

"Yes," she said. "I hope so, too. I appreciate the way you're taking such good care of Bia. I know she does, too."

Aiden glanced back and saw a funny look wash over Bia's face. Had they been talking about him when he arrived? What was there to say?

"Take care," he said, leaving them alone in the foyer.

"There's coleslaw in the refrigerator," Bia called after him.

He felt like an interloper until he found the foil-covered plate of salmon in the oven. They had talked about him coming over after work, and the dinner proved that she had been expecting him. Still, something didn't feel right.

He heard the front door close, and a moment later Bia was standing in the kitchen with her hands clasped in front of her. She looked so damn sexy in shorts that showed off her long shapely legs and a V-neck top that hinted at just the slightest bit of cleavage. It was almost as if Bia was not aware of it. She obviously wasn't aware of the effect she had on him. For as long as he'd known her, she'd never purposely dressed sexy. That was what made her so alluring. She had a quiet confidence that did more for his libido than if she would have gone for the obvious too-short, too-low-cut getup that so many women favored these days. In his book, subtle was way sexier than in-your-face.

He got the coleslaw and dished it onto his plate. "This looks so good. Thanks for making it for me. I'm starving. We filmed at a wedding reception tonight, and the food smelled incredible. But everything was so chaotic that I didn't get a chance to eat."

He recovered the bowl with plastic wrap and put it back in the refrigerator. "Besides, I wanted to save my appetite for tonight."

Realizing how that might have sounded like a double entendre—he'd actually meant it as one—he glanced over at Bia to gauge her reaction. There was that strange look again.

"What's wrong?" he asked.

She stood there for a moment, looking a little vulnerable. Aiden waited for her to answer.

"I ran into your good friend Joanna at the grocery store this afternoon," Bia said.

"Joanna Brandt?"

"I'm not sure what her last name is. The tall blonde you dated a few months ago."

"I don't know if you'd actually call it dating—"

Bia crossed her arms and furrowed her brow. "You see, that's what I'm talking about. Why did *she* think you were dating if you weren't?"

"What are you talking about?"

Okay. Maybe that's what Bia and Maya had been discussing when he'd walked in. He didn't give Bia a chance to answer.

"How is Joanna?" Aiden said. "I haven't seen her in several months."

"Gorgeous as ever," Bia said. "But, sorry to say, she seems to be over you. She says she threw in the Aiden towel a long time ago, but somebody named Lisa is still hot on your trail."

Lisa?

"Lisa who?" he asked, racking his brain, trying to call forth the face.

"Is there more than one Lisa?" Bia asked. "This one's name is Lisa English. Ring a bell?"

"Lisa English? I never even went out with her. She's a friend of Joanna's. Did Joanna tell you I dated Lisa?"

"Let's see if I can remember what she said." Bia put a finger on her chin and looked up at the ceiling as if she were trying hard to remember. "I think it was something to the tune of, 'I have to warn you, Lisa English is devastated that you and Aiden are engaged. You might want to watch your back there. She's not going to go away without a fight.' Yes. That's what she said. This, of course, came after Joanna said she wanted to get a good look at the woman who'd finally stolen Aiden Woods's heart. You should've seen the look on her face when I told her not to worry—that you were still on the market and that this was all just a big farce."

Aiden nearly choked on his dinner. "What? Did you really say that?"

Bia cocked her head to one side, holding his gaze. "Of course not. I'm not stupid."

"I didn't say you were. I just know that Joanna can be a little…"

Bia had her elbow on the table; her chin rested in her palm. She arched a brow at him and moved her head ever so slightly as if saying, *A little what?*

Was she jealous? Aiden's heart gave a little tug at the possibility. If she was jealous that meant she cared. All those years Bia had stood back as he brought different women around—of course, none of them were anything other than friends to him. Except for Tracey. He'd ended up eloping to Vegas with her. She was the biggest mistake of his life.

Bia had never shown the slightest indication that she was bothered by any of the women. Of course, she was a decent woman—she never would have said anything bad about any of them.

Plus, she had been engaged to Duane all that time.

"Joanna can be a little *persistent,*" he finally said. "She has a very strong personality."

"And you think that I'm not strong enough to stand up to her?"

Oh, boy. This was going downhill fast. If he wasn't careful, he was going to dig himself into a hole.

"I'm sure you can hold your own with Joanna or anyone who puts you in an uncomfortable position."

"Which is why you had to jump in and tell the *XYZ* guy that we were engaged? Because I can handle anyone who puts me in an uncomfortable position?"

Aiden set down his fork. "I didn't come here to fight with you, Bia. I'm sorry you ran into Joanna. I'm sorry she said what she said. But the truth is, I've dated lots of women. I'm not dating them now. I can't change the past, and actually I don't want to. Because the one thing I learned from dating all those women is that none of them was right for me. They weren't you."

She stared at him with big eyes. For a moment, she looked a little disoriented. He feared she might get up and walk away. But he'd said it. Said the thing he'd wanted to say since the first time he'd realized he was in love with her. As he waited for her to say something, he looked down at his hands, which were balled into fists in his lap. He consciously relaxed them.

"Aiden, do you think that's because I'm just about the only woman who doesn't find you irresistible?"

Ouch. Not exactly the response he was hoping for. But something in her eyes went counter to the words that were so confidently flowing from those lips that drove him crazy.

His gaze fell to her mouth.

"Is that the truth, B? You don't feel anything for me? Nothing at all? You could just get up and walk away? From us?"

She inhaled sharply.

"Aiden, there isn't an *us,* not in the terms that you're talking about. I'm trying to keep us from making a big mistake and ruining everything."

He leaned in. "So, you're saying that you do feel something? Otherwise there wouldn't be any reason for you to need to worry about *us.* To walk away from *us.*"

She got up and took his plate to the sink. Turned on the faucet, rinsed it and put it in the dishwasher.

He walked up behind her and put his hands on her shoulders. She stiffened but didn't pull away. He leaned in close and whispered in her ear.

"You see, I think the big mistake would be not admitting that there is something here…between *us.*" He kissed her earlobe and then trailed kisses down her neck. She relaxed and leaned back into him, moving her head to the side, allowing him better access. "There's been something brewing between *us* for a very long time. Tell me that's not true, that you don't feel it, too, and I'll walk away."

He nipped at her earlobe, ran his lips over the tender spot where her ear met her neck. Her breathing became heavy and she seemed to stifle a little moan.

But suddenly she pulled away and looked up at him, her eyes dark with need. "It's not that I don't feel anything for you," she said.

Those lips that he'd longed to taste again were

inches away from his. All he had to do was lean in and claim them.

"I'm the only woman who has ever said no to you. I'm just afraid that once you do get what you want, it will be the end of *us*. I'm afraid that you don't really want me, Aiden. You just want what you can't have."

She stood and looked at him. She was so close that they were breathing the same air. She looking at him with an expression that made him want to pull her in close. To show her just how wrong she was about him.

"Did it ever dawn on you that maybe I've dated so many women because I was trying to get you out of my system?"

"No, that's not true," she said.

Her breath smelled vaguely like peppermint and chocolate and he couldn't help himself; he leaned in and dusted a feather-soft kiss on her bottom lip.

"It is true," he murmured. "That's why no other relationship has lasted. I married Tracey because I thought that might be the best way to get over you. But you know how it turned out."

Bia ducked out of his arms. "No, I don't—not other than the obvious. That the two of you divorced. You never told me. Are you saying you didn't love her, but you married her, anyway?"

Aiden crossed his arms and leaned one hip against the counter. "That's not really a fair question."

"It is, Aiden." She grabbed a rag and started wiping down the countertops. "It's a very fair and straightforward question. Did you love Tracey or not?"

This was a no-win situation. "She divorced me, B. So whether or not I loved her is a moot point."

Bia shook her head and smirked at him as if she'd drawn her own conclusion.

"What about you and Hugh?" He held up a hand. "No, wait—don't answer that. It's a rhetorical question. The only reason I brought it up is because you had your reasons for Hugh. I'm not judging you, and I never will. It happened, but it's in the past and that's where it will stay. I just wish you'd give me the same latitude."

She'd stopped cleaning. She was looking at him now with a softer, if not somewhat conflicted, expression.

"I've been up front with all the women I've dated. I've never cheated or promised them something I had no intention of delivering. They were a part of my past just like Duane and Hugh are a part of yours."

He took a step toward her.

"I just need to know that I can trust you. I have more to think about than just myself now. I mean, I'm pregnant with another man's child, Aiden. That's a lot to ask you to take on. And as much as I would love to try on this—this—this…whatever it is that's happening between us—I'm not in the position to test-drive a relationship and potentially make another mistake. What if we take that next step and it turns out terribly? What if we end up hating each other?"

"I could never hate you, B. Give me a chance. Give *us* a chance."

He took another step toward her, and she didn't move away.

"Just tell me you don't want this as much as I do

and I'll never bring it up again. Just say the word and I'll walk away."

She bit her bottom lip, but she didn't say it.

He drew her into his arms and held her, breathing in that familiar floral coconut scent that was so her. She melted into him.

"Stay with me tonight," she said.

He picked her up and carried her into the bedroom.

Chapter Thirteen

There was proving a point, and then there was proving a point. Aiden had stayed. They'd made out like a couple of teenagers and then they'd fallen asleep in each other's arms.

That's as far as it went. It was all very innocent.

He said he wanted her to believe it wasn't just the thrill of the chase. That even though he wanted her so badly it was all he could do to contain himself, he wanted her to believe that his intentions were honorable.

He was not just out to love her and leave her.

Huh.

For a long, heated while, Bia thought that it wasn't *her* virtue that was about to be compromised—she told him he was the one who should be worried.

Yes. The chemistry that had always zinged between them had more than surpassed expectations once they took it to the bedroom. She could hardly wait to see what it would be like to make love to Aiden.

But they were taking it slowly.

With her propensity to get carried away in the moment, in the light of day, playing it safe seemed like a very good idea.

She was sitting at her dressing table finishing her makeup before work when Aiden brought her a cup of decaf coffee.

"Thank you," she said, smiling up at him.

He set the cup down and enfolded her in a hug. "I loved waking up with you this morning. I want to wake up with you every morning."

A spiral of need coursed in her lady parts.

"If you're not careful," she said. "I'm going to drag you back to that bed and have my way with you."

He answered with a deep openmouthed kiss that she felt all the way to her toes. He slid his hands down the vee of her robe and cupped her breasts. A moan laced with all the pent-up want for him escaped.

"What are you doing to me?" she asked, her lips still on his.

He bit her bottom lip. "I'm proving that you can trust me."

Her hand found his desire straining the front of his button-fly jeans. "Oh, wow, I think we need to figure that out pretty quick. Otherwise, I'm afraid we might spontaneously combust thanks to all this…restraint."

"And how," he said, trailing kisses between her

breasts, up her neck and then finishing with a long, lingering promise of things to come on her lips.

"You're going to be late for work if we keep this up," he said.

"That's why it's good to be the boss," she said into his ear.

"To be continued," he said, fixing her robe, covering her up and returning her to her original unravaged state. "But in the meantime, take my truck to work and I'll find that problem that's setting off the sensor in your car."

"Thanks, but don't you have to work today?"

"I do, but we have a later call time because of how late the shoot went last night."

Thirty minutes later, she was on her way to the office and already thinking about coming home and spending another night in Aiden's arms. She wanted to trust him in the worst way.

She thought about what Maya had said last night about taking chances and allowing yourself to be vulnerable. She had a point—a great point—but opening herself up, leaving her heart so exposed and taking the chance of losing this man who was her best friend in the world was such a scary thought.

But then she thought about Maya coming all this way, setting up a business to be near her daughter without knowing how Bia would react, whether she would accept or reject her.

What if Maya hadn't been open to making herself vulnerable?

They both would've lost out on one of the most beautiful relationships—mother and daughter.

Bia smiled at the thought.

She pulled over to the curb and took out her phone to text Maya: I put myself out there. I expect to hear that you've done the same with CJ.

She added a heart icon and pressed send.

The message sailed off into cyberspace, leaving Bia with a warm, giddy feeling. She had just texted her mother for the first time.

She'd spent the night with Aiden, in a manner of speaking, for the first time, texted her mother for the first time. What other firsts were coming her way? Her body responded with a longing that she felt all the way down to her toes.

All in good time. For now, she was going to let Aiden prove his point, that it wasn't all about the thrill of the chase.

Her phone sounded the arrival of a new text. It was from Maya. Well done. I will have an update from my end later today. Stay tuned.

How fun. Having Maya in her life was better than just having a girlfriend to share her secrets with. She had a mother and a friend all in one.

She was about to text back a reply when her phone died. *Huh.* Last night she'd been so swept away, she'd forgotten to plug in her phone.

The memory made her tingle all over.

She could still feel Aiden's lips on her neck this morning. That made her body sing.

Since Aiden's truck was a newer model, she figured the charger was probably in the console or the glove box. She tried the glove box first. When she opened it, a bundle of papers fell out. They'd fallen far enough out of her reach that she had to leave them on the floor after she plugged her phone into the charger.

When she parked at work, she bent down and retrieved them. She was just about to shove them back into the glove box when something caught her eye. The document was a rider to Aiden's homeowner's insurance policy covering a diamond engagement ring.

A fifteen-thousand-dollar diamond engagement ring.

She glanced at the two-carat sparkler on her left ring finger. For a moment she couldn't breathe. She feared a full-blown panic attack was setting in.

The ring was real?

She thought back to what he'd said when she'd asked him if the ring was real: "Sure, I have an extra fifteen grand lying around. I figured you were worth it."

She felt so stupid. She really had thought it was a spectacular piece of cubic zirconia. It was so much bigger and more sparkly than the modest half-carat ring Duane had given her.

Until now, the ring Duane had given her was the nicest piece of jewelry she'd ever owned.

Fifteen thousand dollars?

The ring felt hot and heavy on her hand. Why would Aiden spend so much on it?

Unless he really was serious?

Oh, my God. Is he serious?

Bia did her best to focus on the work she had in front of her. Even though it was the start of a new weekly cycle for the paper's publication, she couldn't afford to get behind.

After the staff meeting where they talked about what they each had on the horizon and Bia had made various assignments of the things she knew were coming up that week, she went into her office to begin writing her editorial.

She had just pulled up the screen and poised her hands on the keyboard when her phone's intercom buzzed.

"Excuse me, Bia," said Candice. "Duane Beasley is here to see you."

She blinked at the computer screen, stunned and a little shaken. *Duane? What in the world?*

"Thank you, Candice," she said. "Please tell him to have a seat. I'll be out to see him in a few minutes."

Why? Why is Duane here? After they'd broken up, he'd taken a job in Boise, Idaho. He'd moved. Far away from her. Far away from the mess that their relationship had become. She hadn't heard from him in two years. What was he doing here?

She opened her purse, powdered her nose and re-applied her lipstick. Not that she wanted to look good for Duane; she simply wanted to look pulled together. She wanted to radiate confidence and let him know that she hadn't lost a single night's sleep since she'd discovered what a cheating sleazeball he was.

And to think she'd almost married him.

But she didn't.

He was sitting in a chair in the reception area. His dark head was bent, a sweep of hair falling across his forehead as he read the most recent edition of the

Dallas Journal of Business and Development when Bia approached.

He looked up, smiled and stood.

"Duane," Bia said. "My gosh, what are you doing here?"

"Hello, stranger," he said, blue eyes flashing in that way she used to find so irresistible. "Long time no see."

Dressed in khakis, a white business shirt and tie, he was still a good-looking guy; there was no doubt about it. Tall but not as thin as he used to be, when he'd played basketball in college. He was still fit, but it looked as if the less active business life was starting to catch up with him.

He walked toward her, and, for a moment, she thought he was going to hug her. So, she stuck her hand out, offering it instead. She hadn't exactly meant it as a handshake, more as a preemptive distance maker, allowing her to keep her personal space.

Because once she got past the eyes and the great smile that used to melt her heart, she couldn't forget that he had cheated on her.

Two nights before their wedding.

Bia's bridesmaids had called everyone on the guest list and told them not to come. The wedding was off.

It was the most heart-wrenching, humiliating time in her life.

Worse than the *XYZ* ambushes.

Yes. Even worse than that.

That's what she thought about as Duane stood there holding her hand in his. She politely pulled it away, took a step back and forced her best neutral smile. She didn't want him to think she was happy to see him, but she didn't want him to think she was unhappy. Neutrality was the best revenge. *I don't dislike you. That would take too much energy. I feel nothing for you.*

Except the need to find out why he was here and then get back to work.

"What can I do for you, Duane?"

"Wow, so formal," he said. "Bia, it's me. You don't have to be all businesslike. We're still friends, I hope?"

Okay, there was no way they were doing this here, out in the open, with Candice watching them, in this building where even the walls, no doubt, had ears.

"Can we go for a cup of coffee?" he asked. "For old time's sake."

"Not for old time's sake, but I can spare ten minutes if you want to go next door to the diner. Candice," Bia said, "I'm going out for a few moments."

Then she turned to Duane. "Wait here while I get my purse."

"Bia, I can buy you a cup of coffee," Duane said.

She waved him off as she started toward the door that separated the reception area from the newsroom. "I need to get my phone, anyway. I'll be right back."

When Bia turned around, she almost ran smack into Nicole.

"Oh!" Bia exclaimed, startled to see anyone standing there. But of course it would be Nicole.

Of course.

The woman stood blocking the doorway, looking back and forth between Duane and Bia.

Bia could virtually see the wheels in the woman's reporter's mind turning, doing the math to see if it added up to what the hunch that was probably gnaw-ing at her gut right about now was suggesting to her. Bia knew what went on inside minds like Nicole's. She had once been not so dissimilar from her subordinate. In fact, that same sort of take-no-prisoners gut hunch was what had led her to the stories that had eventually won her the editorship of the paper.

But it just wasn't so comfortable when you were the victim of the hunch, Bia thought. "Excuse me, Ni-cole," Bia said. "Are you coming or going?"

"I was going," she said. "I have an interview with Brian Collins over at Collins Hardware. They're part-nering with the bank to sponsor the Taste of Celebra-tion this year. I was just heading out."

Bia stepped aside to let her pass. As she went through the door to the newsroom, she cast a quick glance over her shoulder and saw Nicole stop and in-troduce herself to Duane.

"You know what, Duane?" Bia said, interrupting the two midintroduction. "Why don't you just come back to my office? There's coffee in the break room. No sense in us going next door. I'm swamped today. I'm sure our business will be quick."

Duane shrugged and walked to stand next to Bia.

"Goodbye, Nicole," Bia said. "Have a great inter-view. I'll be eager to read your Taste of Celebration piece."

As they walked to Bia's office, Duane said, "So, you're in charge around here, huh?"

"I'm the editor, if that's what you mean."

He nodded as he looked around. Was that supposed to be approval? Irritation roiled in her gut.

"What's up, Duane? Did you just happen to be in the neighborhood? Just passing through? Celebration isn't exactly on your way from Idaho to much of anywhere."

Duane's hands were splayed on his knees. The way he was pitched forward in his seat made him look awkward. Or maybe even a little aggressive.

"I have business in Dallas," he said. "It's part of my territory."

"What are you doing these days?" She asked this in the spirit of making polite conversation, not out of personal interest.

"I'm a rep for Tilton Wholesale Tractor parts. I have the southeastern division."

Bia nodded stiffly. Her hands were folded on top of her desk, until she realized Duane was looking at her ring. She moved her hands to her lap.

"Is it true you and Aiden are engaged?"

Her thumb found the back of her ring and she traced it around to the stone in front. The real, fifteen-grand stone in the ring that Aiden had purchased and put on her finger.

"We are," she said, taking care to inject an enthusiastic upturn into her voice. "Don't tell me you came all this way to congratulate us."

Duane made a noise that was somewhere between a huff and a sigh. "What are you doing, Bia?"

Her email dinged, indicating the delivery of another message. It was the fifth notification she'd heard since they'd sat down in her office.

"Right now at this moment, not what I should be doing, considering today's long to-do list," she said.

She moved her mouse, activating her computer screen and glanced at her in-box. It wasn't that she wasn't glad to see him—

"I'm serious, Bia. Don't make a joke out of this."

She looked up from her in-box and skewered him with the most reproachful look she could conjure.

Why was she trying to be polite?

Actually, she wasn't happy to see Duane, to have him come barging back into her life, to have him sit in her office, taking up time she should be spending on the job she needed to do.

Who did he think he was? After what he'd done, what made him think he had the right?

"Duane, as a matter of fact, Aiden and I are engaged. But, frankly, it's none of your business. You don't get to come in here asking these questions, wearing that face that looks like you're about to tell me I'm making the biggest mistake of my life. I already came through the other side of the biggest mistake of my life. Been there, done that. I'd love to chat, but I have a lot to do."

She stood, hoping he would take the cue and do the same.

But he didn't. The big lunk sat there as if he had no intention of moving until he'd said what he came to say.

Great, this had the potential to get very uncomfortable. She regretted not going next door to the diner, where she could have walked away.

"Why would you want to marry a guy who caused your first wedding to be canceled?"

"What's done is done. We're not going to rehash the

past because it's not going to change anything. Aiden is a great guy. He's always looked out for me—"

"He wasn't looking out for you the night of my bachelor party." Duane's face had flushed. Bia had forgotten how that happened when he got mad.

"What *he* did the night of your bachelor party wasn't what caused us to call off the wedding. *You* were responsible for your own actions, Duane."

Duane stood and slammed his open palm down on Bia's desk. "Dammit, he set me up. He got me drunk and brought that prostitute in to climb all over me. I didn't know what I was doing."

Bia rolled her eyes. "You see, that's the thing about you, Duane—you've never been able to take responsibility for your actions. And, for the record, she wasn't a prostitute, she was a stripper. Aiden may have paid her to take her clothes off, but he didn't pay her to sleep with you. That was a deal you brokered all by yourself. So don't blame somebody else."

"He told you she was a stripper? Is that what he said? If so, your fiancé is lying through his teeth. I just thought you should know. Marrying him would be a bigger mistake than—"

"Than what, Duane? Losing you?"

Duane scrubbed his eyes with the heels of his hands, then raked his hands through his spiky dark hair.

"The guy will stop at nothing to get what he wants. The woman was a prostitute. He got me drunk and set me up. By doing that, he set you up, too. I just thought you ought to know before you made the biggest mistake of your life by marrying him."

Chapter Fourteen

Maya stood outside the Celebration Bed and Breakfast clutching the box of chocolates she'd finished making only an hour and a half ago.

She could've had one of her sales staff deliver it to Charles Jordan, but something wouldn't let her do it. This was a task she had to do herself.

When his order had come in that morning for a dozen salted caramels, with the request for them to be delivered at six o'clock that evening, she decided she would be the one to bring them to him. The order, which had come in five days after her hasty retreat from the pub, felt like a sign. Well, not just the order in itself, but the fact that it coincided with her finding a suitable substitute for the orange essence that she needed for the Borgia truffles.

Borgias had been Ian's favorites.

Maya felt like she was losing her mind, but after she had made the batch of Borgias, a strong gust of wind had blown open the kitchen door. It was a gust of wind she hadn't witnessed since she'd been away from St. Michel.

If she didn't know better, she might think that the winds of love had blown open her door to send a message—that she needed to open her heart and see what was standing right in front of her. Just as she had been telling her daughter to do with the man who was obviously her soul mate.

It was a lot scarier to take her own advice. Especially when she hadn't been able to feel anything remotely like what she'd been feeling since the last time she'd kissed Ian Brannigan goodbye nearly three decades ago.

Was it such a bad thing that Charles Jordan reminded her of Ian? The resemblance in personality was only a hasty assessment. She hadn't known the man very long. It wasn't such a bad thing that perhaps he possessed some of the qualities that Ian had possessed.

That's why she found herself attracted to him.

And there wasn't a thing wrong with that. It wasn't as if she was being disrespectful to Ian's memory. He wouldn't want her to spend the rest of her life mourning and longing for something that could never be.

Or at least that's what she told herself as she pulled open the door of the bed-and-breakfast and marched up to the front desk to let him know she was there.

He was down in the lobby in less than two minutes after Maria, the front desk receptionist, called his room.

She was relieved that he hadn't expected her to bring them up to the room. She'd already prepared an exit strategy: she would simply leave the box at the desk since he had prepaid for the candy.

Actually, it was another little test that she had tucked away in the back of her mind. If he came down to the lobby, it was a good sign and she would stay. If he asked her to bring them to the room, it was a bad sign and she would leave.

As Charles Jordan stood there looking at her through those too-familiar eyes, she knew in her heart of hearts that the winds of love had indeed blown into her kitchen and that she'd read the signs correctly.

"I'm so glad you came," Charles said.

Maya nodded and clutched the box in front of her, grateful she had something to do with her clumsy hands since she felt as awkward and shy as a school-girl.

Why was this so hard?

"Would you like to take a walk?" Charles asked. "We can leave the chocolates at the desk."

He must've sensed her uncertainty, because before she could even answer, he took the box from her and gave it to Maria to hold on to.

They walked side by side out into the early evening air.

"It's the perfect night for a walk," Charles said. "I've been dying to get outside all day. How is business today?"

Finally, Maya found her voice, thanks to how relaxed Charles was and how easy he was making their time together.

"It was good, busy," she said. "But I still found time to make your salted caramels and another surprise."

"A surprise? I love surprises." He slanted her a glance laced with a mischievous smile. "If I wasn't enjoying my time with you so much, I would be tempted to turn around and go back and see what the surprise is. That is, if you brought it."

"I did. They're in the box with your salted caramels. It's the funniest thing. The other day as I was placing an order with one of my suppliers, I came across an orange extract that looks like it could be a fair substitute for the one I used to use for the Borgias. They overnighted it to me. I tried it. And it is almost identical to the one that was discontinued. So not only did I order several cases of the extract, but I used the rest of the bottle to whip up a batch of Borgias."

Charles's brow shot up—another expression that made Maya weak in the knees.

"Are you telling me that I am one of the privileged few who gets to sample your first batch of Borgias after all these years?"

They had found their way to Central Park and were heading toward the gazebo.

"Yes, you are. And I expect an honest assessment. I need to know if they compare to the old tried-and-true. That is, if you can remember. It's been so long. How many years did you say?"

Her stomach did a loop-the-loop as she asked the question. Having been so tongue-tied earlier, she was having trouble keeping her filter in place.

"It's been twenty-nine years," Charles said. "And I still remember the taste of them as if it were yesterday. A man doesn't forget something that sweet and that special."

They were standing under the gazebo now, face-to-face, inches apart. Maya was vaguely aware of people walking past on the sidewalk a good ten yards away. They were there, but not really. All she could see was Charles, looking at her looking at him.

If she squinted her eyes, just enough to blur out the background, to soften the lines, he looked just like—

No.

She took a step back, turned and walked over to the gazebo's rail. She wasn't going to do this to herself. From this distance she could see Charles Jordan.

She needed to focus on *Charles Jordan*.

Not Ian Brannigan.

Charles Jordan.

Charles must have sensed the shift in her mood, because he walked over to the same rail that Maya was leaning against, but he left a good bit of space between the two of them.

"Isn't Facebook a wonderful thing?" he asked. "I was thrilled when I found you online."

If she analyzed his words, he might have sounded a little like a stalker. But he didn't scare her.

"Is that so? How long have you been following me? And should I be worried about that?"

He laughed. "Oh, dear God, I hope you're not worried about it. I promise, I'm harmless. That's why I've stayed away for so long."

Maya's heart started drumming a rapid staccato.

She could hear it in her ears. That's when she realized she'd been holding her breath. She exhaled.

"What do you mean?" she asked, unsure if she wanted to hear the answer.

Charles leaned back on the rail and crossed one foot over the other.

"Twenty-nine years ago, Ian Brannigan was in the wrong place at the wrong time."

All the blood drained from Maya's head, and her peripheral vision went a little white and hazy. She gripped the gazebo's wooden railing as she waited for him to continue. She wanted to ask, *How did you know Ian?* But she couldn't dislodge the words from her throat.

"He witnessed a crime that left him injured and in need of protection. Not only for his own safety, but for the safety of those he loved."

"No, that's not right," Maya said. The words sounded like they were coming from outside her body. "Ian was killed in an accident. His mother told me…."

Charles was looking at her with pleading eyes.

No…it couldn't be. Maya wouldn't let herself believe what she was thinking. If she dredged up the hope that she'd buried so long ago and let herself believe even for a second of a second…and then it turned out that he was…

"Death from the accident was exactly what UK Protected Persons Services wanted everyone to believe. And there was an accident. A terribly disfiguring accident. As far as the world was concerned, Ian Brannigan was dead. But—"

"Ian?"

He nodded. "God, how I've missed you, love."

In an instant she was in his arms. His lips were on hers; his hands were in her hair.

And she knew.

Even after all those years, after all that time apart, looking so different, he still tasted the same and she still fit perfectly in his arms. He was the piece of the puzzle, the piece of her heart that had been missing for nearly thirty years.

Breathlessly, she pulled away, bracing herself to wake from a dream—a dream she'd had so many nights she'd lost track. The dream would be so real; she could feel him, taste him. He was always so alive and then morning's light—the thief that it was—would steal him away. She'd wake up alone with the phantom ache in the place where her heart used to be.

Tonight, with a symphony of cicadas playing in the background and the perfume of night-blooming jasmine in the air, she opened her eyes and Ian was still there. She clung to him as tears streamed down her face.

"Please tell me this is real. Even after all these years, you're not gone. You're really here."

He answered her with a kiss that she felt all the way down to her toes. When he finally released her, she drank him in with her eyes. Her finger traced the scar at his collar.

She had so many questions.

"But why? What happened to you, Ian?"

He told her the story of how when he met her he had been doing undercover work for Interpol. He had been caught in the cross fire of an organized crime operation that he had been trying to take down for several months. In the process, his car had gone off a rocky cliff between Monaco and Nice, France. He had been hurt badly. In fact, he had been close to death. That's when his superiors had made the decision to declare him dead and give him a new identity for his protection and that of those he loved.

"It was too dangerous," he said. "I couldn't subject you and my family to the harm that those sociopaths would've inflicted upon you, your family, my family in the blink of an eye. So they declared me dead, rebuilt my face and gave me a new identity in a new country. The work I had done coupled with the ongoing investigation had helped send away the heads of the criminal organization. Last month, the last dangerous person associated with that organization was executed. It's finally safe enough for me to contact you without putting you in danger."

"Does it mean that we can be together?"

"If you're willing to give Charles Jordan a chance, yes. Ian Brannigan is legally dead."

"No, he's not," said Maya. "He's very much alive in my heart. I just hope that Charles Jordan is willing to hear what I have to say. Because he's missed out on a lot over the twenty-nine years he's been gone."

"We need to talk," Bia said when Aiden got home from work that evening.

The shoot had gone later than he'd planned. They were already over budget for the month, and they still had a week left to go. He was hungry and tired and a little edgy. All he wanted was an ice-cold beer and a kiss from this woman who was becoming the center of his universe.

We need to talk was not what he wanted to hear when he walked in the door.

She was sitting on the far side of the sofa in the shadows of the living room, which was lit by only one small table lamp. She had her feet curled underneath her, and she looked incredibly small sitting there all alone in the dim room.

Aiden immediately knew that something was wrong.

"Is everything all right? Is the baby okay?"

All the possibilities of all the things that could go wrong collided in his head with the result of a fifty-car pileup.

"The baby's fine. But I had a visitor today. Sit down and I'll tell you about it. There's a lot that we need to talk about."

Hugh's family? They were the first ones to pop into his head. Had that attorney—what was his name? Had he told the family and had they come to say they wanted to be part of the child's life?

"Duane came to see me today."

"Duane Beasley?"

That was almost as bad as Hugh's family.

"What did he want?"

"To tell me that you set him up the night of the bachelor party."

Ah, man. Not this again.

He raked his hand through his hair, reminding himself to watch his tone. He shouldn't take out his irritation on Bia. He was hungry, he was irritable and he was tired of this same subject.

"We've been round and round about this, Bia. Duane is a big boy. He's responsible for his own actions. What the heck was he doing here? Thought he lived in Ohio or somewhere like that?"

"He lives in Idaho. But he travels with his job. That's why he was here. He was in Dallas on business. Aiden, did you hire a prostitute to seduce Duane?"

She'd never phrased the question quite that way before. The question had always been whether he set Duane up. Not if he had specifically hired someone with the express purpose of seducing him.

Ah, man. He wasn't going to lie to her.

"Well, I have never hired a prostitute. I hired a dancer for Duane's bachelor party. There's a fine line in that profession. I'm not saying that all dancers or even most dancers are prostitutes. But sometimes they cross the line."

"Aiden, cut to the chase. Did you ask the woman to seduce my fiancé?"

Before he'd always managed to nip this conversation in the bud with the fact that Duane had free will. Tonight Bia was asking another question. Had he asked the woman to seduce Duane?

He looked up at the ceiling. His pulse was pounding in his temples. His blood was rushing in his ears. He looked down at his shoes, weighing his words. Finally he looked back at Bia. Into those eyes that were dark with pain and questions.

Damn that bastard.

"Even if he had a naked woman crawling on him, he should've said no," said Aiden.

"Aiden, just answer my question. Yes or no? Did you tell her to seduce him?"

He could tell that she read it in his eyes even before he could say the word. She scooted to the edge of the couch. Her palms were braced on the cushions on either side of her.

"Aiden, you were married to Tracey at the time. Why did you do it? Why did you set up Duane? Got him drunk, hired a woman to put it in his face? Why would you do that to me?"

"Bia, why would you want a man who would be unfaithful to you?"

"That's beside the point right now. I trusted you, Aiden. I trusted you to take my fiancé out, not to sabotage my marriage. And what about your marriage, Aiden? Why would you do this?"

"Bia, Tracey and I were already separated at this point—"

"So you wanted to break up Duane and me, too? Why? Because misery loves company."

"No, that's not what it was. It wasn't the first time that Duane had cheated on you. I just didn't want to see you get stuck with someone who didn't deserve you. Because you have always deserved so much more."

He wanted to say, "Because I've always loved you," but the words were stuck in his throat.

God, man-up.

"Who made you the morals police?"

"I've loved you my entire life. I realized it too late.

Or at least I thought it was too late, until now. We don't have to keep being the star-crossed lovers, Bia. We can do this."

She took off the diamond ring, set it on the coffee table and gave it a shove. It sailed toward him, went off the end of the table and landed at his feet.

Then she sat back in the corner of the couch, drew her knees up under her chin and wrapped her arms around them. "Just go, Aiden. It's too late for us."

The next morning Bia awoke to the sound of a ringing phone. The first thought that went through her head was, *Aiden?*

Oh, please let it be Aiden. But it wasn't. It was Maya.

"Hello?"

"Good morning, sunshine," Maya virtually sang into the phone.

Bia glanced at the clock. It was seven o'clock. She'd overslept. She'd have to hurry or she'd be late for work. Even so, phone pressed to her ear, she rolled over onto her back and threw her arm over her eyes.

"Good morning," she said, not even trying to infuse the slightest enthusiasm into her voice.

"Did I wake you up?" Maya asked. "I thought you would be up already. Don't you have to work today?"

"Yeah, I do. I had a rough night last night."

"I'm sorry. Were you feeling sick again?"

"No, Aiden and I broke up. I mean, if you can even call it that. If we were even together. I gave him back the ring."

"What happened?" Maya asked, alarm apparent in her voice.

"It's a long story. Maybe we can meet for lunch and I'll tell you. I could use some advice. Speaking of, you never gave me the Charles Jordan report."

There was a long pause.

"Are you there?" Bia asked.

"I am," Maya answered. "Funny you should mention that. Because I do have news."

"Good news?" Bia asked.

"Very good."

"What? Were you going to wait for me to drag it out of you?"

"I wasn't sure if you were up for it right now given the situation with Aiden."

Bia rolled onto her stomach. "Please, I'm dying for some good news. In fact, would you like to meet for breakfast? I'm not feeling exceptionally motivated this morning. Maybe your happiness will jump-start my day. Wow. Maybe I can start living vicariously through my mother."

Bia had to stop by the office before she met Maya. She just had to run in to take care of one call. She'd left the number on her desk.

Good grief, she was scattered. She needed to get herself together and get her head back in the game. Easier said than done, when her heart was heavy with regret.

She'd slept fitfully, waking up every few hours and wondering if she'd done the right thing giving the ring back to Aiden. And the conclusion she came to was of course she had. It wasn't a real engagement, despite the ring and the proposal and the chemistry between them. The fact remained that the only reason he had proposed was to save her from the *XYZ* scumbag.

She didn't need saving.

Maybe she needed to prove that to herself as much as anyone.

Problem was, she had started to believe their PR. If it was going to end sometime, it might as well be now. She hadn't seen or heard from the *XYZ* reporter since Maya had chased him out of her shop. He had probably decided that there was no news here. At least not the kind of news he got paid for raking up. No doubt he was somewhere else turning over rocks to see what would jump out. *Good riddance.*

On her way to work, she thought of something funny and immediately reached for her phone to call Aiden. Then she didn't.

This was exactly the thing that she didn't want to happen. Now everything was messed up. Now she felt weird about calling him for the least little thing like she used to. Because now the least little thing seemed like a big inconvenience.

Not only that, but she needed some space to get him out of her system. That's what you got when you played with fire. You got burned.

But no one was going to save her from this fire but herself.

She parked and made her way into her office, dropping her purse on the credenza behind her desk. As she was moving papers around, looking for the scrap of paper with the number she needed, she noticed Nicole standing in the doorway.

"Did you need something?" Bia asked.

"Where's your ring?" Nicole asked.

Bia glanced at her finger as if she expected to see it there. Of course she didn't, but she wasn't in the mood to deal with Nicole. "It's not there, is it? Don't you have something you need to do? Should I find something for you to write about?"

By now she sounded like the Wicked Witch of the West. But her snark had done the trick. Nicole frowned at her and turned around and walked away.

Within fifteen minutes, Bia was walking into the diner next door to her office. The hostess greeted her with a warm, cheery smile and asked how many would be in her party. Bia spied Maya's red curls across the restaurant.

"Thanks, but I see my party right over there," she said.

She was halfway to the booth when she noticed that Maya was sitting with a man. Bia stopped and did a double take.

That must be Charles Jordan.

Good, Bia thought, she could use a little show-and-tell distraction to boost her mood. Plus, meeting the guy in person she'd be able to get a better read on him to make sure he had good intentions. The place she was in, he better be honorable or she'd personally run him out of town on a rail.

The phrase struck her as funny. She made a mental note to look up the origin of that term when she got back to the office. In the meantime, she put on her best smile and her most generous attitude. If this man made her mother happy, she would be his biggest supporter. She whispered a silent prayer that at least one of them could be lucky in love.

When Maya looked up and saw Bia approaching, she waved. Her hazel eyes were sparkling. She seemed to be glowing with happiness. *Well, somebody must've gotten lucky,* Bia thought. It wasn't quite apparent whether it was in love or lust. Either way Maya was smitten, and Bia's mood was instantly buoyed.

The man stood as she approached. He was tall with dark hair and blue eyes. He had a great smile. Her first impression was that he had a kind face. Bia knew it was early to tell, but something about him made her confident that he was just as smitten with Maya as she was with him.

Maya threw her arms around Bia.

"Um…*Charles,*" Maya looked up at the man and made a face that seemed to indicate that they were sharing some sort of inside joke. "Charles, this is Bia."

Maya closed her eyes for a moment and took Bia's hand.

Tears were in Maya's eyes, but she was smiling so they looked like happy tears. Bia hoped. This Charles had better not have done anything to make her mother cry—

Maya gave Bia's hand a quick squeeze. She took a deep breath, then said, "You don't know how long I have dreamed of saying this. Bia, I would like to introduce you to your father."

Her father?
Her father.

In the span of less than three weeks, she'd not only gained a mother, but a father, too.

It was a little hard to wrap her mind around. But Bia had meant it when she'd said she would be genuinely happy for her mother if things worked out.

And they had worked out in a way that Bia had never imagined.

Charles was the only man Maya had ever loved. Her love for him had withstood nearly thirty years of separation, of giving up a child, of no other man ever measuring up.

Her mind drifted back to Aiden and when he'd told her that she was the only woman he had ever loved. She wanted to believe that but…

How could he love her? She was pregnant with another man's child.

This whole thing had started as a farce. It had blossomed out of the game of chase, of Bia being a challenge. If she put some distance between them now, there might be a chance to save their friendship.

She felt almost panicky thinking about life without Aiden.

Yes, she would fix this, somehow. Just not now. They needed time.

She finished the editorial that had taken her way too long to write. It wasn't stellar, but at least it was done. The words were on paper. She could come back to it and visit it again tomorrow. For now she had to get out of this place.

It was already seven o'clock. It was starting to get

dusky outside. She still needed to stop by the grocery store. She might as well call it a day.

The problem was, she didn't want to go home. The house was cold and empty without Aiden. She wished that they could turn back the clock to the time when things were good.

She wanted to tell him about her father. Heck, she wanted him to meet her father. Wanted her father to meet him. But why? What were they to each other now?

This is my friend, Aiden.

This is my almost lover and former fiancé, Aiden.

This is my pretend fiancé and former friend, Aiden.

None of it felt right. None of it made sense anymore.

She missed him. But she'd messed that up pretty good, hadn't she?

Since she was the last person out of the building, she locked the door. She set her laptop bag and her purse down while she struggled to maneuver the tricky lock. When she finally got the dead bolt to turn, she picked up her things and turned around to leave. She nearly jumped out of her skin at the sight of the all-too-familiar and very much unwelcome face.

"Yo, Bia. Joey Camps from *XYZ Celebrity News.* How ya doin' today, darlin'?"

He trained the video camera on her.

How the heck did this guy do that? Sneak up behind her like that?

"Hey, Bia, where's your ring?"

God! How did this guy know these things? Who was telling him—

Nicole.

The realization came over her in ice-cold waves.

Oh, my God. It has to be Nicole.

She'd been there when Bia had first interviewed Hugh. Nicole had commented on Bia's getting sick in the bathroom. She'd asked her if she'd had a rough night out. Nicole had known Bia was out of the office for a doctor's appointment because Bia had casually mentioned it at the staff meeting. She hadn't realized she'd need to be vague about her whereabouts. It wouldn't have been hard for Nicole to figure out which doctor Bia had gone to. The woman seemed to turn up almost as much as Joey Camps. But Bia would never have been able to put it together if not for Nicole questioning her today about the ring.

Of course. It had to be Nicole.

"So, Joey, did Nicole call you again?"

For a brief moment, Bia saw a flash of recognition in Joey's eyes. Not the look of confusion that would have been there had Nicole not been his informant.

Good old Joey Camps didn't have a very good poker face.

"So, no ring, huh?" Joey asked. "Does this mean the wedding's off?"

How ironic—just yesterday she'd resented Aiden for always trying to come to her rescue. She'd been so adamant about saving herself. About trust and truth and everything she ever thought was good and real and right.

And then today she'd met her father.

A man that Maya had thought dead for nearly thirty years.

So what did it all mean?

What was truth? The things you grew up with? The father who had never bothered to tell her she was adopted? Did that make him any less of a father? Because Charles had been in her life less than twenty-four hours, did that discount him?

Because Aiden had always been her friend, did that mean he couldn't be her lover—her husband?

Did it make any difference how Aiden had exposed Duane for the cheater that he was? Once a cheater, always a cheater, right?

Everything was upside down.

"Since the engagement's off, does it mean that Hugh's your baby daddy, Bia?" Joey whined.

She suddenly realized that she could be tossed and turned by the changes that were taking place or she could grab the wheel of her life and steer it in the direction that she wanted it to go.

"Hey, Joey, I'll make a deal with you. Let me put my purse in the car and I'll give you an interview you will never forget. Just let me set these things down. They're heavy."

"Cool. I'm down with that."

Bia put her things in the car and her keys in her pocket, and rolled up her sleeves. She picked up the garden hose that was lying in its usual heap on the asphalt, turned it on at the spigot—

"Hey, what are you doing?" Joey cried as she drenched him and his camera with water.

Chapter Fifteen

Every time someone new entered the shop, Bia's heart gave a little lurch. Tonight was the party that Maya had originally planned as a post–grand opening celebration—once she got the kinks worked out of the day-to-day operations.

Now that she was ready to show off her shop, the party had morphed into a triple celebration: the shop's opening; the reunion of Bia, Maya and Charles; and an engagement party for Maya and Charles. After all this time the two would finally be married.

Bia owed it to her mom—to her parents….She hadn't yet gotten used to calling them that. She really truly was happy for them, even if she was still mourning the loss of her relationship with Aiden. She was hoping he would come tonight. He'd been invited.

As a matter of fact, Maya had invited him herself. But so far he was a no-show.

Bia's heart ached, but she'd be damned if she would let the smile slip from her face and ruin what should otherwise be a very happy occasion.

The key was to keep busy. She was helping A.J., Pepper, Caroline and Sydney keep the hors d'oeuvres stocked and circulating. She helped fill champagne glasses and made sure that the dessert table was stocked with plenty of Maya's chocolates. If being an editor didn't work out, she figured she could always get a job as a waitress. She cajoled herself with the thought that she sort of had a knack for it.

She was back in the kitchen restocking a tray when Drew walked in. "So I hear your friend was back the other day. The *XYZ* reporter? Is that what you call him? A reporter?"

"Why don't you ask Nicole? I'm almost positive she's the one who has been feeding him information."

Drew's nostrils flared. "Are you kidding? Do you know this for a fact?"

Bia leaned on the counter, looking him squarely in the eyes. "I can't say that I have any hard factual evidence. It's mostly circumstantial. But she really does fit the part. I started detailing all of the events and who might've known. She's the common denominator in all of them. So let's just call it a very strong hunch. The same kind of hunch that helped me help you bring down Texas Star."

Drew stroked his chin contemplatively. "Should you fire her? It is considered conflict of interest if she's giving news to other sources. She signed a no-compete agreement when she came on board."

Bia sighed. "I don't know, Drew. I'll have to think about it. Although, at the next staff meeting, I will review the no-compete agreements and make sure that everyone understands exactly what it means."

"Good idea."

Bia stared down at her naked left hand, at the place where the ring used to adorn her finger. Now it was as empty as she felt.

She looked up a little sheepishly. "Have you talked to Aiden?"

"As a matter of fact, I have. He's taking it pretty hard. He loves you, Bia. If you ever want to talk about what happened…I'm not really good with that kind of advice, but I can listen."

Bia gave him a rueful smile. "And I'm not really good at talking about things like that. So, I don't know if we'd make a very good counselor–patient team. But thanks, anyway. I appreciate the thought."

"At the risk of sounding like I'm giving advice," said Drew. "Talk to him. Tell him how you feel. I think you might be surprised at how much you two think alike."

Actually, no, she wouldn't be surprised. She and Aiden had always been simpatico. What had happened to them?

They'd crossed that line. Now it felt like there was no turning back.

Maya appeared in the doorway. "There you are!" she sang in her lyrical accented English. "Come, come! We need you out here *tout de suite*."

"This sounds urgent," said Drew. "Leave the tray. Caroline will help me fill it when the quiches are done. You go ahead and see what Maya needs. This is your night—well, yours and your family's. Why are you working?"

Because if I don't keep busy I'll make myself crazy.

Bia smoothed her hair, checked the front of her black cocktail dress for crumbs and went to see why Maya needed her so urgently.

When Bia stepped out onto the shop floor, the crowd parted, revealing Aiden at the center.

He smiled when he saw her. And her entire body gave in to the feeling of relief seeing him there. Her first impulse was to walk up and put her arms around him and kiss him senseless, but then she remembered they hadn't even talked since the night she'd given him the ring back.

"There you are," he said. "I have something to ask you."

Bia glanced around, fully aware that everyone was watching them. "Here?"

"Absolutely. This is something all of our friends and family need to see." He walked up to her, took her hand in his and dropped down on one knee.

"Bia Anderson, will you do me the great honor of being my wife?"

The room was so quiet, Bia was sure everyone could hear her labored breathing and the beating of her heart.

Oh, my gosh, what is he doing?

She glanced from Aiden to Maya, who was nodding vigorously, to Charles. "I've already asked your parents for your hand. They said yes."

He was holding the ring between his left thumb and index finger. The brilliant diamond sparkled as if it were connected to an energy source.

She leaned in and said, "Can we talk in private?"

Ever the eternal optimist, Aiden pacified himself with the fact that she didn't say no. Of course, she could be talking to him in private so as not to hurt his feelings, but they were too good together. This time he was not going to let her go. He knew she loved him as much as he loved her. He just did not know what the problem was. He had a feeling he was about to find out.

He followed Bia into the kitchen and up a set of stairs that he didn't know existed in the shop. They led up to what seemed to be Maya's sleeping quarters.

He glanced around the cozy space. A Murphy bed adorned one wall, and a small love seat and chair grouped around a coffee table in the center of the room.

Bia chose the love seat. Aiden sat down next to her.

"Aiden, what are you doing?"

"Last I checked, I had proposed to you. I guess the most accurate answer would be that I am waiting for you to answer me."

"But why?" she asked.

"Bia, I told you once, but I'll tell you again. Hell, I will tell you every day for the rest of our lives. I have never loved a woman the way that I love you. So it's only natural that I would want to spend the rest of my life with you."

"Doesn't it bother you that I'm pregnant with another man's baby?"

"I want a family, Bia. The baby's birth father is dead. I don't know what I would've done if it hadn't been for your father stepping in and serving as a role model for me."

She straightened. "So, wait, are you marrying me out of duty—paying back some perceived debt—or because you love me and want to spend the rest of your life with me?"

"Did you not hear me? I've never loved anyone but you. It's always been you. Well, except for the time I fell in love with my kindergarten teacher. But she wouldn't marry me because she already had a husband."

She smiled and shook her head, love apparent in her eyes. "Yeah, you've always been a player."

"So come play with me, Princess." He dropped down on one knee. "Come play with me for the rest of our lives. Will you?"

"Nothing would make me happier. I love you, Aiden."

They made their way back downstairs. Everyone hushed as they walked into the room.

"She said yes!" Aiden said.

He pulled his bride-to-be into his arms and sealed the deal.

* * * * *

A sneaky peek at next month...

Cherish™

ROMANCE TO MELT THE HEART EVERY TIME

My wish list for next month's titles...

In stores from 18th April 2014:

☐ Expecting the Prince's Baby — Rebecca Winters

& The Millionaire's Homecoming — Cara Colter

☐ Falling for Fortune — Nancy Robards Thompson

& A Baby for the Doctor — Jacqueline Diamond

In stores from 2nd May 2014:

☐ Swept Away by the Tycoon — Barbara Wallace

& One Night in Texas — Linda Warren

☐ The Heir of the Castle — Scarlet Wilson

& The Prince's Cinderella Bride — Christine Rimmer

Available at WHSmith, Tesco, Asda, Eason, Amazon and Apple

Just can't wait?

Visit us Online
You can buy our books online a month before they hit the shops! **www.millsandboon.co.uk**

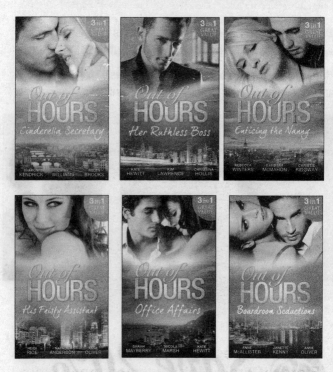

24 new stories from the leading lights of romantic fiction!

Featuring bestsellers Adele Parks, Katie Fforde, Carole Matthews and many more, *Truly, Madly, Deeply* takes you on an exciting romantic adventure where love really is all you need.

Now available at:
www.millsandboon.co.uk

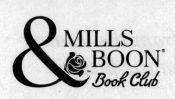 

MILLS & BOON
Book Club

Join the Mills & Boon Book Club

Want to read more **Cherish**™ books?
We're offering you **2 more** absolutely **FREE**!

We'll also treat you to these fabulous extras:

- 🌹 **Exclusive offers and much more!**
- 🌹 **FREE home delivery**
- 🌹 **FREE books and gifts with our special rewards scheme**

Get your free books now!

visit www.millsandboon.co.uk/bookclub
or call Customer Relations on 020 8288 2888